CELESTIAL CITADEL

THE ROGUE DUNGEON BOOK 6

JAMES A. HUNTER

EDEN HUDSON

Celestial Citadel is a work of fiction. Names, characters, places, and incidents either are the product of the author's imagination or are used fictitiously. Any resemblance to actual persons living or dead, events, or locales is entirely coincidental.

JStrode@ShadowAlleyPress.com

CHAPTER I
COMMAND CHANGE

Marek Konig Ustar, spoken of in whispers across Traisbin as the Tyrant King and newly Undead God-Pharaoh of Hearthworld, swept into his war room like a sandstorm. Following him was a small troop of high-level monsters he had acquired along with a slew of Hearthworld powers. Rabid Jackal Fiends carrying bronze khopeshes, Infectious Plague Mummies armed with gold- and black-striped rods and staves, horse-sized skeletal Sacred Bastets letting out bone-chilling mewls as their tails rattled and twitched, and Soul Devourers, huge crosses between crocodiles and overly muscled dogs.

Awaiting him in the war room were his supposedly powerful and loyal generals, assembled from across Traisbin. In truth, they were cringing wastes of breath, weak and pitiful things more concerned with gold, parties, and worthless finery. Aristocratic men and women chosen for their political alliances, strategic positioning, and the strength of their armies rather than themselves. Marek had tolerated them out of necessity. A conqueror had to use the tools afforded to him, and these brittle and rusty weapons were the best this world had to offer.

No longer.

The nobles recoiled in shock and horror at the sight of his new foot soldiers.

This wasn't the first time Marek had invaded a world with an army of strange monsters from across the stars.

His history was a long and bloody one, overflowing with endless horrors and atrocities. Campaigns across the Arcturus Nebula at the head of a legion of wolfmen with slathering jaws and flesh-rending claws. War in the blackest depths of the Empty Expanses with an enormous shark-like race known as the Selachii Hordes fighting at his back. Once, he'd even unleashed a plague of flesh-eating flying creatures with great curling horns that reeked of brimstone on the simple people of Opish. Better than a thousand years ago that was, but he still remembered Opish fondly. It was the dimension where he'd uncovered the first clue that would eventually lead him to the World Stone.

Still, this was certainly one of his most satisfying reveals. Such a wide array of monsters and magic. He savored the moment. That initial confusion and terror came only once a takeover, after all.

The nobles froze in panic. They weren't only responding to the undead Hearthworld spawn, Marek knew. Much of his own appearance had been altered when he'd stepped through the portal into the land known as the Onyx Sands. While arriving in Traisbin had given him the appearance of a handsome but aging noble, Hearthworld had transformed him into a rotting god-creature with flags of torn leathery flesh stretched over bones as black as jet. His face had elongated into a bent and sloping muzzle, as if the skull beneath were melting.

This new, towering form required Marek to duck through the war room doors, and even beneath the vaulted ceilings inside, his massive crescent horns nearly scraped the stonework overhead. A gemstone the size of an ostrich egg floated between their points, crackling with jade lightning and giving off the occasional peal of thunder.

He stopped, thumping his gold-and-lapis falcate staff on the flagstones for emphasis, and let his muzzle stretch into a jackal-like grin while the nobles fought the urge to soil their fine garments.

Even Talise, his treacherous ward, was taken aback, though she managed to cover her shudders much faster than her fellow natives. Recognition flashed in her gray von Graf eyes like candlelight flickering in twin mirrors. Though the girl had changed much in her foray into Hearthworld, gaining golden metallic skin and towering raven's wings, the black waves of hair, those clear gray eyes, and the slightly hooked nose—her family line's defining features—still remained.

"Grandfather," she said smoothly, dipping into a respectful curtsey. "I've gathered your generals, as you requested."

Marek let his gaze roam across the sniveling cowards. To think his campaign for domination of this realm had once depended on such pathetic creatures. No surprise then that it had taken them twenty years to gain control of Traisbin alonc.

"Gracious of you to come at my bidding," Marek sneered.

Several of the noblemen and women flinched to hear the bored aristocratic voice flowing from the rotting throat of this towering Undead God-Pharaoh.

Marek waved a clawed hand at the monstrous creatures surrounding him. "You see before you my new army. As is plain to see, they are far superior to human soldiers. Stronger, faster, with powers and abilities far beyond human ken. And best of all, completely obedient to none but me. Unquestioning, unthinking, and unyielding."

One of the hardier nobles, the Duke of Frahoi, a warrior of

distinction in his youth whose form had run to fat and laziness in his later years, stepped forward.

"Your Eminence," the duke rumbled, "truly you have outdone yourself. These ... eh ... these powerful beasts will certainly bring the last vestiges of resistance to heel. With them beneath my command, surely I will be able to crush what remains of the *T'verzet.* And we can rotate them to the northern front to provide relief against the Sakramors. It's been a bloody winter in the pass, and we've suffered significant losses, even with the magic of the *Burung* at our disposal. The rebels have cut off our supply lines time and again."

Worthless, Marek thought. Always a new excuse with this lot. Always bowing and scraping to curry favor without ever doing anything of worth. Like that lout Lowen. Good riddance to him and all of his countrymen.

"Yes, excellent additions," the other nobles hurried to add, their voices shrill in their rush to praise him. "Brilliant!" "Far superior to pathetic humans!"

Marek smirked. "Ah, I'm glad to hear that you agree. Meet your replacements."

The duke blinked. "Excuse me, Your Grace, but I'm not sure I understand."

"Replacements?" repeated a hennaed older noblewoman.

The other nobles were in a similar state of slow-witted confusion.

Smart girl that she was, Talise was already backing across the room.

"Your services will no longer be required," Marek said. He snapped his clawed fingers.

With an eerie chorus of screeching, the Sacred Bastets led the charge, ripping the head from the noblewoman and feasting on her entrails. The Soul Devourers tore into the fat duke and his screaming fellows, all the while croaking like oversized frogs. At the outer edges of the war room, the Infected Plague Mummies called forth swarms of ravenous locusts and clouds of pestilence to herd any who attempted to flee.

One lesser lord, a grizzled man with a puckered arrow scar on his cheek, was the only one to put up anything that resembled actual resistance. He drew a halfmoon battle-axe and pressed himself into a corner. There was no retreat, the man must have known that, but perhaps he took some small comfort in the knowledge that the monsters wouldn't be able to overwhelm him from the flanks or rear. He knew he was going to die—Marek could see that truth shining in his eyes—yet he would make these new horrors work for his death.

Marek could've killed him in an instant. One spell would drain the life from the man's body. Marek didn't cast it, however. He wouldn't let the man live, but he would honor him with a warrior's death.

The tenacious lesser lord's axe spun and fell, carving through an Infectious Plague Mummy. The creature fell, poisonous dust spiraling out of its split chest cavity. As if it had a will of its own, the dust crawled into the nobleman's nose and mouth. He began to choke and wheeze, sweat breaking out across his creased brow. He would be dead in less than a minute, but still he fought. He swatted aside a bronze khopesh with the flat of his axe, then brought it screaming around in a vicious arc, slicing through the extended arm of a Rabid Jackal and planting it in the creature's exposed throat.

But he wasn't quick enough to stop the Soul Devourer that barreled into him, fangs latching onto one of his legs and crunching down. The noble fruitlessly brought the spiked haft of his axe down into the Devourer's head, but he was too weak from the poison to drive the metal spit through the thick and bony skull. Blood drenched the floor as the Devourer chewed and slurped. A Sacred Bastet ripped the axe from his failing fingers and laid open his throat with razor-sharp talons.

A messy death, but at least the man hadn't embarrassed himself in the end. Few creatures as weak as these humans could hope for more.

Across the room, a Rabid Jackal Fiend loped toward Talise, jaws slavering as it raised its khopesh. Marek could have stopped the creature outright; he had further plans for the brat that didn't call for her bloodied corpse—yet. But seeing her draw her golden rapier and form a ball of the lawless orange magick she'd been born with, Marek decided to allow the charade to play out. Leave his *dear granddaughter* guessing as to his intentions until the last moment.

As the girl and Jackal fell to battle, a scrap of parchment appeared in the air before Marek's eyes.

[Thum, Soul Devourer Level 72 under your dungeon lordship has leveled up! As part of the Dungeon Lord's Tax, you have collected 520 Experience Points!]

Frowning, Marek opened the ethereal tome he had gained as part of this Hearthworld transformation, called a *Dungeon Lord's Grimoire.*

Indeed, in the space displaying his Experience, points trickled in with each of the nobles his undead minions killed. It seemed the fat duke had given the greatest quantity, but from each death, the others added their paltry value to Marek's total, pushing him toward the next level.

Nearly as exciting, Thum the Soul Devourer had gained in power and abilities. He would be stronger, deadlier, and even harder to slay than before, merely by killing off a fat and aging duke. In fact, each of his minions was working toward lethal new strengths with every attack.

[Rekat, Sacred Bastet Level 65 under your dungeon lordship

has leveled up! As part of the Dungeon Lord's Tax, you have collected 312 Experience Points!]

[Hekat, Sacred Bastet Level 67 under your dungeon lordship has leveled up! As part of the Dungeon Lord's Tax, you have collected 129 Experience Points!]

[Mekat, Sacred Bastet Level 72 under your dungeon lordship has leveled up! As part of the Dungeon Lord's Tax, you have collected 201 Experience Points!]

A canid grin stretched the length of Marek's elongated muzzle. The implications of this new magick were world-shaking. In two decades he had only just managed to wrestle a single empire on this planet into his grasp, forced to use cunning and bloody shows of strength in the face of their silly paper spells. But now, with these Hearthworld creatures as his minions sweeping across Traisbin, killing and destroying, constantly growing more unstoppable, nothing could stand in his way.

Ah, but he was getting ahead of himself.

Powerful as Marek Konig Ustar knew he had become, there was still one obstacle barring his path—that upstart Roark von Graf. And unlike that fool Lowen, Marek knew von Graf should never be underestimated. No matter that Marek outmatched von Graf in every way. The same had been true of Lowen, the famed Warrior King Bad Karma of Hearthworld, and a dozen others Roark had defeated, embarrassed, and deposed. Roark was much like the old, grizzled warrior who had made his last stand, courting death face-to-face.

Unlike the grizzled warrior, however, Roark had power, influence, and a penchant for ensuring he was never backed into a corner. There was always a new scheme with that one. And now that the prodigal cur had returned to Traisbin, the Rebel Council would rally round him. Von Graf was likely digging himself into his new location at this very moment, planting every underhanded and overly ambitious trap he could imagine, eagerly awaiting his chance to spring them when Marek attacked.

That was where Lowen's idiotic plans had gone most awry. Attempting to kill von Graf in his own stronghold was a fool's errand.

Even though von Graf was the weaker combatant, on his own territory he was very nearly unstoppable. Knowing this, Marek would employ the wiser course of action—lure von Graf into the open by striking where he was weakest.

Across the war room, a Jackal and Bastet lay dead at Talise's feet, and a pair of Soul Devourers closed in on her from either side.

Experience points trickled in as the last of Marek's human generals died and their corpses were ripped apart by fighting Bastets and shaken down the gullets of Soul Devourers.

"Well, that's the politicking done," Marek said gleefully, dusting his clawed hands together. "Leave her, you fools!" he snapped at the Soul Devourers, as if only now noticing that Talise was fighting for her life. "This is my beloved granddaughter. You are not to harm a hair on her head."

The Soul Devourers croaked out a throaty reply and hopped obediently back to Marek's side.

Slowly, Talise lowered the rapier.

"You're not hurt, are you, my dear?" he asked, taking her hand and feigning concern. Keep her guessing at his intentions until the very end.

"Nothing that won't heal, Grandfather. Thank you."

Amusement tickled him as Talise shook her dark hair from her face and assumed a cool façade as though nothing out of the ordinary had occurred. The golden ichor that had replaced her blood trickled down her cheek from a gash above her right eye, but she was otherwise unharmed. He'd taught her well. Not well enough to best him, but very well indeed.

He nodded. "Excellent. A tragedy averted." Or, much rather, not wasted.

With a thought, Marek chose the ribbon of the Dungeon Lord's Grimoire marked Maps. The pages turned to an enchanted map of Traisbin, laying out the familiar landforms and cities by name. The first change had taken place beneath his very feet. The Imperial palace Marek stood in had been retitled *The Onyx Tomb.* Aptly named, he thought, staring around at the carnage. Far more fitting of a god-pharaoh. He also supposed it was only right to christen such a place with the blood of the weak and worthless.

The second alteration was nestled in the peaks of the Karasu Mountains surrounding Korvo. The Radiant Citadel sat overlooking the city like a protective sentinel.

Marek chuckled. Korvo would be easy pickings, filled with excellent fare for his new legion, and as long as he struck quickly, its citizens would be completely unprepared for an army of monsters beyond their wildest nightmares, just like his worthless generals.

The World Stone Pendant burned icy cold against his chest as he opened a tear in the fabric of space. The violet portal shimmered to life in the dim lighting of the war room.

"Come!" he snapped at his minions. "We've a rebellion to kill."

CHAPTER 2

WORLDS COLLIDE

Darith niet Amstad, second-in-command under Lowen von Reich, better known around his illegitimate family's holdings as the Bloody Bastard of Amstad, floated in black nothingness. No screams, no cackling, no stench of blood and death and smoke. Nothing fun at all.

With nothing to terrorize, Darith might have been bored to tears, but he had no body in this blackness to weep from.

Fear pricked at Darith's mind. What if this was one of the seven hells? An eternity of boredom without anyone else to torment? The last he recalled, that stuffed shirt Roark von Graf had interrupted a perfectly good bloodbath, killing him with waves of dragon flame and a hail of bullets. Darith's father's wife had always told Darith he would end up cursed to the seven hells for his crimes. What if she had been right? What if even now that sanctimonious wench was in one of the heavens, and shoving her off the ramparts at the von Amstad manor hadn't given him the last laugh after all?

A high, eerie note wavered through the blackness, interrupting Darith's rare moment of reflection. It took several seconds for him to recognize the shifting noises as a song, perhaps played on a set of pipes or some type of flute. He'd never understood music. Why did people waste time listening to noise just because it fluctuated? Screams did the same thing, with the added excitement of bright red blood splashing everywhere.

Before the Tyrant King had crushed Traisbin under his wonderfully bloody boot, Darith's noble father had taken care to cover over the numerous trails from Darith's crimes. Purses fat with gold, selling off remaining family members to other lords. All was dealt with as long as Darith never attacked anyone of noble blood. After the Tyrant King came to power, there had been no reason to contain his gleeful violence to the serfs. Darith could hang the flayed flesh of a nobleman's entire family from the ramparts and dance naked beneath it for all that Marek Konig Ustar cared. He'd done just that more than once, starting with his noble father and all of the legitimate von Amstad heirs.

Working for the Tyrant King was a fulfilling career indeed.

Letters glowed bloodred against the black. Darith's lessons in letters had been a boring, painful slog, and he hadn't been able to quit them for good until he'd finished off his third tutor —the third time truly was the charm—but he knew enough to read the word floating in the nothingness.

Respawning...

Joy bubbled up within him, and if he'd had a voice he would have crowed with laughter. He had heard of respawning from other Heralds who'd been killed in Hearthworld. He was going back! Maybe he would be in time for the rest of the battle! And if not, he was becoming skilled at plucking Gargoyles from around the Vault. True, killing the stony creatures wasn't nearly as satisfying as picking off the so-called Heroes of Hearthworld, nor as rewarding as slaying von Graf's minions, but it passed the time much the same.

Instead of depositing him back in the Vault of the Radiant Shield, however, the first word disappeared and more took its place.

[*ERROR!*

Set respawn location, "Vault of the Radiant Shield," not found...

Searching for default location, "City Argentine"...]

[*ERROR!*

Default location, "City Argentine," not found...]

Had Darith possessed the skin to be covered in gooseflesh, he would've shivered with it now. Had they lost? It was an impossible notion. Von Graf was nearly as treacherous in his own way as Darith, but he didn't have the power of Marek's forces. Only a catastrophe of apocalyptic proportions could be responsible for such a turn of events. That line of thinking led him to another, even more disturbing notion. If the Vault of the Radiant Shield was gone, and the nearest city was gone as well, could he respawn at all?

The bloodred letters weren't finished, however. For the first time in his life, Darith was enthralled with reading, devouring every word as it appeared in the void.

[*Searching for default location, "The Hearth – Standing Stones"...*

"The Hearth – Standing Stones" found...

Respawning...]

Darith could've cackled with relief. He didn't know what these Standing Stones were, but he knew that the Hearth was that massive volcanic mountain at the center of Hearthworld. If he respawned there, he could find his way back to familiar territory eventually. And truly, anything at all was better than this floating void of nothingness.

Slowly, the darkness began to recede, and a body filled in around his consciousness with all the appropriate sensations and solidness. The noise from that flute faded away, replaced with short blasts from a nearby hunting horn, the howl of some far-off injured Makaronin, and the scream and clash of an invasion already in full tilt.

Darith blinked, suddenly confused.

He had respawned at the center of a henge of black lava stones jutting up out of an otherwise strangely even street. One of the Standing Stones lay cracked in half with a crushed horseless carriage resting atop it. The blare of the hunting horn came from the twisted metal carriage, droning in time with a pair of flashing lanterns on the front, though Darith could find no hunter within or without sounding the notes or working the lantern shades.

He turned around slowly , surveying the area. Though the sky was dark, with only a sliver of moon showing, lampposts, windows, and magical glowing signs illuminated the area as if it were day. Buildings of glass and metal multiple stories high stood interspersed with the thatch and wood constructions common to both Hearthworld and Traisbin. Strange lights flashed red and blue off the buildings, and the injured howling sprinted closer.

No, not howling, Darith recalled. These were the noises made by the carriages of the constabulary of this world. He was on Earth, the home of the Devs of Hearthworld. Except all of this was wrong. Intermixed somehow.

Pops rang out not far away. Now that he knew where he was, the sound was instantly familiar—the weaponry of this world, guns. Darith grinned. He liked guns. He had several. They were like the deadliest magicks his home world had to offer, yet they required no reading or writing and far less skill than a rapier or axe. Simply point it at the thing you wanted dead and squeeze the trigger—several times usually did the trick, even for the toughest of foes. He pulled the Glock 26 from his Inventory.

Glock 26
Old World Weapon
One-handed Damage: 99 - 108
Durability: 171/175
Level Requirement: 16
Magazine Capacity: 10 Rounds
Current Number of Rounds in Magazine: 0
Semiautomatic Class Weapon: Fast Attack Speed

Empty? He scowled and threw the Glock 26 down with a metallic clanking. That was the only drawback. These guns were mightily effective, but worthless once their projectiles ran out. He would have to find another of the constabulary and steal theirs.

He drew his Broadsword of Agonizing Light and with a mighty flap of his wings took off into the air, heading toward the flashing lights.

As he soared over the lower buildings, Darith caught sight of a familiar location: fortified battlements, parapets, and stone in this sea of fragile glass and metal.

Shieldwall, the new fortress of Roark von Graf's army.

Lowen had attacked the troops stationed there repeatedly before being forced to return to Hearthworld and defend the Vault. Darith wondered whether they had succeeded in driving von Graf away.

When he opened his grimoire to check for messages from Lowen, however, Darith found another ERROR.

[*The account you have entered has been permanently deleted. Messages to this player cannot be delivered.*]

"Eh?" He tried a few more of Lowen's underlings—Viago,

Nitola, and so on. Each time, his grimoire claimed they had been permanently deleted.

Darith landed on a sloping roof high above a battle. Humans screamed and ran while constabulary with translucent shields marked SWAT fought a wallow of Raging Nightboars.

Some residents of Hearthworld still existed, which only made him more curious about Lowen's status. They had somehow made it to Earth, while Lowen hadn't. The only plausible explanation was that von Graf had defeated the Tyrant King's right-hand mage, despite the long odds. Perhaps von Graf had employed the World Stone Pendant, Darith mused. Its magicks were potent, but strange and unpredictable. If that was the case, it might well explain why bits and pieces of Hearthworld were now strewn across the Other World of the Devs.

"If the Tyrant King's right-hand mage is gone, and I'm the right hand's second"—Darith scratched his chin as he did the arithmetic on the Tyrant King's bloody chain of command—"then that makes *me* the new right hand."

He looked from the top of Shieldwall, just barely visible in the distance, to the bloody human-Nightboar battle below.

As the new boss, he was going to need a new army. Maybe, just maybe, those Nightboars could be his first recruits. And if they didn't, he knew lots of fun ways to make piggies bleed.

Albrecht von Herzog slumped in the wingback chair of his study, rubbing at dry, gritty eyes. Nearly everyone in the little mountain town of Korvo had extinguished their lamps and banked their fires for the night, but as usual he was awake, brooding over Traisbin's flagging resistance.

The Rebel Council had been in decline for years before that

bigheaded cockerel Roark von Graf had disappeared, but ever since the night Graf had stormed out some six months ago, the Tyrant King had been taking the resistance apart with a vengeance. Ustars had destroyed Cambry's fabric store and clapped him in the gaol, where the frail old man had died in a matter of weeks. Bran, the barrel-gutted, soft-spoken innkeeper, had disappeared overnight along with his young family. Though Albrecht was certain the innkeeper had gotten wind of danger and gone to ground somewhere far away, he feared the truth might be far bloodier.

Albrecht von Herzog could begrudgingly admit that he was far from the cleverest of mages to come out of his and Graf's class, but even he could trace Marek's renewed assault on the resistance to the night Graf had disappeared. If he'd had any family holdings left to gamble, he'd have wagered that hotheaded fool had gone through with his attempt to assassinate the Tyrant King. Whether it had ended in Graf's death or capture, however, Albrecht couldn't say.

He poured himself another couple fingers of the stinging *asake* alcohol the locals were so fond of.

Morgana had suggested more than once that the Ustars had taken Roark alive and tortured the names of their *T'verzet* compatriots out of him. Albrecht could almost believe it, if only he hadn't known the man. Hadn't seen the hatred burning in his eyes when the Rebel Council had turned down his proposed assassination attempt on Marek. His thirst for revenge was a living thing, a madness that outweighed all reason. Albrecht had known in that single look that Roark von Graf would suffer the seven hells and a thousand more besides before giving up anything the Tyrant King wanted.

In any case, if Graf were betraying people, Albrecht would've been his first choice. Even in their earliest days at the Academy, there had never been any love lost between them. In spite of being the most rusticated of the noble children attending, the boy from the far-flung coastal holdings and the boy from high in the mountains held nothing but contempt for one another. In Albrecht's mind, his continued existence was proof enough that Graf hadn't given them up.

And so, through some other mysterious means, Marek Konig Ustar had whittled the once-strong *T'verzet* down to Albrecht and the elderly merchantwoman Morgana. What a fearsome pair they made, a half-educated mage and a wealthy old maid.

The resistance itself was following suit. Not a night went by when bands of snake-helmed Ustars didn't water Traisbin soil with rebel blood. It didn't matter that their accusations were only correct about half the time, because the raids and executions were so frequent. Slaughter enough people, and you were bound to kill a few rebels by accident. Massacre citizens by the thousand and you could take down a resistance without going through the pesky formalities of inquisition.

Albrecht could say this for the Tyrant King's zealous fervor to stomp out the opposition: as the persecution spread, more and more people who had never considered fighting back were joining the resistance. Even peace-loving folks could only be pushed so far, it seemed. Would it be enough, though? Sadly, Albrecht doubted it very much. He'd always been a realist, and common people, even in great numbers, were no match for the mystical forces that Marek Konig Ustar could bring to bear.

For any chance at victory, they needed nobles—*mages* in truth—and those were in precious short supply.

Albrecht was just sinking into an uneasy doze when a thunderous crash shook his meager rented room. *Asake* sloshed inside his cup. In the coastal land where he'd been raised, earthquakes of greater strength than that were common, but Albrecht had never felt such a thing here in the mountains. Not even the avalanches that closed the pass every year made that sort of ruckus. The next logical option was catastrophe. Perhaps the Tyrant King had finally decided to end it all—scrub Korvo from the map as he had done to so many other cities before.

Outside, someone shouted. Running footsteps clomped along the boardwalk. Another cry went up, and soon panicked voices filled the night.

Albrecht grabbed his pen and a fistful of parchment and sprinted out into the night. Fire was the most likely culprit, some dozing fool knocking over a candle or lamp, but if the Tyrant King were finally riding in to raze Korvo once and for all, he wanted to be prepared. He was their final line of defense, the last mage in the resistance. The citizens of this village had given the Rebel Council a home and hidden them to the best of their abilities despite the danger, and he refused to repay them by running scared, no matter what it cost him.

But outside in the frozen mud of the street, Albrecht found neither violent clashes with snake-helmed Ustari nor billowing smoke and spreading fire. Men and women in colorful night-clothes, with hastily grabbed jerkins and shawls flapping in the icy wind, stood staring up at a glittering structure high on the closest mountainside.

"Where did it come from?"

"What is it?"

Over the roofs of the brightly painted homes and the wall surrounding the village, the ghostly pale structure glowed with a strange inner light. Its construction was stout and strong, like the fortresses of old, all thick stone parapets and squat towers studded with crenellations, though it appeared to be in perfect repair, as if it had only just been finished.

Before Albrecht could begin to analyze how such a construction came to plant itself in the peaks above the old von Graf manor, white lettering as delicate as a spider's thread appeared in the air before his face.

No parchment. No writer. No indication whatsoever of how this strange magick could possibly work. His heart thumped wildly as he read.

[A new Feudal Lord has claimed the territory in which you live! You are now the subject of Roark the Griefer, Lord of the Cruel Citadel.]

"What is this devilry?" someone muttered. Albrecht turned to find a woman waving a hand in front of her face as if to shoo away a cloud of gnats.

A heavily bearded man took a few running steps, then pivoted abruptly. "It won't leave me be! It's followin' me everywhere! A curse on my head, it is!"

Fearful rumbles ran through the growing crowd. Somewhere in amongst them, a young child wailed. An anxious energy seemed to boil within the mass, growing and infecting them like the deadly miasma of a plague. They were all seeing the strange writing.

"Don't panic," Albrecht called, raising his voice to be heard above the murmuring and shouts. "These are letters, no different from the writs used to seal your dead or to strike contracts between you and business partners." It was dangerous to reveal himself as able to read. Only nobles were tutored in the magicks of writing, and all nobles were supposed to be dead or in service to Marek. Still, as risky as such a revelation was, it would be far worse to allow them to injure themselves in their fear. "It says..." He hesitated as he read through the words once more. "It says a new lord has claimed Korvo and the surrounding land. We are all his subjects now."

"Which one?" the butcher's apprentice demanded.

"Aye," a grandmotherly old woman called, "I didn't see no lords and their entourages come along the valley road!"

"Whoever it is, he musta made a pact with something

powerful evil to get through the pass this time a year," the smith agreed. "It's had knee-deep snow for a fortnight."

Albrecht blew out a long breath and glanced back up at the glimmering castle, then let his eyes focus once more on the white letters. That the name was of Lyuko origin made little difference; Albrecht had only known one Roark in his entire life.

Six months ago, the disappearance of Roark von Graf had sent the Tyrant King into a bloodthirsty frenzy that continued without end. Albrecht had a sinking feeling they were about to see just how bad the slaughter could become now that the fool had not only returned, but proclaimed himself a lord in the Tyrant King's face.

CHAPTER 3

NEW WORLD, NEW PROBLEMS

As Roark von Graf stared down from the throne room of the Radiant Citadel at the snow-dusted mountainside above Korvo, a single thought kept returning to him: Marek had the World Stone.

His only edge in the fight against the Tyrant King was gone.

He could give all the rousing speeches and plan to cheat and fight dirty all he wanted, but that pendant had been his only chance. Without it, he never would've survived in Hearthworld. Never would've unlocked his most valuable abilities or allies. Never would've defeated Lowen, who'd been both stronger and better equipped. With the pendant, he'd still been outclassed by Marek, but there had been an outside chance of defeating the Tyrant King. Now Roark and everyone around him was doomed. Marek wouldn't stop at slaughtering him. No, the despot would take down everyone Roark cared about, destroy everything he had built, then salt the earth and hang the corpses as a lesson to the rest of Traisbin.

None of his companions realized yet how dire the situation was. They were all still high on their victory over Lowen and the denizens of the Vault. For them, it was more or less business as usual.

The halls of the Radiant Citadel bustled with the sounds of allied Dungeon Lords, mobs, trainers, merchants, and relocated NPCs going about their lives. Roark had set Yevin and Varek the task of re-establishing a semblance of normalcy within the dungeon while Ick worked at integrating the Heralds who had just come over to the Troll Nation. They were a cagey lot, and they had every right to be. Not a full minute after switching allegiances to save their own hides, they had seen Roark thrashed by their former ruler—who was no longer a simple tyrant, but an Undead God-Pharaoh with all the power and strength Hearthworld could bestow.

Likely more than a few cowards would run back to Marek over the next few days and lose their lives for their trouble. The smart ones would realize going back empty-handed was a death sentence. If they wanted a shot at survival, they would have to bring Marek Roark's head on a platter and pray the despot was in a forgiving mood. If anything, by sparing their lives Roark had increased the odds that he would be assassinated in his own dungeon.

Mac chirped behind Roark, startling him from his dark musings. The Elemental Turtle Dragon leaned his scaly trio of heads over Roark's shoulders. Fiery orange, electric blue, and toxic yellow faces fought for attention, and when Roark didn't react fast enough, the orange one nipped his arm, drawing a bit of blood and making his filigreed Health vial appear for a moment in his peripheral.

"Bloodthirsty beast." Roark chuckled and distributed scratches and hearty thumps between the colorful heads. "All right, boy, no more brooding. We're outclassed and overmatched. Marek's taken our best weapon, but that doesn't mean we can't find a way to outsmart him." He glanced back down at the ruins of von Graf Manor that marred the snowy landscape like a scar in the moonlight. "Whatever we're going to do, we've got to do it soon. Marek won't wait while I get my bearings. This is when we are most vulnerable."

"What we need is more information."

Roark nearly jumped at Randy Shoemaker's quietly determined statement. If he'd been carried away enough in his brooding to miss the Arboreal Herald standing right beside him, then it should be a bloody easy job for Lowen's former troops to sneak up and assassinate him.

Roark glanced sidelong at Randy, waiting for him to elaborate.

His scrutinizing gaze made the Arboreal Herald shift nervously, silver wings rustling. Randy reached up and touched the bridge of his nose absently, then gave an embarrassed chuckle.

"Force of habit," Randy said. "Still hard to believe I won't ever need to wear glasses again." He faltered and cleared his throat. "Anyway. This is your home world, right? Well, we need to know how our magic functions here versus the Tyrant King's. Your magic didn't translate perfectly to Hearthworld, so maybe the same is true moving from Hearthworld to here? Just take respawn for example—death here is forever, unlike Hearthworld. I bet there are other changes too. And if there *are* differences, maybe we can find a way to exploit them. We also need to tally up our advantages and disadvantages. Once we know all the pieces on the board, we can start to devise a strategy that plays to our strengths."

A puff of inky black smoke curled beside him, and Zyra stepped out, carried inches above the floor by her spidery appendages. Though she could stalk from both light and darkness, the Orbweaver Ravager seemed to prefer her Shadow Stalk ability, perhaps because shadows afforded her the most surprise with her midnight blue skin and dark rogue's armor.

"I propose a different strategy," she said. "I say we Contact Poison every one of these Heralds with my Poison of the Rotting Sun, then hang their corroded corpses from the ramparts as a warning to anyone else in this world who would challenge us." Her mismatched purple and green eyes glinted with malice behind the gauzy black veil that obscured her face.

A smirk tugged at the corner of Roark's mouth. "You and Marek would get along swimmingly." He shook his head. "For now, the Heralds are our allies. I swore no harm would come to them as long as they didn't attempt to harm any of us, and I intend to keep that promise. Randy Shoemaker is right. We need more information. The magick of the World Stone Pendant is the one thing that can tip the balance. We can't get the stone back, but there must be a way to nullify or weaken it so that we're not so overmatched."

"Do you think he'll attack again?" Randy asked. "I mean, you told everyone he ran scared when he realized we could hurt him."

The splash of black blood and sliver of health missing from the bar above Marek's head flashed through Roark's mind. The battle had been brutal, even with every advantage, but he *had* hurt Marek. That proved that though the Tyrant King was powerful—especially in his new form—he was not indestructible. Still, the chances of success were slim. The only reason Roark had managed to get the World Stone from Marek in the first place was because the Tyrant King had badly underestimated him. Marek was too devious to make the same mistake twice.

"He'll attack again, but not in the Citadel," Roark replied. "He knows we're too strong here. Just knowing he isn't untouchable—that's too much uncertainty for Marek." Roark's eyes traveled to the village below, and his stomach sank. "I know Marek, better than almost anyone else. He's cunning. He'll try to draw us out. Crush us in the eyes of as many as possible to remind all of Traisbin that he is supreme."

Randy followed Roark's gaze and gulped. "You don't think he would attack innocent people?"

"I don't think so, mate, I know so." Roark spun on his heel and opened the Feudal Lord's Grimoire as he left the throne room behind. Where his Dungeon Lord's Grimoire had only been accessible from his throne, the Feudal Lord's Grimoire could thankfully be opened anywhere.

"We've got to secure Korvo against attack." He found the ribbons marked Floor, Dungeon, and Fiefdom Layout and Design. He selected the last option, and an intricate map of the city unfurled before him. He could see every street and alley, and if he focused closely, each building and house grew larger to show that they were carefully marked with spidery scrawl. In theory, he could make structural changes to the city in the same way that he'd altered FrontFlip Studios back on Randy's home world, but Roark knew from experience that *theory* and *reality* were often different beasts. When he selected the outer stone wall around Korvo and attempted to add ballistae, a scrap of parchment filled his vision.

[*You cannot make changes to Korvo without approval from a quorum of Village Elders.*]

A second, longer scrap appeared.

Grass Roots

The citizens of Korvo are a fiercely independent people. Unlike the chimeras in a dungeon, who instinctively follow the strongest leader, locals must be won over, either by benevolence or bloodshed! If you wish to make changes to

Korvo and its surrounding farmsteads, you will have to establish your rule with the people of Korvo.
Objective: Gain the loyalty of the Village Elders.
- or -
Objective: Slaughter the Village Elders.
Reward: Create and alter the layout of Korvo and the surrounding farmsteads, command and deploy locals, 110,000 Experience
Failure: Die before completing Grass Roots
Penalty: No respawn.
Accept quest? Yes/No

"Bloody damnation," Roark muttered. He didn't have time for local politics; every second they wasted drew Korvo closer to destruction. But what else was there to do? He may have looked the part, but he wasn't a monster like Marek. He couldn't bring himself to slaughter the innocent. Those were his people down there, and though his family estate had fallen long ago, he felt both honor and blood bound to protect them. His father had instilled that duty into his heart and soul.

"We'll just have to go about this the hard way," Roark muttered under his breath.

Flipping to a different page of the grimoire, he dashed off a message to the allied Dungeon Lords, calling them to meet him at the base of the entry stairwell on the first floor, then headed that way himself.

He was certain he could get the people of Korvo to trust him. If any of the previous elders remained, they would know him and surely agree to let him defend Korvo. Most had known him since he was a child sitting in on their meetings with his father. Earning their trust would take time, though, and Marek wouldn't wait long to launch his assault. Which was why they needed to establish emergency defensive positions as quickly as possible. That was where the other Dungeon Lords would come in. They could use Korvo's rugged and inhospitable terrain to create blockades, funnels, and choke points until Roark could speak with the Village Elders.

As he closed the Feudal Lord's Grimoire, a flutter of movement in the corner of his eye caught his attention—a reflection in one of the few leaded glass windows that didn't contain colorful images of deadly winged maidens. A lean, muscular creature covered in purple-tinged onyx scales and coiling tattoos of power moved through the panes, leathery wings folded, horns stretching up from his head.

Roark blinked. On second thought, the Elders might not know him.

The only traces that remained of the man he'd once been were the slight hook to his nose, the dark hair, and the gray eyes he'd inherited from his father. He had grown used to being a monster, but it seemed unlikely that the citizens of Korvo would be able to see past it. The Draconic Chaos Harbinger wasn't even the most fearsome of his shapes; once per day, he could use Draconia Form to become a colossal skeletal dragon, breathing devastating Necrotic and Infernal fire. If they saw that, they would never trust him.

"Admiring your reflection, Griefer?" Zyra teased from her spot on the ceiling.

Roark shook his head and kept walking. "Just guessing at the odds I'll be able to befriend the locals looking like the bloody second coming of the Sky Devourer." He glanced at Randy, who was keeping pace with them. "None of us look remotely human."

Through the gauzy veil, he saw the hint of tooth as Zyra grimaced, disgusted.

"Good," she snapped.

"Not if they think I'm here to bring about the Day of Reckoning," Roark argued. He filled them in on the particulars of his first quest as a Feudal Lord. "If Griff were here, he could be our go-between."

"Still no word from him?" Zyra asked.

Roark's jaw tightened. "Nothing."

Randy's wings rustled anxiously. "But his name is still in my contacts list. That should mean he's still... I mean, that he wasn't trapped when Hearthworld shut down. If he was, it should have grayed out or been deleted. We should be able to find him if he answers his messages."

"But he hasn't. Not yet. And until he does, it's down to us to establish friendly relations with the Village Elders," Roark said. "One way or another."

"Surely when they hear that they're in danger, they'll listen to reason," Randy said.

Zyra snorted. "Oh, of course. Heroes never shoot first and then ask questions when the dungeon's cleared."

Nervously, Randy brushed a hand across the bridge of his nose again. "Well, if we try, anyway..."

"It will have to be addressed later," Roark said, striding into the dungeon's cavernous entrance hall.

For now, the Dungeon Lords were waiting, prowling about and gossiping in growls, hisses, and squawks. They were a formidable lot, ready to rip him or each other apart at the first sign of weakness, but thankfully they were also prompt.

The questions began the moment they saw him.

"What isss it, Feudal Lord?" Shess the Soaring Serpent Monarch demanded. "What isss thisss urgent matter?"

"One assumes it is to discuss the party of attackers gathering at our gates," Rohibim the Deceiver purred, floating in his cloud of Djinn smoke.

"The former littlest Dungeon Lord's already gotten us in

trouble," squawked Drokara the Gullet from her perch on the staircase.

Roark frowned. "What are you all on about? I intended to send you out into the valley to establish dungeons in strategic locations." He glanced from the Harpy to the Djinn. "Attackers?"

With a flap of feathered silver wings, Randy Shoemaker flew to the top of the staircase and looked out into the night.

"Uh, Dungeon Lord—I mean Feudal Lord—we might have to deal with the locals now instead of later," Randy called down to Roark. "There's an angry mob out here."

"What level is it?" Zyra said, drawing her Tattooed Colt 1911s from their hip holsters. "Let's kill the creature and be done with it."

"Not that kind of mob," Randy said. "A... an angry group of humans. Where I'm from, that's another definition for 'mob.'"

Ko the Faceless, Pestilent Mind Scythe, sent Roark images of villagers gathering in the snowy land outside the crumbling walls of the Radiant Citadel. Though their expressions were twisted with fear, the citizens of Korvo were armed with sickles, threshing blocks, and smith hammers. Anything they had been able to lay their hands on it seemed. A few even carried proper weapons—swords and axes—though most were pitted from age or rusted from weather. Here and there Roark recognized a face—hardy, determined folks who had lived their lives in the mountain village.

Ko spoke into Roark's mind. *Relatively simple kills, if you can avoid being overrun. A swarm brings its own unique type of lethality to a fight.*

"We're not killing any of them," Roark said, infusing his voice with a powerful note of authority. The Dungeon Lords were too high level to be affected by his Intimidation, but it wouldn't hurt to remind them who was in charge. "Anyone who harms a villager will answer to me directly. We need those people down there to survive, and they need us, even if they don't know it yet."

"That's going to be a problem," growled Gevaudan the Terrible, scratching at one hairy ear. "Might be, I already sent my pack out to deal with them."

As if on cue, a series of howls cut through the air outside, followed by frantic shouting.

Roark cursed and leapt into the air, winging past Randy Shoemaker and out the door. He had to stop his troops from killing the people he was trying to protect.

CHAPTER 4
PEACE TALKS

Roark soared out of the Radiant Citadel into the icy mountain air. In spite of the darkness, he could clearly see the angry and terrified villagers clashing with the Wolf-Bear Warriors from Gevaudan's pack.

"Stand down!" Roark ordered. "Return to the dungeon!"

But the combatants took little notice of the shouting coming from the sky. Merchants and farmers of Korvo fought the loping, lumbering forms racing around them, attacking, retreating, and herding them into waiting sets of slavering jaws. If Roark didn't stop this now, it would be a bloody slaughter. The creatures of Gevaudan's pack were all in the low to mid-forties and were used to dealing with mail-clad heroes wielding mythic weapons and powerful wizards who could call down thunder or summon minions of their own.

A paunchy man in threadbare linens with a hoe would last all of five seconds. It wouldn't even be a contest.

Roark banked in a tight circle, folded his wings, and dove into the heart of the conflict, where a muscle-bound smith and a Wolf-Bear fought hell for blood in the muddied snow. Roark slammed into fur and flesh, knocking the Wolf-Bear and smith from their feet into the mad scrabble of the battle around them. He thrust his wings out and lifted his arms, palms raised toward the sky. With his scales and horns and skull-studded armor, Roark cut an intimidating figure—one every monster in Hearthworld would recognize at a glance.

Roark stomped his feet, sending a tremor shivering through the frosty earth, and roared. The violet ripples of Infernal Thunder shot away from him, arcing out from his hands in a flashy display of power.

Infernal Thunder
Attack Spell
Range: 40 feet
Casting Time: Instant
Casting Cost: 11% Base Magicka
With a shout of your booming voice, Infernal Thunder shakes the earth, inflicting (2 Damage x character level) and tripping opponents with less than .5n where n is caster's Dexterity.
Note: Infernal Thunder disrupts concentration-based spells when it causes opponent to trip or lose eye contact.
Note: Divine creatures are invulnerable to Infernal spells.

Using the spell was a gamble. Infernal Thunder was designed to temporarily interrupt enemy casters, not to deliver crippling damage, but Roark had no idea how feeble and frail his countrymen were. For all he knew, a paltry 168 total damage could be deadly, but there was no other way to prevent mass bloodshed, so it was a necessary risk.

Men and mobs stumbled and fell, flailing in the rocky mud of the mountainside battlefield. A momentary hush fell over the opposing sides. The Wolf-Bears skittered to the fringes with their tails tucked between their legs at the sight of their Feudal Lord, while the citizens of Korvo openly gaped at the horned, winged draconic man-creature at the center of the disturbance.

"Residents of the Citadel, hear me!" Roark spun on his heel, both to pin each of the Wolf-Bear Warriors with a threatening glare and to get an idea of how many mobs he needed to keep an eye on while he spoke. Hells, Gevaudan had sent a small army. He counted at least thirty. "You are ordered not to harm any citizen of Korvo, on pain of death. Be warned: there is no respawn here. Anyone you kill, and any of you who are killed, will never come back. All death in this land is forever-death."

At the word "death," the smith whimpered and dropped to his knees, praying fervently, "Creator, deliver us from the jaws of this monster from the depths of the seventh hell."

A farmer with a broken sickle dragged the smith backward into the tight circle of citizens. The smith was still crying out desperate prayers as the men closed ranks around him.

"We are here to protect the citizens of this land," Roark continued, raising his voice to be heard over the terrified smith, "not to fight them. Anyone who disobeys this sanction—Dungeon Lords included—will answer to me personally. And, I can assure you, my wrath will be swift and terrible."

He regretted saying the words almost the moment they left his mouth. He knew to the people of Korvo he would sound no different from the Tyrant King they despised. Winning their trust and approval would be even more difficult with such a declaration ringing in their ears.

However, it was the only way. The creatures of Hearthworld—especially those monsters from distant dungeons—respected only strength. Anything less than such a declaration would result in needless death.

Roark took a moment to stare down each of the Wolf-Bears in turn, waiting for a sign that they submitted to his will. One by one, they lowered their heads in deference, amber eyes downcast.

The men flinched as one when he turned to address them.

Seeing the fear in their faces, Roark realized suddenly why the Grassroots quest had allowed him the choice between intimidation rule and winning them over. They were frightened, but they were determined as well. If they thought he posed a threat to their families and neighbors, they would fight to the last man to stomp him out. Down the path of bloodshed, he would soon be ruler over a lifeless mountainside. A tyrant in truth, with no subjects left to terrorize.

Roark folded his leathery wings, trying to look a bit less intimidating and a bit more human.

"Men of Korvo, Marek Konig Ustar is coming. He will slaughter every living soul in the valley and surrounding mountains if need be. My forces and I can protect you and fortify your village against his attack, but we need the permission of the Village Elders to do so." He paused, considering his next words carefully. "We are not the monsters we may appear to be in your eyes. We wish to work with you, not to bully you."

It was a bit hypocritical, he knew, in the face of having intimidated the Wolf-Bears into submission, but he couldn't take the time to explain the intricacies of inter-dungeon politics. Every second was critical.

"It's imperative that I speak with the Village Elders immediately. Are Kareth, Otgerd, and Lonin still alive? They were Elders here when I was a child." There were more, but Roark couldn't remember their names, only their wizened faces.

The smith gasped. "The demon's stealing their names from our thoughts! Kill the monster before he beguiles us into damnation!"

"Shut up, you bloody fool." A broad-shouldered form pushed

to the front of the throng, clothed in what had once been fine robes, which were now going threadbare with use. The hood spoke of a mage, though like the rest of the material it had been patched and was wearing thin in places. "Is it truly you, Graf?"

Hearing the disgraced version of his family name made Roark's hackles rise. After however long he'd been in Hearthworld, he'd forgotten how he hated hearing his family's rightful title dragged through the mud.

"That's von Graf," he growled. "These were my family's holdings before the Tyrant King stole them, and they will be again. If you're going to insult me, then at least have the bollocks to show your face while you do it."

"It must be you." The man pushed his hood back, revealing a familiar visage half scarred by the backfire of a poorly written spell. "I can't believe anyone else would have that much more temper than sense."

"Von Herzog." Roark bit back the urge to return the slur and tried to find something civil to say. Of all those who might've survived to recognize him, Albrecht von Herzog was the last person Roark would've hoped for. He wasn't a bad man. He'd stood up to Marek, after all, even when so many other noble families had bent the knee. Despite that singular positive quality, however, he was an intolerable ass and one of the sloppiest mages Roark had ever known. The burn scars on his face alone testified to his shoddy spellwork. "You're still alive," was the best Roark could manage.

"Indeed I am." Albrecht smirked. "I'm shocked to see the same of you. We thought you'd been killed or worse."

"Sorry to disappoint you, mate." Roark didn't ask who Albrecht meant by "we"; he could only be speaking of the *T'verzet*. "Are... any of the others still in Korvo?" he asked, not wanting to out those still in hiding. Roark had always considered von Herzog to be too mild and cautious for the good of the rebellion, but outing himself like this was a bold move.

"A few," Albrecht hedged. "Things've deteriorated fast since your little tantrum. We've been dealing with what I assume has been the smoke from your fire since."

Roark balled his hands into tight fists, talons biting into his palms. Not without good reason was Albrecht his second least favorite mage on Terho. Though now that Lowen was dead, the fool would have to be awarded first place.

"We haven't got time to test rapiers, von Herzog." It took a monumental effort for Roark to show even a small amount more courtesy than Albrecht had shown him, but he couldn't let the man goad him into losing his temper in front of people who already thought he was a monster. "Korvo is in grave danger. Marek's forces are likely on their way even now. I've got to speak with the Elders immediately."

"Korvo has been in grave danger for *months*," Albrecht said. "Yet suddenly now, after all this time and death, the lost noble comes to its rescue?" He scowled down his burn-scarred nose at Roark. "What's your game, Graf?"

Roark gritted his teeth. "You've never listened to me before, Albrecht, but you would do well to listen now. Marek has changed, gained powers and strength even greater than the ones he had when I left." He hesitated, grasping at a possible tactic for holding Marek off that suddenly occurred to him. It was a risk, but when wasn't he staking his life and the lives of hundreds of others on a roll of the dice these days? "I can stop him, but I need time and permission from the Elders to make changes to Korvo's fortifications. You've got to get them to speak with me. Please."

For once, Albrecht didn't immediately come back with more pointless bile-fueled quarreling. The former noble glared up into Roark's face as if he were trying to see through it to his true intentions.

"Damnation," Albrecht muttered, running a hand along the stubble at his jaw. "If you let us down again..." He glanced over his shoulder at the men of Korvo, then leaned closer to Roark, his voice dropping to a growl. "They might not be the seafolk of my ancestral holdings, but by the Creator, von Graf, I won't let you or any other bloody damned tyrant destroy them. Fail in this, and I'll send you to the fifth hell myself."

Roark smirked. The fifth hell was reserved for those guilty of the worst crimes of betrayal, including nobles who failed or refused to protect the subjects whose safety had been placed in their hands.

"I don't intend to fail," Roark promised. "And if I do, I'll embrace the fires of the fifth with open arms."

Albrecht grunted, then spun on his heel. "This man—er—" He seemed to struggle for words for a moment. "*Lord* is Roark von Graf, son of your former lord, Erich von Graf." He raised a hand to forestall questions. "No, I do not know where he has been, nor do I know how he has come to look as he does. What I do know is that he's returned with new... warriors and magicks... to destroy the Tyrant King."

No grand cheer went up at this, though Albrecht paused as if he'd expected one. The citizens of Korvo looked askance at one another. When no one shouted out a rebuttal, Albrecht went on.

"In my experience, he is brash, impetuous, and foolhardy."

Roark's lips twisted into a wry smirk. Leave it to Albrecht to slander Roark out of one side of his mouth while praising him out of the other.

"But he is not craven and there is no man with greater hatred in his heart for the Tyrant King. He can be trusted," the von Herzog heir said reluctantly. "Return to your homes, men.

And hurry. Those of you who live next to one of Korvo's Elders, wake them and send them to me. I'll have a wagon readied to bring them up to listen to von Graf's proposal so we can devise a plan to protect Korvo against attack."

The words had no sooner left his mouth than a brilliant violet light ripped through the wintry darkness on the opposite side of the village. The shimmering portal illuminated the monstrous shapes spilling from its gullet. Creatures of mangy fur, rotted flesh, and yellowed fangs. Desiccated mummies in golden robes. Enormous crocodilian beasts, which crept along the ground, jaws ready to devour the unprepared. More and more of them came, forming a twisted horde in the valley below.

The clarion call of a war horn rang through the icy air as the glowing portal finally snapped shut. Marek's troops roared in response and charged at the sleepy village below.

Roark cursed under his breath, mind racing.

"Dungeon Lords!" he called, his voice booming off the slopes of the Karasu Mountains. "Deploy your strongest mobs to protect the village immediately!"

CHAPTER 5

INTERNET FAMOUS

For a whole six minutes, mystery portals barfed up Hearthworld landmarks, NPCs, and mobs in and around the greater LA area. Armored horses and merchant carts rained from the sky, while bewildered merchants stepped onto black asphalt for the first time. Thatch-roofed huts and cobblestone inns appeared next to dollar stores and auto shops. Monsters of every shape and size—as well as non-human races like olms and rogs—scrambled for cover or attacked passersby in their confusion. Gunshots, screams, car alarms, and police sirens filled the air as the situation spiraled straight down the crapper.

Scott Bayani, better known as PwnrBwner, and his crew of POSes—PwnrBwner's Poser Owners—didn't have time to stand around watching the absolute shitshow. One of those portals had opened right inside Shieldwall's ramparts, basically giving their well-thought-out defensive perimeter the bird.

"This is total bullshit," Scott griped, bashing some stupid Shroomacat in the face with his Obsidian Glass Mace. The weapon was a helluva lot better than the nail-studded Louisville Slugger he'd started out with, covered in jagged spikes, coated in Poison of the Rotting Sun, and hexed by the Griefer with serious levels of Undead damage. "I made these walls to keep out the douchewads who wanted to kill us."

The Shroomacat rolled right, raking ferocious claws along Scott's silver plate armor, not even scuffing the metal. The Griefer was sort of a chode, but he knew how to make high-quality gear.

"Maybe complain about it some more," GothicTerror deadpanned. She'd taken up a spot slightly behind the portal and was busy sniping feral mobs with an enchanted top-level bow called a Wraithpiercer Arbalest gifted to her by the leader of the Troll Nation. She was using run-of-the-mill arrows, though, all looted from the ArcheryPro since her spelled arrows were long gone, used during the final showdown with the angelic Heralds.

"Eat me, Elvira," Scott snapped. "I'm not complaining, I'm stating a fact. They shouldn't be able to portal inside, period. That's cheating."

The Shroomacat hissed, and Snuff Spores exploded into the air from its mouth. Scott covered his mouth and nose with his mace arm and hit the Storm Winds spell, blowing the spores away before they could get into his lungs and strangle him.

[*Congratulations! Your Spellcasting Skill has increased to Level 8! You can now cast class-based spells for half the Magicka.*]

With Scott's dual-class, he had access to a wider range of spells than most, and now they would only cost him half the Magicka, which was a huge perk. He'd never had to worry about Magicka with his High Combat Cleric alt back in Hearthworld, but as a Ranger-Cleric hybrid, getting enough juice to fuel his array of divine spells was always a pain in the ass. One of the main drawbacks of dual-classing.

He finished off the Shroomacat with a now much cheaper Cleansing Flame, charbroiling the creature into a handful of soot and ash. Didn't hurt that he was getting Experience points through the Dungeon Lord's Tax, too. That was money AF. Making XP while he slept, like some kind of pyramid scheme baller.

"Kaz believes Roark would approve of portaling inside the walls of a stronghold," Kaz replied from behind Scott. "Roark says that in war, there is no cheating, only survival."

"That just proves my point, Kaz," Scott said, glancing over his shoulder at the hulking Hellstrike Knight. "Bullshit cheating is the Griefer's specialty."

Kaz was too busy gently helping a wart-faced old witch limp up the stairs to reply. "Into Shieldwall, please. The wizened crone should watch her step over the threshold, yes. Kaz thanks her for her cooperation."

Scott rolled his eyes and turned back to the portal.

Looked like things were finally starting to slow down. Either Hearthworld was running out of NPCs and mobs to hurl or whoever had opened the portal was finally closing it. Scott was like ninety percent sure all of this had somehow been Roark's doing. That fancy necklace he had—the World Stone Pendant—could do all kinds of wonky shit.

From the corner of his eye, he saw a Venomous Rock Wyvern dive at Kaz's back. Scott turned and fired off a blast of Elemental Fury. Lightning crackled down his arm and nailed the plunging Wyvern between the wings. Direct hit.

Kaz paused from helping little old ladies long enough to finish off the Wyvern with a swing of his Legendary Meat Tenderizer.

Up at the door, 3Trenchcoat_Hobbitses started yelling so there wouldn't be any confusion where new arrivals were supposed to go.

"Everybody on the Griefer's side or just not down with evil, over here!" Hobbitses hit Scott and the other POSes with an orange blanket ward and yelled, "Get *inside* if you're on *our side*!"

He sounded like some kind of nutcase politician screaming slogans at the crowd, but elves, rogs, olms, humans, and various flavors of mob in medieval-style clothes and jankedy-ass starter armor ran for the door.

Not a super smart way to filter out the baddies, but a stricter selection process would have to wait. The feral mobs flooding Shieldwall's front yard were the biggest threat at the moment, aggroing everybody in their cone of sight like rabid racoons on the rampage. Scott would have to deal with the NPCs and mobs who could think and lie and shit later.

With a sizzling sound, the shimmering portal inside the walls shut off like somebody had flipped a switch.

A Greater Livid Rhinosaur halfway through bellowed as the closing portal sheared off its ass-end like an invisible bandsaw. It staggered forward a couple steps, leaking blood all over the place, and bumped into the overweight Ninjastein, who finished it off with his special edition *Bleach* katana, purchased from the Westfield Century City Shopping Mall. Roark had personally offered the weeb a better weapon—one straight from his private collection—but Ninjastein had insisted that he and his blade were bonded in battle. As a compromise, one of the Troll Nation blacksmith apprentices had imbued the dork's shitty weapon with a basic durability and damage rune.

Ninjastein pulled the blade from the corpse and shook the blood from the edge with an anime-inspired flick of the wrist. Scott grimaced. Gross but merciful. And it looked like the flood was over: no new mobs were vomiting into the world like a drunk sorority chick after an all-night bender. They just had to deal with the stuff that had already gotten out, then they'd be set.

Looked like the Poser Owners had that shit in the bag, though.

Ya_Boi_Flappie_Sak planted a blessed hand axe in the skull of a Firestorm Goblin Shaman, dropping it like a bag of rotten meat. Nearby, GothicTerror used an arrow glowing with her newest special ability, Corpse Burst, to turn a flying Aboleth into a bloody *splat* on the wall.

And awesomely, the newly hatched Dragonoids who'd spawned in Shieldwall were helping out. When Scott had first seen them come out of the egg, he'd been pretty sure they wouldn't be useful for anything but running errands or helping Kaz in the kitchen, but they'd grown hella fast, and now a bunch of the strongest ones were kicking major ass on the battlefield.

The tallest one stood just over five feet tall and had deep green scales slashed with orange stripes. Dragonoids fought with their claws and fangs instead of swords or maces, but they were ferocious as balls. The shredded body of a Corpseleg Jackal made a steaming pile at its feet.

Dragonoids weren't *technically* members of the POSes since mobs couldn't join guilds, but Scott was the official Arch-Overseer of Shieldwall, and what he said went, so he counted them as part of his crew. They were good little dudes to have on his side.

He checked the courtyard to make sure there were no other immediate threats. Nothing. That was game over. Home Team – W, Away Team – Eat shit and die. Pretty decent for a bunch of losers who had only started using their Hearthworld powers in the real world, like, a few days ago.

The excitement of winning faded way too fast, as the reality of the situation hit Scott in the gut. This wasn't a few monsters or a handful of Heralds they were dealing with. This was a full-on invasion—one reality smashing into another like a pair of rotting pumpkins. Unless Roark and his whole Griefer crew had been puked out of a portal somewhere in LA, Scott and the POSes were on their own. The only people on Earth with magic powers.

Who knew how far and wide those portals had opened up? They could've covered every continent in rampaging mobs for all Scott knew.

A couple dozen gamers against a worldwide army of overpowered nightmares wasn't a great matchup.

The noise outside Shieldwall's ramparts filtered back in. The metallic clanking of tank treads. The wail of cop sirens. Blue, green, purple, yellow, and red flashed against the usual orange of the LA light pollution. The US military and LA cops were out there trying to fight video game magic with guns and nightsticks and shit. They were going to need serious help. Bullets were effective in large enough quantities, but the humans firing them were glass cannons compared to the armored hordes of Hearthworld.

"Craptastic," Scott muttered. "Right back to square one." He jerked his chin at GothicTerror. "Whoretots, lock it down in here. I'm going up to check outside the walls."

GothicTerror shot him a middle-finger salute, then got to work organizing the last of the chaos inside Shieldwall. She might be a Screamo dick, but she was also an MVP when it came to taking care of guild business. Getting her on his side had definitely been worth the gold.

"Kaz will come, too," the Feral Hellstrike Knight rumbled, following Scott into the building.

Inside, newly arrived NPCs and mobs were milling around the entryway with big shellshocked eyes and fearful whispers. BusterMove and Helen Rose—one of the Frontflip influencers who'd come over to their side—were trying to calm everybody down and direct them toward the cafeteria, but they weren't having much luck. The mobs were scared of the NPCs, and the NPCs were freaked out by the mobs.

A yelling match had broken out between a Matriarch Steamsoul and a quest NPC Scott recognized from the back alleys of Argentine, who had probably led a couple thousand bands of heroes through the Steamsoul's dungeon in search of his lost sword or shield or whatever it was he was always looking for. All around them, hands were grabbing for weapons and wands and claws were being extended and spells prepped. All the place needed was for somebody to sneeze, and it'd go off like a cherry bomb in a high school toilet.

Helen Rose and Buster were in the middle of it all, trying to handle it like Human Resources managers "resolving a conflict," with politeness and without offending anybody.

Fuck. That. Shit.

Scott climbed up on an unlit brazier.

"Yo! Everybody shut up and pay attention to me," he yelled. "I'm the Dungeon Lord here in Shieldwall, so you all better listen up."

The yelling and noise died down as every eye in the room turned to face him.

"Name's Sco—" He stopped short. If his run of crappy jobs had taught him anything, it was that first impressions were important. He was about to introduce himself as Scott Bayani—a loser who worked at Taco Bell and lived in a shitty apartment surrounded by shittier neighbors he hardly knew. No one respected Scott.

But PwnrBwner? PwnrBwner was a beast who'd killed some of the most powerful creatures of Hearthworld, End-Dragon Aczol the Eternal included. PwnrBwner had helped bring down Bad_Karma. PwnrBwner was right hand to a magic-slinging demon wizard from another world. PwnrBwner was a *legend*. These people needed a legend to lead them, not a loser—especially with Roark temporarily out of the picture.

"Name's PwnrBwner," he started again. "Dungeon Lord PwnrBwner." Hell yeah, he liked the sound of that. "I'm not like most assholes who get in a position of authority and turn into a dick."

"Because you were already one," GothicTerror said. She and the other POSes were trickling in the door, probably finished with cleanup in the bailey.

Scott shot her the double-bird, then went back to his awe-inspiring welcome speech.

"Ask anybody who signed on with me, they'll tell you I'm tough but fair, basically a natural leader. You scratch Shield-wall's back and I'll make sure it scratches yours." He pointed at his lieutenant. "Tots, tell them. Do I get you Poser Owners the best loot or what?"

GothicTerror hiked her quiver higher on her shoulder. "We were swimming in it in Hearthworld, and he's broken it up fairly ever since we started gaming in real life."

"Damn right," Scott said. "I only have one rule: you do what I say or you bebop your ugly ass on down the road." He jerked a thumb over his shoulder for emphasis even though the closest street was out the door in front of him. "Them's the terms, folks. If you can live with that, then proceed down this hallway on my right to the cafeteria. That's a big room where there's food, like a tavern but without booze."

A couple of the faces in the crowd darkened.

Scott glanced sidelong at Kaz. "But we're working on getting a brewery up and running. Give it a day or two, and we'll be set on that front, too. Anyway..." He clapped his hands together. "I have spoken. That is all. Get moving."

With a low murmur, the crowd of NPCs and mobs flowed

down the hall toward the cafeteria. Buster stooped to answer a question for an Imp, but Helen Rose shot him a grateful smile.

Damn. It was too bad she was into Randy. Hopefully that little geek was alive and kicking ass in Roark's alternate universe. Randy might've been a nerd, but he was an okay guy, and he'd gone out like a baller, risking his life to save the world and shit. If somebody besides Scott had to get the super-hot famous gamer girl, he guessed he would've chosen Randy.

A tug on his sleeve snapped Scott back to reality.

"Dungeon Lord PwnrBwner," Kaz said, leaning in close, eye to eye with Scott despite the fact that Kaz was standing on the floor and Scott was up on the brazier.

"Dude, you don't have to call me Dungeon Lord," Scott said, hopping down. He reached up and slapped Kaz on the shoulder. "You're OG, generation one of the Poser Owner-Griefer alliance. The rules are different between buds. You can just call me Pwnr or something."

Kaz's huge, soulful eyes watered as he broke into a grin. "Pwnr is so gracious! Truly Roark chose the best hero to rule Shieldwall in his stead!"

Scott shrugged. "I mean, yeah. Obviously. But what's up, Kaz? What did you want?"

"Oh, yes!" The Troll Gourmet turned serious, the terrifying smile evaporating from his ugly mug. "Pwnr, Kaz fears you have been misinformed about how long the brewing of hops requires. Even working round the clock, Kaz must give the ingredients time to foment, to say nothing of the extra care necessary to ensure that Kaz has imparted only the deepest and loveliest of flavors to the—"

"Right, right." Scott glanced around to make sure nobody was listening, then motioned for Kaz to come closer. When the huge Gourmet had ducked down to his level, Scott said, "Don't worry about what I said about the beer right now. That was just a little incentive to keep everybody happy. If we need liquor that bad before your beer's done fermenting or whatever, I'll get a team together to loot a liquor store. Cool?"

Kaz blinked. "No, the process requires a constant temperature well above boiling. Kaz has never attempted to brew anything at a cool temperature."

They headed for the elevators at the end of the converted lobby. Several of the smaller Dragonoids scuttled to move out of their way.

"What I'm saying is we keep the beer timeline between us," Scott said. "That's need-to-know info, and nobody but you and me needs to know right now. Got it?"

Before Scott could get confirmation that he'd gotten through to Kaz, one of the former Frontflip employees slipped between them and the elevators. Scott could remember her trading recipes with Kaz, but not her name, so he just gave her a nod.

She shot him a brief smile, then turned to the Hellstrike Knight. "Hey, Kaz, got a second?"

Kaz bowed deeply. "For Lakshya, bringer of cauliflower curry, Kaz has as much time as is needed."

"So, remember that video I took of you making the Dumptruck Pizza?"

"Yes!" Kaz nodded emphatically. "So Lakshya would know how to make Gry Feliri's greatest invention at home."

Scott rolled his eyes and stepped around her to push the Up button. He didn't have time for more boring chef talk. There was a war going on outside Shieldwall, and now that things were under control inside Scott's domain, he needed to see how bad the sitch was outside of it. He was a Dungeon Lord now, which meant that kind of shit was his responsibility.

"Well..." Lakshya drew out the word like she was trying to figure out what to say. "So, I'm really sorry, I should've asked before I posted it, and I'm a bad person for not asking, but..." She pulled her phone out. "It's going nuts. In like the first two days, it got over nine million views, and it's pushing ten. Fifty percent of people think we're using CGI to disguise you, but with the portals more people are coming around to the idea that maybe you're the real deal, and that's driving the numbers up even higher. Plus, people love the way you talk about food, Kaz."

She turned the phone around for the Troll Gourmet, and Scott leaned in beside him. A small clip of Kaz sprinkling chopped green peppers across a loaded pizza crust hovered over a counter that was steadily ticking upward.

"Son of a bitch," Scott whispered.

"Right?" Lakshya nodded. "He's already internet famous. So, what I'm thinking is we record a few of these, set up a channel for you, get a series going—people love series—and monetize the whole shebang."

"Hell yeah." Scott elbowed Kaz. "You could be a millionaire, dude."

"You've already got the perfect branding," Lakshya said. "The Troll Gourmet. It's easy to remember and it hits the nail right on the head. You couldn't print money faster."

Kaz shook his head. "Kaz does not need money as a reward for teaching others the joys of cooking. Food is its own reward." His eyes glowed as he looked off into the distance. "And such a reward it is," he sighed.

The elevator dinged, and Scott stepped inside, sticking an arm in the doors so they wouldn't close yet.

"I get that," Lakshya said. "Really, I do. You're an artist first, in this for nothing but the passion. But Kaz, you've got to think about it like this: you're not charging anybody to learn from you. You're letting businesses who are going to profit off you anyway pay you to show their ads during your videos. It's only fair that you get something out of the deal, too."

This chick was a wheeler and dealer. Scott smirked. "What'd you say your job was here at Frontflip?"

"I worked in Textures," Lakshya said, then she grinned. "But before that, I was an agent for a midlevel talent agency."

"Of course you were." He rolled his eyes. "This fucking town." He stopped the doors from sliding closed again.

"So, what do you say, Kaz?" She stuck her phone back in her back pocket. "Want to give internet stardom a shot?"

"Well..." Kaz fidgeted with his Meat Tenderizer. "Lakshya is sure the students of cooking won't have to pay to learn?"

"We won't charge them a dime until we see whether merch is a viable option. But that's way down the road. For now, we'll just record a couple more instructionals, your favorite meals, that kind of thing, and see how they perform."

Kaz looked at Scott, his huge eyes puppy-dog pleading for help.

Scott nodded. It was a decent deal, and it could have a fringe benefit that nobody'd mentioned yet.

"I think it's got potential," he said. "Aside from the money piece, we need to be able to get a message out to the rest of the world that not all the monsters walking through their streets are bad. No one's gonna give us the time of day, but with something like this?" He drummed his fingers on the edge of the elevator door. "If we can get the internet on our side, then maybe that'll trickle up to the powers that be."

"So, what Kaz is hearing," the Feral Hellstrike Knight said, "is that such a show will not only teach people the joys of cooking—at no cost—but will also benefit the Dungeon?"

"Bingo," Pwnr said, shooting him a finger gun.

"Then Kaz agrees to try," the Gourmet replied, shaking

Lakshya's outstretched hand. "On the condition that he can show how to make Loaded Wings next."

"You've got a deal," she said. "I'll meet you in the caf about an hour before supper? Is that enough time?"

"Three," Kaz said, holding up three fingers the size of polish sausages. "The secret to Loaded Wings starts with an excellent marinade."

"You're the best, Kaz." She winked at him, then headed over to BusterMove, flagging him down for something.

"Jeez," Scott said, shaking his head. "All right, Kaz, I've got Dungeon Lord shit to take care of. You coming or what?"

"Yes!" Kaz hopped into the elevator, making the whole thing shake under Scott's feet.

"Hope turning this place into a dungeon reinforced the pulleys and shit," Scott muttered, hitting the button for Shieldwall's top floor.

The elevator came out near Scott's badass new throne room, but instead of going in and admiring all his new loot and checking over the list of new troops like he wanted to, Scott forced himself to go straight out onto the battlements.

What he saw dragged him right back down to earth from the high of Kaz's awesome news.

Tanks rolled through the streets, belching fire and shells, trying to take out the biggest mobs, while cops and SWAT desperately tried to fight everything smaller than an elephant with handguns, M16s, and batons—rogs and olms included. Which made the Hearthworld transplants fight back twice as hard with magic spells. It was a total shitshow.

Scott grimaced. Good guys on both sides were probably dying down there, and neither side had any idea that they should've been allies instead of enemies.

Beside him, Kaz let out a panicked whine and tore at his face. "Many good mobs and heroes of this world will be killed, but they do not all mean each other harm! Kaz knows that Naga! It is Srapa the Deatheater. She is very kind. And that Djinn, Teza the Warsworn! He has such wonderful stories to tell and excels at baking cookies. They are not malicious, PwnrB-wner! They should not be killed! What will Kaz and Pwnr do?"

"Basically, the only thing we can do is get our asses out there." Scott blew out a long breath. "We're the only people who really know what's going on. It's gonna suck, but we've got to be the go-betweens. Get the good mobs and NPCs in here with us, protect the humans from the bad guys, explain to the cops and soldiers who to kill and who not to."

"PwnrBwner is right." Kaz's big ears flapped against his head as he nodded. "We must protect them from one another. It is not only the right thing to do, but our duty to Roark and the Shieldwall!"

"Word." Scott leaned on the brickwork and stared down at the chaos, already mentally cherry-picking the best POSes for his street team. "Let's just hope doing the right thing doesn't get us ganked before your cooking video checks start rolling in."

CHAPTER 6
THE VANGUARD

Drawing his new Tattooed Glock 26 and a Peerless Slender Rapier he'd enchanted with Light magicks, Roark leapt into the air and sped toward the village below.

Drokara the Vengeful Metalwraith, Shesss the Soaring Serpent Monarch, Rohibim the Stormbreaker Specter, and their many varied flying minions glided on the air currents around him like cana-hiri falcons heading in for a kill.

On the slope below, Gevaudan, Ishri the Cunning, the Beryl King, and the other Dungeon Lords and the various underlings who couldn't fly raced over the white blanket of snow and ice, dark shapes against the white. A few of the men who had come to confront Roark were doing their damnedest to keep up, desperate to save their families from the raiding army—and likely the troops Roark was leading as well. But the mobs of Hearthworld quickly outpaced their human counterparts, eating up the distance with long legs and ice-gripping talons.

Flashes of jade lightning burst through the streets of Korvo. People screamed in terror as it silhouetted the houses in flickering Undead flames. Fire caught, spreading quickly between the close-packed thatched roofs, but the citizens had no time to fight it. Women darted through the streets, clutching bundled infants and dragging crying children or helping the weak and elderly, all desperate to find a route to safety that didn't lead them directly into the maw of the reptilian Soul Devourers.

Men valiantly fought loping Jackal Fiends a head or more taller than themselves and yowling Sacred Bastets the size of draft horses. Infectious Plague Mummies called down clouds of Pestilence and spewed Plague Spray from outside the fray. Just like the angry throng that had come to confront Roark, the townspeople wielded hoes and scythes and the occasional wood axe. A handful of town guards in boiled leather armor carried halberds and spears, but these were men unfit for war. The young and hardy had been drafted to fight in Marek's bloody crusade, and what remained were wizened graybeards well past their prime. That didn't stop them from fighting, but against such deadly magick and horrific strength, such mundane weapons were next to useless.

Roark felt the absence of PwnrBwner acutely. The overgrown man-child could be frustrating, petty, and unbelievably juvenile at times—almost *all* the time—but no one could doubt his bravery or fighting prowess. This would've been an opportune moment to have the Ranger-Cleric unleash his devastating Light-aligned magicks. Thanks to the peculiarities of Hearthworld's Primal Creation Wheel, the powers of the Undead were completely subservient to the Light-aligned spells and classes, just as Divine power was worthless in the face of the Undead.

Unfortunately, Pwnr and his ragtag guild of Poser Owners were trapped back at Frontflip Studios, worlds away. Roark didn't have any natural Light-based spells at his disposal, but he did have an Enchanted Glock 26. Though Roark's Flash Art Gunsmith skill was far lower than his Smithing, Enchanting, and Cursing skills, the pistol had a fivefold enchantment tattooed into its grip in Old World Flash Art. The blazing sun behind the Goddess of Revenge imbued each bullet with midlevel Light Damage.

It wasn't much against these top-tier Undead creatures, but it was better than nothing.

Roark lined up his shot and fired a volley of the Light-enchanted projectiles into the chest and head of the closest Plague Mummy. Holes riddled the creature, and spidery veins of white light crept across its desiccated flesh, dealing additional damage with every second that passed. Alone, the damage shouldn't have been enough to kill the Undead creature, but as its Health bar flashed, a Pestilent Mind Scythe appeared on a nearby wall and let out a Psionic Shriek. The mummy's head exploded into a hail of black sand, rotting bandages, and bone dust.

"They're weakest against Light magick!" Roark called to his troops, using Infernal Thunder to amplify his shout so those on the ground could hear as well. "Kill anything that isn't human or allied with the Troll Nation. And remember, there is no respawn in this world. If your Health drops, don't wait to drink an Ultimate Healing Potion!"

The Dungeon Lords let out echoing cries, repeating Roark's words down the battle lines, then promptly broke off from the formation. Gevaudan and his pack of Wolf-Bears loped onto a wide cobblestone boulevard, quickly securing it against an onrush of fearsome Undead mobs. The Beryl King and his rocky golems beelined for the walls, attempting to fortify a wooden sally gate and close off a portcullis. Drokara the Vengeful Metal-wraith wheeled right, her lesser wraiths following behind in a tight V formation.

Roark stopped the Stormbreaker Specter.

"Rohibim," he barked, still surveying the carnage playing out on the streets below. Already, the fires were spreading like mad. "Take your strongest Thunderheads and put out the blaze before Korvo is completely destroyed."

The Specter nodded, his smoky form bobbing. "It will be done, Feudal Lord."

Peals of thunder rolled as Rohibim's powerful underlings formed up over the rooftops to unleash torrents of rainwater on the flames licking at the sky.

"Shesss!"

The Soaring Serpent Monarch banked around at Roark's shout.

"Take a host of the fastest mobs and get the people of Korvo to the ruins on the mountainside," he said, indicating the burnt and crumbled remains of the von Graf Manor with his rapier. "Women, children, and elderly first. Guard them there until this is finished."

"Of courssse, Feudal Lord," Shesss hissed, dipping her serpentine head in acknowledgement.

Marek's attack had come quick—much quicker than Roark would've believed possible—and they weren't prepared to stage a proper defense. But they were doing all that could be done, given the circumstances. With the rescue effort begun in earnest, Roark searched the chaos before him for the Tyrant King's nightmarish new form. There wasn't a trace of Marek, which came as a bit of a surprise. Was he sounding out Korvo's defenses before coming after Roark, or was this some sort of trap?

Roark suspected the latter. He wasn't going to turn tail and run, though, not with the lives of so many innocents on the line.

Still, knowing that this was likely a trap, some measure of prudence was called for. Roark continued to circle cautiously high overhead. Powerful though Marek might be, the Undead God-Pharaoh couldn't fly, and Roark refused to give up even the slightest advantage. He was outclassed enough as it was.

Down on the streets of Korvo, blood and fur flew as the Wolf-Bears clashed with Rabid Jackals. The canid warriors snarled, growled, and ripped at one another with claw and fang, then from nowhere the Beryl King's Sarsen Sentinels rolled in to crush the weakened Jackals. It was a wickedly effective pairing that Griff must have come up with; the grizzled old weapons trainer had been the one training the recruits and designing attack teams for the Troll Nation. Not for the first time, Roark wished he knew where in the bloody hells the old man had ended up, or if he had respawned before the shutdown.

An awful racket drowned out the clashing dogs as Drokara's clattering flock of Vengeful Metalwraiths descended on the Sacred Bastets, tearing at the fluttering scraps of skin on the skeletal creatures before taking wing again. With ear-piercing screeches, the catlike Undead leapt and swatted at the metal-winged bird women, momentarily forgetting the bleeding and dying men of Korvo. The Bastets had the level advantage without a doubt, but the Metalwraiths had both a tactical and terrain advantage. They peppered the cat-like creatures with razor-sharp feathers and unleashed their screeching sonic attacks from above, giving the Bastets little recourse.

Roark was pleased with the response of his allies. Their time drilling and practicing together had paid off, and Marek's forces were already caving, clearly unprepared for such a unified show of strength.

That, however, wasn't the most surprising part. The true shock came when Roark realized that he was gaining Experience points from the enemy mobs being killed below.

[Stormwaller, Vengeful Metalwraith Level 58 under your Feudal Lordship has leveled up! As part of the Feudal Lord's Tax, you have collected 289 Experience Points!]

Roark had to read the scrap of parchment through twice to

be certain he wasn't misreading it. Always before he and his troops had only been able to gain Experience and level up from killing the heroes that ventured into the Citadel. Apparently, the merging of Hearthworld and Terho had changed that steadfast rule, and now killing mobs also provided opportunities to grow more powerful. A game-changing discovery—not only for his own forces, but for Marek's as well.

Roark couldn't help but wonder what else might have changed in the process of convergence and whether those changes would ultimately help or hinder him.

On the other side of the village, a child screamed, followed by a serpentine hiss. Roark spun in the air just in time to see a Soaring Serpent Highborn crash into the charred timbers of a burnt rooftop. The little girl the Serpent had dropped limped back to her feet and ran for a man with a bow. As she ducked behind the man's legs, he nocked another arrow and took aim at the Serpent.

"Damnation," Roark growled under his breath. The archer thought the Serpent was trying to steal the girl. The rescue effort was flagging because the people of Korvo simply couldn't tell friend from foe—not while both sides looked like demons from the fright tales of old come to life.

The wounded Serpent Highborn was confused and infuriated by the attack from the humans it had been tasked with rescuing. It slithered and stumbled back to its feet, hissing again at the archer and girl, then lunged like a striking adder.

The archer braced himself, nocking another arrow, but the Serpent Highborn was a powerful level 76, and a member of a species well known for their aggressive nature and venomous bites. The archer stood a better chance of overcoming a pack of wild and hungry Makaronin.

Roark folded his wings and dove in front of the vulnerable humans, conjuring a Necrotic Infernal Shield as he landed. The

Serpent Highborn crashed against the shimmering barrier, still growling and spitting. The impact drove Roark backward into the cobblestones.

"No matter what they do, you are not to harm them!" Roark thundered, his shout booming off the houses on either side, rattling the panes of smoke-blackened glass. "You are here to protect the people of Korvo! Only the Tyrant King's troops are fair game for attack! Am I understood?"

As he spoke, he cast Necrotic Invigoration, returning Health to his allies within a fifty-foot radius and banishing lesser debuffs. The Serpent's red bar sped back toward full Health. Injuries and pain were washed away in a blink, and sense seemed to return to the serpentine creature. It nodded at him, then turned and took wing, swooping off to find less deadly individuals to save.

Roark clambered back to his feet in the snow and shook out his wings. A small gasp from behind made him spin around.

The archer and little girl were staring up at him in bewildered shock. The child fearfully clutched the edge of the man's cloak while he, in turn, held his bow in a white-knuckle grip. Uncertainty wafted off them like the reek from the midden heaps.

"We're on your side," Roark said, sheathing his weapons and holding up empty hands. "I swear it to you."

The little girl burst into tears and pulled the man's cloak up to cover her eyes. The coins sewn into her skirts jingled as she shook with fear.

"You look familiar," the archer said, eyeing Roark, though still not loosening the grip on his bow. "The bodies of the von Grafs was never sealed after they was massacred. We done the best we could for 'em, but none of us townfolks could make up a writ. You ain't one of the family come back from the dead, are you? Lord Erich maybe? You got a powerful likeness to him. 'Cept for the horns and the wings and what have you..."

"Erich's son," Roark said, his voice suddenly hoarse. Something about the man connecting him to his father lit a fire deep in his bones. After all this time, he was home, and these were his people. For one of his own people to recognize his resemblance to the man whose integrity he had always hoped one day to mirror seemed to underscore the rightness of his return. He cleared his throat. "I'm his son."

Finally, the archer eased the tension on his bowstring. "I always told folks one day the von Grafs would come back and avenge all that bloodshed." One hand came off his bow to pat the headscarf of the girl behind him. "Glad to see I wasn't talking out the side of my face. How many of these demons're yours?"

A burst of gold flared in the corner of Roark's vision. A new battle taking place above the rooftops—this time a Malaika Herald and a Pestilent Mind Scythe. He cursed under his breath. He'd been about to tell the man he could trust any of the flying creatures, but if Marek had brought some of the Heralds who hadn't been in the Radiant Shield when Roark defeated Lowen, then that stipulation wouldn't work.

"For now, just get out of Korvo to the ruins of the manor house," he said. Finding a way to differentiate friend from foe to the citizens would have to wait until later. "Get as many people to follow you as you can, but don't stop for anything. And if you're picked up by a flying reptile... don't shoot it."

Gold streaked past the two of them like a meteor as the golden-skinned Herald crashed into the burnt-out husk of the house across the street. A pair of Thunderheads and a handful of Metalwraiths slammed into the angelic being, venomous metal beaks tearing and Elemental Lightning flying in bright arcs of yellow and blue.

Roark froze as he caught the briefest glimpse of raven-black wings in the tussle.

Was it possible?

"Go!" Roark shouted at the archer, waving him on.

As the man scooped up the girl and ran, Roark drew his Tattooed Glock 26 and turned toward the fight. Though the allied mobs well outnumbered the dark-haired Herald, they were no match for her skill with the rapier and her lawless magick. In seconds, two of the Metalwraiths' red bars were flashing out a Critical Warning. Before Roark could intervene, Talise lobbed a crackling ball of orange magic at the closest of the creatures. The Metalwraith dodged too slow. With a screech, the wraith's Health bar ran out and she dropped to the burn-scarred floor of the house, dead.

The sight of the broken creature lying there landed in Roark's gut like a punch. Not just dead, but forever-dead. He'd tried so hard to emphasize the stakes and the dangers, but forever-dead was something these creatures couldn't fundamentally grasp. Not yet. Hearthworld's mobs had experienced a lifetime of respawning; how could they comprehend the *finality* of forever-death? Many more would die before they cultivated the self-preservation instinct.

He shook himself and cast a Necrotic Infernal shield. The purple-and-green wall forced Talise and the Troll Nation troops apart.

"Get out of here, the lot of you," Roark ordered the remaining Metalwraiths and Thunderheads, casting Invigoration to bolster their flagging Health. "I'll deal with the Herald! See to the rest of Marek's forces. And pay attention to your Health! Don't forget that there are no second chances here. Dead is dead!"

The allied mobs acquiesced, disappearing out through the gaping hole in the side of the building.

Talise straightened, but didn't sheath her rapier or dispel the ball of orange magick hovering above her hand. "Roark? You have to get out of Korvo. Marek's come to destroy you. This whole attack is nothing more than a ploy to draw you out."

"I suspected as much," Roark said with a grim nod.

A scowl marred her usually cold, expressionless face. "Then what are you doing here, you bloody idiot? Leave before he finds you."

"I won't let innocent people die for me," Roark snapped, his eyes irresistibly drawn to the dead Metalwraith on the ground.

"Your survival is the only thing standing between Marek and all the innocent blood in this world," Talise said. "Once you're gone, he'll send his monsters tearing through all of Terho. He doesn't need humans anymore. Without you to stop him, he'll massacre them all. How many innocent people will die then? How many thousands will perish without you to stand as the firebreak?"

An aristocratic chuckle sent frost racing down Roark's spine.

The Undead God-Pharaoh manifested outside the burnt-out building, misshapen head grinning down through the hole in the roof.

"I knew keeping you close would serve a purpose eventually, granddaughter," Marek said smoothly. "Observe." Scarabs crawled about under his ragged, decaying flesh as he raised a claw. "If I attempt to kill your brother, you'll throw yourself in front of him, and all I'll have gained is a dead servant. But if I kill you—"

Brilliant jade flashed as the lightning blast of God-Pharaoh's Wrath lanced toward Talise. Time seemed to shudder and slow as death flashed before Roark's eyes. Not his own, but his sister's. Heralds were pitifully weak against Undead, which was precisely the reason Roark had bonded his core with that of Aczol the Eternal, NecroDragon of Daemonhold Deep. He'd used the power of the dread dragon to defeat Lowen. A blast of Undead Energy from a creature as formidable as Marek would be a death sentence for Talise.

She was the last of his blood. His only remaining family. He hadn't found her alive after all these years to simply abandon her to her fate. Not again.

The choice was simple.

With a powerful burst of speed, Roark shot between Talise and the incoming blast, snatching a portal plate from his Inventory with all the haste he could muster.

The Tyrant King's spell slammed into his back, tearing a hole in the armored scales between his leathery wings as if they were no sturdier than wet parchment. Agony detonated through his chest cavity and raced outward along his nerve endings. Instantly his filigreed Health vial dropped to a mere sliver of red and flashed out a frantic Critical Warning.

At nearly the same moment, orange and blue light exploded before his eyes, blinding him to the world.

His legs gave out a moment later, unwilling to support him, and his body crumpled in a heap on cold, uneven flagstones. When the mass of feathers slammed into him, Roark von Graf thought that he had finally died. This time for good.

CHAPTER 7
A REPRIEVE

Roark coughed and tried to blink the flares from his field of vision. Around the phantom lights, he could see the golden flagstones and winding narrow staircase of the Radiant Citadel's entrance hall. Everything was hazy, though, the images and thoughts blurring together around the edges.

"What in the name of Azibek?" Zyra's familiar snarl confirmed it—Roark wasn't dead after all.

Though truth be told, he should have known it from the pain rampaging through his body like a pack of angry Thursr Behemoths. His ribs burned, his skull throbbed, and every breath was a chore—like inhaling through a wet cloth. The sharp, metallic taste of copper lined the inside of his mouth. Surely even the hells couldn't muster that level of all-consuming torture. Worse yet, his Health wasn't regenerating. He needed desperately to drink an Ultimate Health Potion before a stiff breeze knocked the last flashing sliver of red from his filigreed vial, but he could hardly do more than shudder in agony.

"Oh my gosh!" Randy said. Green Arboreal magick flashed

across the back of Roark's eyelids as he prepared himself for an attack. "Uh, battle stations! Unfamiliar Herald in the Citadel!"

Running feet and the clank of swords and armor filled the air. Roark fought for the breath to call them off, but couldn't force a word past his gritted teeth.

"Hold your attacks," Zyra snapped. "You may not see the family resemblance, but that Herald is the Griefer's sister"—the metallic clinking of the Orbweaver Ravager pulling her Tattooed 1911s silenced the room—"and we don't want to kill her unless she's to blame for this." Zyra's voice lilted upward at the end of the sentence, making it a question.

Roark knew he needed to intervene. Zyra wasn't the trusting sort. Azibek the Cruel had been the original Dungeon Lord of the Cruel Citadel, and Zyra had served him as a shadow assassin; winning her over had been no small feat on Roark's part and involved a great deal of poison. Her distrust for all—save perhaps for Roark, Kaz, Mac, and Griff—had only grown over time. No matter how Talise had secretly aided them in the past, Zyra would never fully believe that Talise was on their side. If Roark didn't do something, one of them would almost certainly end up dead.

He steeled himself and pressed a hand against the wound soaking his chest with blood. "Wasn't her," he choked out. "Marek."

Talise shifted, untangling herself from him, and accidentally knelt on his fingers as she stood. He winced.

"Sorry, mate," she said. "Here, drink this."

Cool glass was pressed against his lips. Roark gulped down the potion, for once happy to taste its unpleasant and cloying sweetness. Red liquid flowed back into his Health vial, and the pain began to dull around the edges.

When he opened his eyes, Talise was crouched beside him. A crowd of low- to mid-level mobs made up of Thursrs, Reavers,

Changelings, Imps, Pebblekin, and Bloodleeches encircled them, ready to attack. Randy stood by with Vine Fists readied, and Zyra had prowled silently closer, her Tattooed 1911s aimed at the back of his sister's head.

"Put them down, Zyra." Roark groaned as he sat up. Talise caught his hand and helped him to his feet. "She didn't do any of this. Without her, I would be dead now. Forever-dead," he added for those who still hadn't grasped the unforgiving nature of mistakes in this land. He glanced at his sister. "You cast healing on me as Marek's spell hit, didn't you? But how did you get around my Infernal alignment? Divine Restoration should have finished me off."

"I didn't use Divine Restoration. I called upon the lawless magick I was born with." Talise retrieved her rapier from the floor, where it thankfully hadn't gutted either of them in the portal. "It's faster to cast because it works on instinct rather than decision, and as far as I know it doesn't have an alignment. Not in the sense that the magicks from Hearthworld do."

Roark glanced at the filigreed Health vial in the corner of his vision. It had yet to disappear, which was strange in and of itself. Usually it blinked away the moment it had refilled.

"Zyra is right, however," Talise said. "I am to blame for what happened, at least in part." She slammed her rapier into its scabbard harder than necessary. "Marek must've known I'd turned traitor. Giving you those portal stones was a risk, but I thought I'd covered my tracks well enough. Clearly, I was wrong. I hoped to maintain my cover and continue leaking you information."

She stood and paced, her feathers rustling softly as she walked. "I should've known something was wrong when he insisted I accompany him on this raid. Curse me for an utter fool. It's all so clear in hindsight. Bringing me to the massacre would force you to join the fight, either to stop me from killing your troops or to stop your troops from killing me. It was perfect leverage. How naive was I to think I was deceiving him? The bloody hubris!"

"Ah yes," Zyra purred, slipping her 1911s back into their hip holsters. "I see the family resemblance much more clearly now." The Orbweaver Ravager crossed two of her four arms, planted the others on her hips, and scanned the mobs standing around, awaiting orders. "The Feudal Lord somehow managed to avoid death by stupidity once again, and we needn't concern ourselves for at least another day or so. You can all return to your posts."

Before they could disperse, Roark stopped them. "Our enemy is primarily aligned with the Undead set of magicks. For those of you who don't already have a Light-enchanted weapon, get to the smiths in the Marketplace and arm yourself with one. If you're capable of casting Light spells, find Paragon Yevin and level them as far as you can. You may not need them straight away, but it's best to be prepared for when Marek turns his attacks on the Citadel."

As soon as he finished speaking, the mobs broke into action, scurrying off to do as ordered.

Randy frowned. "What I don't understand is how you portaled into the Citadel. Don't you have wards that prevent that?"

"Portal plate," Roark said. He reached into his belt and pulled free a silver bar that fit easily into his palm. The plate was covered, front and back, with a complicated series of instructions and runes, all linked together using a complex Curse Chain. Previously, the plates had been large and unwieldy, scattered all through the Cruel Dungeon, and used as a sieve to sort and transport incoming heroes by level and even class type to an appropriate level of mob. A level 8 hero who crossed the plate's threshold might be whisked instantly away to the second floor of the Citadel, while a level 20 hero crossing the same plate could find themselves facing down Grozka's blade on the third floor.

They were deadly effective at splitting parties and were just as effective against mobs as men. He'd used a Discordant version to repel Lowen's Heralds and a more benign version to grant allied dungeons access to the Troll Marketplace on Level Five. Over time, Roark and his smithing apprentices had perfected the plates, paring them down in size and material cost to the thankfully small version he held in his hand. There was no telling if all of his plates had survived the merge with the Vault of the Radiant Shield, but at least one of them had. Once he recovered, he'd have to dispatch some of his apprentices to properly take stock of their portal plate situation.

"Luckily, they seem to work here in the same way as they did in Hearthworld," Roark said. A mercy and a miracle both, since he hadn't even been sure any of the plates would work outside of Hearthworld. "Perhaps some bleed-over has occurred to stabilize portal magicks in Traisbin," he mused out loud.

"I suppose theoretically it's possible," said Randy Shoemaker, "but I've been wondering if there isn't a more mundane explanation."

That gave Roark a moment of pause, since his conjecture had been more for his own benefit than for anyone else.

"Obviously we're dealing with a unique situation," the Arboreal Herald continued, "but even in a world where there's magic, the most likely explanation is still going to be the simplest one." Randy's wings rustled, and he shifted uncomfortably under the intense scrutiny of Zyra and Talise.

"I mean, think about it. The Tyrant King didn't have any trouble getting his army here through a portal, and you guys all use portal stones that only he's allowed to create and hand out," Randy said, indicating Talise. "What if the danger of portals is just misinformation he's been spreading? Transporting troops and supplies is a major strategic necessity. If you find a way to cross huge distances that's instantaneous and avoids all ambushes, while your enemy is still relying on old-fashioned means like carts and horses, then you've got a huge advantage over them. Keeping everyone scared of using and researching portals would stop them from ever leveling the playing field."

What Randy Shoemaker said made a certain sense, and Marek was without a doubt devious enough to do just such a thing. So why had Roark never even considered the possibility?

If the Dev was right, it would simplify things enormously. If Roark could create portals that would not only work in Traisbin, but between the worlds, perhaps his friends weren't lost forever. Strange that he'd spent such a sizeable portion of his life avoiding attachments in pursuit of revenge, only to find himself considering tampering with potentially deadly magicks —not in a bid to kill Marek, but to get back a handful of friends from another world. Roark had had plenty of allies in his life—allies could be easily walked away from if the need arose. Friends couldn't be, as he'd too often learned the hard way, and that made them a prime target to be used against you.

And still he was considering transporting Kaz and Griff from the Devs' home world to his? He must have lost his mind in that last transition.

Even ignoring those doubts, it wasn't easy to shake off the distrust of portal magicks. He'd heard the cautionary tales for as long as he could remember. The mages who taught at the Academy had believed wholeheartedly in the instability of portals—or at least professed to believe it. Even his family had thought portals dangerous and warned Roark and his cousins away from ever attempting them. For so many to believe the lie,

Marek had to have poisoned the well of knowledge long before Roark was even born. If that was true, it begged the question: just how long had the tyrant been working his hooks into Terho?

"I don't know, mate," Roark said with a grimace. If he intended to bring his friends through one, he wanted to be absolutely certain of its stability.

"Right, no, I get it." The Arboreal Herald reached for the bridge of his nose, that habit of adjusting his spectacles which he had mentioned, but just as quickly he seemed to realize what he was doing. He pulled his hand back down and clasped it behind his back as if to fight off the urge. "More research is needed."

"Such research is a death sentence," Talise said matter-of-factly. "I've witnessed as much for myself firsthand. I've watched reckless and foolhardy mages attempt to cast portals, only to be drowned at the bottom of an ocean or engulfed in a flow of magma. What you're saying is heresy."

"Heresy's a strong word, I think," Randy said, his silver-skinned cheeks coloring slightly. "And I'm not saying I'm right. The fact that Roark used a portal and wound up as a Dungeon Troll in Hearthworld definitely suggests that there's a kernel of truth there, but in my experience the best lies are always built on partial truths. Maybe they are dangerous, if done improperly, but maybe Marek knows exactly how to properly employ them. That's my working theory, anyway. And it needed to be thrown out there just in case we were missing something. Like, we wouldn't want to go forward discounting a tactic that critical just because of 'heresy.'"

Randy curled the first two fingers of each hand strangely in the air as he said the word.

Talise looked from the alien gesture to Roark as if he would be able to explain its meaning. Roark shrugged. A lifetime wasn't enough to understand the oddities of the humans from Randy's home world.

"I hate to interrupt this fascinating discussion of rumor and conjecture," Zyra drawled, "but we've got a more pressing issue to address."

Roark raised an eyebrow at the veiled Orbweaver Ravager.

"Look at your Health vial, Griefer," she said flatly.

He glanced at the filigreed vial that was still prominently displayed at the edge of his vision. The red liquid inside was steadily dropping. In the few minutes since he'd drunk the Ultimate Healing Potion, he'd already lost a handful of the regained Health.

"What in seven hells?" he muttered, squinting at the ill-behaving vial.

"Curse of the Mummy," Zyra said, gesturing with one pair of hands at him. "My Septic Brewmaster abilities allow me to see active effects, and this one's bad."

Scowling, Roark opened his grimoire to his Character page and scanned the list of effects. At the bottom, the newest one was pulsing with a Necrotic green light.

[*Curse of the Mummy*
You have invoked the wrath of the great and powerful Undead God-Pharaoh! Continue to lose 4x-2y Health per 5 seconds (where x is the level of the caster and y is the level of the cursed) until you or the Undead God-Pharaoh is dead.]

Roark swore under his breath and quickly pulled up the Character page in his grimoire.

Draconic Chaos Harbinger Overview			
Name:	Roark	Level:	86
Gender:	Male	Player Class:	Hexorcist
Type:	Draconic Chaos Harbinger	Alignment:	Infernali
Current Experience:	1,232	Next Level:	330,240
Health:	2,424.250	Infernali Magick:	3,850.000
H-Regen / 5 Sec:	365.825	Magick-Regen / 5 Sec:	189.25
Attributes:		**Stats:**	
Weapon Damage:	163	Strength:	168
Attack Damage:	1709	Constitution:	153.65
Base Armor:	125	Dexterity:	195
Armor Rating:	1342.3	Intelligence:	300
Movement Rate:	2 x Speed of Opponent	World Stone Authority, Greater Vassal	11/60
Critical Hit Chance:	28%	World Stone Authority, Lesser Vassal	85/225
Critical Hit Damage:	(+) 250%	Undistributed Stat Points:	20

Draconic Special Skills:	**Player Special Skills:**	
Rapid-Regen	Spellcraft (Class Skill)	Lv. 15
75% Resistance against normal weapons	Bladed Weapons (Melee Skill)	Lv. 12
Stunning Blow; 22% Chance / Hit	Weapons Specialty: Rapier	Lv. 9
Infernal Necro Shield; Draconic-Hybrid Spell	Calligraphy (Trade Skill)	Lv. 5
Necrotizing Infernal Torment; Draconic-Hybrid Spell	Blacksmithing (Trade Skill)	Lv.13
Necrotic Invigoration; Draconic-Hybrid Spell	Tailoring (Trade Skill)	Lv. 8
Infernal Undead Temptation; Draconic-Hybrid Spell	Enchanting (Trade Skill)	Lv. 17
EXPAND SKILLS LIST	Enchanting Specialty: Cursed!	Lv. 15

Interestingly, he'd leveled up not once but twice, bringing him to level 86—all gained from the Feudal Lord's tax, which siphoned points from the initial skirmish against Marek's forces. Being able to gain Experience from killing high-level enemy mobs was a significant perk. That was the good news. The bad news was that Marek was currently at level 135, so his curse dealt a steady stream of 368 damage every five seconds. Exactly three points above Roark's five-second Health Regen Rate.

He wasn't losing much life, but the drain was constant. The steady *plinking* drip of a leaky roof.

Roark had earned twenty additional stat points, however, and if he dropped all of them into Constitution, it would bolster his overall Health by a hundred points, bringing it up to 2,524.25, and raise his Health Regen Rate up to 375.83 Points/5 seconds.

Just enough to outpace the infernal curse.

The choice was no choice at all. Such a constant drain would mean life or death in any fight, and it would be forever lingering in the back of his mind. If he so much as became engrossed in smithing, creating sigils or flash art, or experimenting with some new magic and simply forgot to re-Invigorate himself, it could kill him. It would be a fool way to die, but it wasn't outside the realm of possibility. He'd been told on more than one occasion that he would forget to breathe when he became absorbed in a project if it weren't involuntary. That was one more headache he didn't bloody need.

He added the points and hit accept.

The real problem was that the additional points were only a very temporary solution to his problem. The curse itself didn't deal fixed rate damage but scaled with character level. As Marek became more powerful—and he would—so too would the curse's power grow. Roark would have to work to keep pace, and he was already starting at a significant disadvantage. If he didn't continue to level, and damned quickly, Marek could pull away, and murder Roark without ever having to step in the same room with him again.

And just when he'd begun to think he might survive this coup on Marek.

He closed his grimoire to find Zyra tapping her chin beneath the veil.

"Perhaps I can brew something up to combat it," she said thoughtfully. "A potion that releases its effects over time? Something in the nature of a poison, but with healing properties rather than deadly ones."

"Let's hope so," Roark said, casting Invigoration to top himself off. The red in his vial slipped back up before finally disappearing. "I don't want to waste any more Healing Potions than we have to. There's no telling if you'll be able to find the ingredients you need to make them here in Traisbin."

Inky smoke puffed beside them, and a low-level Reaver prowled out.

"Apologies, Feudal Lord, but another group of heroes approaches the Citadel," the Reaver said. "All humans. Led by that one with the half-scarred face."

Zyra pulled her Colts again, and Talise her rapier, but Randy caught Roark's frown.

"Albrecht," Roark explained. "He's a failure of a mage and there's certainly no love lost between us, but he's not a threat. And, unless I'm mistaken, that will be the Village Elders with him. If we are to stand any chance of beating back Marek's advances, we are going to need their cooperation—so everyone on their best behavior." He shot a meaningful look at Zyra.

She sighed. "Oh, fine." She shoved her Colts back into her holsters and sarcastically brandished empty hands. "Happy?"

"I'll be happy if everyone walks away from this with all their limbs intact and no cases of Contact Poisoning," Roark drawled.

"I refuse to promise anything sight unseen," Zyra said. "However, if they behave, so will I."

Under the circumstances, it was the best he was likely to get.

With a final glance at the veiled Ravager, Roark strode toward the winding stairway leading out into the snowy night. Albrecht had convinced the Elders to meet with him. Now Roark just had to convince them to trust a monster with all they held dear. Roark worried that defeating Marek's curse would prove the easier of the two challenges...

CHAPTER 8

THESE OLD BONES

Griff cast a weary eye up at the gray light of dawn seeping into the orange-black sky. It had been a long night in a strange land, filled with unusual new monsters and strange conveyances—two things which weren't easy to tell apart here. He'd spent a good hour after being unexpectedly dumped in this world fighting a beast that turned out to be nothing more than a horseless carriage made of metal and the sort of flawless, clear glass he'd only ever heard of in the homes of the wealthiest Hearthworld citizens. He'd been fooled because the cursed things wailed like the dead in the Traitor's Forest, belched fire when it had been beaten badly enough, and had a grown man clearly visible in its belly.

An easy mistake to make, all things considered.

That had only been the beginning.

Later came feral mobs running wild through the streets and terrified folks in strange dress with guns and clubs, wide-eyed and attacking anything that moved. Griff could deal with the first. Even old as he was, he'd spent too much time in the arena to forget how to bring down a rabid Hellskelter or stop a charging Dire Tricorn. It was the second group that truly frightened him. They were probably mostly good folks when you hadn't caught 'em off guard in the middle of the night. Last thing Griff wanted was to end up in a fight for his life with a good man just trying to protect his family from the unknown. The best he could do was try to outpace them, ducking down alleys and hiding in the shadows to avoid drawing their attention.

He needed to find a place to bed down and a stiff drink to soothe the bumps and bruises. Running, hiding, and fighting monsters all night, then tromping around all day was a young buck's game.

He rubbed his dry, gritty eye, then searched the line of blocky buildings again for anything familiar. Unless he'd been imagining things, somewhere along his route last night he'd caught sight of the fancy slate roof of the One-Eyed Unicorn, still as high-falutin' as it'd ever been in Averi City. Under normal circumstances the Unicorn was out of his reach, but just for today he could spare the extra gold for a day's rest and the chance to get his bearings in this strange new city.

From behind him came a porcine snort. "There's somebody down there!" Another snort. "Get him!"

Griff wasn't fool enough to waste time turning around to see who'd spotted him. Get to a defensible spot first, then have a gander for whoever's trying to kill you. That one simple rule had never done him wrong before, and he wasn't about to break it now.

Taking a sharp right turn, he sprinted down a narrow alleyway still wrapped in shadows.

Dead end.

The sharp clack of hoofbeats bounced off the buildings around him, making it sound like his pursuers were everywhere, but he didn't let his fear run away with him. More often than not, a half second's thought made the difference between life and death.

There was a cluster of odd metal barrels and black bags against one wall, the stink giving their contents away, but he quickly dismissed the refuse heap's cover as false safety. His pursuers had most likely seen him duck down here. With the brick wall blocking off the end of the alley, it wouldn't take them long to discover his hideaway, then the only way out would be through however many of them were following him.

A rusty ladder hung down from above. Not quite out of reach, and it led to a series of castle-like machicolations protruding from the side of the building. With their widely spaced iron rails, the murder balconies wouldn't conceal his whereabouts, but most folks—hero, mob, and NPC alike—never quite got the hang of looking up for danger. If the runners after him happened to be a bit smarter than the average mob, Griff had the handgun the Griefer had Tattooed for him, and there was a pair of windows he could escape through or the next level of balcony to fall back on.

Grunting with effort, Griff hopped up and grabbed the bottom rung of the ladder. The ladder and the balcony clanked and groaned as he pulled himself onto it and settled into a crouch.

Not a moment too soon. A small herd of [Nightboars], hulking mobs with stiff bristly hair in a riot of colors and with rings through their notched ears, filled the mouth of the alley. Leading the charge was a big-bellied porker with the nameplate [Pilig Darkswine] floating above his purple-mohawked head.

"He had a shortsword and a buckler," snorted one of the Nightboars. "I saw it. He's definitely from Hearthworld."

"Focus on finding him first," Darkswine grunted. "Then we'll give him the option to join or die."

Griff didn't know what sort of outfit these hogs wanted him

to join, but based on his experience with the Legion of Order's takeover back in Hearthworld, these sorts of posses were rarely made up of fair-minded, even-keeled folks. He wanted no part in their business, even if there was a certain safety in numbers.

"He couldn't have gotten away," snorked another. "There's no way out of—"

Something clinked behind the barrels and black bags. A glass bottle rolled out, catching the meager light.

Darkswine held up a paw. They froze, watching the rubbish heap. Griff tensed as the leader waved a pair of Nightboars toward the pile.

The overgrown hogs dove in and came up with a plump feminine form nearly as large as they were. Blonde, bedraggled hair stuck out from underneath a ribboned maid's cap, and an ample bosom shook with the woman's struggles.

Mai. Sweet, affable Mai—incapable of harming a soul.

Griff scowled. He'd hoped the lass was safe in Flavortown, the tavern she ran with Kaz, but she must've been in Averi City when the portals struck. So much for escaping quietly up the balcony. Mai was like a daughter to him. He couldn't leave her down there alone, his own safety be damned.

Moving smooth and slow, Griff pulled his gun, a handsome piece called the Saturday Night Special.

Superior Saturday Night Special
Old World Weapon
One-handed Damage: 106 - 112
Durability: 99/102
Level Requirement: 16
Cylinder Capacity: 8 Rounds (Enhanced Capacity); .38 Caliber
Revolver Class Weapon: Fast Attack Speed, Slow to Medium Reload

Enchantments: Duty or Death
Effect: +10 Bleeding Damage/Sec, Until Healed
Effect: +5% Piercing Damage against Light and Medium Armor

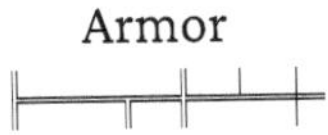

Down below, Darkswine leaned in to snuffle Mai's face. "What have we got here?"

Mai flinched and tried to pull away from him, but one of the Nightboars who had dragged her from her hiding place held her fast.

"Bit of NPC trash from one of the cities," grumbled a scraggly, bearded hog from behind their leader. He gave an exaggerated sniff. "You can smell the heroes on her."

"Yeah, probably been helping raiders take down our kin," added another.

"This soft little barrow?" The boar holding Mai pinched a bit of her side, and she yelped in outrage. "She couldn't hurt a Pixiegnat with a Flail and a Freeze spell. She's harmless."

"Am I now?" Mai stomped hard on the hog's leg, her Soft Leather Boots scraping down his shin hard enough to draw blood. Griff's eyebrows shot up. Maybe she *could* hurt a soul, after all.

The Nightboar squealed and grabbed the bloodied appendage.

"Though you're a mite bigger than a Pixiegnat, to my thinkin'," Mai added tartly, crossing her newly freed arms. "The hams on you would feed a dozen hungry heroes."

"You sow!" The injured and insulted Nightboar came up with a cudgel drawn.

Griff aimed the Saturday Night Special, but couldn't find a clear shot. He cussed silently. Mai was too close in the muddle, and the gun was too new to him. Perhaps when he had leveled his skill with it further, but for now, he couldn't take the chance of hitting her.

Rising to his feet, he stowed the gun and slipped his trusty shortsword and buckler on. It was a far cry from likely that he'd make it down the ladder fast enough, but he had to try.

Luckily, Darkswine grabbed the cudgel before the Nightboar could swing.

"This isn't the Mud Flat Wallows," Darkswine grunted. "We're on a different mission. Here, we don't kill or maim until we know whose side they're on."

The Nightboar let out a disgruntled snort, but lowered his weapon.

Griff froze, one boot on the rusted ladder. What were these lads playing at?

A piggish grin pulled at Darkswine's snout as he turned back to Mai. Griff strained his ears to catch every word.

"So, sweetmeat, who're you allied with? Darith and the Vault of the Radiant Shield or the Griefer and his pathetic POSes? Keep in mind you're a long trot from the safety of the POSes' dungeon, and we own everything between."

Mai looked up, no doubt considering whether she would be better off to lie about her allegiances, and caught sight of Griff. Her plump pink lips made a surprised O.

Griff put a finger to his lips, and she hurried to turn her gaze.

"A dungeon in this world, you say?" Mai inspected a crack in the brick of the opposite wall. "Might be I've heard of it. That's the one they call Shieldwall? Home to all sorts of fearsome mobs and terrible heroes?"

"Maybe a few stupid Trolls are fearsome to a nonessential NPC like you," snorted the bearded hog, "but we eat starter mobs like that with our morning slop."

"Do you, now?" She planted her hands on her wide hips. It

was clear that she was keeping the hogs distracted so Griff could climb down. "Well, here's me looking the prat thinking I'd heard of a Troll Gourmet who served up plenty fine rashers of bacon daily."

Griff didn't let the distraction go to waste. While Mai sassed the overgrown pigs, he lowered himself from the ladder and dropped to the ground behind the Nightboar with the cudgel, stifling a wince at the pain in his joints when he landed. Sure as shine wasn't as young as he used to be.

Nor as quiet, it seemed. The Nightboar with the cudgel spun around, letting out a squeal of shock.

Not one to waste the element of surprise, Griff bashed him in the snout with his buckler. While the boar's brains were good and rattled, he went to work with his shortsword. He wove in and out, hacking and slashing and dodging as Darkswine called the other Nightboars to join the attack.

Griff's mouth pressed into a grim line that was almost a smile. Guns were all well and good, and there was a time and place for ranged weapons, but this was his arena, close-in fighting with a sword and buckler. Footwork and lightning-fast combos. Get in, throw a series of quick but devastating strikes, get out, wear down the Health bar faster than it could regenerate. There was a rhythm to it. A beauty he never got too old to appreciate.

He chipped away at the cudgel-swinging Nightboar, a combo at a time, fending off Darkswine with shield bashes, and getting in some decent licks against the bearded hog in the meanwhile.

Then he saw his opening. Triggering Double Strength Backhand Slice, Griff stepped in and neatly decapitated the bearded hog, shaving a good measure of scraggly hair off his chinny chin chin in the process.

An ascending chime rang through the alleyway.

[LEVEL UP!]
[You have 10 undistributed Stat Points.]

Griff blinked. He'd leveled up by killing a mob? That wasn't possible. Leastways, in Hearthworld it hadn't been. Experience points had been reserved only for the victors in battles against heroes.

Pain lanced through his side and his filigreed Health vial dropped a handful of points. Warm blood ran down his ribs and soaked into his belt.

[You have sustained Bleeding Damage. -2 Health/second for 30 seconds or until you consume a Sufficient Health Potion.]

While he'd been gawking at the level notification like a blamed idiot, Darkswine had darted in and sliced his guts with a simple Off-Hand Combo. It wasn't enough to kill him, but it damn sure hurt his pride.

Returning his attention to the fight, Griff shoved aside all questions about how things worked here. There'd be time for that if he survived. One thing he knew for sure from talks with PwnrBwner and the Griefer—there were no respawns in the heroes' world. Every death was forever. He couldn't afford to die and leave Mai alone and undefended in this unforgiving place. He had to survive at least long enough to get her to the safety of Shieldwall.

For his size, Darkswine was no sorry attempt at a rogue. He was a sneaky brute, light on his hooves and fast enough to leave even a seasoned fighter like Griff winded.

Something whiffed past Griff's ear.

The forgotten Nightboar. The hog cocked back his cudgel for another overwhelming swing, but before he could launch it, Mai crashed a heavy metal bin full of refuse across the top of his skull.

Enraged, the Nightboar spun to attack the pink-cheeked young widow.

Griff threw another shield bash to back off Darkswine, then went after the cudgel-wielding Nightboar. He planted a boot in the boar's spine to Stun him and hacked at the back of that thick neck with his shortsword. The boar's Health bar flashed. He had less than ten percent Health left.

Of course Darkswine wasn't one to ignore the sort of opening Griff had intentionally left for him. Like a gullible little piggy to the slaughter, the leader barreled in as if his Silent Prowl would hide a beast of his size. Though Griff supposed maybe Darkswine could be forgiven for thinking so, considering the old man he was fighting only had one eye left to watch his back with.

Spinning into a bash and slash combo, Griff sliced away the last of the cudgel-wielding Nightboar's Health. He sidestepped the hog's dropping corpse, then ducked under Darkswine's Heavy Cutlass.

A predictable hidden shank to the guts followed, something any rogue could learn on their first day. Griff dashed the blade hand with the edge of his shield and was rewarded with the loud *snap* of Darkswine's wrist bones breaking and a pained squeal.

From his new angle, Griff shoved his shortsword up into the mohawked leader's hairy belly. The stuck pig shrieked and squealed as his Health bar flashed out a Critical warning, then ran dry.

Griff stepped back to avoid the spreading pool of black Nightboar blood and marveled at the influx of Experience points. This place was surely something else.

Mai threw her arms around him, enveloping him in a weepy hug. "Bless me, but I was so scared! I feared you'd be killed, forever-dead, and all because of me."

"You did just fine, lass." He patted the young widow's hair fondly. "We made it out the other side, and that's the part that counts in the end."

"Is it true, what the boars said?" She sniffled and stepped back. "Are we in the heroes' world, same as my Kaz?"

"That's the only explanation that'd make any sense." Griff glanced up at the sun, just beginning to peek over the buildings. He hooked his buckler on his back and stowed his shortsword. "That being the case, we need to get you to Shieldwall. Far as I can figure, it's going to be the only safe place for folks like us."

CHAPTER 9
THE NEW WILD WEST

"Come on, keep it moving," Scott yelled, wheeling his free arm forward like a dude directing traffic. "Follow the chick with the glowing crossbow and the major scream-queen energy."

The frightened refugees jogged forward. They looked like the extras on a post-apocalyptic movie set—dirty and raggedy, but with inexplicably perfect skin, perfect bodies, and white teeth. Except these extras' designer jeans were stained with real blood and ashes and the dirt smeared all over their perfect faces hadn't been carefully applied by makeup artists.

Up ahead, Scott's team—GothicTerror, Kaz, Ninjastein, Flappie_Sak, and a programmer dude named Arjun who used to work at Frontflip—advanced down the street in a loose net around the refugees, keeping an eye out for threats.

The POS rescue teams had been alternating shifts over the last couple days, scouring the streets for refugees of both the human and inhuman variety. With Kaz acting as an eight-foot-tall ambassador, they picked up mobs who wanted a safe place to hide. And keeping Kaz as far in the background as they could manage, they saved humans who couldn't accept that they were going to get killed by game monsters if they didn't get their heads out of their asses and run already.

Working in the food service industry, Scott had already figured out that most people were too stupid to live, but these rescue missions really drove the point home. If he wasn't such a good fucking person, he would've said screw 'em and let natural selection take its course. But as Dungeon Lord of Shieldwall, it was basically his duty to protect the weaker and dumber in his area, so whatever.

At least the loot off the feral mobs was decent. He was making bank. Magic weapons, badass armor, and actual bags filled with silver and gold coins. No more shifts at the Bell for him. Even better, through the Dungeon Lord tax, he got a cut of the Experience gained by everybody below him on the totem pole. Since these rescue runs had started, he'd already leveled up his IRL self once through osmosis, which wasn't anything to sneeze at. Along with that, he'd finally figured out how to access his Character Screen outside of Hearthworld and was stoked to see that his Ranger-Cleric power set wasn't the only thing to transfer over—his level had too.

This alt hadn't started out as powerful as his High Combat Cleric had been, but he'd been steadily leveling up and had just hit 29—as high as he'd ever climbed with any character. He had a boatload of abilities too, most of which he was just starting to figure out how to use on Earth.

Human			
Name:	Scott "PwnBwner" Bayani	Level:	29
Gender:	Male	Player Class:	Soulguard Ranger
Race:	Human	Alignment:	Light/Divine
Current Experience:	18,172	Next Level:	45,240

Health:	934	Divine Magick:	1,060
H-Regen / 5 Sec:	63.05	Magick-Regen / 5 Sec:	49.75

Attributes:		Stats:	
Weapon Damage:	115	Strength:	117
Attack Damage:	394	Constitution:	105
Base Armor:	235	Dexterity:	30
Armor Rating:	840	Intelligence:	78
Movement Rate:	Bonus + 2		
Critical Hit Chance:	22%		
Critical Hit Damage:	(+) 200%	Undistributed Stat Points:	0

Soulguard Ranger Special Skills:
50% Resistance against cursed weapons
75% Resistance against Undead
Blunt Force Barrage: 12% Chance / Hit
Shield Ward: Cleric Spell - Lv. 5
Fast-Healing Blast: Cleric Spell - Lv. 3
Elemental Fury: Cleric Spell - Lv. 8
Solar Glory: Cleric AoE - Lv. 2
Lightning Spear: Cleric Spell - Lv. 5
Elemental Spikes: Cleric Spell - Lv. 1
Holy Reckoning: Cleric AoE - Lv. 3
Powerful Inspiration: Cleric Aura - Lv. 1
EXPAND SKILLS LIST

Player Special Skills:	
Spellcraft (Class Skill)	Lv. 8
Blunt Weapons (Melee Skill)	Lv. 12
Weapons Specialty: Mace	Lv. 7
Heavy Armor (Armor Skill)	Lv. 13
Ranged Weapons (Melee Skill)	Lv.5
Mining (Trade Skill)	Lv. 6
Cartography (Trade Skill)	Lv. 4
Commander (Guild Bonus)	Lv. 4

"Yo, Pwnr," Flappie_Sak called, leaning a hexed Hand axe of Decay against his shoulder. "Straggler."

A superhot chick they'd picked up on Rodeo tottered along behind everybody else. Today's run had been to Beverly Hills, and they'd been dealing with her pampered princess bullshit ever since. First it was the fifteen designer bags she couldn't live without. Then her demand they stop and get an Evian for her stupid purse dog. Now it looked like one of her ridiculously wedged sandals had broken a strap. She was the epitome of too stupid to live, though her sheer hotness made her almost worth the headache.

Only *almost* though.

"You gotta be shitting me." Scott groaned. "Watch our ass end, Flappie, I'll get her."

Flappie_Sak nodded and took the new position.

The scrawny purse dog went nuts, yapping at Scott as he jogged over to the chick.

He ignored the little mutt. "Listen, lady, we don't have time for this. We're just a couple blocks from Shieldwall and the military encampment that I'll probably have to beg to take you off my hands. Now kick those pieces of shit off and let's move."

"Excuse me?" She glared up at him. "These are two-thousand-dollar custom-print Valentina Daravanis."

"Yeah, and you're about to take a serious bath on them. Let's go."

"Fuck you. I'm not going anywhere without these." As she got bitchier, the little dog got more agitated, jumping around and yelping like he was going to rip Scott's face off. "What am I supposed to wear? Some ugly Walmart brand? I would *literally* die."

Scott scowled. They were in the middle of a fucking war zone, he'd been up for like three days straight doing hero shit, and this stupid chick was worried about how she looked. Mobs might be ugly, but at least with them if you were like, "I'm Dungeon Lord, do what I say," those punks respected the chain of command. Humans were just assbags full of more assbaggery, and Scott was done with it.

"No, you dumbshit, you will *literally* die if I leave you here." So he grabbed the chick around her tiny waist and threw her over his shoulder.

She screamed. "What the hell do you think you're doing?"

"Declaring martial law."

"Put me down!" The chick's bony fists thumped against Scott's back and butt. He didn't even feel it through the thick plate armor covering his body. She tried kicking him, but her legs flailed uselessly against his pauldrons. "You Cro-Magnon asshole!"

"That's Dungeon Lord Cro-Magnon Asshole to you."

The purse dog ran alongside Scott, yipping and snarling, but keeping just enough distance so that it wouldn't actually have to attack him. The broken-strapped sandal flew off its owner's foot and narrowly missed knocking the little fart out.

"My shoe!" She went stiff like she was straining to reach it. "Go back and get it right now!"

Scott snorted. "If that rat-thing was a real dog, he'd fetch it for you."

She growled and kicked, her fruitless struggles cranking into high gear. The shifting and flailing knocked Scott off-balance, and he tripped over a curb. He had to throw out a hand at a blue mailbox to keep them both from going down.

The box roared, its letter door snapping open to reveal thousands of glistening teeth as big as butcher knives.

In his rush to get his hand away from those teeth, Scott fell backward onto his ass, the chick on his shoulder letting out an *oof* as the impact knocked the wind out of her.

"Mimic!" Scott yelled, the shock putting a ragged edge into his voice.

The letter box chomped mechanically, every clash of its teeth echoing off the buildings around them like somebody was slamming its letter door over and over again. Scott couldn't get away fast enough with this chick on top of him, and she kept twisting and thrashing, desperately trying to get a glance at what was attacking them—as if she could do a damn thing to help the situation.

"What's going on?" she squealed.

"We're being eaten," Scott snarled. He tried to swing his Obsidian Glass studded mace at the beast, but he was in a terrible tactical position and her crazy floundering made things even worse. "Hold the fuck still."

The Mimic clanged closer, almost chomping the chick's leg off at the knee. Scott just barely managed to swing her out of the way in time. With a grunt, he jammed his mace into the Mimic's jaws. The weapon was made of tough stuff, but the Mimic was a powerhouse. It effortlessly ripped the weapon from his hands and flung it away with a slathering, spiny tongue that looked like it belonged to some hentai creature off the deep web.

The little purse dog squeaked, then darted in like it had been doing to Scott this whole time. Totally a bluff, but the Mimic wasn't having it. The rabid letter box swooped over and gulped down the dog whole.

"Gucci!" the chick screamed.

"Oh shit!" Scott scuttled back farther. "Anybody planning on helping me out, or am I the only one in this fucking guild who does anything?"

An arrow banged into the side of the letter box, its tail vibrating with the impact. A red bar appeared over the Mimic, minus a handful of HP.

"Quit your bitching," GothicTerror said, reloading her Arbalest. "The cavalry's here."

With his free hand, Scott unleashed a sizzling Lightning Spear against the Mimic. "Maybe if I had a team who knew that Hearthworld Mimics are weak against Toxic Rot spells and crushing dam—"

A massive Legendary Meat Tenderizer whistled through the air and smashed down on top of the letter box, crumpling the steel around the hammerhead like an accordion.

The first strike decimated the Mimic's Health bar, but Kaz reared back and brought the Meat Tenderizer down again, flattening the creature into scrap metal. Its last trickle of Health ran out, and an option to loot popped up.

"Thanks, King Kaz," Scott said.

The huge blue shitkicker cocked his head like a confused dog, big ears flapping. "Kaz is not a king, PwnrBwner."

"It's from *Kong vs. Gojira 19*, this movie about—" The chick on Scott's shoulder caught sight of the former Troll and flipped her shit. "You know what, forget it. Help me out here."

Kaz hurried to scoop up the screaming, crying chick. Unlike Scott, Kaz was big enough to hold the flailing woman like a baby across his chest. Not that she reacted to that any better than being thrown over a shoulder, but it was probably a more comfortable ride.

Grunting, Scott climbed back to his feet, snagged his obsidian mace, then checked the loot on the dead Mimic. He snorted at the contents.

Along with a handful of gold, a Cracked Sapphire, and a pair of Biteproof Gauntlets, Scott pulled a shaking, jittery purse dog out of the letter box.

When she saw it, the chick stopped fighting Kaz and threw open her arms.

"Gucci, baby!" She sniffled, face all streaky with mascara. "Come to Mommy, sweetie!"

The dog practically jumped out of Scott's arms. Ungrateful little mange factory.

They made it the last block and a half without any more nasty surprises. Scott relaxed a little as he got eyes on Shieldwall and the military's tanks and tents camped out around it. Best part of the day—unloading the civilians.

Couch_Warrior3000, a Poser Owner who had gotten called out by the National Guard when shit IRL started to go sideways, met Scott's team at the line. He'd been acting as their go-between with the military.

"Where'd you pick these folks up?" Couch_Warrior smirked at the designer clothes and bleached teeth as his fellow National Guard ushered the refugees toward the tents. "Louis Vuitton?"

"No takesies-backsies," Scott said. "They're your problem now."

Couch_Warrior snorted, then turned serious. "Dude, you heard about Mike Silva?"

"What about him?" Scott asked warily.

Mike Silva was the CEO of Frontflip, the game studio whose headquarters Scott and the Poser Owners had taken over and the Griefer had transformed into Shieldwall. Total cock knuckle. Even after being told he was dooming three whole universes if he did it, the dickhole had un-soulbound Roark's World Stone Pendant. All this monster invasion shit could probably be laid right at Silva's feet.

No news about that douche was good news.

"He's still pissed about Frontflip, and he's making waves with the higher-ups in the government. He says you stole his property."

"I took it over. There's a difference. Anyway, if you run away like a little bitch, you don't get to complain about people stealing your shit. Tell him I said to suck it and he can't have Frontflip back."

"He doesn't want the campus back, he wants money," Couch_Warrior said. "I guess his usual law firm was destroyed in the Merge—that's what everyone's calling it now, the Merge. Anyway, now he's rounding up lawyers outside the containment zone to sue your ass for five point six million in stolen property and damages."

A cold fist gripped Scott's balls at the number. Five point six million? He'd never see that much money in ten lifetimes. There was no way he could pay that, and it wasn't like he had a crack legal team to get his back.

Then he paused and started to laugh. What the hell was he worried about? The dick wobbler could sue him for ten billion dollars for all Scott cared—Silva couldn't touch him. Scott

Fucking Bayani was a Dungeon Lord now. In this slice of the world, his word was law. Silva's lawyers were welcome to march in here and try to collect, but all their fancy Harvard and Yale degrees combined wouldn't get them past the outer wall.

"Obviously Silva hasn't noticed that things have changed around here. Hiding behind lawsuits, legalese, property values —that shit's ancient history. If he wants that money, he'll have to grow a pair and face me man-to-man."

"But... the lawyers... They'll sue your ass off, dude."

Scott sneered. "This is the new Wild West, brohole. Out here, you take what you want or you get the hell outta the way. Far as I'm concerned there's only two rules. Whatever I say goes, and you keep what you kill." He glanced up toward the looming edifice of Shieldwall. "That puppy's mine now." At least it was until the Griefer showed back up, but the military didn't need to know that yet.

He turned back to Couch_Warrior, who was still obviously struggling with the concept of Scott not giving a fuck about being sued. "Anyway, I ain't got time to deal with that. Your military buddies are probably gearing up to storm this area and take out the mob menace. I've gotta get the rest of the good mobs inside Shieldwall before they take out a bunch of dudes they don't know are on our side."

That snapped Couch_Warrior out of his daze. "Actually... that's not happening. They sent the order down a few hours ago." He hesitated, glanced away, and shifted on nervous feet. "We're pulling out," he finished after a second.

Scott blinked. "Come again?"

"So, you know how it's been like a little over a week? Well, the government's already sunk a ton of money into trying to clean up the LA area of bogies. But there's no putting a lid on this short of nuking the city. The monsters are spreading fast and creating new dungeons by the hour. There are already sightings as far north as Ventura and as far south as Oceanside, even though the bulk of them came through here. The Marines are putting up a helluva fight out of Pendleton, but it's a lost cause. We've already lost the Naval Weapons Base outside of Fallbrook."

Couch_Warrior ran a hand over the stubbly hair on his head.

"It's bad. There are some dangerous weapons buried out that way, and if these monsters get ahold of them, it could be a nightmare. We can't afford any more losses like that. So, it looks like the top brass has switched gears. This is a containment mission now. They want to keep this thing from spreading out. They've already deployed the entire Pacific fleet and a huge number of Coast Guard cutters—that'll be the western edge of the quarantine zone. Keep the mobs contained to the land. And now they're pulling us out and they're going to build a containment wall to the east. A big one."

Scott stuck up a hand. "Let me get this straight. They're going to pull you guys out—"

"Yeah." Couch_Warrior nodded.

"And build a wall."

"Yeah. They're already mobilizing the Army Corps of Engineers."

"To build a fucking wall around LA? How stupid are these jizzbrains? Half the mobs can fly!"

Couch_Warrior shrugged. "Not just LA. My guess is the cordon's probably gonna encompass most of southern California by the time they're through. As for the aerial mobs, they'll probably just shoot down anything that tries to fly over. They've got harriers running raids from the fleet aircraft carriers. Everything inside the containment zone is going to be under lockdown."

"After the evacuation's done," Scott said.

Frowning, Couch_Warrior jerked his head at his buddies, who were already busy pulling up stakes on one of the tents. “The evacuation’s done, dude. Orders came down from on high. We’re pulling out ASAP. Not just us either. Local police. Paramedics. Fire department. LA belongs to the monsters now.”

“But that’s bullshit! What about all the assholes still trying to get out of this place?”

“They’ll have to get to the wall themselves,” Couch_Warrior said, his face dark. “We’ve been ordered not to interfere. Just put everything toward getting the hell out of here.”

Scott dragged a hand down his face. “Great! Just great.” He started backing away from the encampment. “I was about to get a nice hot bath and some gourmet food, courtesy of Kaz, but now I’ve got to put off what I want to do and be the big fucking hero.” He stuck his fingers in his mouth and whistled. “Poser Owners, get your shit together. We’re about to move out. Uncle Sam’s done with this place, and we’re all that stands between the people of LA and death. Again. Time to move our asses!”

CHAPTER 10

THE BLESSING

While Zyra directed the Village Elders to the Throne Room, Roark laid out his plans on a massive dark wood table near the chamber's intimidating and beautiful onyx-and-gold hearth.

He had wanted to escort their human visitors through the Radiant Citadel, both to see who, if any, of the Elders he remembered were still alive and to show that he wasn't a threat to them, but Zyra had waved that away as utter nonsense. No Feudal Lord worth his land received commoners himself; this was what he had subordinates for. If he was going to be stubborn about it, she would fetch them.

When Roark had said, "I thought you said you were finished playing fetch for Dungeon Lords," the Orbweaver Ravager had responded over her shoulder, "One of these days, I'll find a poison that even your precious Feverblood Ring can't protect you against, Griefer."

Zyra had also suggested that he await them on his throne, regal and intimidating, like a true Dungeon Lord, but Roark refused to sit around for appearance's sake. Mobs he had ordered forward were out there dying. And even if that weren't the case, the Elders weren't Dungeon Lords, impressed only by strength and posturing, they were humans. More, they were Korvo citizens. Roark couldn't hope to bully them into agreeing to his plan. The folks of his home were a jolly, colorful lot most of the time, but when pushed, their spines turned to forged steel and they dug in their heels.

Hopefully, Zyra wasn't purposely trying to frighten the Elders too much. Convincing them of his plan was going to be hard enough as it was.

Perhaps he should check on their progress. He glanced at the Feudal Lord's Throne. From it, he could remotely view any of his mobs, be they in battle down below in Korvo or escorting elderly men and women through the Citadel.

A thought occurred to him: Could he view mobs of the Citadel who were in the home world of the Devs? Kaz and the troops he'd sent to aid PwnrBwner at Shieldwall?

Before he could attempt it, however, a rustle of wings brought his attention back to the Throne Room.

Randy Shoemaker landed gracefully beside the huge map-covered table.

"I don't know if I'll ever walk again. Flying is so efficient and... *fun*." He reached for his nonexistent spectacles, then stopped himself. "Sorry, I keep getting caught up in all the things I can do now. This is the new normal, and it's so much better than the old normal. But Ick is on his way, like you asked." The Arboreal Herald looked over the parchments spread across the rough-hewn surface of the table. His eyes widened and he leaned closer to a map of Korvo covered in sigils. "Is this what I think it is?"

"As a Dev of Hearthworld, you ought to know its magicks better than I do," Roark said blithely. "Didn't you help design it?"

"Well, not exactly. You see, as head programmer, I—that's

not really important now, I guess. I was involved in making sure things like the magic didn't conflict with the other components of the... um, Hearthworld, but..." Randy cupped his chin and frowned. "I've never seen the magic used like this before. Or on this scale."

Roark smirked. "Neither have I, mate."

That was why he needed Ick to scrutinize his plans before he put them into action. With something of that size and power, there was a very high possibility he could kill them all.

He'd hoped the Nocturnus would make it to the Throne Room first so they could discuss and refine his schematics, but when the doors opened again, it was to admit Zyra, Albrecht, and a bare handful of elderly men and women doing their level best not to look terrified by the alien environs of the Citadel and its inhabitants.

Of course Zyra wasn't helping. The Orbweaver Ravager was using Wall Walk to stride across the ceiling above their heads as if she were on solid ground. Her snowy white ringlets hung down, but her lacy black veil, armor, and holsters all hung upward like gravity pulled them toward the sky rather than the planet beneath their feet.

"Your Lordship." Zyra sank into a deep bow—upside down—before him. "The Village Elders of Korvo."

"Thank you." Roark started to address them, but stopped awkwardly when he realized the elderly portion of their little company was still hobbling slowly across the shining Throne Room floor. Probably best to wait until they were well within hearing distance.

Roark took a moment to assess them. He recognized the merchantwoman Morgana, a member of the T'verzet and, like Albrecht, a transplant to Korvo. Her piercing green eyes gave little more than a flicker of surprise as she twisted the opal ring on her gnarled finger. It was a symbol of her former seat on the Council of Ancients before Marek's blood-drenched takeover. Roark wasn't fooled by her lack of recognition. Morgana was a woman who never missed anything; likely, she already well knew that he was who he claimed to be and was planning appropriately.

The only other Elder Roark recognized was Otgerd, a man who'd already been one of the oldest citizens in Korvo when Roark was just a boy. Now impossibly ancient and fragile looking, the hunched Elder tottered over his thick wooden cane precariously, as if he could fall and shatter into a thousand pieces at any moment.

Lastly came a knobby man with a prodigious amount of ear hair and a woman with a long nose and flesh as thin and wrinkled as onionskin. They leaned on one another for support and bickered under their breath as they shuffled across the shining floor.

While the Elders were still making their way to the map-strewn table, the Throne Room doors opened again, allowing Ick, the Witchdoctor of the School of Night, to enter. The Elders edged subtly away from the Nocturnus's spidery form, though after Zyra they seemed slightly less surprised by Ick's rubbery tentacles of hair and multitude of limbs.

"Feudal Lord," Ick buzzed through his mandibles, bowing deeply over clasped hands. He began to remove chairs from his Inventory and set them on the glistening Throne Room floor. "Your sister thought it wise to send me with some seating for our esteemed guests."

Seeing the surprise on Roark's face, the Nocturnus grinned. "She did not believe you would have the same practice at seeing to the comfort of those honored elders of advanced experience and wisdom."

"I'm glad she thought of it," Roark said, silently cursing himself and thanking Talise. The lack of hospitality was an oversight that wouldn't have happened when he was a child; his mother had always been there to see to the Elders' comfort when they met with his father. Too much of Roark's time had been spent fighting wars and racing to stay one step ahead of his enemies. If Kaz were there, the Gourmet likely would have had an entire meal laid out for the guests. A meal, courtesy of the Hellstrike Knight, would've done much to ease their minds.

The Elders of Korvo, however, were too busy to notice his blunder.

"Advanced experience!" The onion-skinned old woman let out a dry cackle and clapped Ick on the shoulder. "That's a sweet-smelling way to say we're dusty old skeletons. I like you, lad, bug face or no."

The knobby-jointed old man whose arm she leaned upon snapped, "Hush yourself, Adra, you're showing yourself a vulgar nag again."

"Hells, Fitzl, I don't have to be polite. I'm advanced. Right, bug-face?"

Ick chuckled. "Correct, honored senior."

While the elderly couple bickered and jested with Ick, Roark and Randy began arranging the chairs around the table.

With a disgusted sigh, Zyra snatched the menial task away from Roark.

"Go do something lordly," she hissed under her breath.

He watched a moment to reassure himself that the veiled Ravager wasn't about to Contact Poison the Elders' chairs and withhold the antidote until they agreed to his schemes. As nothing deadly was forthcoming, he joined Albrecht and Ick in helping the Elders into the seats.

Morgana accepted Roark's hand without the same hesitation her fellow Elders showed. Her sharp green eyes scrutinized his jet-black talons and purple-tinged onyx scales, then lifted to meet his gaze.

"What manner of demon are you?" she asked as he handed her into a chair.

"I'm no demon. I was and still am Roark von Graf. This form is called a Draconic Chaos Harbinger, and it's only the latest in a long line." Roark felt a small smile form at the confused looks the Elders gave him. He clasped his hands behind his back and strode to the head of the table. "Honestly, I've changed so many times that now and then even I forget what I look like. The how is something I don't fully understand myself, but the what I can explain easily enough: The night I failed to kill the Tyrant King, I escaped through a portal into another world. The magicks of this other world changed me into a small creature known as a Troll, and since then I have been gaining strength and abilities and progressing through stronger and stronger forms."

"I mightn't see as well as I used to," Otgerd said, aiming a knobby finger at Roark, "but I never forget a face. Those are von Graf eyes or I'm a twice-damned polecat."

"Who cares who he is?" Adra interjected in a phlegmy voice. "His demonfolk saved my great-nephew, dimwitted slow-top that he is. I watched it carry him to safety, cradled in its big scaly arms like a babe."

"Another'n was fighting them dead cat creatures," Fitzl said. "A thing like a cairn a' rocks come to life. Some'a the men attacked the rock man, but it never did turn on them, just kept fighting off the cat things."

"Aye, it appears you're working for our good," Otgerd said, rubbing his knobby hands together as if he were trying to drive away a chill. "But why drag us old folks all the way up here? Perhaps as hostages to keep the village in line?" His ear hair waved in the breeze as he shook his head. "I can tell you now, son, it won't work. They listen to our wisdom from time to time, but they can live without us easily enough. Come to it, they'll see the prudence in leaving us to our fate."

"I don't have any intention of using you as hostages," Roark said, "though I'd be willing to wager that the four of you are worth more to the people of Korvo than you know. When I was a child, my father sought your counsel on multiple occasions because he recognized the value of your combined experience."

Adra snorted. "Our advanced-ness, you mean."

Roark allowed himself a smile. "Advanced-ness, then." He shuffled through the maps until he found what he was looking for, then pushed it into the middle of the table. "Korvo," he said, gesturing to it.

As one, the Elders leaned in, blinking rheumy eyes and trying to get a better look.

"Right now, Marek Konig Ustar is below, trying to raze the town to draw me out," Roark explained. "You saw his armies—undead creatures such as the Sacred Bastet you spoke of, Fitzl. Marek knows if he kills me, this world is his. For all his power, Marek is a cautious monster, and he knows attacking me here, in my seat of power, is a risky endeavor—one he is likely to fail at, just as Lowen failed before him. Instead, he is baiting me. Attacking Korvo is his way of drawing me out. He won't stop until it works... or we make Korvo more trouble than it's worth."

Roark triggered the Illumination spell he had prepared, lighting up several new constructions he'd added to the map. Glowing towers at intervals along the village wall marked out a massive sigil.

"Ah, Discordant Inversion and Deflection." Ick's mandibles clicked gently as he studied it. "Apologies, Feudal Lord, but this web is much larger than any I have seen. You are trying to keep out an army?"

"No. Just one person," Roark said. "Or more accurately, one item. The World Stone Pendant. I studied it at length while it was in my possession. There's still much I don't understand about it, but I'm familiar enough with its energy signature to create the cast." At least, he hoped he was. This was new territory not only for him, a relative newcomer to Discordant Inversion, but for Ick, too, since the Stone's lawless magick wasn't part of the Primal Creation Wheel the Nocturnus understood so well.

"What the bloody hells does all that mean?" Adra demanded.

"Aye." Fitzl nodded, digging at one ear. "We ain't all mages, ya know. Speak it plain."

For their sake, Roark forewent the much longer and far more nuanced explanation—one involving power structures, dyads, and magickal nodes. "This sigil will rebound the World Stone, forcibly expelling the Tyrant King from Korvo as long as he doesn't abandon the stone—which he will never do. He lost it once. As long as he lives, he'll never let go of it again. Marek is more powerful than me, but if we can effectively remove him from the battlefield, his army won't be able to take Korvo or attack my fortress directly."

"A thousand apologies, Feudal Lord," Ick said, gesturing at the sigils with two of his spidery limbs, "but to cast a Discordant Inversion of this size with only one's own Magicka..." He faltered and dry washed chitinous hands, causing an arid rasping sound that made a few of the Elders shudder. "To power its web would almost certainly kill one."

"Er, yes, well..." Roark frowned down at the map. His calculations had led him to a similar conclusion each time he'd checked them, but he'd been hoping Ick would disagree. "Is there no way around that?"

"Actually, there might be," Randy said, ignoring Morgana's affronted scowl as he leaned over her shoulder to get a better look at the schematics. "Hearthworld spells tend to work a little like cars—or, um, I'm sorry, I can't think of an equivalent just now that you guys might recognize. But my point is, Discordant Inversion uses your reserve of Magicka like a car uses its engine. To power something hundreds of times bigger, say an aircraft carrier, the engine's got to be enormous or you'll never get it to move."

"You've got an idea to move it, though?" Roark asked, eyeing the Arboreal Herald. Though several of the words were foreign to him, he understood the principles of what Randy was getting at.

"Maybe. See, the buildings in Hearthworld sort of come with their own Magicka built in," Randy explained. "It worked out as the most efficient way to shape and reshape the layouts, but it's also why we had to limit those changes to one major overhaul per day. It's massive compared to say a Dungeon Lord's Magicka, but it's still finite. If you could tap into that, though, you could theoretically use the Citadel itself to power the Discordant Inversion sigil."

"Can you show me how to do it?" Roark asked, planting his fists on the table. "As a Dev of Hearthworld, you must know the proper spell to write to... tap into it, as you said."

Randy's face colored faintly. "I—I mean, I did design the system that integrated all of this stuff in the first place, so... I think so? It might take a little trial and error, but—"

"How long?"

"I'll get on it right now," Randy said.

"This is all very fascinating, von Graf," Morgana said, pursing her wrinkled lips, "but it sounds as if you've got the solution to your problems already in your minions. Otgerd's question remains: What do you need from us?"

For a brief moment, Roark wrestled for the words to explain the arbitrary rules governing Hearthworld's magicks, but he came no closer than he'd ever been to understanding them. Instead, he went with the simplest explanation.

"I'm the Feudal Lord of this territory," he said, "but I don't want to bend Korvo to my will. I'm sure you've all had enough of that with Marek. I've laid out my plans for you so that you, the Elders, can either approve of them or reject them. I want to protect Korvo, and I believe this is the best way to do it. If you give me permission to make changes to the town, I can not only rebuild what Marek's armies have destroyed, but reinforce and build up the battlements already in place, as well as cast the Discordant Inversion to keep him out."

Morgana squinted at him. "How many men will you require to do all that?"

"None." At their disbelieving expressions, Roark spread his hands. "Such is the magick of Hearthworld. They may be complicated and strange, but they are reliable, and in many cases instantaneous. However, it cannot be done without your blessing. That or your deaths, and I refuse the latter option. You are my people, this is your town, and I will either have your help willingly or not at all. Regardless of how I may look, I won't let Marek make a tyrant of me."

"I've heard all I need to hear and more than I care to try to follow," Adra said, puffing up her lumpy little frame. "All Elders in favor of granting this big goat-horned scaly thing permission to make changes to Korvo?"

Otgerd fixed Roark with a rheumy glare. "You ain't gonna tear down the tavern or some fool nonsense like that, are ya?"

Roark stifled a startled laugh.

"No." He cleared his throat and forced a solemn expression. "I promise you I won't be doing that."

"I'll say aye, then."

"Aye," Fitzl agreed.

Morgana's keen gaze still raked Roark's face as if she were trying to tear her way inside. Finally, she nodded.

"Aye," she said.

"That's it, then." Adra coughed up a bit of phlegm, then continued. "Fix up what you'll fix up and cast your spells, mage-thing. Us advanced folks give you our blessing, such that it is."

CHAPTER 11
FURY ROAD

Scott sprawled out across the best chair in Shieldwall, legs over one arm, head over the other, and a mug of lava-hot coffee resting on his gut. The chair was one of the last left behind from when the room had been Frontflip's employee lounge, an ugly barf-green color and the kind of awkwardly shaped furniture only interior designers and tech companies thought was cool. Flipside, though? Comfortable. As. Balls. Whenever Scott had a shift off between rescuing the refugees of LA and running the dungeon, he spent it in this little slice of heaven.

Over on the far wall, the latest version of the Infinitab projected a constant stream of news covering the shitshow that was LA's new normal. Shots of burning cars, looters ransacking the transported Avery City apothecary where Scott used to buy his potions, and people fleeing for their lives from killer Ettins and Dire Sabercows. Interspersed among that montage of carnage were flashes of the enormous containment wall the Army Corps of Engineers was setting up. Under it all ran this little red ticker asking stupid questions like *LA Panic: rift in time and space brings about alien invasion or viral marketing by movie studio finally goes too far?*

And that was just the nationally syndicated crap.

At least those jerks were keeping tabs on the situation from a safe distance. The indie news bloggers trying to get their street journalism picked up by a major broadcaster were sneaking into LA by the dozen. The Poser Owners had already had to rescue three of those morons just over the last couple days. Having people interview him and put the real story out there should've been awesome, but they kept digging around, trying to find something screwed up about his motives to do an exposé on. He had literally just saved their lives and they were trying to make him look like the asshole. Scott scowled. Total crock of shit.

He rolled his shoulders and squirmed deeper into his favorite chair. The heat prickling his palms through the mug would've already lulled him to sleep if he couldn't hear the constant rumble and murmur of a couple hundred mobs, NPCs, and LA natives jam-packed like sardines into Shieldwall. He tried to tune it out, but then another frickin' fight broke out in the cafeteria, some dude yelling and a Kobold doing a weird croaky bark.

A contingent of stumpy, scaly feet came slapping down the hall—Shieldwall's Dragonkin running to settle whatever the hell problem those two had with each other before it ended with dismemberment or some shit.

Scott grunted with annoyance. This place was getting hella cramped. The bulk of the military had pulled out the same day Couch_Warrior gave him the news, and the rest followed pretty damn quick, so they had nobody to pawn the human refugees off on. On top of that, they kept picking up more Hearthworld creatures and NPCs. Word was getting around that Shieldwall was a safe spot for friendlies, but that wasn't working in their favor.

Scott had already used his formidable powers as Arch-Overseer of the Dungeon to add new places for the arrivals to bed down, but they were being overrun. Fights and arguments were constantly breaking out over petty shit like blankets or who took the last of the pepper or cutting in line at the john. If they didn't figure out how to deal with this many people soon, some awesome and all-powerful Dungeon Lord was going to snap and total party wipe this whole damn place.

The lounge door banged open.

"Read the sign," Scott growled without opening his eyes. "Dungeon Lord's Lounge. Do not disturb. Shut the door on your way out."

"You got it, guy who's not the boss of me." Instead of getting lost, GothicTerror plopped down on a shapeless purple couch and started checking the chipped black nail polish on her nails.

"Fine." Scott kicked his legs around to sit up, then drained the lava in his mug. "But if you're gonna be here, you're gonna work. So, riddle me this, Tots—"

"Nessa," she said.

"Nestots."

She rolled her eyes, but dimples appeared in her cheeks. She was trying not to laugh, which was just one of the weird differences between her real self and the deadpan dark elf she mained in Hearthworld. She also didn't have the standard smoking hot perfection of a game character, but even with the little extra curviness and couple of blemishes, she was pretty decent, in that girl-next-door way. Plus, those pale blue eyes were crazy awesome against her dark brown skin.

Scott steered his brain back on track. "We've got two hundred too many people here, with more showing up every day. We can break the POSes into escort parties and shepherd the humans out to where the army's setting up their containment zone, but that'll take, like, twenty trips, and we'd lose half of them to their own stupidity. Not to mention it would split our forces and make us sitting ducks if Silva ever grows the nads to come in and try to take back Shieldwall."

"What I'm hearing is two problems," GothicTerror replied, sticking two fingers into the air. "One, you're a stupid, soft-hearted sucker who can't turn a bunch of refugees away. And, two, they can't stay here or they risk bringing everything down for everyone."

"Hey, I could totally turn them away if I wanted to," Scott said, although that option hadn't occurred to him until she mentioned it, "but I'm too magnanimous of a ruler to pull something shitty like that. So, what else is on the menu?"

She tapped her thumb on her chin while she thought about it. When they'd met, her nails were Goth perfect, shiny and black. Fighting a war had chipped the polish, but there was still enough left to see the little skull she'd painstakingly painted onto them.

"We're basically looking at a transportation problem," she finally said. "We need to move two hundred or more people, what, like seventy miles?"

"Seventy miles of hostile mobs, abandoned cars, and wrecked-up roads," Scott said, gesturing at the images the news was running. "It's basically Mad Max's Fury Road out there. A standard city bus ain't gonna cut it."

"Maybe Fury Road is the answer," she mused. "What if we found an abandoned bus and modified it? I mean, we have all these amazing dungeon mob blacksmiths and rune crafters on hand. A bunch of Roark's apprentices are dying of boredom downstairs just looking for something to do. We could have them add a cattle pusher and spikes and guns and enchant them to the gills. Something like that would make it. How many people can fit on a bus at one time?"

Scott grunted and shook his head. "Not two hundred."

"It's still not a terrible idea. Even if we only got thirty or forty people out, it would ease the load a little."

"Oh shit." Scott snapped his fingers as something better occurred to him. "Forget the bus idea. What we need is a tow truck. A big-ass rig. The kind of heavy-duty truck they send to tow semis—because that's what we're going to do."

GothicTerror cocked an eyebrow at him.

"Shut up before you say anything." He held up a hand to stop her. "One, a fifty-three-foot tractor trailer will haul a ton more people than a bus. Two, we can weld some steel panels onto the sides for extra armor and throw on, I don't know, some spikes or whatever it was you said. Plus turrets, get the offense and defense covered. Three, a semi and a bus will get stuck if we end up on a road that's too screwed up, but a wrecker can just winch itself out and drag out whatever else it's pulling."

She flipped her hair out of her face. "I'm not a mechanic, but that doesn't sound legit at all. I'm pretty sure winches have limitations just like everything else."

"Still shut up because I'm not done." Scott was on a roll now. They could argue over the details after he'd gotten it all out. "It would be an enchanted winch, so it would work. Plus, if we get it going fast enough or even just throw it in low gear, it'll plow right through any abandoned cars or debris and shit. And having the tow truck pull the semi would give us even more hauling room, too. We'd have the passenger seat of the truck, the cab of the semi, and the whole trailer to cram people into. Best of all, I already know where to get the whole setup."

He waited.

This time GothicTerror didn't jump in.

Scott threw up his hands. "Jeez, would it kill you to toss in a

'Where, Dungeon Lord PwnrBwner, wherever will we get a wrecker, semi, and trailer?'" he asked in a breathy, falsetto voice.

"I thought I was still shutting up. Also I would never sound like that." She rubbed her eyes and leaned back against the purple couch cushions. "Also also, I can't tell whether that's the dumbest most needlessly complicated idea I've ever heard or you just veered into galaxybrain territory."

"I am all galaxybrain, Tots. To answer the question you didn't ask about where we'll get a tow—I know a guy. He works nights for a company that does emergency highway service and wrecker rescues for big rigs. Dude even knows how to weld. Between him and the smith apprentices the Griefer left behind, we'll have the rig up and ready to roll in no time. We've been buddies since grade school, and we used to party together in Hearthworld, so he'll already know this monster invasion thing is for real."

GothicTerror sighed. "If this idea isn't as stupid as it feels like it is, then it might actually be the solution we need."

"There's just one problem." Scott glanced over at where he'd left his phone charging. "Kevin might not be super psyched to hear from me. We didn't part on the best of terms. Last time I saw him in-game, he was acting like a punk because of the hit Bad_Karma put out on me, and I told him so. I also told his sister to go blow BK—maybe that she was a bitch, too, I can't remember."

"There's that sparkling personality everybody loves," GothicTerror said.

"What, was I supposed to lie? I call it like I see it. Mistakes were made on both sides. Shit happens." He ran his hand angrily through his hair. "Anyway, I'm not even sure the wonder twins will still be in the valley. They're not braindead like most of the idiots hanging around here waiting for somebody to save them."

"Only one way to find out." GothicTerror stretched across the arm of the couch and handed over his phone. "Call your friend up and ask him."

Scott didn't want to—it was one thing to be mad at your friends for abandoning you and to assume they were mad at you, too, but it was another thing to know for sure they hated your guts. On the other hand, Scott didn't want to look like a wuss in front of Nessa, either, so he dialed Kevin up without any outward hesitation.

It rang and kept ringing. Scott blew out an annoyed breath. Of course Kevin wouldn't pick up. Kellie was probably standing right there, telling him not to.

Just when Scott was about to give up, somebody answered.

"Hello?" It was Kevin, a.k.a. Dude_Farkowitz, a.k.a. one of Scott's two real-life friends. "Scott?"

An involuntary grin broke out across his face when he heard the dweeb's voice. He hadn't wanted to think about it beforehand, but part of him had been worried that Kevin wouldn't answer, not because he and Kellie were mad, but because they were dead. Kinda dark, but definitely a possibility with some of the things Scott had been seeing out there in the streets. Anyway, finding out they were alive was a good start.

He shot GothicTerror a thumbs-up, then leaned his elbows on his knees.

"Dude, Kevin, where are you?"

"On a call. Overturned tanker on the 605. We just got it moving again, but with the way everybody's panicking..." He sighed. "They're gonna need all wreckers out here all night. What about you? Did you get out of LA yet? Before, Kel said she couldn't get you to answer your messages on Hearthworld, then they shut the game down and now all this stuff with monsters... We thought maybe you'd been..."

"It's going to take something a helluva lot more OP than fantasy MMO mobs to kill me," Scott said.

"Then where have you been?"

"It's a long story. I'll fill you in on it sometime. For now, though, I need a favor."

There was a split-second pause on the other end of the line.

"A favor like the times you needed the answer to number four or a favor like that night you wanted me to fix the axle on your mom's car so she wouldn't know you drove it off that embankment?"

"Hypothetically," Scott glossed over the implied accusations, "if somebody needed to tow a semi and full trailer from LA to, say, Ventura, could the Winch Witch do it? Let's assume, for the sake of this totally hypothetical question, that the winch is also enchanted and magically reinforced. And how soon could you get her downtown to the old Frontflip campus?"

Kevin didn't say anything right away, so Scott went for broke. "And since you're coming this way anyhow, bring one of the semis and trailers from the tow yard with you."

"You want me to cut work while I'm supposed to be helping clear highway, and then as if that wasn't enough to lose my job, you want me to steal a semi and trailer from my boss's tow yard?"

"It's on your way, asshole!"

GothicTerror gestured violently for him to cool it.

Scott rolled his eyes and forced himself to calm down. "Look, dude, this is some hero-level shit I'm asking you to do. And it's not like you're going to have a job here in a week, anyway. This is the end of LA as we know it, maybe the whole west coast. This is your chance to be the big shot who saves the day, Kev. Don't blow it like you did in third grade. Remember?

When Tommy Jackson stole your Rebel Galaxy Outlaws lunch box and you let him walk all over you for like a year until I saved your ass?"

"You're such a dick," Kevin said. Then, with a reluctant sigh, "Kellie and I'll be there in a couple hours."

CHAPTER 12
BATTLEMENTS

The moment the Village Elders were escorted out of the Throne Room, Roark opened the Feudal Lord's Grimoire and set to fortifying Korvo's defenses. There were many more options available now than when he was a simple Dungeon Lord, and five times the Layout Points to spend —five thousand, five hundred to be exact. Moats and machicolations. Turrets, towers, and forward outlook posts. Enormous drawbridges presided over by reinforced gatehouses. Hells, he could even add a series of internal walls, transforming the city into an elaborate labyrinth if he chose.

There were also a number of town upgrades available. He could instantly build a barracks to house the city's forces, not that Korvo had any forces to house, or install a melee training ring and adjacent archery range. Neither were currently worth the points, considering the circumstances, but certainly something to look into later. Other options like expanding the smithy or tacking on an enchanting workshop would prove more useful. And those were only the mundane fortifications—there was also a bevy of mystical options, from Divine siege cannons to formidable Infernal ballistae. The collapsible acid pits in particular caught his eye.

Naturally, each upgrade was more expensive than the last, and even with the additional points to burn, there was no way to unlock all the available options.

Which meant every single feature Roark added needed to pull its weight twice over. Automated siege weapons were practical and brutal, but he could manufacture such weapons on his own, given enough time and manpower. Zyra could make tubs full of acid without much effort, and the Beryl King and his forces could call forth pits in the earth and bedrock without the hours of digging other mobs would require. Instead, Roark focused his efforts on physical fortifications that he couldn't reproduce on his own and the structures needed to form the magickal warding barrier against Marek.

Though it was patching a pail after the milk had drained away, the first thing Roark added was stronger battlements. Korvo had an exterior retaining wall, sufficient to keep out wolves or other natural predators, but it wouldn't stop a human army, let alone the monstrous forces Marek had brought to bear against the city and its inhabitants. He fortified the outer curtain wall, making it twenty feet tall, then created robust ramparts and crenellations to help protect the guards. Since he was modifying an existing structure instead of crafting one from scratch, it cost substantially less—only five hundred of his available points.

The pair of concentric rings he added outside of the city's existing wall were far more expensive. Eight hundred points apiece. For a scant one hundred additional points, however, he lined those walls with sharpened wooden pikes called Abatis. The troops he had on the ground were well on their way to emptying Korvo of Marek's forces, so his energy was best spent making it harder for new waves to get into the city.

[As Feudal Lord over a Septic Brewmaster, you have the option to add Poison Assortment to Abatis Line at no extra cost.

Add Poison Assortment to Abatis Line? Yes/No]

There was no mention of the types of poison in this assortment or whether it would ignore allies, but Roark selected yes and made a mental note to send word to the villagers to have a care around the rough-hewn timbers when he was finished.

These new outer walls weren't as wide as the inner curtain wall—certainly not wide enough to support foot troops—so he added a series of archer towers for one hundred points each, dropping him down by another seven hundred total. These towers weren't an afterthought, but rather were meticulously and strategically spaced according to an intricate pattern that Ick had helped Roark design. A pattern that would ultimately power and maintain the massive Discordant Inversion sigil Roark was attempting to craft.

If things went according to plan, at any rate.

Next, he turned his sights on the city gates, fortifying each with iron and timber and narrow corridors full of switchbacks to funnel invading armies one at a time through the sally ports. Within each corridor, he added murder holes for his defenders to attack invaders from above with little chance of retaliation. These alterations ate through six hundred more points, bringing his available total down to two thousand points. A costly but worthwhile endeavor since the gates were a natural weakness that Marek and his forces would seek to exploit.

[As Feudal Lord over a Gourmet, you have the option to add Boiling Oil Pots to the Murder Holes at no extra cost.

Add Boiling Oil Pots? Yes/No]

It seemed having friends helped in more ways than one. Eagerly, Roark agreed to the option.

Similarly, the Disorienting Echoes option came courtesy of being allied with a Renowned Bard, Soileau in this case. In certain areas within Korvo and the walls, Disorienting Echoes would warp the sounds of battle to become so chaotic that it had a 15% chance of confusing enemies and causing them to attack one another.

In the killing fields between the main and secondary walls, Roark sprinkled in Black Powder Charges, compliments of his new Flash Art Gunsmith skill—though these were not free additions. Each Charge cost a mere handful of Layout Points, but they would pay back in full the first moment an army tried to charge through the space, taking a devastating chunk out of the closest mobs with every detonation. When he had a little more time, perhaps he could spend it smithing the charges himself and reallocate those Layout Points to something else.

For the time being, however, he selected their placement carefully on the map of Korvo, installing them in the most likely traffic ways between the walls.

In the center of the city, rising like a watchful sentinel, he added the linchpin Mage's Tower. It was a beautiful creation of stone, wrought iron, and rune-etched stained glass. A winding staircase in the interior of the building led to an enormous crystalline prism set at the apex of the tower. From a distance, the structure almost looked like a lighthouse, but this great prism wasn't lit with a roaring fire meant to illuminate treacherous coastlines in the night. It was designed to harness and tie the archer towers together—a hub to direct the complicated magic they were about to unleash.

Roark had already fashioned a hundred different script plates that would adorn the interior of the Mage Tower. Matching script plates would be placed within the gates and along the outer walls. Not only would this vast structure keep Marek out by powering the massive Discordant Inversion Spell, but it would likewise serve as a supercharged version of the Hero Sieve that Roark had created so long ago for the Cruel

Citadel. Enemy mobs of a certain type, level, or elemental alignment would instantly be ported to the newly established dungeons scattered across the mountains and forests surrounding the city—all occupied by the powerful Dungeon Lords who had followed Roark over from Hearthworld.

That wouldn't stop the invasion, not entirely, but it would disperse Marek's forces and buy Roark additional time to figure out how to stop Marek for good. And the Dungeon Lords were only too happy to grow even more powerful off the experience of mobs weak to their particular skill sets.

With the bulk of his essential projects done, he spent the scant three hundred points he had remaining to upgrade the town's smithy and tack on an enchanting workshop. They would need armor, weapons, and a way to enchant them all if they were going to equip the townsfolk. Churning out that many items would be next to impossible without a little help, especially since many of Roark's most talented apprentices were stuck in Shieldwall with PwnrBwner and Kaz. He needed to train some new talent, but perhaps that was something the townsfolk could help with.

And that spent the last of the Layout Points.

Roark checked over his selections again with a critical eye, searching for weaknesses. There were more than he liked, but this was the best possible configuration with the resources he had at his disposal. Satisfied with his workmanship, he accepted all changes. The customary warning appeared.

[You have changed the layout of the Village of Korvo! Changes will take place immediately, but no further changes can be made within your Fiefdom for (24) hours. Are you sure you wish to proceed?
Alter the Village of Korvo? Yes/No]

Roark didn't immediately select yes.

Randy Shoemaker was still tinkering with calculations for the final spell form. What they were attempting was a complicated bit of magick, and working out how best to use the Radiant Citadel to power the Discordant Inversion was no easy task. Roark had explained that the layout of the sigil towers was nonnegotiable—the School of Night Magick was a finicky and dangerous thing, requiring the utmost precision in its physical components—as was the Mage's Tower that acted as the central node. But that didn't mean the Citadel itself couldn't be altered.

On the off chance that Randy's designs required adjustments to the dungeon itself, Roark didn't want to be forced to wait another day to put the cast into effect.

Interestingly, following the Layout options was a Troop Management section that had not only the massive roster containing the names and levels of all allied Dungeon Lords, but Korvo natives and their occupations, which Roark supposed functioned as their class. Like the Hearthworld troops, their status—Alive or Dead—was given, but under the space marked Level, each local had only a "–".

Roark could access the character sheets of all those within his dungeon, but when he tried to select Albrecht's character sheet, he received a strange notification.

[ERROR: That action cannot be performed. Player "Albrecht von Herzog" incompatible.]

He tried again with the village smith and received the same response from the grimoire. All of the villagers he selected were shown as Incompatible, whatever that meant.

An awkward throat-clearing nearby pulled Roark from his

musings. Randy Shoemaker had returned. This Error would have to be a mystery for another day.

Roark closed out of the Feudal Lord's Grimoire. The Arboreal Herald was carrying an armful of rolled parchments, worth a veritable treasury in Traisbin, and yet so plentiful in Hearthworld that the Citadel spawned them automatically. That wonder never ceased to amaze him.

"Okay. I think I've found the most efficient method for the Discordant Inversion cast." Without waiting for an invitation or even acknowledgement, Randy Shoemaker laid out his parchments on the table and launched into an explanation, his hands waving frantically as he spoke. Unlike many of the rebels and Dungeon Lords Roark had worked with, Randy Shoemaker wasn't interested in meaningless pleasantries, he simply wanted to get down to business. It was something Roark admired about the Arboreal Herald: a single-mindedness to match his own.

"To start off with, I had Ick demonstrate and explain the method for casting a Discordant Inversion web, then I broke that down into its component tasks. Those I sorted based on whether they had to be done in a specific sequence, could happen at any time, would take a massive amount of Magicka versus small, had to be done by an entity with a physical, ambulatory body or could be done by a ... well, not really code now that the Citadel exists in real time and space, but a stationary building, anyway." Randy snorted and leaned conspiratorially closer to Roark. "I've never felt so much sympathy for a task coordination program before."

Completely lost, Roark nodded. "Right... Task coordination."

"Exactly. That's where you have to focus in something like this. I can't just evenly divide up the steps and say, 'Roark, you do this half, and the Citadel will do this half, and we'll have a

Discordant Inversion by five o'clock.' It's not that simple. Your strengths are going to be things like the physical motions required for the cast—which is why you'll be assigned the task of going through the forms—and the designing of the sigils themselves, which you already did." Randy tapped the map of Korvo.

"On the other hand, the Citadel's strength lies in its enormous reserve of Magicka and its inability to tire. Which is why we're going to use that immense power to sort of kick-start the initial cast, then maintain the spell power over the days and weeks ahead. We'll also divert some of the routine operating energy from the dungeon's reserve to power the sigil plates in the central Mage's Tower, which, in turn, will constantly scan for the presence of the World Stone—holding the Web ready until the Stone's energy signature is detected. All of this will weaken the Citadel, but the trade-off is a more secure Korvo as a whole."

Randy glanced sidelong at Roark. "Obviously that's the thousand-mile view of the process. It gets a lot more detailed and complicated the more you dive into the nitty-gritty. I don't want to bore you with too much of it, because believe me, I can." The Arboreal Herald smiled wistfully down at his plans. "There's something so satisfying in the order of it all. People make life needlessly messy because they don't follow their own internal logic, but I could always count on the architecture of a well-made system to make sense."

"That I can understand," Roark said. Smithing had been much the same to him, a refuge of sanity in a world of chaos, fighting, and death. "This, though..."

He gestured to Randy's careful, precise writing spaced neatly across the rolled parchments. Some phrases like *"Stance of the Patient Hunter: postures to cast, priority 1 of postures, physical"* and *"detect: World Stone Pendant"* made a measure of sense to him, but others were little more than gibberish strung together from familiar words, such as *"fuel cast, active: magicka-lake."*

"It's about as dense as fog to me, mate," he admitted. "And if I'm honest, I'm surprised you didn't have any adverse reactions writing it all out. Here in Terho, magick adheres to the written word. A misspelling or poorly placed comma can quite literally blow your head off."

Randy's silver cheeks darkened a few shades, and he shuffled his papers sheepishly.

"I did actually try a few spells before getting down to business. Nothing dangerous! Minor stuff... kind of hungry... thought it would be easier to summon strawberry Pop-Tarts than make them out of nothing..." His wings rustled nervously. "I can see how the slightest inattention to detail could easily be fatal in this system. But I was very careful and specific when I wrote the spell to clean it all out of your study; there shouldn't be any stickiness left behind."

Roark frowned. "Stickiness?"

"Right, so, Discordant Inversion!" The Arboreal Herald clapped his hands together. "Ick explained to me the basic principles of Discordant casting—utilizing the elemental mechanics of the Primal Creation Wheel to turn the strength of an opponent back on them. It's a perfect application of equal and opposite reaction. The more powerful your enemy is, the more powerful the Inversion, and from what you've told me, the World Stone is incredibly powerful."

"Too right, mate. I don't know enough about the Stone to say where all that power comes from, but I intend to remedy that once I know that Korvo's safe." Roark cast his mind to the elderly Morgana and her former seat on the Council of Traisbin. "And I believe I know where to start." He nodded at Randy. "But first we need to deal with the business at hand. Let's get on, shall we?"

"Yes, of course." Randy reached for his lost spectacles, then when he realized what he was doing jerked his hand back down to brace on the table. "So, to do something like this, we've got to have four components. You and the Citadel are the processors, for lack of a better word, and I'll be functioning as the routing mechanism. Basically, every task I've got in my notes"—he tapped the precise script covering the parchment—"needs to be sent to one of you based on your capabilities.

"That's my job, allotting the tasks in order to each of you, receiving the completed versions, and routing them through the central Mage Tower and out to the archer towers, which will function as our fourth component—final storage. There, the completed tasks will come together to form a single massive activated Discordant Inversion web. At least in theory. That or we blow everything up, create a giant magical feedback loop, and likely kill ourselves. But probably the first thing."

Though not everything the Arboreal Herald was saying made sense to Roark, he could see the overall picture of how Randy meant it to work—and the problem Randy wasn't mentioning.

"For you to sort through all this," Roark said, "you'll have to be connected to all three of us, won't you?"

"Well, yes, essentially. I'll be using a modification of my Arboreal Herald powers for it—sort of like an overpowered Telepathic Message function."

"And you'll be incapacitated while this goes on?"

"Er, yeah, that's one of the downsides. I'll have to be completely focused on the routing and coordination."

"I've cast these Discordant Inversions before, Randy. Your attention can't waver for a second, and you can't hesitate. That means I'll be tied up with the cast, and I have to assume it means the same for the Citadel."

"Well, on a magick level, but essentially..."

"So you're saying the three of us will be defenseless for however long the cast takes. That's a weakness... not even a weakness, but a fatal flaw. I have no doubt in my mind that Marek will be waiting in the wings for me to pop out of the Citadel. And the moment I do, he will strike, just as he did before. He'll kill me before I ever get a chance to finish the cast."

"Yeah, about that." Randy reached for his missing spectacles and shuffled his feet uncomfortably. "I was sort of hoping you would have a plan for that."

"Who needs a plan?" A curl of inky smoke rose from the opposite side of the table as Zyra stepped out of the shadows. "The Griefer's got an army. If the two of you can figure out how to power this cursed monstrosity without killing yourselves, I'll make sure you're protected long enough to pull it off."

Roark glanced at Zyra for a long moment, studying her face. She was confidence and resolve in equal measure. *Trust me, Griefer.*

He shifted his gaze to Randy. "Well, what are we waiting for? It's time to enchant all of Korvo."

CHAPTER 13
THE WINCH WITCH

Scott was in the john when somebody double-tapped a train horn outside. That was always how it went—the second you sat down, the repairman, delivery guy, or your buddy with the tow truck you'd been waiting on all day—instead of the two hours he'd promised—finally showed up. And of course, five seconds later, your Dragonkin dudes started banging on the door.

"A great beast trumpets its challenge at our gates, Dungeon Lord PwnrBwner," Larry, the Dragonkin who'd been on watch, croaked through the door. "What shall we do?"

Scott rolled his eyes. Larry was a cool guy, but not a self-starter. "We talked about this, right? When the Dungeon Lord is indisposed, you go find GothicTerror. I bought myself a Lieutenant Uberbitch for a reason. The least she can do is make sure I get to take a crap in peace once in a while."

"Yes, of course, Dungeon Lord!" Scaly feet slapped on the stone floor as the Dragonkin scrambled off to find Nessa.

When Scott joined them outside after finally handling his business, the Winch Witch and her haul had been pulled inside the Shieldwall Gates, and Kevin had somehow managed to parallel park all ninety-eight feet of it flawlessly alongside the front entrance. Scott had to give him props for that. He himself couldn't even parallel park a Kia. But then, when you were a boss, you could just get underlings to handle all the shit you weren't good at. High-powered businesspeople called it delegation, instead of just being lazy.

The big rig Kevin had towed down wasn't in too bad shape. The driver's side corner of the trailer was a little crumpled, and a front tire on the semi was blown out, but it was off the ground, so that didn't matter. The left fender was smashed up, and the whole shebang was muddy, as though Kevin had dragged it out of a ditch. In spite of all that, she looked like she would haul a shitload of people.

Anyway, the semi wasn't the main event. Scott crossed his arms and admired the sixty tons of steel, cranes, stabilizer jacks, and heavy-duty rigging. The Winch Witch's purple and green flame decals practically glowed in the afternoon sun. Pure badass mechanical power. She made the people and Trolls standing around her cab look like malnourished kittens.

Scott couldn't help but grin. "Now that is what I'm talking about."

At the sound of his voice, Kevin and one of the Troll Smiths the Griefer left behind turned around.

"Scott, hey." Unlike his Hearthworld avatar—who was damn near seven feet of elf-gold skin, magic, and muscle—Kevin was a skinny birdlike dweeb IRL, all arms and legs and Adam's apple, plus a nose like a big honkin' beak stuck smack-dab in the middle of his narrow face. He shoved his hands in the back pockets of his jeans and gestured with one elbow to indicate Shieldwall. "This place is amazing. A real-life medieval fortress."

"Yeah, who'd you steal it from?" Kellie asked, eyes narrowed as she came strutting around the front of the Witch. She was basically the mirror image of her brother, but with longer hair and boobs and a row of eyebrow rings to draw attention away from the family schnoz.

"Mike Silva, actually. Why, you gonna tattle on me?" Scott shot back in an equally nasty tone as he came down the steps. He looked Kel up and down. "Funny, I don't remember inviting the worst Farkowitz twin."

"Guys, don't do this today, please," Kevin begged, sticking his hands into the air.

Kellie ignored him and planted her hand on her hip. "I round out the party, Scott. It's not the Alameda Assholes without me."

Scott smirked. Their little three-person gang hadn't been called that since the haters in junior high tried—and failed—to take them down a notch. It was turning into Nostalgia City up in here.

"Fine," he said, trying not to sound too happy about it, "the Assholes ride again. But FYI, you two are playing with a major handicap." He stuck out his hand and cast Elemental Fury. It wasn't his most powerful spell, but the arcing blue lightning crackling down his arm looked freaking impressive. "Here's what you missed. Anyone who sided up with Roark the Griefer before the Merge"—he swiped a hand around, indicating the fortress and the mobs—"now has access to legit magic. I was playing my Cleric-Ranger when the Griefer knighted me, so those are the powers I have now."

"It's true, then?" Kevin said, eyes wide and excited. "Hearth-world magic merged with the real world?" He glanced at the Troll busy giving the Winch Witch an enthusiastic once-over. "I mean, I knew something serious was going on, but... real magic. It's like a dream come true."

And right there was the whole reason Scott had such a soft spot for the dorky bastard. Kevin could be a punk sometimes, but he got just how awesome this was. Everyone else was running around, wailing and whining about how this was the end of the world. Maybe it was for some, but for Scott and people like him, this wasn't the end, this was a whole new beginning. For the first time in his life, Scott was on the top of the dog pile instead of stuck at the bottom, wedged beneath some lard ass who hadn't showered in four months.

"You're damn right it is," Scott told him. "Bad news for you and your freakshow sister is that I don't think normies can level up or unlock powers."

Of course, Kellie couldn't just believe him. She immediately stuck out her hands to cast something from her NecroKnight. Surprise, nothing happened.

Scott rolled his eyes. "Like we haven't already tried that like a hundred times. So far as we can tell the only people with powers are the Griefer's followers or the NPCs and mobs who came over from Hearthworld. There's a silver lining though. Magic items still work, even on normies without classes. I can strap you guys with some of the Cursed and Enchanted weapons and armor Roark left behind. It won't be like having your own powers, but it'll keep you alive even against some of the nasty things running around out there. We just need to get the rig ready to roll and then we'll be out there living the dream."

Scott gave them a brief rundown of the sitch with the refugees and his plan for getting them to the edge of the containment zone.

Kevin rubbed his chin. "It's not the worst idea you've ever had, but it's not going to go as easy as you're thinking. I don't know how far you've been from Frontflip lately, but it's insane out there. There were sinkholes and buildings on fire—and I had to back out of a few streets because somebody set up hedgehogs. Like legit, metal hedgehogs from World War Two.

Can't even guess where someone would get something like that. I even had to unhook the tractor trailer a couple times and pull abandoned vehicles out of the way before we could get through. This isn't your average run, and things are getting worse out there, not better."

"Pfft, like I was born yesterday. That's where this guy comes in," Scott said, calling over the Reaver Shaman who had been enthusiastically inspecting the rigs. "Kevin, Kel, meet Cranko. Dude's got mad Smithing skills, and he's a top-tier Enchanter with the Troll Nation. Magic items aren't the only thing that work here. Cranko and his boys are gonna help us clean up the rig, trick it out with some badass spells, and then we'll be golden."

Cranko shot the wonder twins a nod as he wiped his deep blue hands with an oil-stained rag. He turned to Scott.

"The skeleton of this contraption is still strong," the Reaver said. "Repairs and enhancements will be extensive, but much of the material needed can be scavenged from the area surrounding Shieldwall."

"Whoa, whoa, whoa," Kevin said, getting all up in arms. "Nobody but me is doing anything to the Witch."

"Take it easy, dweeb," Scott said. "Nobody's going to mess with your girlfriend without your say-so. Most of the repair work's got to be done on the big rig, anyway, right, Cranko? For the tow truck, I'm thinking mainly Enchantments—extra horsepower, unpuncturable tires, and one of those things on the front, like old-timey trains had."

"Cowcatchers," GothicTerror said, rocking up from wherever she'd been hiding.

"Yeah, a cowpusher," Scott said. "But let's add in a flamethrower and some badass spikes."

Kevin frowned, but didn't immediately say no, which to Scott was basically the same as a yes.

"She's your baby, Kev," Scott said, clapping him on the shoulder. "You're gonna decide what she needs to get through that war zone out there; Cranko's just there to assist you and get you materials. And let's not forget how awesome this is. This is a new chance for us. This is our world now, and with a little help, you'll be the one guy in all of LA who can get around out there without worries."

"The cowpusher's a pretty good idea, actually," Kevin mumbled. "There's a surprising amount of small debris out on the road. It's too small to drag, and it takes forever to get out and move it, but you can't leave it because it could damage a tire or bounce up into the undercarriage." He thought about that a second. "While we're at it, I suppose it wouldn't hurt to armor plate the whole undercarriage to protect the belly of the Witch from debris."

"And from mobs attacking from underneath," Scott said.

Kellie cocked a pierced eyebrow at him. "From where, the sewers? What is this, a heist movie?"

Scott stabbed a finger at her. "That's exactly the kind of shitty attitude that'll get you killed out there. These monsters are just as dickish and crafty as they were in Hearthworld, except now our whole planet is their dungeon. If you're partying with us, you better get your head out of your ass and in the game."

"Fine, whatever," she snapped. "So where do we get these magic swords and armor you promised? And what's the healing potion situation?"

It was as close as Kellie would ever get to an apology and spoken like the tanked-up rog she mained.

"Jenkins." Scott caught the eye of the Dragonkin at the door and nodded him over. "Kel, go with this guy. He'll show you around and get you kitted out from the armory." Scott glanced over his shoulder. While he and Kellie had been arguing, her brother and the Reaver Shaman had snuck over to the Witch and crawled underneath to get a better look. Two pairs of boots stuck out from under the truck, one Obsidian Glass, one Redwing. "Kev can get his gear later on when he's done nerding out with Cranko."

Kellie headed off with the Dragonkin, Scott headed over to the tow truck to see how the wrench monkeys were getting along.

"... with that kind of weight, it'll have to be welded to the chassis," he heard Kevin say under the truck. "Attach it anywhere else, and you run the risk of it breaking off the first time you fire it."

Scott crouched down on his heels to find them flat on their backs deep in discussion.

"I know *weld*," Cranko said. "It is when you join two pieces by hammering them together with flux and molten metal. But I do not know *chassis*. Please explain."

"It's the frame, the skeleton, like you said earlier." Kevin pointed out the visible part to the Shaman. "If you want to attach something and make it strong enough to—" Kevin finally realized Scott was there and looked up. "Dude, you're going to love this."

"Okay, I'll bite. What?"

"Cannons."

Scott grinned. "See, I knew you were the guy for the job, Kev."

"Wait 'til you hear the best part. Cranko says he can Smith them so they're also part flamethrower."

Flat on his back, the Reaver Shaman gave an awkward horizontal shrug. "It is not so hard with the plans for weapons of this world that Lord Roark unlocked for his apprentices when he created the new Gunsmith class. The modification to this cannon is nothing more than a standard Explosive Fire Rune...

with a bit of a Cranko twist." The Shaman's serrated onyx fangs gleamed as his mouth pulled into a wolfish smile. "Fire Enchantments are my specialty."

"You do whatever your little pyro heart desires, Cranko," Scott said. "I want this thing to scare the piss out of every mob and looter in the city. When they hear this beast coming, I want unfriendlies to sprint for cover, trying to hold their fear-induced diarrhea in. I want to put the fear of PwnrBwner into everybody for a hundred miles, so even when these runs are over and done with, everyone and their brother knows not to dick around with me or Shieldwall."

Kevin's excited grin faltered. "That's kind of... intense, isn't it? I mean, even with everything going on, this isn't Hearthworld."

"No, it's not," Scott said. "The time for playing games is over. This is the new reality, and everybody west of the Rockies is going to know who runs it. Now get this shit done—I've got a dungeon to run and a world to save."

CHAPTER 14
KAZ'S HEART

Kazko the Troll Gourmet was a simple creature. He loved his friends, creating good food, and the plump and wonderful apple of his enormous eyes, Mai. Since Hearthworld had been destroyed and the portals had closed, however, Kaz had lost contact with two of those three things—his friends and his sweetheart.

However, he had faith that food was the solution to this difficulty, as it had been to every other trial and tribulation he had experienced so far in his sentient life.

"Today, Kaz would like to show you how to cook Stuffed Pepper Soup, a delicious dish Kaz just tasted for the first time two days ago, thanks to wonderful Heather, who came to Shieldwall on her way to escape from this city known as Los Angeles. She is not native to this place originally, she assures Kaz, which is fun because Kaz is not either. One visitor to another, Heather was kind enough to share her recipe with Kaz."

He picked up one of the kitchen knives thoughtfully provided to him by Lakshya and made eye contact with the camera. That glassy circle was Kaz's student, she had frequently reminded him when he began making these instructional segments, and he had quickly learned to treat it as if he were speaking to one of his apprentices.

"To begin with, Kaz must dice the five large tomatoes and cook them down." He chopped the red fruits and then scooped the pieces into the pot. "Do not fear that you will not have enough fluid for this to become a soup." He held up one large handful of tomato, giving it a gentle squeeze so that seeds, pulp, and juice ran between his fingers into the pot. "As Gry Feliri is so fond of saying, 'trust the ingredients to do the job for you.' They may look insignificant, but these delicious vegetables—or are they fruits? Kaz cannot get a straight answer out of anyone on this subject—are filled with liquid which will become the base of our soup."

Kaz went on, chopping fragrant green peppers and slicing bright yellow corn from cobs. From behind the camera, Lakshya gave him encouraging nods and signaled now and then to draw out his explanations to make this "stream" as she called it longer and trigger something called "algorithms." Kaz had no idea what either term meant and didn't much care, but he was happy to do whatever was needed to reach more students with his love of good food. Besides, enough could not be said on the matters of choosing the right herbs for a dish or the debate of whether to add meat or no meat.

Though Kaz worked diligently and explained each step with wonder and enthusiasm, his mind was not fully focused on the work before him. Or perhaps it was more correct to say his heart.

For while Lakshya and PwnrBwner might hope for these cooking videos of Kaz's to make no small amount of gold and to spread the word that the mobs of Hearthworld were not all savage beasts, Kaz had his own agenda in making them. One completely unrelated to cooking.

He finished browning the hamburger—a red meat the former occupants of Shieldwall had stocked in abundance in the walk-in coolers—and stirred it into the simmering pot, then added the finishing touch.

"The salt," he said with great satisfaction. "No dish is complete without the salt. Just taste it and see."

Picking up a bowl, Kaz ladled the Stuffed Pepper Soup and held the dish out for the camera to close in on.

As Lakshya began to back out once again, Kaz tried a bite.

"So scrumptious!" he said, closing his eyes and letting the flavors burst over his taste buds. "The green florality of the peppers and the hearty strength of the hamburger are an excellent combination you will not want to miss."

Lakshya nodded, then twirled a finger in the air, the signal to speak the ending lines they had practiced so diligently.

"Kaz is so glad you joined him here on the Troll Gourmet. Cooking is a delight for everyone, Troll and hero alike." Instead of going through the agreed-upon conclusion, however, Kaz left the script behind. "Food is a gift to the ones you love, Kaz has always felt this. And now, Kaz is missing the one he loves." He took a shuddering breath to stave off the tears and looked soulfully into the unblinking eye of the camera. "If Mai is safe inside the Citadel, then Kaz is very glad, but if Mai is out there somewhere in this strange world listening, Kaz is here at Shieldwall, waiting for her." He sniffed. "Kaz hopes these videos he is making will not only help others find the joys in cooking, but that they will help find Mai as well, wherever she is, and guide her back to him."

Griff and Mai crept through the strange city, avoiding the spreading fires, destruction, and roving gangs of mobs who had already pledged their allegiance to Darith. The Herald's faithful were easy enough to spot; they went about with crude gold wings riveted to their armor and terrorized anyone they could find. They seemed to be spreading unfortunate quick, too.

Each new section of the city they came to was the same. They found badly approximated paintings of shining golden wings scrawled across stone buildings, metal carriages, and the few thatched huts and wooden carts that had escaped the fires. Other factions seemed to be breaking out as well. Toadlike symbols, crossed daggers, and something that resembled a three-headed hydra with one of its heads missing all marked off territories of differing gangs.

Griff was beginning to think this new world was nothing but lifeless rock below and foul-smelling fog above when they finally came to a stretch of open green.

"The town square?" Mai asked, stepping hesitantly toward the grass.

"Not likely, lass." Griff laid a hand on her arm, stopping her from going any farther, and surveyed the scene. Strange trees with swaying, branchless trunks stretched up to enormous shaggy fronds that jutted out in every direction. Griff had never seen their like before. More of the rock paths crossed the grass, dotted here and there with metal benches; in the distance, another forest of buildings hemmed it in. "It's got no hint of a market nor portals, and I don't see a single board for postings."

Mai gasped, and Griff instinctively pulled his sword and buckler.

"Water," the young widow whispered. She slipped from his grasp and headed for a gleaming lake.

"Don't be in a hurry, lass." Griff caught up with her. "Might be something nasty waiting for us at the water's edge."

He hadn't seen freshwater since coming to this world, and though he'd been careful to ration out the few ales and brews they'd been carrying between them, he was as parched as he'd ever been. Still, that was no excuse for carelessness, especially in a strange and unpredictable land such as this. It was the way of ambush predators to wait until their prey had dropped its guard before attacking, and watering holes were notorious places for monsters to lie in wait. Unseen until it was too late.

Mai slowed beside him and together they approached a wood structure along the lake's shore, a squat little building with a pier stretching onto the gentle waves. Nearby stood a weathered statue of a woman, human or perhaps elf, Griff couldn't tell with the hood covering her ears.

As if to confirm his fears, on the opposite side of the pier, half hidden by the little wooden building and half submerged in the waters, lay the massive skull of a Landwhale Calf. It had been picked clean of meat.

Something moved in the corner of Griff's eye. He spun around, ready to fight for their lives. Approaching them was a massive swan, half again as tall as he was. It bobbed on the currents, gliding silently across the placid surface of the lake before bumping against the land.

Griff waited warily, muscles coiled.

The bird beast made no move to attack. Its feathers didn't even rustle in the breeze.

When it bumped against the shore with a hollow thud, Griff finally realized he wasn't looking at a mob but some odd sort of boat.

"Oh, thank God!" A man in the strange fashion of this world —skin-tight britches, multiple scarves, and a knit cap—not a bit of it with any armor rating or practical utility—stood up from a hollow in the back of the swan ship. "I yelled for like two days, and nobody came. I was starting to think maybe I was the last living person in LA."

"Ah, ya poor dear." Mai helped him out and onto the grass.

"You must be starving. Come along, and we'll get you a bite to eat."

As soon as his feet touched solid ground, the lad's knees buckled. Griff and Mai caught him before he collapsed in a heap.

"Whoops. Guess I need to get my land legs back. I've been hiding out on that thing for a while. Not very comfy, but the walrus dogs couldn't climb into it while I was out on the water, so I stuck with it."

Griff's intuition prickled. "Walrus dogs?"

"Yeah, a whole pack of them. Big sons of guns, the size of a Great Dane, but blubbery, with these huge tusks." He raised his hands to his mouth and stuck out two fingers, like downthrust fangs. "I heard the rumors about mutant alligators in Echo Park Lake, but that was mistaken identification, I guess. Believe me, these things don't look remotely reptilian. Mean as hell, though. They went after that crawling whale thing over there like a herd of piranhas." He turned to Mai. "You said something about a snack?"

Griff suppressed a shudder. "We'd best make tracks first, lad. If the beasts in this water are what I think they are—"

An eerie howl went up from behind the wooden building. The calm waters on either side of the swan boat exploded, and a pair of Tusk Cabras burst forth, shedding water as they lunged at the humans on the land.

Griff shoved Mai and the armorless young man out of the way and put himself between them and the Cabras. The lumps of blubber and tooth weren't the strongest mobs of Hearthworld, but they were damn troublesome. They tended to move in packs and could overrun a fighter if he was caught alone.

Shoving his buckler into the faster Cabra's swinging tusks, Griff hacked down onto the weak spot at the back of its neck, then spun toward its friend. Three more of the blubbery beasts were following hard, charging forward on thick leglike flippers, spreading out to surround their little party.

Another eerie howl went up from behind the wood building, and the lad let out a yelp.

"Back in the swan!" He slammed into Griff's blind side, nearly knocking the older man off balance and into the rending tusks of the oncoming Cabras. "Oh crap! Swan's blocked."

"Aye, it is," Griff muttered, slashing at one chomping Cabra and crushing the skull of another with a fierce swing from his buckler while activating his Shield Bash ability. He shoved a spare Obsidian Glass sword into the lad's hands. "Keep 'em from surrounding us and we'll be all right."

The lad didn't look like he even knew how to hold the weapon. Griff would never get used to this new world's heroes. They were so much softer and more fearful than the ones he'd met in Hearthworld, with none of the swagger and killer instinct. Honestly, he couldn't imagine how this whelp of a man had survived as long as he had. Surely there were monsters and threats in this land aside from those that had migrated over from Hearthworld?

"Too late, dude," the lad said.

From behind them came a feminine grunt and the dull clang of iron on bone. Griff kicked away a Cabra and spun around to find Mai swinging a cast iron frying pan at an advancing Alpha Matriarch Tusk Cabra the size of an ox.

"There's the ma, then," Griff said under his breath. "Hold the pups off until we can run for it," he told the lad, then sprinted to Mai's aid.

Spotting the sudden motion, the Alpha Matriarch swung its huge frame around to face Griff. The undulating dewlap beneath its tusked chin filled with air, and the enormous beast trumpeted. He'd tangled with an Alpha Matriarch, though only once before, and he'd never forget her Bellow Blast attack—

which dealt out concussive sound damage in a two-meter cone. Griff threw himself into a dive, narrowly avoiding the wave of force, then rolled to a crouch. He feinted right, then darted around Mai's side, only to be knocked back by a glancing blow from the Alpha Matriarch's tusks. He absorbed the brunt of the assault with his buckler, then planted his shortsword in the heavy dewlap.

The pouch of air deflated with a high whine. The Alpha Matriarch mirrored Griff's movement, slashing its tusks and pawing the air with its front leg-flippers. One well-timed swipe nearly took his head off, but he threw himself into a roll and came up several lengths away. The Alpha Matriarch let out a wheezing bellow, now devoid of its enchanted power, and followed. Not the fastest of beasts on land, it was slowing down even more as it fought for breath.

Powerful and deadly though they were in a water fight, Tusk Cabras weren't made for the chase. Add to that they were territorial beasts mainly interested in defending their chosen watery homes, and he, Mai, and their new acquaintance could probably get out of this without having to face down the whole pack.

"Run for it!" Griff yelled as he dodged another swipe and gave the Alpha Matriarch a bloodied shoulder for its trouble. "Far edge of the green! Move now!"

Poor swordsman though the lad might be, he was a born sprinter. He easily outpaced Mai to the strange branchless trees, then hunkered there in the safety behind a bench. Mai ducked behind it a moment later, blonde flyaways from under her cap hanging tangled in her flushed face.

"Come on, Griff!" she called, a panicked break in her voice. "Hurry!"

Griff didn't need to be told twice. As the Alpha Matriarch charged again, he leapt, using the last of his stamina on Flying

Leap. With the grace of a Reaver Bat, he soared over the rampaging Tusk Cabra's head and landed with a heavy thump on its back. He planted his shortsword in the weak spot at the base of the beast's skull, driving the blade down to the hilt with his body weight.

With a final breathless roar, the Alpha Matriarch stumbled and dumped forward. One of its tusks broke off with a snap. It kicked, one final spasm of muscular power, then went still.

Griff swung his leg over, knocked aside a clumsy attack from an overeager pup, then half limped, half jogged away from the water.

Mai was leaning over the bench, eagerly waving him on. When he made it to the young widow, she threw her arms around him and sobbed onto his shoulder.

"I hate this world, and I want to go home!" She whimpered like a lost child, her large frame trembling.

Griff patted her plump shoulder consolingly. "Don't fret now, lass. We'll find the Griefer's stronghold and Kaz, and you'll feel a sight better. I promise you that."

"Kaz?" The lad used the borrowed Obsidian Glass weapon like a common stick to push himself back to his feet. "As in the Troll Gourmet from that cooking show?"

Mai's weeping stopped abruptly, and she lifted her flushed face.

"You know my Kaz, dear?"

The lad shrugged. "I just spent two days hiding on a boat with nothing to do." He reached into his back pocket and pulled out a strange rectangle. "I had to watch something. Besides, he's super soothing to listen to. Like watching those ancient history programs about Bob Ross painting."

The lad held the rectangle out for Griff and Mai's inspection. Nearly the whole thing was taken up by the image of the

Feral Hellstrike Knight pulling loaves of bread from some strange version of an oven.

"That's who you're looking for, right?" The lad glanced at the image. "Oh, whoops. Volume's down. Just a sec." He squeezed the sides of the rectangle.

A little at a time, Kaz's voice grew louder.

"The freshest of bread," he rumbled, leaning over and sniffing the hot loaves before letting out a satisfied sigh. Then the big Troll's face fell. "Kaz is certain that you will love fresh bread as much as he loves it. For most, it is a scent to warm the loneliest of dungeons, but for Kaz, it is a reminder of his lost Mai. Kaz and Mai used to bake bread often together in the Citadel, along with many other delicious staples of a healthy and balanced dungeon diet."

Mai sniffled and put a hand to her lips.

A tear slipped out of the Gourmet's eye as he looked out of the rectangle. "Wherever Mai is, Kaz loves her and misses her. Kaz hopes she is safe in the Citadel, but he fears she is out there somewhere in this strange and dangerous world. Mai, Kaz is at Shieldwall, and he hopes that if you see these videos, they will help you find your way back to him."

"Oh, Kaz," Mai whispered, reaching out to touch his face.

The moment her fingers touched the strange rectangle, however, the image transformed into a series of painful, strobing lights and blaring noises Griff could barely recognize as music.

"You must've hit the Play Next button," the lad said, taking the rectangle back and blessedly silencing the awful racket.

Mai spun around to face Griff. "I've got to get to him."

"We'll get you there, lass," Griff said patting her shoulder reassuringly. He fixed his piercing glare on the young man who'd let the borrowed sword drop into the grass like a discarded bit of refuse. Picking it up, he asked the lad, "You're from this land, true? Do you know how to get to Shieldwall? It's home of the Griefer's forces and the Devs of Hearthworld."

The lad frowned. "Hearthworld devs?" After a moment of blankness, he snapped his fingers. "Oh, you mean Frontflip. They're the studio that made the game. Yeah, it's downtown." He waved a hand vaguely to the left.

Griff considered the Obsidian Glass weapon for a moment before making up his mind. He'd served as a hero escort through many a dungeon during his days in Hearthworld; it was about damn time a hero escorted him to his goal for once.

"Can you take us there, lad?"

After a moment, the young man sighed. "I guess it's the least I can do. You guys did save me." He nodded down at the rectangle in his hand. "Plus, the video descriptions all say that you should head their way if you're stuck in LA right now, so I guess I'm going there anyhow." His fingers danced over the rectangle and after a brief pause a map appeared on its face, marking the final quest location. "Looks like we're heading this way."

CHAPTER 15
MASS ENCHANTMENT

Roark stood in the snowy bailey of the Radiant Citadel, watching Zyra's troops take their positions in and around the outer wall. The day was clear and bright, the sun glinting off the snow like knives, but one by one they disappeared into a puff of golden smoke, courtesy of the Invisibility potion the Septic Brewmaster had prepared. The potion worked on a similar principle as her Diurnal Prowl, making it possible for the drinker to hide within pools of light, but didn't allow them to cross distances within it as her Prowl abilities did.

When he'd asked Zyra whether that was due to her limitations as a Brewmaster, she had grinned. "A necessary precaution. If I give up all my best secrets, what's to stop the ambitious ones from coming after me?"

Below, the fight still raged on in Korvo. The sigil towers studded the battlements, awaiting the Discordant Inversion cast. The added fortifications had slowed the Tyrant King's forces significantly, and the allied mobs were quickly culling them from within the city. The problem now was keeping them out. For every Sacred Bastet or Soul Devourer Roark's troops killed, Marek and the World Stone spawned five more. Until they rid the area of the Tyrant King, they were fighting a war of attrition, and that wasn't a war they could win. Not even with all of the allied dungeons throwing their support behind the endeavor.

Marek was just so damned powerful.

Next to Roark, Mac was curled up in a patch of sunlight, snoozing despite the battle going on below. On his other side, Randy Shoemaker was shivering from boots to the tips of his silver wings in spite of the unseasonably warm weather.

"Nervous?" Roark asked him.

"Huh?" Randy blinked, then looked down at his arms hugged around his torso. "Oh! No—well, a little—but it's more that I'm used to Southern California weather. Sunny and seventy-five on a cold day." He chuckled. "I used to get razzed about that when I went back to Minneapolis for Christmases and Thanksgivings."

At Roark's questioning look, Randy explained, "Holidays in my home world. You usually spend them with family, but I just had my grandparents. I stopped visiting Minnie when they passed away. Honestly, I sort of forgot what the cold felt like." He glanced out at the snow-covered mountainside, wings shuddering with another full-body tremor. "It's kind of beautiful if you can get past your body thinking it's dying."

Gold smoke smelling faintly of coquelicot blossoms curled from a sunray beside them, and Zyra Prowled out on the spider legs protruding from her back. She didn't seem bothered by the cold, though Roark couldn't say whether that was due to her spawning in the chill dankness of a dungeon or her natural cold-blooded disposition.

"I still think this would be better done inside," she said in lieu of a greeting. "Easier to defend you both if I don't have to watch out for a hail of arrows. One lucky shot is all it takes. And even a powerful Feudal Lord is susceptible to an unlucky roll of the dice."

Randy grimaced and shook his head. "Heart of the Forest requires me to have line of sight of each of the principals."

Though Zyra's face was hidden behind her lacy veil, the Herald quailed when she shot him a lethal glare.

Roark stifled the urge to smile. "Even ignoring that, the cast is too large for a confined space. Ick and I both tried to find a way to shrink it, but came up empty handed. This is the only way forward."

"That doesn't mean I have to like it." The Orbweaver Ravager pulled one of her 1911s and checked its magazine. "Just get this over with before all this open space and sunshine becomes an issue."

"Ready?" Roark asked the shivering Arboreal Herald.

Randy wiped his hands on his armored thighs and nodded, then took a deep breath and blew out a stream of white. He shifted so that the Citadel, Roark, and Korvo were all within his field of vision, then held out his hands palms up and relaxed.

When he breathed out again, it wasn't the white haze of warm air, but a cloud of translucent emerald energy that quickly grew and solidified into gnarled, rootlike protrusions rising from his fingertips. Without warning, the roots plunged into the snow-laced dirt beneath the Arboreal Herald's feet.

Something grabbed Roark's ankle.

In spite of having been warned by Randy how Heart of the Forest worked, Roark still flinched as the green shoot wrapped around his calf.

[Arboreal Herald Randy Shoemaker has requested to open a connection with you. Do you agree? Yes/No]

Casting a watchful eye down-mountain at the war-torn Korvo, Roark quickly allowed the connection. Below, much larger roots were sprouting up from the earth. The biggest of the lot erupted from the earth near the Mage's Tower in the center of Korvo, wrapping around the outside of the tower like a python made of vines and leaves. Small roots branched out from the tower, crawled through the earth, then ensnared each of the seven archer towers along the walled perimeter. Roark knew he would find much the same if he cast a backward glance at the Citadel.

Under normal circumstances, Randy had explained to him, Heart of the Forest would only allow him to coordinate between living members of his party, but with a small modification to the spell's understanding of "party"—made possible by the looser rules of Traisbin's magick—he had been able to include nonliving structures as long as they contained a measure of Hearthworld's Magicka.

The tremble working through the ground roused Mac from his slumber. The Elemental Turtle Dragon lumbered to scaly feet, one head examining the roots drilling into the ground, another watching the battle play out on the field below, the third nuzzling Roark's free hand, looking for scratches. Roark was only too happy to oblige.

Okay, connection to the Citadel's Magicka pool is open, Randy's voice came through the mental connection. *Begin the form for the cast whenever you're ready.*

Roark nodded, but didn't immediately rush into the postures required to weave the Discordant Inversion despite the urgency for speed. The odds of him achieving this cast on his first try were slim —even small, simple Inversions had taken him time and massive efforts of will to learn—but to rush would further pare down his chances of success to nothing. He patted Mac's head one final time, then pointed at a section of stone pavers far enough away that the Turtle Dragon wouldn't interrupt his spell.

Mac chirped grumpily, but trundled away and plopped down, his spike-studded tail curling around his body.

Roark closed his eyes and took deep, deliberate breaths. Emptying his cup of distractions, as Ick liked to call it. It felt unbearably slow, but he forced himself to remember that following the proper steps would save him time in failed casts, no matter how it chafed. He could take as long as it required, he told himself. Randy was making certain the Citadel and Towers were moving forward with the rest of the tasks that would eventually make up the spell. All he had to do was focus on the one task presented to him at a time.

When he was centered and focused, Roark dropped into *Stance of the Patient Hunter*, holding it for a moment before throwing himself into the dizzying series of forms collectively known as *Wrapping the Struggling Prey. Stillness in the Breeze* followed, a bone-jarring stop that quickly flowed into *Creeping Across a Dewy Web.* With a burst of speed and power, he leapt into the air and spun, *Falling on the Unsuspecting Quarry*, then drew himself up into *Stance of Defending Against the Angry Retaliation of a Wounded Enemy.*

Every motion and posture of the School of Night had been crafted for the Nocturnus frame—eight spider's limbs as well as humanoid hands and feet—and so every step of the cast required Roark to work multiple times harder for the same results. Within moments, he was sweating, with steam rolling off his Draconic Chaos Harbinger form and breath raking his lungs in heaving gasps. But it was working. He could feel the thrum of the arcane energy building in the air around him.

With a final shout of power, Roark threw himself forward, fists outthrust in *Repelling the Stronger Opponent.* And just like that the tenuous energy... dissipated. Scattered to the winds before he could harness and channel it. He'd missed the landing, though only barely. Thankfully the spell didn't blow up in his face, which was an equal possibility.

Sweat dripped from Roark's jaw onto the snow.

Uh, Randy started, but Roark interrupted him.

A failed cast. I'll get it this time.

It's not that—

"Looks as if you're attracting some attention, Griefer," Zyra purred. "Tell me, can your Tyrant King sense when spells are being directed against him?"

A look down the mountainside showed a sudden shift in the battle. The gout of dark shapes of the Tyrant King's army veered suddenly away from the new battlements surrounding Korvo and charged at breakneck pace up the mountain toward the Citadel.

"Bloody damnation," Roark cursed under his breath.

Gulping down a lungful of air, he returned to the starting posture for Discordant Inversion. It was a damned sight harder forcing himself to focus and move slowly knowing that Marek was likely on his way to the Citadel. If he didn't get this cast right, they were doomed. He didn't have the power to face off against Marek directly. Not yet.

He managed to keep his concentration flawless through the first half of the form, but as he leapt into *Falling on the Unsuspecting Quarry*, the first of the Tyrant King's undead hordes exploded out of the tree line, sweeping out in an arc like an invading plague of locusts.

Within sight of their target, the mobs gained a second wind, picking up speed. Jackals, the fastest of Marek's troops, yipped and barked at one another as they raced over the rocky ground, kicking up white tails of snow behind them.

Focus, Roark ordered himself, clamping his eyes shut tight. He was nearly there. Only a few motions left. It had to work this time.

There would be no third chance. Hopefully Zyra's forces were up to the challenge and could buy him the time he needed. He heard the shouts of the Reavers, Nagas, and Imps breaking free from their Invisibility and leaping on the attackers from the Citadel's walls.

This time, when Roark fell into the final stance, thrusting out his fists in *Repelling the Stronger Opponent*, the arcane energy swirling around him snapped into a meticulously woven web of power—though it existed only inside his mind. When he opened his eyes, no glowing web floated before him, yet he could feel every strand of the spell radiating outward, covering the city and the Citadel in its protection.

Instantly, he felt the Discordant Inversion ripped away, like a rapier wrenched from his hands mid-duel. Unable to hold himself upright, Roark dropped to his knees in the snow, sweating and shaking. In spite of his exhaustion, he couldn't help but grin. He'd done it, though whether the Web would actually work against Marek or the World Stone remained to be seen. The rest of his spells were up and running, however, which was a good sign.

Outside the walls, Zyra's army battled back the monstrous Undead. The few that made it through the open gates were in for some nasty surprises. Brilliant flashes of light blinked across the front lines as enemies stepped across portal plates and were whisked away to distant dungeons where Roark's allies waited to pounce. Roark stood on shaky legs—still feeling winded and weak from the cast—and scanned the city and the air for any sign of Marek. He'd been so sure that the Tyrant King would be waiting, ready to strike the moment he saw an opportunity. Nothing. No sign of the decaying God-Pharaoh.

Was it possible that he'd read the situation wrong?

No sooner had the thought entered his head than a violet shimmering portal tore space and time inside the Citadel's bailey.

The nightmarish form of the Tyrant King stepped out of the tear mere feet from Roark.

For a fraction of a heartbeat, Roark's eyes met Marek's. The Tyrant King's mouth opened to let loose with a murderous spell or one of his bored aristocratic taunts—Roark never found out.

Before Marek could utter a sound, a thunderous crack shook the air.

An enormous darkly radiant web of Discordant Inversion and Deflection flashed from the sigil towers below, bursting forth to cover the entirety of the mountainside like a net, from Korvo to the crumbling golden top of the Citadel—so much larger than Roark had originally intended.

Immediately on its heels, a sapphire blast exploded from the amber-colored World Stone Pendant around Marek's decomposing neck.

The force of the Inversion threw the Tyrant King miles down the mountainside, until Roark could just barely make out the bright red Health bar floating above the despot's head.

A grim smirk twisted Roark's face. Watching the Tyrant King on the receiving end of a malicious spell for once was a nice change of pace.

Nearby, Randy dropped Heart of the Forest and whooped. "It worked!" He slapped Roark on the back. "You did it!"

"We did it," Roark corrected him, without ever taking his eyes off the Tyrant King below.

The Undead God-Pharaoh's stance was hunched, fists clawed with fury. He made a single move to step closer, only to find himself forcefully hurled back again, losing another considerable chunk of Health the moment he tried to cross the web. Obviously sensing that this was not a defense he could bully his way through, Marek opened another portal and disappeared, taking a good measure of the tension screwing up Roark's muscles with him.

Without Marek to continue spawning new troops, Zyra's hidden army quickly killed off the majority of the remaining mobs attacking the Citadel. The few who weren't assassinated were the ones smart enough to retreat. Not that they made it far. The Orbweaver Ravager's forces tore through their fleeing ranks, and when they made it to the gates, the portal plates wouldn't just let them leave. They were instantly ported away, directly into the waiting jaws of enemy dungeons.

The last of the tautness drained from Roark's limbs, leaving euphoria in its place.

He wasn't the only one excited about the victory. Beside him, Randy fidgeted from foot to foot, wings fluttering a little, face beaming with the aftereffects of the adrenaline.

"You modified the cast so it would include the Citadel as well?" Roark asked.

"Oh right, that!" The Arboreal Herald bounced a little in place and explained excitedly, "I hope you don't mind—I know it took a little longer than we'd planned, but when I saw they were coming this way, I just assumed the Tyrant King would follow, so I was able to assign the Citadel an exponential expansion routine and route the Inversion back through it."

Roark snorted. "Mind? No, I don't bloody mind! It saved our lives, mate."

Randy let out a relieved chuckle verging on hysteria. "Thankfully it didn't freeze up on us." As soon as he said it, Randy seemed to realize just how high the stakes were. "Oh gosh!" Randy's wide, terrified eyes met Roark's, white showing all the way around. "We could've died!"

His legs wobbled beneath him, and only Roark catching his arm kept him on his feet.

"Could've but didn't," Roark said with a wry grin. "In my book, that means we won."

Though he didn't say so, he knew that removing Marek and

the World Stone from the battlefield was a hard-fought victory, but it was also a temporary one. Sooner or later, the Tyrant King would find a way to break through the Discordant Inversion with the Stone. When that happened, Roark intended to be prepared. He would need to be. Marek was not only more powerful, but Roark was still suffering under the effects of the Curse of the Mummy. The trickle of Experience coming in thanks to his Feudal Lord's Tax kept him from dying on the spot, but Marek would only get more powerful the longer this went on.

The key to defeating Marek lay with the World Stone. That was the God-Pharaoh's single biggest advantage. If Roark could figure out a way to strip him of that forever...

Well, he might just have a shot at killing the bastard for good. Roark stared down the mountainside at Korvo. The Troll Nation was finally making headway in cleansing it of Marek's remaining troops.

Somewhere down there was an Elder who'd once served on Traisbin's Council, twisting her opal ring and waiting. Waiting for him to ask what only someone trusted with the deepest secrets of Terho's history would know: the origins of the World Stone.

CHAPTER 16

RAVINGS OF A MADMAN

Heavy cleanup was already underway in the streets of Korvo when Roark arrived. Locals in their brightly colored clothing, smeared liberally with ash and blood, worked alongside the smaller allied mobs. Together, they put out the last of the fires, wrapped and laid out the dead in the square, and sifted through the charred remains for salvageable food to pass around the village. Meanwhile, the strongest men, aided by towering Thursrs, Rock People, and Wolf-Bear Hybrids, cleared the streets of the heaviest debris so carts could pass and carefully lifted chunks of wall and roof, freeing those who'd been trapped beneath.

After days of fighting, the sight of the two groups cooperating did Roark good. The transplanted Troll Nation had proven their intentions to the townspeople, and in turn, the townspeople had begun to trust them.

Stranger still, it wasn't only the allied mobs and Dungeon Lords who acknowledged Roark as he, Randy, and Zyra passed through Korvo. Word had spread of his true identity, it seemed. Though the hardy, proud mountain people didn't bow and scrape like the lower-level Citadel mobs did, the citizens hailed him as Korvo's long-lost son, calling out to him in the streets. Despite looking like a demon pulled from the Lore books of the Lyuko travelers, he was offered friendly open smiles and courteous, though shallow, bows of respect.

"Lord Roark, welcome home!"

"Way to run off that Ustar bastard, Lord Roark! Just like your father in his day!"

"Bless you, Lord Roark, bless you!"

Roark received the praise and well-wishes with some chagrin. He didn't feel equal to it considering he was the reason they'd been attacked in the first place. The rows of corpses wrapped in colorful blankets in the square were on his head. The destroyed homes and places of business were down to him as well. The best he could manage was a grim smile in response to their greetings and the occasional stop to help with a bit of the backbreaking labor. Roark may not have been equal to Marek in strength or raw power, but as a Draconic Chaos Harbinger he was still a force to be reckoned with, stronger than even the biggest and most powerful of the Thursrs.

So it was that he arrived at the inn much later than he'd intended and in more than double the time the same walk would have taken uninterrupted.

Korvo's only inn, the Flagstaff, was long and squat and conveniently situated near the southern gates, where weary travelers and merchant caravans would lay eyes on it as they first entered town. Roark was glad to see that the building had weathered the onslaught unusually well. A few spots on the roof's thatching were blackened and burnt, and the stable had been crushed beneath a massive chunk of the old wall, which had broken off from the city's previous defenses sometime before Roark had created the new battlements. Otherwise, the structure was untouched.

An elderly merchantwoman had taken up a semipermanent

residence there not long after the Council of Traisbin was deposed by Marek, claiming she was returning to her roots shipping goods through the pass to either side of the Karasu Mountains. In fact, this was not only a clever disguise, but a booming trade for the old woman. With most of the von Grafs dead, she'd quickly become the wealthiest resident of the city. That success had allowed her to fund most of the *T'verzet*'s more expensive activities. From what Albrecht had told him, the old woman was still living there, and with Bran gone she had become a sort of de facto innkeeper.

And, if Albrecht could be believed, she also happened to be the only person who might know the true origins of the World Stone Pendant.

Folding his leathery wings, Roark ducked through the low door. The common room was warm and cheery, a bright fire burning in the hearth, but still it took a moment for Roark's eyes to adjust from the brilliant sunlight outside.

"I expected you earlier," Morgana said.

She was seated close to the fire, not in one of the rough-hewn chairs that filled the room, but in an expensive-looking high-backed seat with thick cushioning. A small throne in its own right.

Roark wove through the tables to join her. "I was ridding Korvo of an infestation. Took a bit longer than I would've liked; the king of the rats was tougher to drive out than I expected."

The elderly merchantwoman's eyes gleamed with barely suppressed humor. "You've changed much since last we met, von Graf." She looked over his monstrous form and lifted a fine porcelain cup from a gilded table beside her. She took a long sip of something that smelled of equal parts tea and *asake* and considered him for a moment longer. "I sincerely hope those changes aren't only superficial," she said.

"I'd like to think I've learned a thing or two since my rather impetuous attempt on Marek's life. How to lead and govern. How to delegate. That strength isn't the only way." Roark paused, lips pressed into a tight line. "That I don't know everything."

"I have my hopes," the old woman replied, before taking another sip of tea, "though I have learned through a long and painful life that words are both easy and cheap."

"Unfortunately for you," Roark said, "you don't have many better options. Marek is more powerful than he's ever been and growing stronger by the day. If we don't make our stand now, we'll never have another opportunity."

"Still a little impetuous, I see," she amended, though she did so with a soft smile. "Such is the curse of youth." She stole a sidelong look at Randy and Zyra. The Orbweaver Ravager was eying every potential hiding place for threats, while the Arboreal Herald stuck close, eager for the information they could only get from Morgana. "What you want to know, I can't discuss with outsiders present. In truth, I shouldn't even be discussing it with you."

Her words irked Roark. He had grown, had changed during his time in Hearthworld, yet the fact that they'd kept this information from him for so long was irritating. Perhaps, if they had shared with him then all they knew, they wouldn't be in this ugly, desperate situation at all. Roark was willing to admit he was wrong about certain things, but they'd been wrong to keep the truth from his ears.

"Why bother, then?" Roark asked, fighting and failing to keep the frustration from his voice. "Why not continue keeping your secrets while Marek runs roughshod over the land, just as you and the rest of the Council of Traisbin did these last twenty bloody years?"

Morgana twisted the opal ring on her gnarled finger. "Six months ago, a hot-tempered youngster stormed out of the fabric store with nothing but revenge and death on his mind. As one might easily imagine, his idiotic scheme to assassinate the Tyrant King—with nothing more than a knife, mind you—failed." She locked eyes with Roark. "You tell me: in a time of war and desperation, would you want potentially devastating information in the hands of those with nothing but courage? Or would you choose to place it in the hands of those with courage and wisdom in equal measure?"

Much as he hated to admit it, the old bat had a fair point. "But what makes you think I'm the man to handle this potentially devastating information now?"

"For one, you are right. We *are* running out of time. Marek finally resembles the monster he is in truth, and the forces he has at his disposal are like nothing I've ever seen. And I've seen much in my years. Desperation makes all of us a hair impetuous, I suspect. For another, you have an army of monsters at your back, and that has to count for something. But there is also more to it than that. Before all of this happened"—she waved a hand at his demonic appearance—"you gladly ran off to die the moment you caught a whiff of the Tyrant King."

Morgana's gaze grew distant as if she were looking down the long hallway of time.

"During this raid, however," she continued, "you saw the attacks for the obvious lure they were, and rather than letting your hatred for the Tyrant King control you and bumbling into his trap, you directed an intelligent, strategic counterattack that ultimately drove him away." Her lips pulled into something halfway between a grimace and a smile. "You also haven't threatened to burn the inn down around my ears for doing nothing with this information all these years, which if I recall correctly, you did threaten to do to the fabric store the night you stormed out."

"Give me some time and I may yet," Roark replied. He

glanced again over his shoulder to his friends. "You can demand they leave if you like, but the moment we're done here, I'll only relay everything you've told me to them. They may be outsiders from another world, but they're some of the bravest and strongest people I know. And they're loyal. Sometimes to a fault," he finished, looking at Zyra. "I couldn't have come this far without their help. I certainly can't finish this without them."

"Told you so," Zyra said. At Morgana's scandalized expression, the Orbweaver Ravager gave Roark a sarcastic bow and added, "Feudal Lord."

Roark snorted. One moment she was insisting he act with all the pomp of his title to intimidate the locals, the next she openly mocked the position. At times, he suspected Zyra might be flipping back and forth depending on what would annoy him the most in any given moment.

"Indeed." Morgana eyed the veiled Ravager. "If they are to be part of this with or without my protestations, then let's note that I protest and move forward without wasting any more time. You're here about that stone Marek wears about his neck?"

"The World Stone Pendant," Roark confirmed.

Her wrinkled lips twisted into a smirk. "Very good. You've managed to learn in six months what it took years for the Council of Traisbin to eke out." She twisted the opal ring. "We were as slow-moving as the Turtle Islands in Labrange Lake, and that was our downfall. By the time we had discovered a scrap of new information, debated its veracity and consequences, discussed potential action at nauseating length, and decided to move, it was too late."

Roark bit back the urge to say she'd brought the same glacierlike pace to the T'verzet, but the sharp old merchantwoman must have caught something in his expression, because she spoke as if she'd read his mind.

"You believe it was the same with the Rebel Council." She shook her head. "The simplest of questions, a yes or no, would take months, and often end up being irrelevant by the time it was decided."

"This lesson in governing is enlightening," Roark said, unable to quite keep all of the sarcasm from his voice, "but it isn't why I came here today. I need to know where the World Stone came from."

"Of course," she said. "Forgive an old woman her digressions. I just wanted you to understand why we did nothing with the growing threat of Marek Konig Ustar while we still might have stopped him. Mistakes were made, there is no denying that. And like you, I am big enough to admit that I don't know everything."

"I apologize. Please continue."

She graciously dipped her head in acknowledgement. "You recall the rumors that Marek came from the West, yes?" She waved a gnarled hand. "Patently false. No records or accounts were ever found that confirmed that Marek was from Traisbin—or Terho at all, for that matter. The true Council did, however, find one far-fetched drunkard's claim of an eerie light on a cold, clear night. When delved into, the timing fit perfectly with the earliest accounts of Marek."

She raised a brow as if to accuse Roark of some wrongdoing. "Many of which come from your mother's people, the Lyuko. The travelers speak in hushed tones of a lost caravan last seen entering the mountains with a man matching Marek's description who wore an amber stone around his neck. He had it already, you see. Years later, the bloodbaths began in the West, hence the rumors, but our theory was that he came from another world entirely, from a planet far beyond the stars."

"The eerie light the drunk saw in the sky." Roark nodded, recalling the moment the Tyrant King had nearly killed him after his battle with Lowen. "He said our world wasn't the first he'd conquered—called himself the world eater."

Morgana shifted in her chair, pulling her shawl tighter about her shoulders.

"Just so. Tell me, von Graf, how would you find the origins of a man and magick not of this world?"

The bottom dropped out of his stomach. "Portals. Then you knew all along that they're harmless."

"Harmless, no. Written incorrectly, they are every bit as deadly and unpredictable as you've been led to believe, and written to a place you've never been or seen can be just as lethal. We lost more mages than returned to us, and the few who did return were... no longer human."

"That's why you weren't surprised to see how I'd changed," he guessed.

She acknowledged this with a slight cant of her head. "There are more worlds... indeed, more universes full of more worlds than we can dream of. It was a miracle we found any answer at all."

Roark leaned forward in his seat, his body and wings tensed with anticipation.

"Many of these other worlds had been destroyed by Marek in one form or another. These were where most of our information came from. The Council had our mages follow it through deaths and transformations, until finally we arrived at the end —or rather, the beginning. The Tower of Creation."

Roark opened his mouth to speak, but Morgana held up a trembling hand.

"Let me speak this through to the end. I hope to do this only once and never be forced to relive it again. There is a space at the center of all worlds, all universes, every reality, *connecting* them, but not *of* them. It is like the eye at the center of a great storm. And there stands the tower, binding all of creation together. It is the source of all magicks, great and small, and it powers everything we know, everything we think we know, and everything we don't know at all."

She visibly shuddered.

"To see it... Well, you cannot grasp how truly insignificant we are, nor how incredibly meaningful each and every living being in every world is. We are known, von Graf, known to our core, and that is the most horrible and beautiful thing anyone can experience." She clutched her shawl tighter. "I cannot grasp how Marek managed to stand before it, unmoved and unbent by the power of its presence. For that alone I would name him monster. But it is worse than that. He found a way to carve a piece from the tower."

Roark frowned. "You're not telling me the World Stone is part of this Tower of Creation?"

Strands of Morgana's wispy white hair wafted as she nodded. "As far as we can discern, it is the one and only piece *ever* taken from the Tower. His task couldn't have been an easy one, fracturing reality rarely is, and from what we've learned, he nearly died in the attempt. He spent centuries recovering before he was able to begin his storm of destruction on the very world that had nursed him back to health. It is a husk now, like so many others left in his wake.

"Fortunately, we found a few scattered living creatures able to communicate what had happened. He'd hoped to destroy every living thing on the planet to hide the origins of the stone, and in his arrogance, he thought he had, but unbeknownst to him a precious few escaped. They told of the rantings of the battered, nearly dead man their elders nursed, ravings about the strange amber stone he never let out of his grasp. 'It wants to go back,' he would cry in his feverish delusions. 'Too close and the Tower will be healed. I'll never go back, you'll never be whole.'"

As the implications of the ravings sank in, Roark's heart thrummed faster in his chest.

"If he returns to the Tower, the stone will be reabsorbed," he whispered in a hoarse voice. His mind raced, everything Morgana had said and everything he knew about the stone and Marek blasting around inside his skull at once. "It's not the sole source of his power, but it is his greatest advantage, and it nearly killed him in the taking. If reabsorbed, he wouldn't be able to break another piece off easily..."

Roark jumped to his feet, knocking over the chair with his leathery wings.

"Bloody hells, that's it!" He gave the old woman a gracious, though rushed, bow and took her frail hands in his. "Thank you, Morgana. Thank you for entrusting this information to me, and most of all, thank you for waiting until now. It never would have worked before, but I would've bloody charged off and tried to do it anyway—likely dooming all of Terho in the process. You were right to wait."

Morgana frowned quizzically. "You believe you've found an answer."

"I found it in Hearthworld," he said, letting go of her hands and striding toward the door. "I just didn't know it at the time."

"Will you kill him?" she asked.

Hand on the latch, Roark let out a laugh that sounded a bit mad even to his own ears.

"If this works, one of us isn't coming back." He flung the door open. "And I don't intend it to be me."

CHAPTER 17
WAR MACHINE

After the initial discussion of what the Winch Witch would be expected to do and what sort of defense and offense would be feasible on a land battlecruiser her size, Scott was pretty much excluded from the rebuilding process. That was fine with him. He hadn't gotten into Dungeon Lording to sling wrenches and micromanage. Scott was a big picture guy, top of the corporate food chain, delegator type. He came up with the ideas and assigned them to underlings who could get the job done without his help, because he had Dungeon Lord shit to take care of.

After all, he was basically running the last beacon of civilization between Ventura and Baja. That was a lot of work. When he wasn't handling disputes between refugees and mobs or organizing salvage runs to fulfill Kevin and Crank's shopping list, Scott was literally saving lives with the Poser Owners. With the military gone and the local police forces scattered, every too-stupid-to-live civilian became Scott's responsibility. From sunup to sunset, he was clearing out Best Buys of Ravenous Ghouls or kicking in the teeth of Bog Goblins who'd turned the Whole Foods into a bastion of depravity.

Even that was like trying to bail water with a colander. Even with the portal to Hearthworld shut off, the dungeons were multiplying like bunnies in the springtime.

The constant governing and Dungeon Lord duties and rescue missions were a complete one-eighty from the life Scott was used to—which had mostly amounted to finding ways to fill the time between shifts at the Bell. But he handled the weighty responsibility exactly like he'd always assumed he would—like a G. Roark had been right to leave him in charge. The hundreds of civilian lives he'd saved were proof of his absolute badassery.

Pimping out the wrecker and tractor trailer took a lot longer than Scott was expecting it to. Even with magical assistance from Crank and his helpers, the job lasted three days. Kevin insisted certain things be done the old-fashioned Earth way, especially when it came to the Winch Witch, and since she was his baby and he knew more about engines and drive shafts and that type of crap, Scott let the dweeb have his way. The semi and trailer didn't need to run, though, they just needed to not fall off when the wrecker pulled them, so Crank and the other smiths had free run of that half of the job.

Finally, after a mind-blowing supper of the best ham 'n' beans and cornbread Scott had ever tasted thanks to Kaz, a little Dragonkin came running into the cafeteria to get him.

"Dungeon Lord PwnrBwner, the smith and the *mechanic*"—the little dude sounded out every syllable of the unfamiliar word Kevin had probably taught him—"say it is finished. They humbly request your inspection of the mighty Winch Witch."

"Sweet." Scott wadded up his paper napkin and banked it off the wall into the trash can. Or at least onto the top of the trash getting ready to overflow that particular bin. There were rotations assigned to trash pickup and disposal for Shieldwall —that piece of infrastructure had become necessary almost immediately after Scott took charge of the place—but it still blew his mind how fast the garbage piled up with hundreds of mobs, refugees, and dungeon staff eating three to four square meals a day plus snacks.

Luckily, if Kev and the wrecker were ready, then they were about to solve that problem. Shuttling out eighty percent of the people clogging up Shieldwall would cut down on the trash PDQ. And a ton of the other administrative headaches that were constantly following him around. The Hearthworld mobs and NPCs were all pretty chill—mostly because they knew their place in the hierarchy—but all the dumb civilians treated Scott like he was a hotel manager instead of a warlord saving all their sorry asses from certain death.

"Lead away, Harvey," Scott told the Dragonkin, following the little dude out into the hall.

As they wound their way through the torchlit corridors, people recognized Scott and tried to hijack him into even more of their petty, small-time concerns. He wasn't having it. He had big-time high-concept problems to solve right then, and they didn't include him slowing down for the plebe stuff.

"Dungeon Lord, the coffee machine in the second-floor lobby isn't putting out hot water anymore!"

He didn't even slow down. "Dungeon Lord on a mission, bro. Find GothicTerror."

"Dungeon Lord, the kobolds are fighting with the gang-bangers from Riverside again!"

"You know who would be great at handling that? Gothic Terror."

"Dungeon Lord, the toilets in the west hall—"

"That's definitely a GothicTerror job."

Delegation ruled.

To be fair, it helped that his Lieutenant Uberbitch was pretty great at handling all the minor things that added up to huge stupid problems without freaking out about how much he sent her way. Scott even thought about leaving her at Shieldwall when their wrecker convoy pulled out, but ultimately decided that he couldn't spare such a vital part of the POSes. Not when they didn't know how much resistance and firepower they'd be facing on the road to the containment wall.

Instead, he'd let one of the less talented fighters hang back and keep things afloat while they were gone, somebody like that glass cannon Tomahiro or that dweeb Arjun who just wanted to draw everybody kitted out in their weapons and armor for "character references."

When they reached the lobby, the Dragonkin threw his weight into the massive reinforced door and held it open for Scott to go first.

Outside, thick black cables snaked across the churned-up dirt from high-powered work lights. The lights had been scavenged from a nearby Department of Transportation shed, and would have been worthless with the rolling blackouts raging through the city as LA's infrastructure fell apart, but Kevin and one of the goblins who apprenticed as an Enchanter under Crank had come up with a solution: generators powered by a magical rune system. Turned out having a wrench monkey on call was pretty handy, especially when you needed your phone charged.

The Witch sat at the center of the work lights, shining in the brilliant wattage like the grand prize on some insane apocalyptic game show. *Tell them what they won, Johnny... A brand-new war machine!*

The Witch's cab and windshield were now reinforced with armored plates of solid steel with gaps cut out at eye level for the driver and spotter in the passenger seat. More armor plates had been riveted down the sides of the semi, and barnacle-like pillboxes for spell slingers and archers had been welded onto the sides of the trailer. Kevin had talked about wishing for one of those big-ass snowplows the DOTs had in colder states, but Scott thought the cowpusher they'd rigged up on their own was better.

Two giant metal blades had been welded together in the middle to form an enormous knife, which rose higher at its center than the Witch's hood. Both sides scooped back like the barrel of a wave and tapered off at the edges, so anything that got caught up would quickly tumble out of the way without getting dragged under the wrecker and hanging her up. And thanks to Crank's ingenuity with the pneumatics, the pusher could be raised and lowered if they ran into some majorly uneven terrain.

Planted squarely on top of the Witch's roof and welded to the light bar was a turret mounted with a .50 cal machine gun that Crank's apprentices had mysteriously "acquired" after the army moved out. One of Roark's enchanting apprentices had carefully carved a flash art tattoo onto the barrel—a dagger piercing a palm while a fanged serpent coiled around the wrist—granting the weapon additional penetration power and adding in poison damage to anything lucky enough to survive a direct hit. The toolboxes farthest forward had been opened up and equipped with flamethrowers, which could be controlled by the spotter from the safety of the cab.

The wheels on the middle axle—currently raised and off the ground to avoid digging the bailey up any more than necessary—had been swapped out with scoop-lined steel wheels that looked like they'd been stolen off a steam engine from hell. Supposedly those would give the beast extra traction if she needed to haul the semi over some really jacked-up roadways.

Vicious-looking foot-long spikes sharpened to a razor's edge had been added to all the outrigger legs, and every rim on the Witch and the semi had been fitted with serrated spinners of death—gleaming metal grinders that stuck out a good yard from the hubs, ready to chew up anybody that got too close and spit out a fine pink mist.

Best of all, mounted on the cowpusher was a big, fat stogie of a cannon barrel. There was also some kind of rotating drum magazine for charges as big as bowling balls.

Scott stopped on the top step and whistled through his tooth. "Damn, son. That's beast AF."

Kevin rolled out from under the Witch on one of those mechanic sliders.

"She's a beauty, amiright?" he said, grinning like a goober. "Want a tour?"

"Hells yeah." Scott hopped down the steps. "Show me all the awesome aftermarket features you guys added."

That made Kevin light up like the Christmas Quesadilla Scott and his dick of a manager had to mount on top of the Bell's sign every year. Not that he'd ever have to do that again. No more bullshit jobs for this Dungeon Lord.

Kevin climbed up on the Witch's newly armored fender and flipped open the hood.

"Okay, check this out."

Scott looked longingly at the flamethrowers and turret. "The boring stuff under the hood isn't really the features I meant."

But Kevin was too caught up in his boner for the Witch to notice. "Basically, she started out with a base of five-fifty HP—"

"You can just say horsepower, dude. Nobody thinks you're cool just because you abbreviate."

"—but with the enhancement Crank's Enchanters came up with, I figure she's closer to seven or even seven-fifty now. Pretty excellent for a 40-ton, right?"

"It's decent," Scott said. He had no idea if it was decent or not. He wasn't a motorhead.

Not that Kevin cared. He rattled right along.

"And you know how we were trying to find a way to keep her cool with all this armor boxing her engine in? Well, some of the guys in Enchanting also came up with these modified Ice and Water runes." He pointed out a pair of silver medallions mounted along a section of chromed out piping. "It took some testing, but they were able to get it working like coolant, just on the outside, to keep the heat from building up in here."

"What about the cannon and the flamethrowers?" Scott asked, trying to steer the conversation back onto something he actually cared about.

Kevin waved a dismissive hand. "They're controlled from inside the cab. Rune to pneumatics. Whatever. Check out her new braking system—"

"Yeah, I'd rather not, dude. This is all cool for somebody who likes dumb nerd stuff, but it's super lame for a baller-ass warlord like me. What I really want to know is how many shots does the cannon have, and what are we firing?" He rubbed his hands together as he talked.

Deflating a little, Kevin slammed the hood back down.

"It's an eight-shot rotating drum," he said, considerably less enthused. "The payload is alternating solid steel balls with a sort of dragonsbreath-grapeshot mix the apprentices came up with." He tapped at an etched tattoo of a sacred heart with flames billowing out the top, an open eye in the center, and a pair of wings protruding from the sides. "That bad boy grants each shot additional fire damage and significantly increases range. She's accurate up to half a mile. Crank says its powerful enough to punch a hole through the hide of an ancient Dragon."

"Fuckin' A!" Scott slapped him on the back. "That's what I'm talking about! How do we reload?"

"That's a longer process," Kevin said. He pointed to the .50 cal on the roof. "If we had a cannoneer on the hood, they would risk getting shot down by the gunner back there. Not to mention, they'd be in the way of the driver, and there's no reasonable way to store reloads up front. Basically, we have to pull over and do everything manually."

Scott rubbed his chin and nodded, picturing how it would go down. "We'll be sitting ducks until the job's done, so conservative is our friend on the cannon fire."

"Exactly."

"Still, that's pretty fucking impressive, man. Now how's about we take this beast for a spin, see how it handles?"

"But you still haven't seen the no-puncture Enchantments they put on the tires or the interior of the semi and the—"

"Bor. Ring." Scott climbed up on the driver's side step and clapped his hands together. "Throw me the keys already."

Kevin kept them clenched in his fist. "Nope. No way. You're not driving."

"Dude, what the shit? I'm an excellent driver."

"The Witch is an eighteen-speed," Kevin explained. "Her transmission is completely different from the manual in a little car. Besides, she's finicky. No one but me behind the wheel. Period."

Scott scowled. "I bet you let Kellie drive it."

"Kel barely passed on a nine-speed. She's not touching the Witch."

"Augh, fine, whatever." He jumped down. "Have you tried her out yet?"

Somehow Kevin's grin came back even bigger and gooberier than before.

"We just got back an hour ago. She's a monster, dude. She couldn't have come out better."

"Anything left you've got to do to her?"

"I was just checking her over and making sure she was ready to go when you got here."

"Good. Do whatever you have to do to get her ready to roll out, then make sure you get some sleep tonight. We're going on a road trip at dawn. It's high time I offload some of my problems. And by problems, I mean all the dickheads taking up space inside my awesome dungeon."

CHAPTER 18
ABANDON SHIP

From the Winch Witch tour, Scott headed straight back to the cafeteria and climbed up on a table. The low murmur of voices intermingled with the sounds of clanking silverware, plastic trays sliding across tables, and footsteps ringing on the stone flooring. Scott raised a hand overhead and unleashed an arc of Elemental Fury that split the air with a thunderous boom. In an instant, a tense hush fell over the room as every eye turned toward him.

"Yo, everybody pay attention, I've got a big announcement," he said, no need to yell since he had everyone on the edge of their seat. That was Command Presence, and Scott had it in spades.

"Silence," one of the Dragonkin barked, even though everyone had already shut their traps. "The great and powerful Dungeon Lord PwnrBwner wishes to address you!"

Scott jerked his head at the Dragonkin. "Thanks, Chad. Good effort."

The Dragonkin tried to shoot him a scaly thumbs-up like they'd worked on, but it still looked like more of a threat than a friendly gesture.

Scott looked back out at the masses of refugees and mobs gathered before him.

"You're probably wondering why I brought you all here," he said. "Well, it's because I'm a hero and saving people is what heroes do, end of story. But even the greatest of heroes eventually run out of space. That's what happened here. You've all probably noticed that we've got a big-ass truck and trailer out in the bailey"—he shot a look at the kobolds and gang members—"well, those of you who haven't been too busy pissing each other off to notice anything else.

"It's my buddy Kevin's. And that big, beautiful beast is the ticket out for those of you who can't hack it here in the new wild Wild West. Believe me, I get it. It's not what most of you are used to, this kill-or-be-killed shit. That's no life for pansies, so no shade, if you don't want to stick around, you don't have to. Everybody who wants out will have their chance—"

GothicTerror stepped up. "Not everybody."

Scott scowled down at her. "What? Why the hell not?"

"Couch_Warrior3000 got back to me." She held up her phone to show him a long-ass text. "He said the army's only letting humans through the containment wall. No mobs or NPCs allowed. They're pulling aside anybody looking to get out who's got magic, magical weapons, scrolls, or potions on them. CW says he hasn't seen anybody who's been taken for questioning released yet."

"No big deal," Scott said, shrugging. "The only human-looking people here with powers are NPCs and those of us the Griefer made his Vassals in Hearthworld, and we all want to stay anyway. Everybody else can just drop their weapons and magical items when we get within sight of the wall."

"Um..." Arjun stepped forward with his hand raised. "I actually don't want to stay here. I've got family on the other side, and..."

Scott rolled his eyes. "Okay, yeah, obviously I should've seen that coming. Arjun wants out. Anybody else?"

Helen Rose stepped forward. "Like you said, most of us aren't really cut out for this kind of life. I mean, I don't want to grow old fighting monsters."

"Yeah, that's not what I signed up for," Three_Trench-coat_Hobbitses said. "I thought saving the world was going to be a one-and-done type situation."

"You too, Hobbitses?" Scott said, dumbfounded.

"Et me, bud," he said.

Beside him, Ninjastein and Flappie_Sak were nodding along in agreement. Hell, half of the original Poser Owners wanted out! What the shit was going on here?

"Seriously, dude," one of the guerilla journalists Scott had personally saved from the jaws of a Flame Revenant spoke up. "All the Starbucks are shut down from here to Bakersfield. Just look on their websites if you don't believe me." His eyes went wide, showing whites all around like some kind of psycho. "I haven't had a Nitro Cold Brew in three days. This isn't fun anymore. I don't want to live in the new Wild West. I want civilization."

A gang member on the other side of the caf yelled, "Yeah, and the last time I stopped in Trader Joes, a Sorrowflayer almost ensnared my mind. It tried to drink my soul out. Shit was traumatizing. I'll probably have PTSD."

"This place is a shitshow," a chick yelled. "I say we let the monsters have it. That's obviously what the government thinks we should do or they wouldn't be cordoning it off."

Scott shook his head and ran a hand through his hair. "I can't believe this. Are you telling me you idiots want to go back? You want to, like, get crappy dead-end jobs just like before and work for minimum wage and—"

"I had an excellent job," someone in the back hollered.

"With benefits!"

"Fuck your benefits!" Scott snapped. "You still had to get all your thrills from video games and movies until you died of old age and boredom. What the hell kind of life is that even?"

"A safe one," Helen Rose replied.

A chorus of agreement backed the gorgeous social influencer up, which just fucking figured since that was her job before all this Hearthworld-Earth Merge shit kicked off.

"A safe one?" Scott couldn't believe what he was hearing. "I think I'm gonna hurl. Which Hallmark rom-com bullshit movie did you get that from?" He threw up his hands. "You know what? Whatever. Forget it. Pick the dumbest option if that's what you want. It's your life—if you can even call it a life." He hopped down off the table. "Dawn tomorrow, everybody who wants out be in the bailey and ready to roll! If you're not there, you get left behind!"

Scott ignored the requests and questions from a bevy of Dragonkin who swarmed him in the hall, and instead just shoved his way through, infuriated. What a load. These idiots had their pick of half the west coast and they wanted to run home to Mommy Civilization. They could be anything out here, live like fucking kings off the swag, and they just wanted their Starbucks and Wi-Fi.

He veered into the former employee lounge, where the Dragonkin knew better than to follow, and slammed the door behind him.

With a pissed off grunt, he flopped down in the comfy chair and shut his eyes.

After a few minutes, he wished he'd grabbed a coffee before he headed in here. If he went back out after that awesome storm out, it would totally ruin the effect. Besides, the chair was too comfortable. Even mad, he just wanted to stretch out in it for a few hours and take a nap.

The lounge door opened and closed a lot softer than he'd done it. There was only one Uberbitch who would have the figurative balls to waltz into the Dungeon Lord's lair like that.

He cracked one eyelid.

"Coffee?" GothicTerror asked, holding out one of two steaming mugs.

"Obviously," he said, sitting up and grabbing it.

"Hey, no need to thank me, even though I had to go all the way downstairs to the one in the back of the building since the machine on the second floor's not working anymore."

He gulped down a scalding mouthful. "At all?"

"It's done for," she said, like that was all they had on the Running Shieldwall agenda to talk about. "Something about the heating element. One of the Enchanters the Griefer left behind tried to rig something up, but it busted the reservoir. They said they couldn't work on two projects at once and have them both come up roses—meaning they were focusing totally on the wrecker and, yeah, they were ticked that I kept asking them to take care of other little stuff."

Scott blew out a disgusted breath. "Get what you pay for, I guess."

"I guess." She shrugged and blew on her coffee.

"Like those morons in the cafeteria. We'll all be better off once they're gone." He downed another swallow of liquid lava and came up even more pissed than before. "I just don't get it. Even some of the POSes want to leave. They have what basically amounts to fucking superpowers and they want to bow out. They've got this golden opportunity just handed to them, and they want to throw it away to go back to their shitty daily grind. It's insane. I don't know what the hell's wrong with them."

Instead of trying to tell him that was what normal people would want, Nessa huffed a laugh.

"You probably would've made a great old-timey prospector

or gunslinger," she said.

"Bet your ass I would have," Scott said, nodding. "Six-guns on both hips and one in the chamber in case anybody thinks they're big enough to square up."

GothicTerror smirked. "I don't think one in the chamber is how six-guns work. But what I meant is, you get that there's risk, but you also think the possibility of reward is worth it. Like the homesteaders who would burn their houses down, collect the nails, then head west and live the dream. You're not in this for the safety of what you know, you're in it for what could be out there."

"Nope, I know what's out there," he said. "They do, too, it's the exact same thing that was in Hearthworld. Mobs, gold, levels, and awesomeness. We're not talking imaginary gold that may or may not be buried under some hill two thousand miles away. We're talking literal gold dropped by mobs two blocks over."

"Yeah, but we're also talking about literal death if you screw up," GothicTerror said.

"That's got to be better than the alternative," Scott said. "Living bored and soft and dying anyway."

She nodded. "Yeah, maybe."

He shot her a glare. "You're leaving, too, aren't you?"

GothicTerror looked at the wall like she was peering into the future.

"I've got less than a year left on my fine arts degree, and I should be able to get a job with basically any art review blog or gallery I want, then eventually start showing my own art. Which is awesome. I love painting. It was kind of my life before this whole thing blew up."

She'd sounded like she was going to go on, but when she didn't, Scott prompted her.

"But...?"

"But I've kind of started to realize that it wasn't that fulfilling. Art's more of a side effect of life, you know?"

Scott snorted. "Yeah, no. I don't know."

"Well..." She shifted on the shapeless purple couch. "You can't really make genuine art unless you're living life. You can try, and it might even look good, but really all you're doing is regurgitating the stuff you think you should be putting out there. You're not coming up with anything new and meaningful to say. The way you do that is by living life, finding out who you are. Struggling."

Scott sat forward, slicing a hand through the air while he tried to process this new side of the cute Goth chick sitting across from him.

"Are you telling me you want to stay out here and fight for your life so you can paint pretty pictures?"

GothicTerror threw back her head and laughed.

"I don't know if they'll be pretty," she said when she calmed down. "But yeah, I guess that's basically what I'm saying."

"Because shit can turn ugly out here real fast."

She raised an eyebrow at him. "Now you want me to leave?"

"No!" He said it a little faster than he should have if he was playing it cool. He shook his head and sat back. "I just want to make sure a floofy-poofy artist tot like you knows what she's getting into."

"Please," she said, rolling her eyes. "I've saved your ass like a hundred times already. You wouldn't last a week out here without me."

"Whatever! I think you're forgetting which one of us made it to Dungeon Lord here."

"Yeah, now go back and imagine doing that without your Lieutenant Uberbitch," she said. "Without me, it never happens."

Scott kept arguing with her, mostly because he wasn't into

backing down, whether the loser he was fighting with was right or not. But also because it was kind of fun having somebody to rag on who could dish it back out. Anyway, it was good to know she wasn't planning to run scared back to "normal" life, either. Nessa wasn't just cute, it turned out she was cool, too.

Or at least he thought so until about twenty minutes later when she finally decided her coffee was cold enough to drink.

She took a dainty sip and grimaced. "Ugh, what I'd give for this to be Mountain Dew."

"Hold. The eff. Up." Scott couldn't believe what he was hearing. "You'd rather have that glowing sewer runoff than coffee? What the hell is wrong with you?"

"Screw you, I've got refined tastes." Then she laughed. "Okay, so it's my guilty pleasure. The Bell used to make this sixteen-flavor Suicide totally out of Dew." She did a chef's kiss and sighed. "Amazing. I used to drink, like, three a day before all this."

"Barfola."

"Have you ever even tried one?"

"No, because I'm a sane person." And because once you'd had enough of any kind of drink thrown back in your face by dickwads who thought they were funny, that drink lost whatever appeal it might've started with. Scott shook his head. "I'm going to have to rethink my whole image of you. Mountain Dew is, like, the least Goth thing I've ever heard of." He thought about it for a second. "Unless you count that it's basically killing yourself slowly with toxic waste. That's pretty emo."

"Probably why they call it a Suicide," Nessa said.

Scott snorted. Fine, she was still cool, even with sickeningly bad taste in beverages.

They ended up joking and talking most of the night away, even though they were both supposed to be grabbing some Zs before their big deadly road trip in the morning.

CHAPTER 19
ROAD TRIP

Scott grinned and sucked in a breath of the early morning air as he strode out into the bailey. He couldn't tell whether it was just his imagination or LA was less of a smog cloud since the Merge. He'd stayed up most of the night talking to Nessa, but he felt great. Like an awesome raid had come together perfectly under his leadership—or like it was about to.

Refugees wandered around, rubbing sleep from their eyes and downing coffee from their one working coffee machine—after Scott finally shuffled these dweebs out of his territory, he'd raid a Bed, Bath, and Beyond to rectify that situation. Honestly, he couldn't wait to have them all gone. As he glanced around at the squares of flattened grass, churned mud, and rolled-up sleeping bags, it seemed like that feeling was mutual. A bunch of folks had slept outside overnight to make sure they wouldn't miss the bus out of LA. Scared little pansies.

Nope. Scott stopped himself. He wasn't going there again. Like Nessa had said last night, he should pity them. These losers thought they could be happy going back to the soul-crushing nine-to-five, working to make somebody else rich, instead of living the dream out here like a bunch of badass motherfuckers. Whatever. More Wild West for him.

A stumpy little Imp in a chef's hat scampered up to Scott with a tray of burritos steaming in the already warm SoCal air.

"Would Dungeon Lord PwnrBwner care for a slice of the Troll Gourmet's brand-new Invigorating Breakfast Burritos?"

More of Kaz's cooking apprentices, both mob and human, were scattered throughout the road trip crowd, passing out breakfast to those preparing for departure. Not only would these sheeple be missing out on all the loot and freedom they could handle, they also weren't going to get any more of Kaz's culinary creations once they crossed the border back into human civilization. That alone would've made Scott want to stay.

"Don't mind if I do." Scott grabbed one off the tray and took a huge bite of perfectly seasoned home fries, melty cheese, spicy sausage, and crunchy bacon. He groaned at the excellent mix of flavors. "Aw, hell yeah! This is even better than the Bell's Breakfast Fiesta Special."

"I shall give your compliments to the Gourmet, Dungeon Lord," the Imp said, bowing deeply before scurrying off.

One of the journalist douches stalked past, vlogging into his cameras about the "harrowing journey we're about to begin" like anybody but him gave a shit, but even that couldn't get Scott down this morning. There was something so kick-ass about taking off on a road trip. Plus, all those journalist nutsacks were about to be somebody else's problem, and that was the best breaking news of all.

He spotted Nessa hanging out over by the battlement with her DnD buddies, Ninjastein and Flappie_Sak. All three of them were armed and armored up, ready to rock. When she saw him, she shot him a shy smile. Scott toasted her with his rapidly disappearing breakfast burrito, and she waved hers back. He hadn't had a girlfriend in a while, but mutual burrito toasting? They were basically dating by anybody's standards.

Swallowing another big bite of tortilla-wrapped heaven, he made a quick stop by the front of the Winch Witch, where Kevin was head and shoulders deep under her hood.

"How's she looking, bro?" Scott asked, climbing up on the fender next to him.

"Good," Kevin said without coming up for air. "Just giving her a final once-over, then we're ready to hit the road."

"Sweet. Keep up the good work." Never let it be said that the great PwnrBwner didn't know how to praise his staff when they deserved it. Scott downed the last of his burrito and wiped his mouth on a bracer. "That means it's time for me to do some Dungeon Lording."

He hopped off the wrecker and jogged up the steps of the building, then squared his shoulders and faced the milling crowd.

"All right, people," he yelled. The low rumble of conversation died out as everybody in the bailey turned to face him. "If you're going out on today's bus, form an orderly line at the back of the semi-trailer." He checked to make sure Kellie and Cranko were in place at the doors to keep everything moving neat and tidy. "Listen to your flight attendants and do what they say. Don't push or shove or start shit, or they are authorized by the power vested in the great Dungeon Lord PwnrBwner to kick your ass off the transport. Got it?" He pretended to wait for an answer, then nodded. "Awesomesauce. Load up." He jerked his chin at the foot of the stairs. "Poser Owners and Frontflip Vassals of the Griefer post up over here to get your convoy assignments."

That got everybody moving in the right direction. Another job well done. Being a leader was a pain in the ass sometimes, but the way Scott saw it, it was easier than any of his asshole managers had ever made it sound. Basically all you had to do was lay out your orders clearly and threaten to curbstomp anybody who didn't follow them.

While Kellie and Cranko loaded people into the converted trailer, Scott huddled up with everybody who had access to their Hearthworld abilities.

"We're going to stock the pillboxes on the sides of the trailer with alternating magic users and heavy hitters so we've got a good spread of long- and short-range attacks. Leading the pack on the driver's side, ScreamoTots will bring the archer-undead spellslinger combo, Flappie_Sak watching her back like usual, and bringing up the rear on that side, BusterMove with blood magic. On the passenger side, front to back: monster wizard Tomahiro with Ninjastein protecting his squishy ass, and last but not least Helen Rose playing sky scout and raining down AoEs on anybody who gets in our way."

Even though Scott rattled them off like they were no big deal, the assignments hadn't been random. He'd put a lot of thought into where each person should go based on how their abilities complemented those of the people in the pillboxes around them, what he'd seen of their situational awareness, the way they worked together on rescue or salvage runs, and the best ways to balance out their respective weaknesses. Helen Rose, for example, could fly and rain down insane weather-related spells, but she could only stay up in the air for forty-five seconds as of her last level, and like Tomahiro, she was squishy as balls. A serious hit from a mob and she'd be dead, so he needed to keep her either up high or down in the protection of the pillbox, but never anywhere in the middle.

It was genius-level strategizing, but even then there were some people who weren't happy with his killer plan.

"Wait, what about me?" Arjun nodded toward the semi. "I've got some serious spells and I'm basically half tank."

"Yeah, but you're also half asleep, dicking around with your drawings and stuff," Scott said. "This is life or death, broheme. I hate all of those people"—he hooked a thumb toward the line snaking into the trailer—"but I'm also responsible for their survival. We all are. They don't have powers like us, and the mobs of Hearthworld will skewer 'em and slow roast 'em over a fire if we screw this up. We're not messing with the possibility of you daydreaming when you should be slinging attack spells. Besides, I need you in the semi's cab on the radio with Kevin. If the Winch Witch gets into trouble, your Shadow Puppets are going to buy him the time he needs to get out and fix things."

Three_Trenchcoat_Hobbitses raised his hand.

Scott stopped him right there. "Hobbitses, before you say anything, you're going in the cab of the semi with Arjun and the Ultimate Magicka Potions. We're not dicking around with our healer." He stabbed a finger at Helen Rose. "When we get into the shit, our Druidic Skyguard's going to shoot straight up into the air to get an eye on the action below. Helen Rose, you have Message, right?"

She nodded. "It came with my class."

"During the firefights, you'll keep in contact with Hobbitses and call in healing for whoever needs it. If it gets real hairy or you're not sure, just have him cast Blanket Heal. I know it's got a long cooldown period, but better to be safe than dead."

Arjun still looked all mopey. "And where are you going to be, Mr. Boss Guy?"

"I'm the original triple threat, son—Ranger and Cleric attack magic, clerical healing spells, and ranged shooting perks for days." Scott pointed at the .50 cal turret on top of the Winch Witch. "Obviously, I'm running the big fucking gun."

"I could run the gun," Arjun said.

Instead of telling Arjun that he couldn't even run Scott's jockstrap, Scott said, "Not up for discussion," probably because he was growing as a person and shit. "Now everybody get where you're going, familiarize yourself with your new digs, and get comfy. We've got eighty miles of rough road ahead of us, and we're rolling out as soon as this bitch is loaded."

It would actually be more than eighty miles—with the wrecker and semi's added defensive and offensive measures bulking it up and out, Kevin had had to find a route that didn't take them under bridges and overpasses that were too low. Kevin was used to that, though, since he towed big rigs for a living. Scott wasn't worried. Of all the people on his team he trusted most, Kevin was just below the great shit-kicker Kaz and his Uberbitch lieutenant. Kevin would find a way to get them out of the city.

With only a little more grumbling, the Poser Owners broke up and climbed into their assigned seats. While Scott watched, old rescue run pros like Buster and Ninjastein helped the new kids like Tomahiro and Helen Rose, who'd spent most of their time as magic users defending Shieldwall, settle in and figure out how to get off shots while moving or fight from inside their pillboxes.

Up at the front two pillboxes, GothicTerror and Flappie_Sak got busy coordinating some kind of Undead Chaos-DPS ranged combo with her compound bow and his Enchanted Obsidian Glass throwing axes. The thought that Flappie_Sak of all people was planning to bail when they got to the border gutted Scott more than he wanted to admit. He had some good people in his crew, and if they left it wouldn't be the same without them. Still awesome, because Scott would be around, but fractionally less awesome.

Metal crashed behind Scott like a bomb going off in a restaurant supply store.

He spun around, mace in one hand and a Lightning Spear crackling in the other.

Kaz was standing at the top of the stairs looking down at the pair of apprentice chefs scrambling to pick up all the pots, pans, and cookware they'd just dropped. Nearby, Lakshya and the dude she'd gotten to work as her cameraman hovered, getting every second of this for the internet crowd.

Kaz sighed and rubbed at the bridge of his nose with his enormous sausage thumb and finger like he was at the end of his rope.

"Please believe Kaz, apprentices," the Troll Gourmet said, in one of those I'm-doing-my-best-to-be-nice-to-you-morons voices. Except his was a lot nicer than Scott's ever managed to sound. "While Kaz loves these fantastic spatulas, mandolins, and whisks, and thinks they are wonderful additions to any kitchen, it must be known that these things are not necessities."

Kaz's voice softened and his eyes shined as he held up a huge stockpot in one hand and a box full of ingredients in the other. "Campfire cooking does not require fancy methods to taste delicious. In fact, when space is limited, just the opposite is necessary. We must pare down our methods to the bare bones, yet still find ways to extract the ultimate flavor from them."

"Love it! Cut it there," Lakshya told the cameraman. "That's going in the trailer for season two. We'll call it Troll Gourmet: Road Warrior Chef. No, wait—Foodscape from LA. Curry Road?" She sliced a hand through the air. "We'll workshop a name later. For now, Kaz, you just keep being you."

Kaz shifted, his big ears twitching uncertainly. "Kaz is not sure who else he could be, Lakshya."

"Just ignore her, dude," Scott said. "It's how phonies in the business talk—they just string together a bunch of crap and act like it means something."

Lakshya shot him an annoyed look, but he ignored her and took the stockpot from Kaz to free up one of the big guy's arms.

Scott glanced from the handful of utensils in the pot to the single box of veggies and spices Kaz was packing.

"Think this'll be enough to feed everybody?" he asked.

"No," Kaz said in a weirdly cheerful tone, "but it will make an excellent base for the meats and foraged food we will find along the way. This is part of Kaz's plan for the road trip shows —to teach cooks everywhere to think outside of what foods spawn in their home dungeons. Taste adventure awaits around every corner!" he said, waving his free hand in an arc like he was painting a rainbow in the air.

"Dammit, we missed it!" Lakshya came running up behind them, camera guy in tow. "Say that again, for the cameras, Kaz. It'll make a perfect bumper."

Scott glared at her. "You and Lens Buddy aren't coming. We've already met our quota for douchebags filming shit," he said, jerking his head at one of the guerilla journalists vlogging her way past.

"Uh, yes we are coming," Lakshya said, hands planted on her hips. "One, because we need footage for season two, 'Foodtrip'—okay, no, I don't like that one—and two, because I'm not coming back."

"Me either," the cameraman said.

"Grant either," Lakshya continued, hiking a thumb at the cameraman. "And with this new hit show under our belt, we'll be able to get work wherever the new Hollywood pops up."

Scott started to argue, but Kaz pulled him gently aside.

"PwnrBwner, please allow Lakshya and Grant to come along," the huge Troll Gourmet pleaded. "For Kaz's sake." He pursed his lips for a second, shooting his documentarian shadows a look over his shoulder, then whispered to Scott. "If Mai is lost somewhere in this dangerous, strange land, she will not know how to find Kaz unless Kaz keeps updating her on his location. What if she comes to Shieldwall only to find Kaz gone?

What if she loses hope?" Kaz's ears drooped and his eyes went all watery. "Please, PwnrBwner."

Scott rolled his eyes. God, he was such a giant softy for being an absolute murder-machine. "Fine. They can come."

Kaz literally leapt with joy, just about dropping his spice and veggie box in the process. "PwnrBwner is truly a benevolent Dungeon Lord!"

Lakshya smirked.

"But I'm not doing this for you losers and your dumb show." Scott stabbed a finger at her. "This is one hundred percent because Kaz is my boy."

"What's good for the Troll Gourmet is good for his producers," Lakshya said.

"Whatever," Scott sneered, packing Kaz's stockpot in the trailer. "Just don't slow us down and don't get killed."

CHAPTER 20
A LONG REST

After his conversation with Morgana, Roark installed an additional portal plate by the stone stoop outside Korvo's inn both for his and the Village Elders' convenience. If his feudal lordship were to continue, they would likely be seeing much more of one another.

"I'm going to stay behind for now," Randy Shoemaker said, shuffling his silver wings. He nodded toward the walls. "I'd like to inspect the sigil towers up close and personal and make sure the background processes are running like they should. I also want to execute a couple of stress tests on the spell plates in the Mage's Tower—make sure they aren't siphoning more of the dungeon's Magicka reserve than they ought to be."

Though Roark didn't know what the Arboreal Herald was referring to, he thought he understood the gist. The more time he spent around the man, the easier it became to understand the strange language of the Devs.

"You're making sure the Discordant Inversion is still set and waiting?" Roark guessed.

"Exactly. Based on our calculations, they should be able to

support it for months without a recast, but I'd rather be safe than sorry."

"That's a sentiment I can appreciate. Let me know what you find out."

Randy nodded. "Shouldn't take much more than a couple of hours. I'll give you a full report when I get back to the Citadel."

Roark clasped forearms with the Arboreal Herald, then he followed Zyra onto the portal plate. In a flash of blue, they were returned to the corresponding plate in the Troll Nation Marketplace.

The hustle and bustle of the shops went on as always, but there was a thinness to the activity, a stillness that put Roark's teeth on edge. Too many faces were missing from the crowd. Half the usual number of hammers rang at the smithy. The allied mobs training in Griff's arena huffed and grunted in muted tones. A childlike laugh rang out near the old crone's magickal herb garden—a Hatchling Naga playing with the reflective properties of Glass Leaf—but the glares of the closest mobs shushed him. The Hatchling cleared his throat and awkwardly slithered away.

It was like the whole of the bloody Troll Nation was in mourning.

Roark's black mood intensified as they passed Flavortown. A bright warm glow spilled from the windows into the street, but the inn looked unbearably cold. Mobs and NPCs alike still queued up down the street, but the line no longer wound around the block, and the usual energy of excitement had gone out of the waiting parties. They looked as if they were performing a chore.

"Something wrong, Griefer?" Zyra asked.

He raised a brow at her. "Am I that obvious?"

"If you want to hide what you're thinking, wear a hood. Your face doesn't have the knack for it." Her veil shifted slightly as she turned her head to follow his dark gaze toward Flavortown. "It is sort of desolate without the big guy around, isn't it?"

Roark snorted humorlessly. "Like a damned funeral rite. But I intend to remedy that as soon as possible. If I get started immediately, I should find a way to bring Kaz and Griff and the others back to the Citadel."

His empty stomach chose that moment to growl loudly. It seemed that forever-death was not the only change in returning to his home world. Food had become a necessity once again. But without Kaz's excitement painting every meal with color, eating was just another duty that had to be performed to continue the fight against Marek. There was no joy or excitement in it. And though he still had Zyra and Mac with him, he was missing his friends—Kaz, Mai, Griff, even PwnrBwner. He hoped they were faring well at the Shieldwall.

"Perhaps after you've eaten," Zyra said.

"I can eat later," he grumbled.

"Don't be stupid, you're here now. Come back later and you'll only be wasting time and effort."

Without waiting for his reply, the Orbweaver Ravager strode around the back of the inn.

Reluctantly, Roark followed her between the enormous brewing vats. He knew for a fact he could run for a good long while on an empty gut, but he wouldn't be functioning at the top of his ability. If he were going to do something as potentially deadly to his friends as write a portal to bring them back, he wanted it done right and without any distractions.

Kaz's most trusted apprentice, a one-armed Lamia named Nubbi, met them at the back door, looking both harried and dispirited. When he saw Roark, however, the drooping spines of his head crest perked back up.

"Feudal Lord!" He snatched off his Cap of the Sous Chef and

eagerly ushered them into the kitchen. "What can I do for you, eh? You tell ol' Nubbi what you're hankerin' for and I'll get you fixed right up, yessirree!" He waved his cap at the roasting spit. "The Peiking Wildfowl is most excellent today, Feudal Lord! Or perhaps you'd like the Roasted Rotatos with Kaz's famous Bacon and Brown Sugar Demi-glace! Or if you're of a mind for some—"

"A bit of bread and cheese will be fine, Nubbi," Roark said. "I'm in a bit of a hurry."

"The great Troll Gourmet would never have heard of it! Serving his dearest friend the scraps we wouldn't foist off on a wandering traveler? No, that broth won't gel, Feudal Lord, it won't!"

Roark opened his mouth to protest, but Zyra slipped her hand into his and squeezed. In addition to the welcome distraction of her touch, a row of hidden needles pricked his palm through her black lace hand wrappings.

[*Feverblood Ring has resisted Poison Scratch.*]

"Bring him both, Nubbi," Zyra said. "The Wildfowl and the Rotatos."

The Lamia beamed with joy and scurried off, shouting orders to his fellow apprentices about sauces and plating.

Roark shot the Orbweaver Ravager a sidelong glance. "If I didn't know better, I'd say you were concerned for my well-being."

A soft snort made her lacy black veil flutter.

"They need this distraction as much as you do, Griefer," she said. "Look at them. They're at loose ends without Kaz, nearly as brokenhearted and broody as you are."

Roark scowled. "I'm not broody."

"Brood any harder and you'll hatch a chick."

"In any case, if I truly need a distraction, I can think of several more interesting ones to spend our time on," he said, squeezing her hand tighter. The hidden needles dug deeper into his palm, and a few drops of blood dripped from between their fingertips.

Zyra chuckled. “You’d best eat first, then. You’ll need all your strength for that.”

MUCH LATER, Roark found himself facing down another discovery of the differences between life in Hearthworld and Traisbin. He lay beside the fireplace in his study with Zyra on his chest, her multiple spidery legs draped across him and her four human arms wrapped around him. Her veil had been discarded for the time being, and her snowy ringlets tickled his jaw.

Under normal circumstances, the Orbweaver Ravager was as cuddly as a fistful of poisoned daggers and showed all the affection of a cornered feral cat. It was only these rare peaceful moments alone when she would allow him to hold her, and Roark didn’t intend to let a single second of it go to waste.

Suddenly, Zyra sat bolt upright and scrubbed at her eyes with one pair of her human fists.

“What did you do?” she hissed. Panic filtered through her usual calm, but it was quickly edged out by cold fury. One of her human hands fumbled for a dagger that wasn’t there. Finding it tossed aside with the rest of her armor, she grabbed Roark by the throat. “Did you put some slow-acting toxin in my food? Or was it contact poison? A single needle while we were occupied?”

“What are you talking about?” Roark choked out.

“You poisoned me, you underhanded Jotnar trash!” As she spoke, her wide, mismatched purple and green eyes slipped closed and her head drooped, her pixielike chin bumping against her chest.

For a heartbeat, her grip on Roark's throat went slack. He stole the opportunity to break free and get outside of her reach.

"Like seven bloody hells I did!" he snapped.

His voice caused her to jerk awake again.

"My eyes won't stay open, my head's so heavy I can barely keep it up..." She scrambled on weakening legs toward their pile of knives and pistols and clothing, and snatched a 1911 from the top. "A moment ago, while we were lying there, blackness closed in around me and I felt myself floating away. I was dying, forever-dead!"

Finally, Roark's startled brain caught up to what was happening. In Hearthworld, he'd never seen a Troll sleep and had never needed any himself. In Traisbin, however, it seemed that in addition to food, sleep was another biological necessity. Zyra and he had been on the go since arriving in Traisbin. It was a miracle that they hadn't passed out from sheer exhaustion sooner.

He raised his hands and crept incrementally toward the furious Orbweaver Ravager.

"Zyra, I would never poison you," he promised. "And not just because poisoning is *your* specialty. I love you. I would never hurt you—I swear it on everything that's sacred."

"Then why..." She wavered on her feet, head bobbing again, the arm gripping the 1911 dropping toward the floor.

In a flash, Roark shot forward and caught her, twisting the gun from her grasp before she accidentally—or purposely—used it on him. The impact startled her awake again. Luckily for him, without the 1911, all she had were her fangs and Poison Scratch, and several passionate interludes had proven those weapons well and truly ineffective against his Feverblood Ring.

"You're not dying!" He had to shout to be heard over her

thrashing. He winced as a Poison Scratch laid open his cheek. "Listen to me, Zyra, you're falling asleep! It's not death, it's rest, slumber." She went still. Roark plunged ahead before his opportunity ran out. "You've surely heard of sleep—it's why they have beds at inns and bedrolls in bandit caves."

She scowled up at him. "I've only ever floated like that when I was sent for Respawn."

"Here they call it drifting off to sleep. Do you remember the Sleeping Death poison you made for the prison break from Chillend?"

She squinted suspiciously, but that quickly morphed into a jaw-cracking yawn.

Roark hurried to explain. "You were only asleep then, not dead. Here in Traisbin, sleep works in much the same way, except that it's not caused by a poison. Everyone needs rest, even Trolls apparently."

"Will I wake up?" she asked in a small voice that squeezed his heart.

"Yes."

She drew a hidden blade and pressed it against his throat. "Swear to it."

Gently, he pulled the blade away, then directed her into the heavy leather chair with him and arranged her multiple sets of arms and legs.

"I promise you'll wake up when you've had enough rest," he said, raking a strand of snowy white hair out of her eyes. "And you'll feel better once you have."

"Will you stay with me?"

He nodded. "I'll be right here when you wake up."

"And if I don't wake up, you'll wake me."

The realization that in bringing Zyra to his home world, he had started an invisible countdown toward a day when one or both of them wouldn't wake up hit him like an icy fist to the solar plexus.

He had to clear his throat before he could reply.

"Of course."

This finally seemed to be enough to allay Zyra's fears. She curled up in his arms, snuggled her face against his chest, and drifted off to a peaceful sleep.

Roark, however, found himself unable to do the same. He sat awake, listening to her soft breaths and wondering if he'd done the right thing, bringing the Troll he loved to a world where if she wasn't killed by a rival or in battle, she would still eventually come face-to-face with forever-death. Roark didn't have a good answer. He pulled her in tighter, taking in a deep, coquelicot-scented whiff of hair and savoring her warmth. Whether it was a good choice or not, he had to selfishly admit that he was glad she was there beside him.

CHAPTER 21
CALL OF THE WILD

Roark finally managed to doze off. He slept fitfully until Zyra woke. She climbed off him and out of the chair using her multitude of spidery limbs and crossed the room to the weapons and armor strewn about.

"I've an idea for a brew," she said, all her limbs working together to dress, buckle, and holster her. The childlike fear and vulnerability were gone from the Orbweaver Ravager. She seemed unwaveringly focused on this new brew. "Something to hold off sleep."

"That already exists here," Roark said, standing and stretching. His back popped a few times. "It's called coffee. Tea works as well, but it's not quite as effective. Though they can only keep you awake for so long before your body collapses." He smiled wryly. "I know from experience."

Zyra stood up from tying her holster to her leg and flipped her snowy hair out of her eyes.

"I'm not looking for half-solutions," she said. "I'll find something that will keep you wide awake and focused until you're ready to sleep."

Roark laughed. "The alchemists of Traisbin have been

working on that for centuries. The closest they've come so far is a drug called uraka, and unfortunately, the side effects are far worse than the benefits."

"*They* weren't Septic Brewmasters of unparalleled genius." She shot him a fangy but adorable grin, then slipped her lacy black veil over her face, once again hiding the cuteness that she considered her greatest weakness. "I'll find the answer, and it won't take me centuries."

She headed for the door, then suddenly stopped and came back, lifting her veil aside just long enough to give Roark a strangely sweet kiss on the jaw. Before he could ask what it was for, she spun on one spidery limb and disappeared.

Rather than swinging closed behind her, the door rebounded off a slight visual distortion. With a disgruntled chirp, Mac dropped his Camouflage and appeared on the ceiling. He was stuck half in and half out of the doorway, his Elemental Turtle Dragon frame too wide for the narrow, pointed top of the arch.

"You'll have to come down," Roark said. "It's wider at the bottom."

Mac grunted and released his hold on the gleaming stones of the ceiling. Two thousand pounds of scales, spikes, and waving blue beard shook the room as he slammed onto Roark's chest, knocking the both of them into a heap of legs, heads, and wings.

The air woofed out of Roark's lungs. The weight alone would have killed a human, but with his Chaos Harbinger Health, Mac's impact only stole away a sliver of the red in his filigreed vial.

"You bloody overgrown pup," he coughed out, grabbing Mac's orange head and wooling it around, much to the jealousy of the blue and yellow. "You're going to do me in one of these days."

The door flew open again, bouncing off the wall, and one of the guards Zyra kept in rotation over Roark's study burst in.

"Where's the enemy?" Crusher demanded, waving his Obsidian Glass Halberd around, eyes wild. "Somebody fired off a tank round in here, I heard it!"

"It's just a silly Jotnar and his Turtle Dragon," Zyra's voice called down the hallway, though there was no sign of her.

Roark chuckled and shoved away the dragon heads vying for his attention.

"Everything's fine, Crusher, just a bit of roughhousing," he said, trying to drag his arm out of the mouth of the blue head. Delighted, the blue head shook like a wolf trying to rip off a chunk of meat from a carcass.

The Bonesnap Behemoth rolled his eyes as if this were the sort of thing he ought to have expected from the same Feudal Lord who'd spent countless hours nearly killing himself in this very study with his experiments. With a put-upon sigh, Crusher withdrew from the room and pulled the door shut behind him.

Roark wrestled his way out from beneath Mac. The yellow head, obviously not finished playing, nipped at Roark's black-scaled arm. With a laugh, he wrestled it around for a few moments longer, the blue and orange heads joining in gleefully.

"All right, that's enough, you bloodthirsty beast," Roark said, giving each head a final vigorous beard-scratch. "We've got portals to write."

Mac squeezed around him, trying to bar his way to the bookshelf lining the wall of his study.

Roark cocked an eyebrow at him. "You want Kaz back, don't you? He's the one who cooks the Saberboar bacon."

The heads somehow managed to blink all six eyes out of sync. With a round of reluctant grunts and chirps, Mac finally allowed Roark to pass.

Though he didn't have access to Hearthworld's WikiLore

anymore, Roark did still have the books he had collected while he'd been there. He spent a moment searching the shelf for *Portals, Portals Everywhere,* a tome he'd found on portal travel. A small part of him was still amazed by the fact that he was standing in front of more books than anyone in Traisbin had ever seen, a treasure trove by any noble's standard. As the feeling of wonder passed, he dragged the massive volume over to his desk and propped it open.

The problem came when Mac tried to squeeze into the heavy leather chair behind Roark. The arms snapped off, and the whole frame buckled beneath the creature's considerable weight. Unperturbed, Mac went to the fireplace and curled up in front of the fire, resting his orange head directly in the flames. Within seconds, he was asleep.

"I'll just stand then, shall I?" Roark said, voice dripping with irony.

Mac didn't stir. The uncanny beast's napping habits, at least, seemed unaffected by the shift to Traisbin.

Without his chair, Roark stood hunched over the desk as he read *Portals, Portals Everywhere.*

Six months ago, according to the timeline Albrecht had come up with, Roark had attempted to write a portal to a run-down pub in the port city of Zariston, a place called the Hearth of the World, which doubled as a resistance safe house. Rather than step through to the top floor of the pub, he'd been deposited in Hearthworld, at the top step of the crumbling staircase leading down into the Cruel Citadel.

He rolled back his shirtsleeve to reveal the faint silver scarring that showed through the purple-tinged black scales of this new form.

A portal opens in front of me, leading to the topmost floor of the Hearth of the World.

His arms were covered in those faint silvery scars, the oldest going back decades to the night his family had been slaughtered, but the portal spell was the first that had gone awry. Either he'd been unaccountably lucky or that half-finished Academy tutorship he'd gotten had well paid for itself.

If portal spells could be written correctly, what had caused his to go awry that night? He could see nothing wrong with the lettering, spelling, or punctuation, and he'd been as specific as possible about the location where he'd meant to arrive.

Or had he?

He frowned down at the lettering again.

According to Morgana, there were hundreds if not thousands of universes one could travel to via portal. The Tower of Creation existed somewhere at the center of them all, and they extended like millions of spokes around the hub of a wheel. What if his home world, Hearthworld, and the world of the Devs existed one after the other side by side? He hadn't specified which Hearth of the World in which of those universes he'd meant to travel to. Had that lack of direction sent him careening into Hearthworld instead of the seedy resistance pub?

Before he could analyze the possibility further, a scrap of paper with the familiar scrawled writing obscured his vision.

[*Curse of the Mummy*
You have invoked the wrath of the great and powerful Undead God-Pharaoh! Continue to lose 4x-2y Health per 5 seconds (where x is the level of the caster and y is the level of the cursed) until you or the Undead God-Pharaoh is dead.]

"Damnation!" Roark blinked away the text and checked his Character page.

Draconic Chaos Harbinger Overview			
Name:	Roark	Level:	95
Gender:	Male	Player Class:	Hexorcist
Type:	Draconic Chaos Harbinger	Alignment:	Infernah
Current Experience.	1,232	Next Level:	399,000

Health:	2,819.250	Infernali Magick:	3.940.000
H-Regen / 5 Sec:	423.325	Magick-Regen / 5 Sec:	193.75

Attributes:	
Weapon Damage:	163
Attack Damage:	1754
Base Armor:	125
Armor Rating:	1527.3
Movement Rate:	2 x Speed of Opponent
Critical Hit Chance:	28%
Critical Hit Damage:	(+) 250%

Stats:	
Strength:	168
Constitution:	223.65
Dexterity:	195
Intelligence:	300
World Stone Authority, Greater Vassal	11/60
World Stone Authority, Lesser Vassal	85/225
Undistributed Stat Points:	0

Draconic Special Skills:
Rapid-Regen
75% Resistance against normal weapons
Stunning Blow; 22% Chance / Hit
Infernal Necro Shield: Draconic-Hybrid Spell
Necrotizing Infernal Torment; Draconic-Hybrid Spell
Necrotic Invigoration: Draconic-Hybrid Spell
Infernal Undead Temptation; Draconic-Hybrid Spell
EXPAND SKILLS LIST

Player Special Skills:	
Spellcraft (Class Skill)	Lv. 15
Bladed Weapons (Melee Skill)	Lv. 12
Weapons Specialty: Rapier	Lv. 9
Calligraphy (Trade Skill)	Lv. 5
Blacksmithing (Trade Skill)	Lv 13
Tailoring (Trade Skill)	Lv. 8
Enchanting (Trade Skill)	Lv. 17
Enchanting Specialty: Cursed!	Lv. 15

Roark had gained considerable Experience through the Feudal Lord's Tax, leveling up nine times over the course of Marek's assault on Korvo. He'd dumped all of his new Stat Points into Constitution, raising his total Health to 2,819 points and increasing his Health Regen Rate considerably. Clearly it still wasn't enough. Marek must have leveled up out of the range of Roark's enhanced Health Regen, which was a frightful notion. Just how powerful had Marek become over the past days and weeks and how many innocent lives had he extinguished to make such extraordinary gains?

With another curse, he slammed his grimoire closed. At the fireplace, Mac's blue head gave an admonishing chirp at the disturbance, then lay back down.

Roark needed to grind out another level or two to get ahead of Marek and avoid the constant sapping of the Mummy's Curse. When the Tyrant King had pulled out of Korvo, however, he'd taken what remained of his armies. Other than a few spies stationed at the mouth of the valley, whom Roark had given his own spies specific instructions not to destroy, as he would need them later, there were no enemy mobs to kill. Griff was the only trainer with a high enough qualification in Weaponry to help Roark level up his Rapier and Dagger skills, and the old man was still lost, whether in Hearthworld or the Devs' home world he couldn't say.

The only remaining option was to kill humans or animals, like Marek's troops had done to gain their levels, but Roark loathed the thought of resorting to either path—the humans for obvious reasons and the animals because there were very few in Traisbin that could stand against him at his current strength. As strange as it might seem that he of all people would balk at an unfair fight, the idea of hunting down something weaker than him put him off. His father had never allowed such poor unsporting behavior on his lands.

Moreover, how much experience would such a creature even have to give?

No, that was an untenable option. But he needed to do something. Marek would only get stronger the longer this war raged.

As if the mountains themselves had heard Roark's thoughts, the high, eerie howl of a lone maka-ronin warbled in through the study window. The call of the king of the wolves joined with the crackling of the fire in the hearth, and it was as if Roark were transported back through time and tragedy to the simplicity of childhood winters, sitting safe by his father's knee and shivering at the cry of the wolves that roamed the mountains. And he wasn't the only one affected. On more than one occasion, he'd seen even his older cousin Dirk fail to suppress a shudder at the ghostly sound.

Uncle Gareth, who had loved nothing more than a good fright tale, never failed to launch into the story of the time he,

Roark's father, and their brothers had nearly been killed by the great maka-ronin that ruled the Karasu Mountains.

Five skilled hunters with spears and magick had been no match for the king of the wolves. Maka-ronin were terrible creatures, as cunning as any man, fiercely loyal to their pack members, and murderously territorial. They were also large enough to give even Macaroni in his current Evolution pause, and their pelts were nearly impervious to normal steel. Legend held that only enchanted silver could so much as draw blood, though that was likely a load of rubbish. On the night the von Graf men had come across the maka-ronin, only Lord Erich's daring and quick thinking had made it possible for them to escape.

Gareth always finished the story with, "You lads may see him for yourself someday, if we stumble upon His Majesty on one of these hunts. Just hope your uncle Erich is leading the charge."

"I'll be leading from directly behind your uncle Gareth," Lord Erich would say, his face somber, but his gray eyes twinkling with a silent laughter. "He's the most likely to get stuck in the beast's craw."

Later, when putting him to bed, his mother had cursed Gareth for frightening Roark and attempted to undo the damage.

"The Great King is nothing to fear, my *milyy syn,*" she said as she ran her fingers through his dark hair. "The travelers, we have an agreement with him. He lets us pass through his mountains, and we do not harass his kin. If you meet him, he will smell your Lyuko blood and let you go free."

"But half my blood is Father's," he replied in a small voice, "and Father said von Grafs have been hunting the mountain forest for generations. What if the maka-ronin smells that in me instead?"

She hesitated a moment, then tossed her head. "Bah! Von Graf blood is strong, but cold like their mountains. Lyuko blood burns like fire and passion." She tapped her chest, then his to indicate his heart. "The Great King, he will only smell the traveler part of you."

That had done little to reassure him, but on all the hunts he'd ever been on with his father and uncles, the only sign they had ever seen of the maka-ronin had been massive paw prints they often left behind in the snow. That and the occasional stag's corpse, savaged almost beyond recognition.

The maka-ronin's howl hung in the air of the study, making the hair on the nape of Roark's neck stand up once more. A beast five armed men couldn't wound—moreover, one they had barely escaped with their lives. One Draconic Chaos Harbinger versus a maka-ronin might be a more than sporting fight.

A coal popped and Mac stirred in the fireplace.

Roark almost woke the Elemental Turtle Dragon to ask if he wanted to go hunting, but snapped his mouth shut at the last second.

He had the strangest sense that the maka-ronin's call had been meant only for him. A challenge to the newly arrived Feudal Lord from the Great King of the Karasu Mountains.

Working quickly and silently, Roark stripped off his Glock 26 and Obsidian Glass weapons, leaving them in a heap on his desk. If he was going to do this, he was going to do it as his father had, and all the von Graf men before them.

He found a simple Iron Spear in the Radiant Citadel armory, then snuck out into the icy mountain night alone.

CHAPTER 22
SOMETHING FISHY

Dragonkin cranked open the massive gates on Shieldwall's battlements and cheered as the Winch Witch and her load lumbered out of Shieldwall and onto the streets of LA. Scott figured that was deserved. They cut a pretty badass post-apocalyptic figure, especially with him decked out in Obsidian Glass armor and riding in a .50 cal turret on the wrecker from hell. Honestly, this was the shit Lakshya should've been filming. All the production value of a hundred-million-dollar blockbuster, without the cost or the shitty CGI, hastily slapped on in post-production.

But whatever.

The fastest route in Scott's opinion would've been to take the 110 to the 101, slide over to the 405 and out to the north for smooth sailing to Ventura, but according to Kevin they would hit a bunch of low-clearance spots the Winch Witch couldn't make it through going that way.

Instead, they were going to have to parallel the 10 on about a million side streets all the way to Culver City, *then* hit the 405 and shoot up and out. It was going to take a little improvising on the 101 in downtown Thousand Oaks because of another low underpass situation, but Kevin assured Scott that wouldn't be a big deal and he'd done it a hundred times before when he was on call. Worst-case scenario, they could blow up the underpass with the front cannon and use the POSes' powers and the Witch's cowpusher to clear the rubble.

Overall, it was a pretty circuitous route, but supposedly they would steer clear of hang-ups and most likely run into fewer abandoned vehicles since the smaller streets were less traveled than the bigger roads out of LA.

Scott had cocked an eyebrow at Kevin when he said that. "There are less-traveled roads in LA?"

"Relatively!" Kevin said, going into defensive mode.

"Jeez, dude, no need to jump down my throat. I was just asking."

Kevin had loosened up a little then. "Sorry. It's just, you know how to lead a party and be a Dungeon Lord. I know how to drive a big rig around this city."

"That's why you're here, Kev," Scott said. "There's no better man for the job. You know I'd tell you so if there was."

That had made the little dude snort. "Yeah, I know you would. You're a total asshole, but at least no one can accuse of you being dishonest."

Scott shook off the memory as the Winch Witch rumbled into forward and forced himself to keep his head on a swivel. There was no telling what they would run into out here.

Just based on their rescue missions, the mobs had been in constant shift, new gangs moving in and out on the daily, so he had to be prepared for anything. He'd even heard chatter about a small army being gathered up by some nameless figure. Refugees said the dude looked like some kind of angel, with massive wings and golden armor, but was scary as hell. The rescued NPCs had confirmed what Scott had already figured out —this new boss was one of the Malaika Heralds the Griefer's little war had left behind. As if Scott wasn't having to clean up enough of Roark's mess already.

Scott saw evidence of mobs everywhere. Fat slime trails oozed across roads and up the sides of buildings. Random palm trees had been gnawed around the spiky base—in some places until they'd come crashing down. The tops of those were nowhere to be seen, just the points of their chewed-off trunks sticking up out of the mulch like a broken bone.

Inhuman eyes shined down dark alleys, in the shadows behind broken and boarded-up windows, and out of the darkness of storm drains. It freaked Scott the fuck out. Whenever he spotted a new pair of eyes—or trio or sextuplet of them—he swiveled the BMG their way. Maybe they hadn't been planning to jump the Witch in the first place, maybe they were just innocent mobs living their best life on the abandoned streets of LA, but Scott wasn't taking a chance. Anything with ideas about attacking thought twice when they saw the .50 cal swinging their way.

Metal shrieked and crunched as the Witch shoved aside abandoned cars and even one flaming dumpster full of burning trash, but nothing stopped her.

The convoy made it to the southwest corner of Exposition Park before the first ambush.

E.P. had seen better days.

The stadiums had developed this layer of grunge, like they'd been sitting empty for hundreds of years already instead of just a couple of weeks. The green spaces had overrun everything else, creeping in between the walkways with enormous jungle plants that Scott recognized immediately. They came from the Jungles of Eternal Night, and many of them were man-eaters. A bunch of the dense foliage had also spilled out onto the road, covering the asphalt in dead brown Joshua trees, tangled vines, and weird, spiky plants that looked like overgrown agaves.

The Winch Witch downshifted and pushed on, her big blades shoving the debris out of the way and off to the sides like the jungle version of a snowplow.

But the lush greenery turned out to be cover for the ambush. Gronions—these musclebound crosses between a catfish, an onion, and a World's Strongest Man competitor—popped out of the jungle in the park and from behind the foliage barrier criss-crossing the road. There were two dozen of them, working in teams to try and hem the Winch Witch in. Unfortunately, they were doing a decent job of it. A Gronion Shaman wearing a grass skirt and a filthy shawl chanted and slammed a gnarled staff onto the asphalt, summoning a wall of vines ten feet thick that would be impossible to pass through, even for the Witch.

Scott whipped one hand forward and unleashed a searing Lightning Spear that slammed into the Shaman's throat and dropped the creature on the spot. But the damage was already done. They were stopped.

The rest of the Gronions uttered a gurgling war cry as they bolted for the wrecker, waving tridents and chain nets with treble hooks welded into the weave.

"Let's do this, Poser Owners!" Scott called over his shoulder.

He swung the gun around and picked out a target. His Foe Slayer ability kicked in, slowing down the charge of the body-builder catfish until it seemed like it was barely moving. At the same time, different parts of the fish's body lit up, alerting Scott to weakness points.

[*Head – 89%*]
[*Torso – 90%*]
[*Left Arm – 43%*]
[*Right Arm – 48%*]
[*Left Leg – 31%*]

[*Right Leg – 28%*]

Obviously, he was going with the headshot. With a thought, Scott selected the fat, mustachioed lump stuck to those yoked-out shoulders, sans neck, and squeezed the trigger. The gun barked, kicking in its mount while it barfed out fire and lead. Three or four rounds—there was no way to be sure with how fast the gun fired—tore through the monster's deformed body. There was no satisfying rag doll animation, just IRL blood and bone and gore splattering everywhere.

More Gronions were on that first one's tailfin, flooding out of the jungle and closing in fast. They needed to get the rig moving, but that wasn't going to happen with the vines clogging up the roadway. Kevin and the cab crew were on that like flies on shit, though. Flamethrowers poked out from the front of the rig, remotely controlled by Cranko, and spewed thick ropes of magically enhanced flames.

The vines sizzled, but they were too thick and wet to catch fire like that.

Scott was ready. Time to turn up the heat.

He opened a leather pouch riding one hip and pulled free a trio of glass vials filled with a black, tar-like substance. Pitch. The stuff inside was a Ranger specialty and burned hotter and faster than napalm. He hurled the bottles into the tangle, one right after another, and watched the glass bottles break and the pitch splatter across the thorn-studded vines. A second later, a tongue of flame ignited the brew and the whole hedge went up in the bonfire to end all bonfires. The blaze would take care of the hedge barrier before long, but they needed to hold out until then.

Off to both sides, spears banged off the wrecker and the trailer, a lot of them aimed the way of the awesome gunner who'd just shot down one of their fish buddies and torched their roadblock.

Scott took that personally. But then Scott took pretty much everything personally.

With a grunt, he picked his next target—a big flathead about to wing his barbed net up onto the turret—and took that fishman out, too. The .50 cal was death incarnate and chewed through the creature's waist, separating the torso from the legs. Gross, but also oddly satisfying.

[*Congratulations! You have leveled up your Ranger Foe Slaying Skill to Level 6! You can now take down two enemies at a time. While in Targeting View, select two marks within 6 feet of one another on the horizontal axis. Shots will be made in immediate succession. Select the same mark twice to activate Double Tap.*]

"Sweet," Scott said, blinking away the notification.

We've got more inbound, Helen Rose's voice said in Scott's head thanks to her Messaging Ability. *I see three dozen at least. Looks like they were holed up in the Swimming Stadium. In Hearthworld, Gronions are vulnerable to fire magick. Do you think it works the same way here?*

Scott glanced to the vines burning merrily in front of them. *Yes,* Scott snapped, targeting the next closest Gronion and the head of the one just behind him. *Now relay that info to Cranko! He's the one up front operating the flamethrowers.*

Oh right. Sorry.

Don't apologize, just get it done. Scott took a second to glance toward the front of the rig again. The vines were as charred and twisted as those Blacksnakes fireworks he used to play with as a kid, and it looked like they would come apart just as easily, but they were still burning like crazy. No way would Kevin run the Witch through that while it was still on fire. Scott shot Helen Rose one last message. *And then put the vines out with Torrential Downpour so we can get the rig moving again.*

He figured only a couple seconds had passed since the ambush started, but they were already about to be overrun. Spells were flying behind him—he caught the boom of GothicTerror's Exploding Corpse perk as it took out a net-thrower, and the flash and bang of Tomahiro's Shrapnel Lightning Bolt knocking over a handful of the muscly bastards—but there were too many Gronions, and they just kept coming.

As the Foe Slayer View flashed off, a burst of rounds slammed out of the BMG, nailing each of the fish Scott had selected, taking them both out of the fight for good.

"Sweet ass sweet!" Finally, something useful from the Ranger side of his dual class.

But there wasn't any time to celebrate. The fishy warriors were almost on them and until the rig was rolling, they were sitting ducks. Scott had to trust that his team knew what they were doing—even though he figured there was only about a fifty percent chance of that—and keep as much pressure on the approaching monsters as he could. Scott found his next shot, a big chonker, twice the size of the other Gronions, decked out in heavy plate armor crafted from colorful coral. The fish freak looked like it could bend a steel I-beam in half and take a bite out of the middle.

If Scott had learned anything from the Griefer, it was that there was no such thing as overkill when something outleveled you.

He hit the Double Tap, focusing all of his firepower on the charging behemoth fish.

Turned out he was right not to dick around. Rounds slammed into the creature's torso, but they didn't turn it into pink mist and chum. That coral turned out to be tough as shit—the tanked-out fish didn't even slow down. It shrugged off the shots and slammed into the side of the Winch Witch, rocking the wrecker on her wheels. With a ground-shaking roar, the

Gronion scrambled up the side of the wrecker, heading straight for Scott's turret.

Scott drew his mace in one hand and pulled out another glass pot of pitch from the bag at his side. The Gronion was close enough that he could smell the stench of onion on the thing's breath. In the split second he had between being overrun and killed, Scott smashed the glass container down on the creature's blocky, weirdly smooth head; black liquid splattered out and sluiced down the monster in tiny rivulets, dribbling into all the coral armor's nooks and crannies.

All down the side of the Witch, the flamethrowers finally belched to life once more. The pitch-soaked Gronion caught like a burning gas station. It let out a gurgling howl and tumbled off the wrecker's side, rolling on the street and slapping at the fire with its big flat fin-hands. More fire sprayed out in an arc, torching the other creatures encroaching on the Witch.

A thundercrack split the air overhead a second later, and thick rain clouds materialized at the front of the wrecker, unleashing a torrential monsoon directly onto the vines blocking their path. The hellish blaze flickered and died, leaving only gray embers of flash-fried foliage in its wake.

The Witch rumbled and lurched into gear, and the flamethrowers belched again. Scott stowed his mace and hurled more vials of pitch at the oncoming Gronions. Musclebound fishmen burned, screeching and gurgling in pain. Turned out, seeing their buddies burst into flame was a great deterrent for the fish dudes bringing up the next wave of the charge. They turned around and noped right back into the safety of their overgrown jungle.

They're telling the ones in the foliage to retreat, too, Helen Rose Messaged excitedly.

"Hell yeah!" Scott hoisted himself up to get a better vantage. All along both sides, the Gronions were melting back into the trees, while the few that remained burned on the ground, slowly dying. Shots from the back of the trailer picked them off, not leaving anything to chance. Scott glanced back at the Poser Owners, searching for any obvious damage to them or the rig. *Anybody hurt back there?* he sent to Helen Rose.

Ninjastein's got a fishhook in the back of his hand, and Tomahiro took some spear damage, but nothing fatal. Hobbitses is healing them now.

"Okay, decent," he said, but he was mostly talking to himself. It wasn't bad for the convoy's first encounter. Nobody died, and the Winch Witch hadn't been disabled. She was moving forward again, bulldozing through the burnt foliage as she rumbled down the street.

The slow-moving trailer shifted as Kaz hopped out of the back, followed by his stupid film crew. Heedless of the danger they'd just survived, the Troll Gourmet ran around scooping up an armload of catfish chunks.

"Gronion fries up beautifully in a pan or can be added to stock for a delightful fish stew. And best of all, it does not even need the aromatics one would have to add to a meat that is not naturally seasoned," Kaz told the camera as he scooped.

"Get your big ass back in the trailer, Kaz!" Scott yelled. "We just got on the road, we're not making a pit stop for snacks!"

"PwnrBwner should not worry, Kaz has already gathered enough for tonight's stew!" The Troll Gourmet waved a handful of fish meat, then hopped back into the trailer and helped Lakshya and the camera guy back inside.

Back in the pillboxes, the newbs were joking around and slacking off, but the rescue run veterans knew better than to drop their guard out here. It didn't matter that they'd just kicked the first round of ass; Round Two could strike at any second.

Scott pushed himself up and raised his voice so the POSes could hear him.

“Cut the celebration, losers! We made it twenty minutes without anybody dying, big whoop. There’s still eight hours to go. Eyes on the road, spells and arrows cocked, nocked, and ready to rock. Let’s do this!”

CHAPTER 23
SUICIDE RUN

The Shieldwall convoy made slow but consistent progress through the streets of LA. The city was a disaster zone like something out of one of those shitty summer blockbusters. Scott idly wondered where the new Hollywood would be, since everything from the Sunset Strip to Little Armenia belonged to a gang of Smogsouled now. And not just there. The effects of the Merge could be seen down every street—tucked away in big box stores, under bridges, and in ritzy neighborhoods and slums. The majority of Hearthworld's infrastructure was confined to the ten square miles surrounding Shieldwall, but the game's monstrous residents had spread fast.

A lot of the smarter mobs were busy doing their own shit, setting up dungeons, carving out territories for themselves, pushing back against the Heralds of Destruction who were sweeping up mobs and Hearthworld natives into their ranks. Most of them didn't want to fuck around with a target as formidable as the Winch Witch. They did hit a couple minor hiccups after the Gronions. A herd of Rampaging Rhinocorns defending their territory, which apparently consisted of a destroyed strip mall, and a spike strip thrown down by some

Goblins in Crenshaw that the POSes sent running for the hills in about ten seconds.

The Winch Witch wasn't fazed by any of it.

The Enchantment-reinforced tires rolled over the Goblin's spikes like they were made of wet cardboard. Scott's .50 cal bullets all but bounced off the Rhinocorns, but they backed off when they couldn't even make a dent in the armored steel plates down the semi trailer's side and Arjun's Shadow Puppets lured the lumbering morons off to fight imaginary trespassers in their parking lot.

Around noon, Scott spotted a gas station with an attached Taco Bell. The windows had been busted out, and one of the Taconator decals flapped in the breeze, but he called down to Kevin for a pit stop. While the driver and his Reaver spotter climbed out and stretched, Scott had the POSes post up around the Witch.

"We'll go inside in shifts," he said. "Tomahiro and Ninjastein, clear the bathrooms before we send in the refugees. Flappie, Buster, and Helen Rose, keep an eye on the Witch and the surrounding area. Skullcandy, you're with me."

"Can't go to the ladies' room by yourself?" GothicTerror asked with a blistering smile.

Scott shot her a flat look. "Do you ever get tired of nobody thinking you're funny?"

"As long as I make myself laugh, what do I care?"

Scott snorted. He did have to take a leak, but he could've done that anywhere—one of the many perks of being a dude—and it wasn't the real reason he'd wanted to stop here. He was keeping the truth close to the breastplate for the time being.

He and GothicTerror headed around back of the semi and opened the trailer doors. Scott was expecting a mass of pissed, smelly, grumbling refugees, but what he found instead was a crowd enraptured by a bubbling stockpot over a blue Sterno fire.

Kaz stood over it, explaining as he stirred. “Many chefs, like Kaz, may think that because salt is so good in small amounts, large amounts must be even better. However, with naturally salty creatures like Gronion, moderation is the key to successful—”

“Hold on, Kaz, cut,” Lakshya said, holding up a hand to stop his food monologue. “We lost our hobo cookfire light.” She glared toward the back of the trailer. “Who the hell opened the door?”

“Yo, nutsacks,” Scott said. “We’re stopping for a potty break. You’ve got ten minutes and we’re back on the road. Anybody who’s not in the truck when time runs out gets left behind.” He looked around the trailer from one set of eyes to another. “If I were you losers, I’d get my business done now.”

With an annoyed sigh, Lakshya said, “Cap the Sterno can and take ten, Kaz. We’ll finish this sequence later.”

Scott rolled his eyes and headed for the gas station with GothicTerror at his side.

Ninjastein poked his head out from around the side of the building, probably where the station’s bathrooms were, and shot Scott a wide thumbs-up.

“Bathrooms’re clear. Super nasty, but no mobs.”

Scott nodded. “Use it if you have to, then switch out with the POSes on Witch watch. Tots and me are gonna grab some road trip snacks.”

“Not much selection,” the fat guy said with a shrug. “Tomy and I already checked out the C-store.”

“We’re checking again,” Scott said.

One of the automatic doors on the front of the station had been busted to pieces, and the other one was hanging on its track by only one runner.

Nessa nocked an arrow, and Scott pulled his mace, just in case anything big and bad was waiting for them inside.

Stale air and the stink of rotten chocolate milk punched Scott full in the nose as they walked in. The stuff in the cold cases must've gone bad during the blackouts. Luckily, milk and gas station sushi weren't what Scott was looking for. The stuff he was after would probably survive a nuclear blast, just it and the cockroaches.

Like Ninjastein had said, all the snacks, beer, candy, and soda had already been looted from the gas station racks. Even the crappy health stuff like the kale chips and garbanzo bars were gone. People must've been desperate to sink that low. Torn wrappers crinkled under their feet as they moved from aisle to aisle.

"Pretty picked over," Nessa said, thumbing the string of her compound bow with a muted *twang*.

"Come on." Scott jerked his head toward the doorway connecting the gas station and the Bell's dining room.

The breeze blowing into the gas station from the Bell stunk like taco seasoning, but not decay. Scott always figured the brown gloop he was shoving into tortillas was probably more chemicals than actual meat, and here was confirmation of that theory.

The roll cage was down, standing sentinel over the treasures the Bell had to offer, but a crushing blow from his mace broke the mechanism holding it in place. Scott grabbed the metal grating, but before he could pull it up, Feral Senses tingled, raising the hairs on his arms.

He jerked back a split second before something skittered across the doorway and shot under a broken table.

"What the crap was that?" Nessa asked, arrow trained on where it had disappeared.

"Purple, furry, and fast," Scott said, still scanning the dining area. “Do you hear slurping?” Feral Senses was picking it up big-time.

She shook her head.

Scott crept forward—silent even in his heavy armor thanks to his Ranger Wilderness Stealth—and peered through the cage.

The dining room was dusty and cobwebbed, littered with quesadilla wrappers and plastic cups. The cash register lay smashed to pieces halfway between the counter and the door.

It only took him a second to locate the source of the slurping.

On the drinks machine, a furry red ball about the size of a grapefruit clung to the drip tray, noisily sucking up soda. As it gorged itself, the furball’s head bumped the dispenser arm for Mountain Dew Baja Blast, spilling out another snoutful.

A mob tag appeared over the furball’s head.

[Vent Trabble]

GothicTerror pulled up beside Scott.

“Trabble?” she whispered. “Is that one of those things from the volcanic vents in Enterprise Grotto?”

Scott nodded. “That one is.” His eyes roved the shadows at the perimeter for the thing they’d seen first. “I don’t know what the purple thing was.”

A scrabbling sound snapped his attention back to the drink machine. The Trabble was swelling up like a balloon, being shoved by its growing mass off the drip tray. Hundreds of clawed feet, crammed into its round belly like a scrunched-up centipede, scrambled frantically to hold on. Scott watched in fascination as the expanding creature’s lava-red fur mottled with Baja Blast blue, then morphed into a bright purple.

Scott grimaced. “Sick. I knew that stuff was toxic waste.”

“It is not,” GothicTerror growled. “It’s probably just bad for Trabbles.”

"You would say that. You like that crap." He straightened up and dropped the Stealth and whispering. "Let's punt some Trabbles."

"Wait, Pwnr, what are we even doing here—"

He jerked the roll cage up. Just like in the Grotto these things called home, the noise instantly drew hundreds of the little red dudes out of every conceivable nook and cranny. Half a dozen big purple ones that had obviously been indulging in the Mountain Dew emerged from under broken tables and behind the counter.

For a split second, nobody moved.

Then all hell broke loose.

The Trabbles charged, thousands of tiny claws clicking on the dirty tile.

Scott waded into the tsunami of fur, alternately kicking like he was trying to score the game-winning forty-yard field goal and swinging for the fences with his mace. Most of the smaller Trabbles were so low-level that they exploded on contact. Tufts of red fur floated through the taco-scented air.

One of the big purple dudes was bearing down on him fast, but his hands were full with the flood of little furballs. For every ten he exploded, there were twenty waiting to take their place. They swamped up his knees and started gnawing on his armor.

That was how they got you in the Grotto—by overwhelming numbers. If one of them managed to get through the plate, they would all swarm inside through that hole, then eat you alive from the inside out. Not a pretty way to die, even in a game.

An arrow glowing green with Undead Chaos Damage streaked past, slamming into the oncoming purple ball. It let out a screaming, farting sound like a balloon deflating, but kept charging toward Scott. A round mouth filled with concentric jaws like a lamprey's yawned open wide, the lines of razor-sharp teeth churning in opposite directions. Scott had seen some shit, but he had to admit these things were a lot freakier in real life. Thanks to his stupid cousin Marcus, Scott had developed an immense dislike of Furbies as a kid. The furry, bat-eared creature toys from the old days had made a huge comeback when they were in elementary school. Marcus had hacked into their speech boxes, making them turn on at random times and whisper horrific shit like "We will devour your soul" and "Scott is a turd nugget."

These little Trabble freaks were too close for comfort.

He backpedaled away from the purple hell floof, preparing to unleash a concentrated blast of Elemental Fury.

The floor rumbled as GothicTerror beat him to it, casting Hungry Grave instead.

Hungry Grave

Area of Effect Spell

Diameter: 40 feet

Casting Time: Instant

Casting Cost: 12% Base Magicka

Undead thieves from beyond the grave snatch your enemies and pull them kicking and screaming into unending darkness.

Targets take 4x Undead Damage, where x is the caster's level.

Targets with Strength of 50% or greater than the caster's can Struggle to break free.

Targets with less than 50% of caster's Strength are instantly killed.

Note: Hungry Grave does not affect caster's allies.

Cracks streaked across the tile as rotting zombie hands burst through. The undead extremities started grabbing Trabbles left and right and jerking them down into the ground. Puffs of red fur popped up as they exploded. One dead hand snatched at the purple Trabble. It struggled, but before it could break free, GothicTerror nailed it with another arrow. It popped, showering the surrounding Trabbles with teeth, guts, and purple hair.

"Decent," Scott said, bashing a bunch of the little red dudes off his left calf.

"Better than decent," she said, turning another struggling purple ball into a pincushion. "I saved your life."

"Take it easy, Tots, you killed a trash-tier fuzzball. This isn't a Medal of Honor situation."

They shot, kicked, and bashed their way through the rest of the furry flood, until they'd culled it down to a handful of little red Trabbles scrambling around like panicking roaches. Then it was just a curbstomping game.

"Suck on that, you hairy little Furby testicles." Scott squashed the last one. It burst with a satisfying pop. "Don't mess with the best."

He swatted a tuft of drifting fur out of his face, then headed for the counter.

GothicTerror picked a stringy bit of Trabble out of her hair. "Are you going to tell me what we're doing here, or is that top-secret Dungeon Lord business?"

He hopped over the counter and grabbed one of the few extra-large cups still in the holder, along with its corresponding lid.

"I needed to get something." He went to the Dew-only drink machine the Bell workers used to fill drive-thru orders—which also happened to be the one the Trabbles hadn't been glugging out of—and checked the ice dispenser. Water dribbled out, so that wasn't happening, but when he shoved the cup under the first Dew spout, frothy Code Red bubbled out just like always.

He hit the Baja Blast next, then the Lightning Fury, the bright green of Original, all the way across the board until he had mixed in all sixteen flavors.

Scott slapped the lid on and spun around, holding out the cup.

"One sixteen-flavor Mountain Dew Suicide," he said, setting it on the counter in front of GothicTerror.

She stared at the drink for a second, then grinned.

"Scott, did you stop here just because I said I missed Taco Bell's special Suicides?"

He smirked. "Don't be stupid. I love the Bell. It's one of my all-time favorite places to hang out. I would've stopped whether you were here or not."

Nessa laughed and picked up her cup. Then she hesitated. "Is it bad that I saw what this did to the Trabbles, but I'm still not grossed out enough to not drink it?"

"Yes," Scott said. "But not as bad as liking that sludge in the first place."

"Thanks," she said. But she sounded sincere about it, which made Scott smirk a little wider.

Mission accomplished.

"Whatever. Drink up," he said, heading back into the gas station, past the sea of furry corpses. "Our ten minutes are probably up by now. We need to get back on the road."

Nessa caught up to him, slurping happily on her cupful of Trabble-mutating toxic waste.

Outside, the refugees were loading themselves back into the truck and Kevin and Crank were just slamming the Winch Witch's hood.

Kevin shot Scott a thumbs-up. "All the runes are working perfectly. She's ready to go."

"All right," Scott said, clapping his hands together. "Let's get this show back on the—"

Out of nowhere, a Malaika Herald swooped down from the sky and hit the three-point landing between Scott, Nessa, and the Witch. Scott recognized the jerkwad right away from the Heraldric assault on Frontflip. It was the bald douchebag who'd been Lowen's right-hand psychopath. Scott had sincerely thought this guy was dead, but apparently, he'd survive the battle. He'd also obviously leveled up since then, since he had the glowing red boss tag floating over his head to prove it.

[Darith]

"Here I was stumbling around this city like a chicken with its eyes gouged out looking for Frontflip, and now Frontflip's come to me," he sneered. He stuck his fingers in his mouth and whistled. "Get 'em, boys!"

CHAPTER 24
KING OF WOLVES

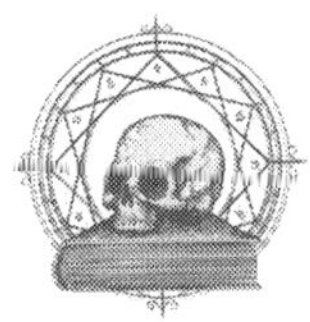

Roark loped easily through the forest, spear in hand. The wind whispered in the trees, interrupted by the occasional hoot of a distant owl or the rustling of foliage off in the distance. A bed of fresh, powdery snow and centuries of pine needles cushioned every step. The moon shined through the trees, turning the upper branches into spiny silhouettes and affording him just enough light to search the snow for tracks. Small game trails crisscrossed the forest floor, a hare's leaping path, the feathery disturbance of a woodduck, the divided hoofprints of a hind and its fawn.

All desirable prey for small predators such as foxes, tanuki, and the stout mountain cats, but of little consequence to a maka-ronin. A hunter that large required much more substantial prey.

Where the snow deepened, Roark found a set of snowox tracks. The markings were a tale written into the ground by nature, easy enough for any competent hunter to read. The unevenness of the prints suggested the snowox had an injured rear leg, while the scuff marks high along the trunks of nearby pines suggested it was a large specimen—easily nineteen hands tall. Roark followed the lumbering trail to a stony brook edged in ice. At the edge of the water, the ox had veered sharply down-mountain at a run, clearly spooked by something.

With their heavy curved horns, bulky slabs of muscle and fat, and long sweeping fur, one would never suspect the snowox could outrun a grown man at full sprint, but it was one of the more dangerous beasts that populated the Karasu Mountains when frightened or provoked. Splintered branches, broken saplings, and a muddy churned-up path through the snow marked the ox's panicked headlong plunge. A mature hard maple had been nearly uprooted, the long white tangle of fur clinging to its scraped bark evidence of the culprit.

Farther downstream, the reason for the normally docile beast's breakneck pace became clear—wolf prints burst out of the water and onto the trail. In his Draconic Chaos Harbinger form, Roark well outsized a human man, but these prints were larger across than his boot was long, and tipped with sharp claws that had dug into the mud and rock beneath the snow for extra purchase. The trail was fresh, untouched by the latest dusting of snow.

Blood soon littered the path, telling its own tale. A pitched battle. A desperate flight. A mad dash for safety even while badly wounded. The wolf prints followed. Droplets of blood transformed into great splashes of red and torn clumps of snowox fur. No additional wolf tracks joined the first set, which struck Roark as curious. The maka-ronin hunted the huge beast alone—a deadly gamble, even for a predator of his size. The snowox would outweigh the king of the wolves by tons, and in its struggle to survive it could easily strike a crushing blow that, if it didn't outright kill him, would leave the maka-ronin lamed and lead to a slow and lingering death.

Most wolves wouldn't have taken the chance without a

pack. Either desperation or foolhardiness had driven the maka-ronin to risk this hunt.

Roark felt a grim smile tug at his lips. Often enough in his own life, the line between the two had been too thin to differentiate, and death or dismemberment had felt like a small price to pay for a chance at victory.

Abruptly, he came out of the trees and nearly ran headlong into a deep ravine cut into the mountainside by untold centuries of spring melt. The kill site lay below, a muddy wallow of crimson snow and gore.

The ox's carcass had frozen over, pale pink crystals of hoarfrost growing on the exposed ribs and innards, a sign that the kill had taken place hours earlier, but Roark felt certain the maka-ronin was somewhere close by. After that clever play of herding the ox off the cliff, the beast wouldn't soon desert his hard-won meal. The deadly risk had yielded him days' worth of food, and that was not a gift to be squandered.

No sooner had Roark thought this than he heard the muted crunch of compacting snow.

Slowly, deliberately, he turned.

The king of the wolves crouched behind him, ready to spring.

Nose to tail, the beast was nearly as long as Roark was tall, lean and rangy, but with muscles like coiled steel beneath its battle-scarred hide. The deep red glint of drying blood on its muzzle shone in the moonlight.

Bright yellow eyes burning with hatred glared back at Roark, completely devoid of any recognition or understanding his mother had been so certain the "Great King" would have for her son. He looked every inch the fearsome monster his uncle Gareth had painted in those wintry stories.

The maka-ronin's black lips curled back in a snarl to reveal imposing yellowed fangs dripping with bloody saliva. Down its shaggy neck and back, the beast's hackles were raised, prepared to defend its meaty prize.

"I know how you feel, mate," Roark answered in his own low growl. He let out a humorless chuckle and hunkered down, tightening his grip on the spear. "Believe me, I do."

He'd stood in the maka-ronin's place time and time again and learned the hard way that with every new victory came not peace, but more challengers. Such was the life of a predator, a fighter. Down every road there was always another looming threat, a stronger enemy vying for the prize. To rest on past victories was to ensure future defeats. This was the cold, hard reality of life.

The wolf leapt, snapping for his throat. Roark dodged, letting the fangs slip past him by a hair, and struck out with the Iron Spear. It sliced through the maka-ronin's ruff without puncturing its hide.

The wolf switched directions faster than a fencer, twisting back on itself, and snapped at the spear's haft. Roark jerked the weapon out of its reach, then lunged with a bastardized *imbroccatta* thrust *dalla spalla,* from his shoulder. The maka-ronin yelped at the bite of iron as the tip of the spear gashed its shoulder, but the beast continued its forward attack undeterred. The massive wolf slammed into Roark, its claws ripping into his chest. At the last second, Roark managed to interpose the haft of the spear between the beast's slavering jaws and his throat, but the sheer momentum of the attack drove them both to the trampled, muddy snow.

They rolled a short distance before bashing sidelong against the steep rock of the ravine's southern wall. The maka-ronin took the brunt of the impact, offering a sharp yelp as a large boulder slammed into its side. But the beast quickly recovered. It bit and gnashed at Roark, trying to get past the makeshift barrier of the spear, its claws digging and tearing at his scales.

Roark could see that the tumble had taken a toll, however. Though still fierce, the beast's movements had taken on a slowed, dazed quality.

In that moment, Roark knew he could end the fight with a word or a spell. His Infernal Necrotic Breath would tear through the beast's fur and flesh, but this wasn't just about winning. This was about the battle. About pushing himself. He hadn't brought his enchanted weapons or armor for a reason, and he intended to finish this fight fairly. This magnificent creature was a native son of Korvo, just as much as Roark, and he deserved to have a chance to win the day. But that didn't mean Roark would pull his punches—the beast deserved respect, not pity.

Seeing an opening, Roark pulled his legs up under the wolf's belly and shoved with both feet, throwing the maka-ronin's massive body over his head. He and the beast scrambled to their feet at the same time, lungs heaving out great white clouds of steam into the night air.

They lunged as one and continued their bloody dance across the ravine. Man versus beast—though Roark wasn't sure those words applied to himself anymore. He was as much beast now as he was man. And good thing too, since he never would've been able to stand against the great wolf as a mere human. They were perfectly matched in that moment, agility for agility, strength for strength, determination for determination. It was a thing of brutal beauty—a bloody shame that only one of them could come out of this alive.

Through clenched teeth, Roark cursed the Tyrant King who'd made this fight necessary. The despot would never know nor care about this struggle beyond the delight of having caused one monster to slay the other at the end of his bloody puppet strings. The thought made Roark sick to his soul. No matter which of them survived, he or the wolf, the mountain would lose one of her children tonight, and for what? A handful of Experience points? The scramble to keep up with Marek's damned curse?

The true hell of it was that Roark couldn't stop.

How he felt was nothing in the face of all that stood to be lost. Unless he kept up his level, Marek could easily strike him down, then nothing would stand between the would-be conqueror and taking this world and so many others besides, destroying everything and everyone Roark loved in the process. Roark was the last line of defense, and he couldn't fail, no matter how much he hated the price of this particular victory.

A howl went up nearby, and the maka-ronin answered it with a snarling bark that shook powder from the snowy branches overhead.

Out of the corner of Roark's eye, a shadow blocked the moonlight at the top of the ravine. Some ancient instinct or intuition instantly recognized the graceful movements of a smaller wolf as it slipped down the steep side of the gully toward their battle.

A chorus of howling sang through the forest.

Three... then five... at least ten other wolves calling out to their king.

Over the sound of his own harsh breathing and the maka-ronin's growling and panting, Roark heard the soft pads of feet racing across the snow and bounding off jutting boulders. Soon he was facing down not one massive wolf, but a pack of them. Small and large, they harried him, darting in from the flanks and tearing at his heels and wings and back. They never stayed long enough for him to launch a proper counterattack, melting away the moment they drew blood. Death by a thousand cuts. All the while, the maka-ronin pressed the frontal attack, keeping Roark on the defensive.

It hit Roark all at once what he was seeing. A coordinated

attack, a trap sprung with himself at the center of it. The king of the wolves wasn't alone after all. The beast had hunted the Snowox not out of desperation, but to test himself, to push himself—just as Roark had. This was his pack, and they had come to his aid in his hour of need. The fight had never truly been one man versus one wolf. Like any good gambler, the maka-ronin had loaded the dice in his favor long beforehand.

Roark let out a sharp bark of laughter. "Don't intend to lose tonight or any other night, do you, mate?"

In answer, the maka-ronin leapt, bounding off a tree trunk, then launching himself at Roark's throat once more.

"Neither do I." Knowing he couldn't win against so many foes without the use of his powers, Roark triggered his Infernal Necrotic Shield.

A dome of green-and-purple light erupted around him, protecting him from the snapping fangs and tearing claws that were coming at him from every side. The massive wolf slammed into the barrier of infernal energy, and a few of his subjects yelped as they did the same at Roark's back and flanks. The barrier would only last so long, though. Roark threw back his head and unleashed a shout of Infernal Thunder. Violet rings raced outward from where he stood, sending tremors through the earth that knocked many of the encroaching wolves from their clawed feet.

But it was an attack meant to disrupt, not to kill. There wouldn't be a loser here tonight—Marek and his curse be damned. Roark would deal with the consequences himself rather than dragging this beast and his pack into it.

Unfurling his leathery wings, Roark leapt into the air. Only icy blue Downdraft arrows filled the ravine, the cold pooling in its depths, but with his Draconic flight abilities, he no longer needed to fear the effects of the air currents. With powerful wingbeats, he quickly soared over the heads of the pack, leaving them staring up at his scaled form.

The maka-ronin wasn't so easily outmaneuvered, however. The uncanny beast raced up a craggy wall and leapt off, colliding with Roark in midair. They plummeted toward the dirt in a clumsy spin. Spikes of pain shot through Roark's shoulder as a set of massive lupine jaws clamped down, puncturing his draconic scales. The maka-ronin shook its head viciously as they fell. The sound of tearing meat and snapping scales filled Roark's ear.

They crashed down in a snowbank, one of Roark's wings pinned awkwardly beneath them, and instantly the pack fell on him, ripping, tearing, and clawing. The red liquid in his filigreed Health bar drained by the handful with every bite, made worse by Marek's damned Mummy's Curse.

Out of other options, he triggered his ultimate ability, Draconia Form. The ability was undeniably powerful, but with a twenty-four-hour cooldown timer, he had to be wise about when best to deploy it. Considering the circumstances, however, he suspected that there would never be a better time.

Splintering agony seared through his bones as his frame stretched and distorted to accommodate the NecroDragon's leviathan size. His strong jaw elongated, wicked onyx fangs bursting from his gumline, while his wings seemed to stretch forever outward, their leathery membranes dissipating into spiky, bony protrusions. Fingers and toes lengthened; ebony claws the size of shortswords jutted from their ends. Bony spikes erupted from his spine, connecting to a lashing lizard's tail that outsized even the tallest trees on the mountain. By the time his wings stopped growing, they were big enough to block out the silvery light of the moon; each scale covering his massive torso was the size of a kite shield.

He was no longer just a monster, but a living force of nature, impossibly powerful, at least for a short while.

Wolves were thrown aside as their formerly manageable enemy filled the ravine, now in the form of an enormous skeletal dragon. They'd had a chance when he was only a little bigger than a man, but now they were facing down a creature without equal in all the land of Traisbin.

Roark straightened his huge lizard's skull and bared his fangs at the pack.

[*Congratulations, you have unlocked Intimidation Level 4. With Intimidation, beings with an Intelligence of less than .5 x your Intelligence suffer Fright for 60 seconds. Sometimes a big enough bark is all you need...*]

Whimpering and squeals echoed off the stony walls, and all the lesser wolves scattered, leaving the noble maka-ronin to face this new foe by his lonesome. Even bloodied and exhausted from their battle, the king of the wolves still refused to accept defeat. He limped forward, growling, hackles raised, ready to attack again.

Roark braced himself for the detestable job of destroying such a magnificent creature. The twisting purple and green flames of his Infernal Necrotic Breath roiled upward from the furnace in the breast of his exposed rib cage, casting dancing shadows on the mud and snow.

But over the growling came a strange sound. A small yip that morphed into a wavering howl. The cry was undeveloped but strong, determined.

Roark craned his neck to see between his massive bony wings and the spikes lining his broad back.

In a nearly hidden cave mouth stood a tiny maka-ronin pup. A second joined him and lifted its voice to the sky, then a third.

Their little muzzles dripped with snowox blood, and the last had to drop a chunk of red meat before joining its brother and sister in chorus.

A sleek she-wolf slipped out of the shadows and herded the pups back inside, nipping at the flanks of the strongest willed, the prince who would someday become king of the wolves, before he finally retreated into the safety of the cave.

Mentally, Roark cursed himself to the seven hells. His bone-spiked tail whipped behind him in frustration, splintering a small copse of trees farther down the chasm. He didn't know where he would get the Experience points he required to fend off Marek's curse, but he would be damned to the lowest circle before he became the bloody tyrant that slaughtered this family.

He turned back to the encroaching king of the wolves. The beast was facing down the largest predator he must have ever seen, but still he prowled forward, fangs bared, ready to defend his family with his life.

The maka-ronin crouched, then charged, no sign of fear. Roark batted him down with a carefully calculated swipe of one enormous paw, retracting his claws as far as possible to avoid accidentally eviscerating the wolf. Pinning the maka-ronin to the muddy ground, Roark spread his bony wings and battered the air. The powerful thrusts kicked up a whirlwind of swirling snow and fallen branches while simultaneously sending a few of the remaining pack tumbling backward.

With the agility of a dragonfly, his Draconia Form took to the sky, leaving behind the proud maka-ronin and his pack.

Roark was still soaring over the trees toward the mountain's peak and cursing himself for a fool when the countdown timer blinked a frantic warning in the corner of his eye. His time as the skeletal dragon was about to run out. With eagle-sharp eyes, he found a snowy clearing that glowed in the moonlight as if it were a beacon beckoning him down. He banked easily in spite of his size and glided into a graceful landing in the center of the glade. Mere seconds after his feet touched the ground, his body returned to its Draconic Chaos Harbinger form.

"Bloody damnation," he growled under his breath, running a hand down his face. "Now how the hells am I supposed to keep up with Marek's curse?"

"Son of the Mountains," said a soft feminine voice from the trees behind him, "I may be able to aid you in this."

CHAPTER 25

A KALEIDOSCOPE OF WORLDS

Roark spun around to find himself alone in the clearing except for a large black crow resting on a broken branch at the edge of the tree line.

In a flurry of ebony feathers, the crow leapt from the branch and fluttered to the snowy ground, transforming in midair into a beautiful woman. Her dark, broad face matched the paintings of the fierce warrior peoples of ancient Traisbin that he'd seen in his Academy history lectures, but her smile was soft and kind, almost motherly. Inky feathers were tied throughout her wavy locks, the hair so black it took on an almost emerald sheen in the moonlight. A wide necklet of polished mountain rock and yellowed bone hung down to cover her chest, while more of the crow's dark plumage had been woven into a shifting, green-black skirt around her legs.

There was something so familiar about the woman, but Roark couldn't pin down why he felt that way.

"Who are you?" he asked.

"You are not afraid?" She canted her head to the side like an inquisitive bird. "Not surprised to see a crow turn into a woman?"

"You just saw a dragon turn into a demon," Roark returned, gesturing at himself. "Something tells me neither of us is easily shocked anymore."

Her smile widened, showing off teeth blackened by *maho* resin. According to the history lectures, chewing the resin had been part of an ancient ritual practiced by the mountain tribes, though no one in the modern era was certain what the ritual did. Roark had a feeling that if the elderly mage who'd taught history were there, Old Palver's heart would have burst with excitement. Finally all his speculations and questions about ancient life could be answered.

"You are a demon in face only," the woman said, reaching out and brushing his cheek with motherly affection. Her fingers were as soft as down feathers, but cold as the mountain air. "No true demon would have spared my son."

Moments passed before Roark realized she meant the maka-ronin.

"You're the mother of the wolf?" He squinted and tried to hide his skeptical tone. He doubted he was successful.

"In a way, I am yours as well, Son of the Mountains, as I am your sister's and I was your father's. I am Karasuno. All creatures born in this place belong to me." She swept both arms to the sides and spun in a slow circle, feathers rustling as she moved.

She dropped her arms and passed by him, drifting to the center of the glade with all the grace of a bird on the wing. A fire was burning there, crackling and hearty as if it had been there all along. There was no fear or worry in her steps. She'd seen what Roark was capable of, yet she freely offered him her back —a sign of trust amongst beasts of the wild.

Roark followed, racking his brain for what little of the old languages he could remember outside of what he'd had to learn for certain magicks.

"Karasuno, meaning 'of the Karasu'?" he asked.

"That is very close," she said, nodding. Instead of elaborating, she seated herself beside the fire, seemingly unbothered by the cold snow beneath her, and gestured for Roark to do the same. "Please."

"It's not my intention to be rude, but I don't have time to sit." He checked his filigreed Health vial to see how far it had drained since his arrival. "Every second I tarry..." His voice trailed off. He blinked to make sure he wasn't imagining things.

The red in his vial had frozen.

Karasuno flashed her gentle smile at him. "Do not fear time, Son of the Mountains. Once you set foot in my clearing, you left time behind with the others. At least for a little while. For now, you are with me, and we will sit."

"But how—"

"What is time to the mountains?" Bones and rocks clacked softly as she shrugged. "Nothing. Sit."

Bewildered, Roark lowered himself to the frosty grass across the fire from her.

Her long black hair and crow feathers slid over her bare shoulders as she nodded her gratitude. A stick appeared in her hand, and she set to stirring the coals with it.

"You are the shaman for your people," she said, a slight lilt to her voice that could almost have been a question.

Roark had become so accustomed to Hearthworld that he said, "I'm a Hexomancer—" before it occurred to him that she likely wouldn't understand or care about the intricacies of the magickal class system from another world. He stopped himself. "What I mean is, no, I'm not a shaman."

"I know the many worlds, Son of the Mountains, but I speak in the language of my home. In your day, what used to be called shamans are now called nobles. They are rulers of land and people, drenched in ink and learning by rote." She stopped digging in the coals and leaned forward as if to impart a great secret. "But once they were the spiritual protectors of their tribes, of these mountains.

"They walked where no others could go, between the smoke and the fog, between the fire and the light, and returned to their people with knowledge no man could know." With her stick, she reached into the coals and dragged something sizzling onto the snow. "You are a shaman, Son of the Mountains, I see it in you. You know of the worlds beyond the world, but you do not know how to walk between them where you need to go. The knowledge you gained in Hearthworld is not enough alone. You must have the missing pieces. Tonight, I invite you to share in the secret knowledge shared by all shamans who have come before you."

"The secret knowledge is how to safely travel through a portal?"

"Walking between worlds is as simple as following a game trail," she said. "Arriving where you wish to arrive, however, is not."

Roark considered this. "Marek knows the trick. Is he a shaman?"

"Perhaps in the world of his birth, he once was," she said. "But now he is a detestable creature of greed and contempt. His every step makes my granite crawl. He does not belong here. His presence is a foreign irritant, yet until now he was but a bad dream to me as I slumbered deep in the heart of the mountain." She paused and looked up from the coals, eyes gleaming with fiery malice. "That has changed. His innate magick was also powerful—and amplified a thousandfold by the power of the World Stone—but the abilities he unlocked in this Hearthworld..."

She faltered, lips turning down at the edges.

"He has become an existential threat to this world. To all

worlds. When he transitioned back to Terho, bringing his monstrous army with him, his sheer presence was enough to wake me from a rest that has lasted a thousand years or more. Left unchecked, he will burn all of creation to the ground and declare himself the emperor over the ashes. You fight to rid my mountains and this world of him, but you refused to destroy your brothers and sisters to do so. This is why I offer you aid, Son of the Mountains, so you will rid our world—all worlds—of his vile ambition."

She picked up the thing she'd dragged out of the fire. It was a lump of black resin, still bubbling in places. Untroubled by the residual heat, she held it out to him.

"Will you journey with me on this most sacred pilgrimage, Roark von Graf, Son of the Mountains?"

Take a Little Trip and See

You have proven yourself a true Son of the Mountains, and as such, Karasuno has invited you to share in the secret shamanistic knowledge of walking beyond your world.

Objective: Chew the maho resin and complete the ancient ritual

Reward: Secret Knowledge of the Ancient Shaman, ??? Experience, Class Change, unknown boon granted by Karasuno

Failure: Refuse to partake in the ancient ritual

There are more worlds than these. It is time to see just how many more.

Accept quest? Yes/No?

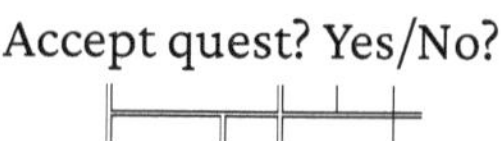

Although the Experience was undefined, Roark imagined it would be enough to get him to the next level and hold off the slow drain of the Curse of the Mummy. Or, at least, he hoped so. Still, he didn't immediately accept the quest. This could be an

answer to his problems, yet he had learned well that playing with magick beyond mortal understanding was a good way to end up dead. Moreover, making deals with questionable creatures of ancient myth and legend could have hidden barbs with terrible consequences all their own. The Lyuko had many such stories about lost and weary travelers bargaining with spirits of the forest.

Bargains for life, for riches, for power and fame. Bargains struck with the best of intentions only to unleash a metaphysical wildfire that burned through their lives and turned certain victory into bitter defeat.

The bones and stones clacked again as her head cocked in that corvine way. "Do you fear what visions or dreams may come?"

Roark glanced at his frozen Health vial once more.

"Among other things," he replied. "Like a true Son of the Mountains, I know that trust is earned, never given. And I'm sure you know of the stories told about the spirits of the forest. About the deals they make. What's to say I strike this bargain only to find myself whisked away for a hundred years?"

"A prudent consideration, worthy of one of my children. My intentions are pure, but ask questions three, Roark von Graf, and I shall answer true."

"Let's start with a simple one. Is time moving outside this clearing?" he asked. Marek could be formulating a way to destroy or get past the Discordant Inversion—hells, he could already have found a way. The Tyrant King could be slaughtering Korvo and everyone in the Citadel while Roark sat there with Karasuno.

She raised a slim, pale finger capped with an obsidian talon. "That is not now, Son of the Mountains, that is later."

"And that is not an answer," he said.

When she laughed, the sound was like birdsong, "But it is

the truth," she said, before falling silent, content not to discuss the matter further. Instead she waited for him, as patiently as a mountain outwaiting an obstinate, short-lived century.

"Then tell me why I should trust you."

She smiled, black teeth gleaming in the firelight. "Because I am telling you the truth. Even if I could offer some further proof, what would you accept?" She cocked an eyebrow. "The reason you will say yes is because you have no other options. You are a desperate man. When a forest fire runs wild, the deer and the wolf both flee from it, side by side, because there is nothing else to be done." She raised another clawed finger. "Your final question now."

He grimaced, not in any way mollified by the answer. She had a fair point—what evidence would he accept? A writ, signed by a lord? A sacred tome? If she was who she claimed, then she was older than the oldest books. She was right, there was nothing she could say or do to prove the veracity of her claims. He had few options left, and those were running out every second.

"Is it possible that doing this will kill me?" he asked finally.

She *tsked*. "There is nothing certain in life, except that death waits for all. You and I both know that the greatest rewards only come with the greatest risks." A third finger joined the first two. "Now, decide."

Roark reread the quest and went through what he knew.

First, he needed that Experience, and if she was telling the truth, then he also needed the piece of information the quest would supply. Second, she was clearly powerful in her own right, and if she meant him harm there were countless other ways she could do so. Why this farce unless it was no farce at all and she was being honest? Third, if Korvo or his friends were under attack, there was nothing he could do about it right now without jeopardizing his final plan to deal with Marek. This was a gamble, and it was still distinctly possible she was lying, but he'd never been one to shy away from a risk so long as the payout was worth it.

Resolved that he wasn't going to get any more information, he accepted the quest.

Karasuno reached through the fire, the flames having no effect on her flesh, and held the resin out to him.

Roark took it, biting down on the tarry lump with the wicked onyx fangs of the Draconic Chaos Harbinger. It tasted like the sharp scent of cedar in the fall, the bitter bite of a stormy winter wind, the cold refreshing spring melt, and the warm earthiness of a summer mushroom all blended into one. The flavors burned down his throat and settled in his belly like the molten rock at the center of a planet.

Immediately, the fire began to darken from bright, flickering orange to a cold blue. As he watched, the flames receded, drifting father and farther away from him—and not only the flames but the small wood fire itself. The two bodies sitting beside it. The clearing. The entire mountain range. All of Traisbin, and the whole planet of Terho and all its sister planets and moons and giant raging stars. In seconds, Roark was looking down on that universe from somewhere *outside.*

Surrounding Roark was a whirlwind chaos of endless universes. Shimmering galaxies, blazing suns, spiraling nebulas in shades of blue and purple, red and orange. Cosmoses and realities without end in every direction. Each one rotated at its own speed and carved its own path through the void, every possible plane and trajectory occupied at every moment, and every universe held millions of trillions of living creatures, great and small, all immeasurably insignificant and all infinitely vital at the same time.

The enormity of it all assaulted Roark, sending his head spinning. He felt himself plunging wildly, but couldn't tell whether he was falling up or down or being thrown to one side. Clamping his eyes shut tight, he flung his hands out, reaching for something solid, something he could comprehend and grasp hold of. An anchor in the impossible largeness of it all.

Cold fingertips as soft as feather down brushed across his knuckles, then closed around his hand with gentle firmness. He clutched Karasuno's proffered hand like a life rope thrown to a drowning man.

"No. Not like that. You are trying to see too much," she said. "I know you are eager to know all, but if you stare at the whole forest at once, you do not see anything—not the beetle on the log, nor the snake attacking the nest, nor the wolves in the den. Breathe, Son of the Mountains, and look only to the worlds where your foot has tread before."

Roark opened his eyes, forcing himself to focus on nothing but her face. "How am I supposed to find them in amongst all the others?" he asked, his voice reedy and scared in his own ears.

"How do you find your way back to your mountain home when you stand in the center of a vast grassland? How do you turn your face toward it when you drift on a wide-open sea?" She smiled. "Your instincts remember the trails you have traveled to get where you are. Do not fight them. Not yet."

Taking a deep breath, Roark braced himself for the mind-crushing vertigo and turned to face the infinite whirlwind of realities once more.

For a moment, the chaos overwhelmed him again, but something tugged his attention to his right. He turned his head and found the soaring buildings, metal horseless carriages, and strange technology of the world of the Devs. It was a miniscule pinpoint in the cosmos, a single snowflake in a blizzard, but as he focused on it, the raging snowstorm of worlds faded until that sole snowflake was the blizzard. Until it was everything.

The universe was infinity big, but *his* universe was much smaller.

Tiny really, especially when seen next to the vastness of reality.

His world was a handful of relationships, it was familiar corridors that he'd walked a thousand times, the workbench he'd labored over, drafting his plans, and the smithy where he'd hammered out blades before quenching them. It was Zyra's alchemy shop. The von Graf manor house where he'd grown as a boy and where he'd fled from Marek's bloody retribution. His knowledge of the world was vast, but his experience of it was so laughably small. Hearthworld was gone, he could see—a dark void in space and time like a missing puzzle piece.

He glanced down on the world of the Devs. Randy's world. PwnrBwner's world. Even that world was *vast* but there were golden threads dashing along the surface. He picked one thread up and followed it back to Shieldwall, though this was not the Shieldwall as he remembered it. Roark inspected the new battlements PwnrBwner had installed and examined the Dragonkin the dungeon had spawned in his absence. From there, he searched and found the de facto Dungeon Lord and Kaz ushering a strangely dressed group of people through a wasteland of debris and monsters.

Roark wanted to call out to them, get closer and help them, but a visceral strike of intuition told him they would neither see nor hear him if he did.

Another world pulled at him, slightly up and to his left. It was Terho, the tiny blue and green planet threaded with veins of black corruption that he knew instinctively came from Marek's evil. The cloud might not be visible with the naked eye, but here, outside of reality, he could see it. It reminded him of Blackvein fever. It often started from a small cut, not properly treated. The fever came first but it wasn't long before the creeping black veins spread upward from the wound site, dancing along the surface of the skin like ugly bolts of lightning, invariably leading to the heart. Those who contracted it nearly always died.

Marek was just such an infection and if he wasn't contained, he would spread to the heart of Terho, claim it as a victim, then spread to other worlds.

He followed the final pull to Hearthworld, once a vibrant universe filled with life, now a dark and empty void. A puzzle missing a piece.

"It is not the first world Marek has brought to ruin," Karasuno said, her voice cold and dark with hatred.

Anchored by the worlds he was familiar with, Roark followed her gesture to countless voids mixed in amongst the living worlds. Utterly, achingly lifeless, all because of Marek. Roark's clawed fingers curled into fists at his sides.

"This ends now," he vowed. "Marek won't take another one. Not as long as I live."

"I believe you are right," Karasuno said, the joy of a proud mother filling her voice. "It is why I brought you here. But first your vision must grow. Expand outward. Now that you have seen the trees, it is time to see the forest. Then past the forest to the mountain which they reside upon."

He listened to her words, letting his consciousness stretch. It was painful, a dull headache throbbing beyond his eyes, as a bone-deep chill stole into his limbs and filled his body. But he persisted, pushing his senses ever outward, trying to see everything. And the longer Roark looked out at the turmoil, the more it began to resolve into something he could understand. Though at first glance the whirl of infinite universes looked like madness, it was actually a finely tuned clockwork in constant motion. All around him, realities brushed against one another without ever stopping or slowing down. And what was more impressive, without ever colliding. It was all perfectly timed, perfectly measured, a vast endless engine of realities working together.

"Terho isn't side by side with Hearthworld—not now, anyway," he said as the realization dawned upon him. "They passed by one another the night I wrote the portal." He frowned out at the movement of the universes. "Their positions aren't fixed points in space and time, they're fluid, like the movements of the planets or the colors of a kaleidoscope. The question is, how do I get from one to the other without ending up in whatever reality is closest at the moment?"

"By starting from the only truly fixed location," Karasuno said.

She tugged lightly at his hand, and Roark let her turn him around.

A massive structure loomed over them, a colossal, jagged mass of amber that glimmered with iridescent light; around it was a cornea of purples and blues that looked like the eye of a giant god. The stone hummed with unimaginable power. The whole universe was a spider web, each galaxy and world like a drop of dew suspended in the early morning. This stone was the center of the web, the anchor miring every strand in place. But it was *broken*. Even though the stone was massive, the size of a small moon, Roark could feel more than see that a piece was missing.

A small chunk the size of a fist.

With her free hand, Karasuno gestured to the glowing amber monolith before them.

"The Tower of Creation," she whispered, awe buzzing beneath the words.

CHAPTER 26

THE TOWER OF CREATION

"The Tower of Creation is the only point in everything that exists, did exist, or will exist that does not move," Karasuno explained. "All of existence spins and rotates relative to the Tower. Like true north, it is the starting point for finding the way to any world you seek. Every shaman who fruitfully walked the worlds before you has found their way through the Tower of Creation. Do you see?"

Roark considered this for several long seconds. In some worlds, those seconds passed as eras, and in others it was as no time at all.

Finally, he nodded. "Portals can be written without it, just as you can start a journey without knowing which way north is. The difference is ending up somewhere unintended—which I did when I wrote mine that first night."

"Or arriving at your destination irreversibly changed," she said.

"Again, as I found out." He raised one hand and turned it over, examining the wicked onyx claws. "And as the Council of Traisbin's mages learned the hard way."

The bone and rock necklet clacked softly as Karasuno nodded.

"The Tower is a navigational reference," Roark said, glancing once more up at its gleaming amber façade. "So, how do I use it?"

"The shamans that came before you directed their walks between worlds in many ways," Karasuno said. "Some danced a doorway into being, others drank it into their mind or drew it with blood or dirt or cast the stones or lay the sticks until they presented the correct shape. You, Son of the Mountains from the time of ink and parchment, will write your journey."

"How?" Roark asked, trying to keep the frustration from his voice. This was why he preferred to learn things from books.

Karasuno gestured to the Tower. "Ask it. You have used a piece of the Tower before—its ways are more familiar to you than most, even if you do not realize it. And as you know it, it knows you. Ask it once more and it will whisper its secrets to you."

He cast a doubtful eye at the gleaming stone structure. It glowed with the same light the World Stone took on when its magick was activated, that hum of life and power thrumming beneath the surface like a massive heartbeat he could almost hear. What was more, he could feel it there, even when he shut his eyes. The Tower was looking into him, down to his very soul, seeing every awful thing he'd done to take down the Tyrant King and before, when he was nothing but a scared child running from his past and a cowardly youth avoiding the war he knew was his destiny.

Murders, lies, thefts, betrayals, unholy alliances, one virtue after another forsaken and cast aside. Some in the service of revenge and some in the service of nothing more than himself. When everything was stripped away and laid bare before him, the man at his core seemed as dark and as blood-drenched as the despot he was trying to destroy. Roark recoiled from the awful revelation, unable to hold his ground in the face of what he had become. He'd told himself over and over again that he would do whatever he had to in order to defeat Marek Konig Ustar, but seeing himself reflected back in the Tower's stark light of honesty...

It was too much to face.

"Do not be afraid," Karasuno said, squeezing his arm gently. "The Tower knows you."

"That's what I'm afraid of," he said in a voice that was embarrassingly unsteady.

She gave a soft chuckle. "The Tower does not hate you, Son of the Mountains. It sees your desire for good to triumph over evil and the struggles you have fought to make it so. What good you cannot see in yourself, it sees in you."

Still, he hesitated.

"Does the Tower of Creation belong to the Creator?" he asked.

This time, Karasuno's laugh was one of pure delight. "Like I belong to the mountains," she said.

He shook his head in wonder. "How in the seven bloody hells did Marek ever manage to stand before this?"

"It is easy when one does not recognize their own stains as stains," she said. "You confront the truth of what you are. This is why the Tower loves you and why it hates Marek."

Taking a deep breath to steel himself, Roark stepped forward and placed his right hand on the Tower. It was the way he had first used the World Stone—by placing his right hand on Kaz's shoulder and waking him to sentience. He'd done the same for every Vassal he'd created. It stood to reason that this was the way one communicated with the Tower.

A chaotic series of images filled his head, an onslaught too great to grasp in its entirety. He saw Marek—and somehow he *knew* it was Marek, though he wore a different face, a different skin—whizzing through the space around the Tower of Creation on a golden, horseless chariot powered by runic magic. At his back was an army of horrors. Wolfmen in golden armor with powerful crushing jaws. Creatures with squid-like heads, tentacles trailing down their robed chests. Mages carrying swords and spears that buzzed with arcs of blue lightning. Huge siege weapons that floated through the cosmos.

Arrayed against the vast horde was a pitifully small number of men and women, both human and monstrous. They wore no uniforms, commanded no siege weapons, and had no underlings to do their bidding. Some wore furs, while others wore armor made from bone or stone or steel. Burning runes were carved into the flesh of a creature made of wood and grass. Prismatic magic danced along the outstretched hand of a minotaur. A great cyclops with a magical club resting against one sloping shoulder prepared to hurl sigil-etched boulders—their version of a siege weapon. Among them was a woman with blackened teeth, covered in dark feathers.

These were the great shamans. Magickal beings of earth and forest and stone and stars, come to make one last desperate stand against a tyrant who would rule not just a world but all of them.

Chaos erupted and the power of their magicks was too much for Roark to understand. Spells flew and blood fell, transforming into nebulas of stars. The shamans fought tooth and nail, the battle raging for a day, then two, then three. They lost the line an inch at a time and made Marek pay for it with bodies. But that was a price Marek was only too happy to pay—he was a creature with loyalty only to himself. On the fifth day, the shaman guardians broke, just long enough for Marek to assault the Tower directly. Using a drill powered by the souls of a hundred conquered worlds, he harvested a single chunk of the Tower for himself.

The World Stone Pendant.

The vision flickered and faded to bitter ashes in Roark's mind.

"I was there that day," Karasuno said. "The process nearly killed him. On death's door, he fled with his prize in hand, leaving his army behind to be slaughtered. Not that he ever cared. I know not which world he fled to. When he finally arrived on Terho, I had been slumbering for more than five hundred years, recovering from a war that had nearly killed me. A war that did kill more great shamans' spirits than I can bear to tell. We all have our failings, Roark von Graf. Our deep moments of shame and regret. The Tower, it understands the frailty of our small lives."

She fell silent as he stood there, palm pressed against the stone, feeling warmth and protection radiate into his hand. Despite her reassurances, Roark still waited for the crushing weight of condemnation to rain down upon his head. Instead, he felt a hand grip his shoulder, firm and strong and too large to be Karasuno's.

Memories of his father he'd assumed long forgotten suddenly resurfaced. Lord Erich wasn't a man for drawn-out speeches or displays of affection. Whenever the man had wanted to convey his approval, Erich had simply grasped him by the shoulder and smiled down at his son, a gesture that never failed to fill Roark with a sense of accomplishment.

On the heels of this came understanding. The constant motion of existence unfurled like a map in Roark's mind, showing the endless turning of the universes within universes, and at the center, a rune of power, shining like the Traveler's Star in the sky over Traisbin.

Roark realized with a start that he'd seen something very

similar to it before. Every portal stone Talise had stolen from Marek for him had an icy blue rune marked in its center that very nearly matched it. Nearly, but not quite.

The rune on the portal stones was corrupted, or maybe the Tyrant King had simply misunderstood what he'd seen. Either way, Marek hadn't inscribed his portal stones with the true rune for the Tower of Creation. As such, Marek could only accurately travel to or within worlds he'd visited before. When he wanted to open a portal to a new reality, he had no choice or control over where he ended up and no way to know what he would become when he stepped out the other side.

Silently thanking the Tower, Roark pulled his hand away and stepped back, the true rune still glowing in his mind like a sunrise promising a new and better day to come.

Karasuno's maho-blackened teeth showed in a wide grin.

"You see now," she said, beaming proudly. "You have learned the secret knowledge of the shaman. And now... Now it is time for you to use it."

WITH A SHARP INTAKE OF BREATH, Roark opened his eyes in the clearing. Powdery flakes of snow and ash dusted across his scale-plated legs and clung to the tips of his lashes. The moon and stars hadn't changed position overhead, so little to no time had passed on his journey between worlds, but the fire was long out, the coals cold to the touch.

Karasuno was nowhere to be seen. The only hint she'd ever been there at all was a crow feather on the undisturbed snow where she'd been sitting.

The feather ruffled and twisted, but wasn't carried away by the wind. As Roark looked at it, a brilliant green luster flitted across its dark surface. An eerie note drifted on the air, similar to that strange, haunting flute music of Hearthworld's respawn period.

Roark leaned across the dead fire and plucked the feather from the snow.

[*Congratulations! You have completed the quest Take a Little Trip and See!*
You have gained Secret Knowledge of the Ancient Shaman, the Divine Soul Shaman Class, and the boon Protection of Karasuno. The mountains themselves fight in your favor!
Warning: Protection of Karasuno is dependent on your treatment of the mountains and her children. As it has been granted, so also can it be revoked. You have seen the gentle side of the Mother of the Mountains, but harm her children for meaningless sport or for the sake of your own ambitions and you will see true viciousness.]

Roark's mouth dropped open as he read through the notification, a wave of shock rocking through him like a Stun debuff. He'd just been granted a boon from the literal heavens. He'd just forged an alliance with the mountains beneath his feet and managed to unlock a new class, even though he didn't know what it entailed yet. And, with the Secret Knowledge of Portal magicks finally opened to him, he would be able to reconnect with his lost friends stranded at Shieldwall and perhaps even stop Marek for good.

Still reeling, he blinked the scrap of parchment away. The crow's feather caught fire in his hand, burning up in a flash of green flame. As the feather was consumed, the fire sank into his palm, then flashed across his scales a moment later. The emerald sheen bled into the scales, adding a deep green shadow to their purple edges.

[*You have unlocked the .error (): WXRLOCꝀ Class Specialty: Divine Soul Shaman!*

Only those who have walked among the pillars of creation and journeyed to the great tower at the heart of existence may walk the path of the Divine Soul Shaman. Divine Soul Shamans hail from many worlds, come from many different walks of life, and are masters of magicks untold, yet the power locked within at the Tower of Creation eclipses them all.

Divine Soul Shamans are masters of all lesser magicks; they gain the benefits of their new class while retaining all of the abilities and bonuses from previous classes. Divine Soul Shamans are masters of reality, capable of navigating all of creation through the use of potent portals. Portal Magick costs 25% less Magick to cast, and portals gain a 50% stability bonus. Permanent runic totems may also be inscribed on secondary items, such as parchment, metal, or stone, without the risk of degrading over time.

Upon changing classes, the Divine Soul Shaman gets a Tower of Creation Experience bonus equal to 20,000 EXP multiplied by their current character level. Additionally, they also gain access to the Divine Soul Shaman spell Portals of Infinity, which can be used as a cantrip, meaning it does not consume a regular Grimoire spell slot.

Warning: Players can only have (1) Class Specialty at a given time. Are you sure you would like to add Divine Soul Shaman? *Yes/No?*]

Roark read through the description, a sense of hope reigniting in his belly. He would be a fool to say no. He hit yes, and an ascending chime rang through the clearing. Golden light flashed, and warmth and vitality washed through Roark's limbs as his filigreed Health vial—no longer frozen—refilled to the top.

[LEVEL UP x 4!]
[You have 40 undistributed Stat Points!]
[*You have reached Level 99! You may choose to Evolve into an Undying Dragonblood Seraph!*
Warning: Troll Evolution is irrevocable. Once an evolutionary path has been selected, a Troll cannot change to another path. Select "Yes" to choose the Undying Dragonblood Seraph path; select "No" remain in your current form, Draconic Chaos Harbinger.
Note: The Undying Dragonblood Seraph path is the capstone evolutionary form of the Necro-Dragon-Jotnar Infernali Hybrid!
Evolve into Level 99 Undying Dragonblood Seraph? Yes/No]

Once more, Roark accepted, knowing he would never receive such a godsend again.

Time seemed to lurch and slow as a new prompt appeared, this one accompanied by an image of himself floating in the air, rotating slowly. Well, not *quite* him—at least not as he was. This new version had six wings protruding from his back, and instead of leather, they were covered with silky black feathers with an iridescent greenish sheen, just like Karasuno's. The sickly pallor to his skin had transformed to a pale luminescence like a pearl glimmering in the light of a moon. His flowing black hair was now strands of pure silver that hung down to his shoulders in a sheet. His horns swept dramatically away from his face before curving upward sharply. Hovering above their points was a halo of crimson fire.

He squinted. Not a halo, but a miniature portal through space and time, and in its center the Tower of Creation. Watching over him as its chosen Guardian.

His eyes burned with a pale red light, and though his wicked fangs had vanished, his talons remained, still as sharp as a chirurgeon's scalpel. The scales covering his body had given way to heavy armor that looked to be crafted of overlapping plates of gleaming, pearl-white bone and sheets of ropy red muscle that glistened with unnatural light. Dragon skull pauldrons rested upon his massive shoulders while gauntlets covered in retractable curved spikes protected his forearms. An assortment of shriveled, cursed heads dangled from one hip, and his Peerless Rapier of Dancing Death, with its elegant golden basket hilt, was sheathed at his other—ready to be drawn at a moment's notice.

Seven hells, but he looked deadly. A force of nature to be trifled with only if one had a death wish. It was brilliant.

Working quickly, Roark opened his grimoire and divvied up the sudden massive influx of points. Though it pained him to add more points to an attribute that went so against his class, he allocated twenty points to Constitution so that he could keep pace with Marek's infernal curse. Ten points went to Intelligence, increasing both his Infernali Magick pool and its Magick Regeneration rate. Five points apiece went into Strength and Dexterity, rounding out his overall stats. When he aimed his final blow at Marek, he wanted it to hit, and he wanted it to hit *hard.*

Roark carefully checked over his stats and abilities one more time to make certain he hadn't missed anything.

Undying Dragonblood Seraph Overview			
Name:	Roark	Level:	99
Gender:	Male	Player Class:	Divine Soul Shaman
Type:	Undying Dragonblood Seraph	Alignment:	Infernali
Current Experience:	1,232	Next Level:	431,640

Health:	2,949.25	Infernali Magick:	4,080
H-Regen / 5 Sec:	445.825	Magick-Regen / 5 Sec:	200.75

Attributes:	
Weapon Damage:	163
Attack Damage:	1784
Base Armor:	125
Armor Rating:	1587.3
Movement Rate:	2.5 x Speed of Opponent
Critical Hit Chance:	32%
Critical Hit Damage:	(+) 300%

Stats:	
Strength:	173
Constitution:	243.65
Dexterity:	200
Intelligence:	310
World Stone Authority, Greater Vassal	11/80
World Stone Authority, Lesser Vassal	85/225
Undistributed Stat Points:	0

Draconic Special Skills:
Rapid-Regen
75% Resistance against normal weapons
Stunning Blow; 22% Chance / Hit
Infernal Necro Shield; Draconic-Hybrid Spell
Necrotizing Infernal Torment; Draconic-Hybrid Spell
Necrotic Invigoration; Draconic-Hybrid Spell
Infernal Undead Temptation, Draconic-Hybrid Spell
Raise Thralls; Draconic-Hybrid Spell
Infernal Necrotic Breath; Draconic-Hybrid Spell
Draconia Form; Draconic-Hybrid Ability
Dragon's Flight; Draconic-Hybrid Ability
Transmutation Tricks; Grimoire Unlocked
The Art of Glamorous Makeovers; Grimoire Unlocked
Portals of Infinity; Divine Soul Shaman Spell
Draconic Leadership Lv. 7

Player Special Skills:	
Spellcraft (Class Skill)	Lv. 15
Bladed Weapons (Melee Skill)	Lv. 12
Weapons Specialty: Rapier	Lv. 9
Calligraphy (Trade Skill)	Lv. 5
Blacksmithing (Trade Skill)	Lv.13
Tailoring (Trade Skill)	Lv. 8
Enchanting (Trade Skill)	Lv. 17
Enchanting Specialty: Cursed!	Lv. 15

Satisfied with his choices, he accepted all the changes and felt his body shift and change, energy suffusing his limbs and burbling out from his center as feathers took shape, horns lurched and twisted, scales receded, and spurs of draconic bone and fire-proof tissue emerged. He dropped to the ground, sending up a small puff of powdery snow, and stretched his newly acquired wings and his formidable new muscles. Marek had more reason than ever for fear—Roark was not only massively stronger, but he'd unlocked several new abilities. In addition to the Portals of Infinity Spell and Undying Soul, granted to him by his class change, he had three other powerful new abilities.

Portals of Infinity: As a Divine Soul Shaman you have ascended, becoming one of the Tower Guardians, a grave calling, with grave responsibilities. You are expected to protect the Tower from those who would destroy it, but the Tower also entrusted you with the secret rune of power, Ithel the All Rune. With Ithel as a guidepost, the universe is an open book to you and so are the hidden mysteries of stable portal magick.

Planar Flight: Thanks to your Draconic heritage, you may take wing from any location without draining your Stamina. Red Updraft and blue Downdraft arrows no longer have any effect on you. In addition, while flying you can activate Planar Flight, which drains half your Stamina, but allows you to travel at ten times your normal speed for ten seconds.

Redeemer of the Fallen: As a Tower Guardian, Freedom Fighter, and Dungeon Lord, you have been blessed by the Tower of Creation with the special ability Redeemer of the Fallen. Bring the souls of the fallen their final justice by seeding their spirits in new Dungeons. You may raise as many Redeemed Warriors as are available within the selected Dungeon Zone; all Redeemed Warriors keep their skills and classes at the time of death and have 5n HP, where n is the caster's Character Level.

Draconic Seraph: You have touched the power of the heavens and it has left an indelible mark upon both body and soul. Once per 24-hour period, leave behind your lowly lesser form and reign supreme

over land and sky as a Draconic Seraph, a creature equal parts light and shadow.

Undying Soul: The Soul of the Divine and the Soul of the Damned reside within you. Once per 24-hour period, trigger the effect Undying Soul on yourself or an ally, preventing them from receiving a mortal blow for one minute. While under the effect of Undying Soul, a person cannot be killed, but neither can they kill another.

Undying Soul had some pragmatic uses—especially in a world without respawns—but with a 24-hour cooldown period, it would serve best as a last resort when things turned especially dire, not a catchall protective measure. Portals of Infinity, on the other hand, changed everything. With that, he could step between worlds and be reunited with his friends once more, no matter how far away they were. And, even more important, it would be the instrument of Marek's undoing, which had a certain sense of poetic justice to it. Portal magic had brought Marek here, it had whisked Roark away from certain death and into the waiting arms of Hearthworld, and now it would deliver Marek into a grave of his own making.

Roark had a plan. A daring, bold plan. Albrecht would almost certainly call it foolhardy. Zyra might call it suicidal. His nemesis turned ally, PwnrBwner, would call it ballin'.

The fact that he was doing something that Pwnr would approve of was somewhat concerning, but taking out someone as powerful as Marek didn't come without risks. Legions of them.

Roark closed the grimoire and turned toward the shining shape of the Radiant Citadel below, the kernel of a plan forming. With the rune of power, *Ithel,* blazing in the forefront of his mind, Roark set off, eager to end this war with Marek once and for all. There was quite a bit of work to be done first, however. Like the clockwork of creation he'd just witnessed, he had hundreds of intricate pieces to set in motion. The odds were still overwhelmingly in favor of the Tyrant King, especially in a fair fight.

Luckily, fighting fair wasn't in Roark's repertoire.

CHAPTER 27
MAD BUTCHER OF LA

Darith stuck his fingers in his mouth and whistled. "Get 'em boys!"

A horde of monstrous creatures surged forward, fangs bared, claws flashing, weapons and spells poised to kill.

Scott ducked under a massive swing from an immense two-handed Zweihander, then lashed out with his mace. Blunt Force Barrage kicked in as the blow landed, stacking 12% more damage on top of the weapon's already boss-level Light Damage. The mace caught the attacking Valbat in the gut, doubling the lanky humanoid bat-creature over. With an execution-style Lightning Lance to the back of the Valbat's head, Scott finished him off.

[LEVEL UP!]
[You have 10 undistributed stat points.]

Hells yeah, he'd leveled up! Pulling off a sick combo like that in real life was the kind of shit that should've made the news. Stupid guerilla journalists never videoing when they should be.

Unfortunately, he didn't have time to gloat about the golden glow that shined from his skin or lament that Kaz was internet famous instead of him. His Feral Senses was tingling, which meant something was coming at him. He blinked away the notification and fastballed a vial of tar-like Ranger Pitch right into the chest of an oncoming rog. The green-skinned NPC slipped and slid, trying to keep its balance, but Scott triggered Lightning Spear. Crackling arcs of blue electricity set the pitch ablaze, sending the enemy rog screaming and sizzling to the deck.

Ninjastein pirouetted through, moving with the grace of a dude half his weight, and sliced the flaming rog's head off with his mall katana. The weapon definitely didn't suck as much as it had, now that the big guy had sharpened it and leveled up his Two-Handed Skills enough to make it count.

Across the gas station parking lot, Nightboars, Valbats, and even a handful of elves and rogs that asswipe Darith must've recruited battled with the Poser Owners.

Kellie and Kevin were at the back of the semi-trailer, protecting the refugees from the attack, which was ballsy as hell since neither had magical powers of their own. Sure, they were kitted out in magically enchanted armor, which imbued even normies like them with some extra strength and vitality, but it wasn't the same. They also weren't alone, which made a difference. Hobbitses was lingering nearby, chanting, hands weaving through the air, casting a powerful buff to keep them alive and in the fight.

Even so, Scott didn't like the dweebs fighting without some backup that had some extra stopping power.

"Ninjastein, get your ass to the back of the trailer, stat!" he yelled.

The big guy shot him a nod and sprinted off to help the twins. To be on the safe side, Scott shouted out the cast for his

Clerical blanket buff, dropping a dose of Powerful Inspiration on his party.

"For Shieldwall! For PwnrBwner! FOR THE SALT!" Kaz roared as he bowled through the swarm of Nightboars with his Legendary Meat Tenderizer, smashing skulls and breaking bones. Even big sumbitches like the rog NecroNight were hurled away like rag dolls with the impact of the Troll Gourmet's massive swings. Kaz might've seemed like an overgrown teddy bear when he was talking about food, but when it was time to brawl, the Troll Gourmet was a murder machine.

Scott scanned the place for GothicTerror, but she had disappeared somewhere in the melee. The best he could find was her precious Suicide, now a syrupy mess staining the pavement, plastic cup crunched to pieces under stomping boots and hooves.

Up front, the flamethrowers installed in the Winch Witch's toolboxes belched and flambeed an enemy charge.

I've got eyes on the ringleader, Helen Rose messaged Scott. *He's—oh shit, he's making a dive for Tomahiro!*

With one of the other benefits of Feral Senses, Scott's eyes locked on the streak of wings and assholery shooting toward the trailer in less time than it would've taken a regular human to register what Helen Rose had said. Tomahiro was on top of the trailer, blissfully unaware of the strike careening toward his back while he fired off devastating Thunder Tsunamis and Shrapnel Lightning Bombs. Obviously, Darith wanted to put a stop to one of the heaviest magical hitters on the POSes' team, and he couldn't have picked a better target. Tomahiro was the quintessential glass cannon—one hundred percent damage output, zero percent damage resistance.

Scott whipped out his Obsidian Glass bow and nocked his last two Solar Glory arrows. The Griefer had enchanted these for taking down Aczol the Eternal NecroDragon, and though a handful of his apprentices were still at the Shieldwall, none of them could do what Roark could. These arrows were the closest thing to magical homing missiles Scott was likely to ever get his hands on. Needed to make 'em count. Sighting down the arrow shaft, he triggered his Ranger perk Foe Slayer. His target slowed to a crawl, allowing Scott to get a lock on the flying douchebag's torso—a full 87% chance to hit.

To be on the safe side, Scott triggered Double Tap.

Good thing he did, too. The first shot just barely missed Darith's chest, but the second one slammed into the spot just under the Herald's armpit.

The arrow exploded on impact, the blast so bright that Scott had to squint and shield his eyes with one hand. He only heard the boom and the insane peal of laughter that followed.

When he looked back, the Solar Glory had only knocked a handful of red off the dick's Health bar. That blew chunks, but one-shot one-kill hadn't been the only thing Scott had been going for. He'd been trying to draw aggro, and the psycho seemed only too happy to comply.

Darith flailed to a stop in the air, wings slapping, and spun around to grin at Scott.

"Yeah, that was me, you overgrown chicken nugget," Scott sneered. He beckoned. "What's the matter, brohole, scared? Come at me."

Darith giggled. "I can't wait to play skip rope with your innards. But not before you tell me where your master is. I'll finally do what Lowen never could."

"Good luck with that, douche nozzle. Roark is halfway across the galaxy, and he's probably kicking Marek's teeth into the back of his throat, which is still better than what I'll do to you. Fuck around with me and I'll rip off your head and shit rainbows down your neck."

"Von Graf is gone?" the giant insane idiot asked. "Banished back to our home world?"

"That's what I said, isn't it?"

A feral grin stretched across the Herald's face. "Then all that stands in my way of dominating this world is little old you. Even better."

With a primal howl, the Herald folded his wings and shot toward Scott like a bullet.

Scott managed to fire off one more Double Tap, then speed-switched to his mace. The arrows hit true, but didn't explode, so the damage they caused was negligible at best. Add to that the fact that this psycho clearly had more than a couple of screws loose, and there was no scaring him off.

Scott wished like hell he'd spent that last Ranger perk on Clever Dodge, but it was too late for that. With a shout, he shrouded himself in Holy Reckoning.

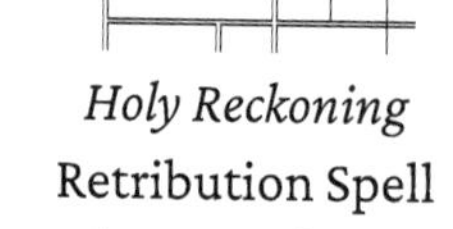

Holy Reckoning

Retribution Spell

Casting Speed: Instant

Casting Cost: 0% of Base Magicka on cast, 9% of Base Magicka upon triggering.

Holy Reckoning assures that your enemies will not attack you without reprisal. Attackers take 50% of all damage dealt to the caster.

Note: Holy Reckoning can only be cast by Divine-aligned heroes.

Darith hit Scott like a cannonball of wings and armor and fury.

He had about half a second to see the notification that

Darith had triggered the Clerical Retribution Spell before they slammed into the side of a gas pump. Pain exploded through Scott's skull, and black washed in from the edges of his vision along with the roaring sound of the ocean.

When Scott blinked open his eyes, his Health bar was flashing out a critical warning and agony roared through his stomach like a wildfire tearing through a canyon. A blood-soaked Darith loomed over him, cackling like an evil mustache-twirling villain while he thrust a big-ass dagger down, over and over again. He'd cracked open Scott's breastplate like a crab and was busy hacking his guts to pieces, giving exactly zero fucks that every blow was chopping into his own Health bar thanks to Holy Reckoning.

[*You have been Concussed! Suffer 25% Penalty to Dexterity and Wisdom for 1 minute or until you drink an Ultimate Healing Potion.*]

[*You have taken Severe Bleeding Damage! Suffer -5 HP per second for 1 minute or until you drink an Ultimate Healing Potion.*]

Based on his screaming filigreed Health vial, Scott didn't have a minute's worth of HP left to lose. His head spun and his hands fumbled as he tried to grab for one of the potions he'd brought along.

An arrow sizzling with Undead Chaos Damage streaked past, leaving crazy green contrails in his blurry vision. It slammed into the side of the Herald's head, making him shriek and stumble sideways, buying Scott a moment to breathe. Though breathing was real hard at the moment, on account that most of his insides were now on his outsides. What a shitty way to go out, Scott thought. Still, a gut full of dagger *was* better than grinding away at a meaningless job that he hated until he died alone and in his underwear of a heart attack at sixty.

If he had to go, at least it would be as a badass and a hero.

A slightly fuzzy GothicTerror appeared between Scott and

the howling Herald, another arrow already nocked and ready to rock.

"He's... too psycho," Scott choked out, blood spluttering between his lips. "Get refugees outta here... Tell Kev... haul... ass..."

Darith stumbled forward, cackling and howling. That Undead Damage had done a number on him, but it hadn't slowed him down. If anything, he was picking up speed.

GothicTerror cast Mirrored Simulacrum, becoming three perfect duplicates of herself. All of them aimed their Undead Chaos Combo shot at the sprinting Herald.

"No. Run," Scott croaked at her. Dying was one thing. But he couldn't handle it if Nessa kicked the bucket IRL because of him. He wasn't ready to deal with losing somebody like that. Better for her to live. To get away and help guide the rest of the POSes to safety. "Fuck... off... Tots..."

"Not gonna happen." The trio of GothicTerrors let their glowing green arrows soar. "This jizzbrain spilled the last Mountain Dew Suicide in LA. He has to die."

Brilliant light seared across Scott's retinas as Darith flared with light, then dodged all three of GothicTerror's arrows like a tail runner making a fool out of a defensive line. In retaliation, the psycho yanked out a chromed-out Colt 1911 and squeezed off an overload of shots at the center Nessa like he had all the ammo cheat codes in the world to waste.

That Nessa flickered, then disappeared.

"Guess again, cockbreath," the GothicTerror farthest to the left said. She thrust out a hand and blasted the area at the Herald's feet with green light. "Jump Scare lets me move between duplicates. And this—"

Skeletal hands burst through the concrete of the gas station parking lot, grabbing for the closest enemy.

"—this lets me get handsy," she finished.

Scott's numb fingers finally bumped up against one of the Ultimate Healing potions he'd brought along.

"That pun sucked so much," he groaned as he yanked out the potion. "Leave the jokes—" He choked on a throatful of blood, finally hacking enough of it out of the way to finish the thought. "Leave them to me, Tots."

"Hey, good idea," she said, rolling her eyes, "use the last of your strength to insult the person saving you."

Her undead zombie hands latched onto Darith's boots and ankles, clawing at his legs. Their ragged nails left deep scratch marks in his armor. But instead of panicking or tripping over himself to get free—both of which Scott had seen mobs do when GothicTerror used the spell in their rescue missions—the nutcase giggled and started stomping on the hands like he was trying to beat the all-time high score on Squash-A- Bug.

Nessa took her chance, firing off another volley of Undead Chaos arrows while her remaining duplicate cast Necrotic Depletion, a super-slow drain Health spell that dealt steady DPS over time. A sick-looking aura engulfed the Herald, and a green haze sucked HP from his red bar and deposited it into hers. A little at a time, it started refilling the chunk Darith's bullets had taken out of it.

Scott was still fumbling with the damn cork in the Ultimate Healing Potion. Stupid blood loss and stupid numb fingers. Getting your guts sliced and diced was the worst.

Nessa snatched the potion out of his hands, ripped the cork free, then upended the bottle into his mouth. He chugged it—lamest keg stand ever—and immediately warmth and feeling returned to his limbs. His insides pulled back together, washing the pain away, and sealed up, leaving only a ragged hole in his armor as a reminder of just how powerful Darith was.

"I would've gotten it," he said, sitting up.

"Sure you would've." She gave him a hand, pulling him to his feet. "But we've got places to be tomorrow."

Just then, Helen Rose's voice popped into Scott's head. *The rig's being overrun. This douchebag brought a legit army.*

Yeah, I noticed. Tell Kevin to get the refugees the hell out of here, Scott sent back, searching the ground for his mace. It was lying next to a gas pump with blood splatter and a Ranger-Cleric-shaped dent in the side. *Nessa and I'll catch up as soon as we deal with this dickface.*

The connection cut off while the Druidic Skyguard relayed the message to the crew of the Witch, and Scott snatched up his dropped weapon.

Nearby, Darith was actually making progress with the grasping, undead hands. Yellowed bone crunched and splintered under his golden boots. Huh. Maybe stomping on the zombified hands was the way the developers had originally intended for people to escape that spell. It was surprisingly effective.

But before the loser could get free, Scott thrust out his free hand and spammed Darith with a deadly combo of Lightning Spear and Elemental Fury. The ratio of damage output to Magicka-usage was decent because of his last level-up, but against a Herald, they weren't the big guns, just something to keep him distracted. In Hearthworld's game of magical Rock, Paper, Scissors, Undead magic ate Divine magic's lunch every time.

As GothicTerror was about to demonstrate.

She traded her bow for her Cursed Crook and Rod set. They were exact replicas of the ones she'd gotten in their raid on the mummy pyramid in the Onyx Sands, black-and-gold Egyptian-style weapons, glowing toxic Mountain Dew Original green. They came fully furnished with two new Summon Undead spells from Hearthworld's final Expansion Pack and a metric asston of Necrotic Damage. Pretty sweet, and she had Scott to thank for it, because he was the one who'd introduced her to the benefits of being a Poser Owner.

GothicTerror raised the glittering weapons and, calling out a string of words that were definitely not English, she dual cast the Summon spells. The concrete beneath Scott's feet rumbled, and the smog overhead darkened, swirling into an angry looking thunderhead. A hot wind blasted through the parking lot, scouring the place with black sand from out of nowhere. The sand spun into a bunch of tiny dust devils, whipping up two slavering Rabid Jackals and two shambling Plague Mummies.

The sand blew away again, gone as fast as it had come, and the summoned creatures sprinted at the Herald, who was still mired in grasping undead hands.

Nessa hunched over with her hands on her knees, breathing hard.

Scott shook his head in disbelief. "What the hell? I thought you were going to flood this place with an army of the dead."

"How about you go eat a ginormous dick?" She panted. "The pharaoh we ganked for these things was a level 63 Cursed War Priest—they take a crapload of Stamina to dual-cast. A fifth of my overall for every pair of creatures."

The Plague Mummies weren't fast enough to get within arm's reach before Darith emptied his pistol into them, blowing fist-sized holes through their bandages and desiccated bodies. Their Health bars hit zero, and they exploded into a poof of dust and brittle wrappings.

Luckily, the Rabid Jackals were way more effective. They sprinted around the Mummies while Darith was riddling them with bullets, and closed in on him from behind like a pair of hunting rottweilers. The first one leapt and ripped into his wing, tearing out a mouthful of feathers. The second one latched onto the Herald's shoulder and growled, shaking his head like a junkyard dog.

The Message connection with Helen Rose opened again.

Kevin said he's not leaving without you, she sent, worry in her voice.

Tell that dweeb it's not up to him, Scott snapped. *I'm the boss here and I say GTFO. He's got the life of every person in that trailer in his hands. They're counting on him to be the big damn hero right now and burn rubber.*

I'll try, she replied.

Don't try, Scott snapped. *Just get it done. You're the social influencer. Influence him.*

Jesus. How was it so hard for people to understand that there wasn't trying in war? You did or you died.

While the Rabid Jackals tore at Darith, he hacked at them with the big-ass knife he'd been using to slice and dice Scott's guts and clubbed their golden-blood-soaked muzzles with the butt of his gun. His Health bar was plummeting, but he didn't seem to be getting any weaker. Even weirder, the psycho kept giggling like some kind of nutso serial killer.

"These doggies are a mighty fine trick," the douche said, grinning at GothicTerror crazily. "But I've got a good one, too. Want to see it?"

"Let me guess, all we've got to do is come back to your van to see it?" She rolled her eyes. "Forget it. I wouldn't even go if you were offering candy, and I love candy."

Darith's Health bar strobed out the Critical warning as it dropped below 10%.

Instead of freaking out and trying to save himself somehow, the Herald howled with laughter, doubling over and holding his guts.

Scott's hard-earned instincts from thousands and thousands of boss fights suddenly kicked in.

"Oh shit." He stowed his mace and double-fisted Lightning Lance and Elemental Fury. The purple in his filigreed Magicka bar dropped like crazy, plunging toward empty, but they had to finish this asshole ASAP. "Tots, kill him before—"

An intense bloodred glow shined from the Herald's torn and bloody skin, growing bigger and brighter every second.

"Freaking bullshit boss cheats," GothicTerror growled, spamming a double-dose of Necrotic Drain and Miasma of Death, even though they both knew it wasn't going to stop the oncoming tsunami of sewage they were about to eat.

As the last of Scott's Magicka ran out, a quest notification popped up in his face.

The Mad Butcher of LA

The only way out of this city is through the new boss of its mean streets, Darith niet Amstad, the Mad Butcher of LA.

Objective: Use all the resources at your disposal to kill the Mad Butcher.

Failure: Die at the hands of the Mad Butcher.

Restrictions: The only rule out here is there are no rules.

Penalty: Death, no respawn.

Reward: Title Warlord of the West, 50,000 Experience, 1,000 gold, Custom Scaling Item

Accept? Yes/No

"This is the new reality, and I want everybody West of the Rockies to know exactly who runs it." ~ PwnrBwner

Who or whatever was making up these quests must be a serious nutsack. Throwing his words back at him like that? Total dick move. Still, there wasn't any way around this. If he was going to stay in Shieldwall and run LA, he was going to have to take out Darith sooner or later. And based on the way this freak had leveled up over the past week, the sooner the better.

Scott accepted, and the notification disappeared—

—just in time for him to see Darith's body explode in a shower of golden ichor and feathers and Evolve into his final boss form.

CHAPTER 28
BATTLEFIELD REUNION

"You're certain we're getting closer to Frontflip, Trevor?" Griff asked, eyeing the lad wearing the baggy stocking cap and oddly tight pants. No maneuverability in a pair of britches like that, Griff thought for the hundredth time, no protective value either. The people of this world were a curious sort to be sure, though Griff had been working with Trevor over the past several days, doing his damndest to set the lad on the right path. He'd looted some modestly enchanted leather armor off a pack of goblins, and Trevor was now wearing it over his chest—though he had several colorful scarfs draped around his neck which he refused to discard even though they could pose a visibility threat and created the perfect handle for an enemy to grab in combat.

They were designer wear, Trevor insisted, which seemed to pass as his excuse for keeping them. Curious indeed.

Trevor had an obsidian blade on one hip, courtesy of Griff's Inventory, not that it would do the lad much good against any enemy that had an even passing understanding of battlecraft. Trevor was a nice enough sort, but Griff had never seen a slower study—not to mention the boy was as soft as a feather and rather lazy to boot. No desire to practice the sword forms or try any of Griff's physical training regimens.

"Are we getting closer or not?" the old man prodded again.

He and Mai stood at a crossroads, waiting while the lad squinted in each direction.

"I mean, yeah, definitely," Trevor finally said. "I'm pretty sure this is the way downtown." He held up the lifeless black rectangle he'd been consulting as if it were an oracle's clairvoyance orb. "I could tell you how close we were if my phone hadn't died."

Mai scowled. "If you knew the layout of your own land, you wouldn't need a map to find your way around."

Griff shot the young widow a warning look. The lass had a sharp tongue when she was frightened or frustrated, and these had been some of the most frightening and frustrating days Griff had ever lived through—and that included the siege against the Vault of the Radiant Shield. But just because tensions were running high didn't give her the right to lash out. The lad probably felt unmanned enough not being able to find his way around his own city.

Truth be told, Griff was starting to suspect the directionless wandering was a symptom of a larger problem for the folks here in Earth. Seemed like most of them were lost in one way or another—unable to protect themselves, find food for their bellies, or even a path through their own world. Griff wasn't one to pray to the gods regular-like, and he sometimes forgot to make offerings on the Volcanic and Lunar Solstices, but he hoped greater wisdoms than his own were directing fate. If they were, maybe it hadn't been a bad turn that brought him here. Maybe it had been a bit of divine intervention in these folks' favor.

Heavens knew they needed someone like him to show the

way, especially against the creatures that had once called Hearthworld home.

The lad stabbed the dead phone like a sword down one of the roads. "It's that way. I'm positive. Hundred percent."

Mai threw her hands up in disgust.

Before she could say anything too harsh, Griff stepped in. "We just came from that way, boyo."

"Dammit!" The lad deflated, eyes dropping back to the black face of the phone. "I'm usually better with directions than this."

"Sure, and I'm a dainty Summer Sylph, I am," Mai muttered under her breath. She scrubbed quickly at her eyes, trying to hide a tear. "We'll never get to my dear Kaz like this."

Griff patted her wide arm.

"Don't fret, lass." His eye swept the intersection's tallest building. A line of pipe had been attached to the bricks, extending down from the roof. He wasn't a Ranger or Stalker by any means, but he knew a few basics of survival. "I'll clamber up there and get a lookout. Should at least give us an idea of what we're heading into." And keep them from blundering into another nest of Chrysalizards, like they'd done only a few hours ago.

On his way past, Griff clapped the lad on the shoulder. "Give me a boost, son."

The lad leaned against the brick wall. Stepping on the boy's bent thigh, Griff reached up to the closest handhold he could find on the pipe and started shimmying up.

He was halfway to the top when he heard the crackling thunder of an Elemental Fury spell. That was trouble. There were few creatures powerful enough to cast magick of that sort, and none of them were the kind they wanted to square off against. The three of them wouldn't survive long against a Thunder Drake or a Greater Air Elemental. But Elemental Fury was also a spell common among Clerics, which meant it was possible there were heroes or other residents of Hearthworld up ahead. Either of which could prove just as dangerous in its own way.

Everyone was frightened, and many of the citizens of Hearthworld had joined up with the Heralds of Destruction, led by none other than Darith, that bald chap who'd been right hand to Lowen.

"Duck in somewhere 'til I see what we're up against," he called down to the others.

While they squeezed into the alleyway, Griff scrambled up the pipe. His wiry arms shook with exhaustion and effort as he pulled himself onto the roof.

Green, blue, and bloodred lights flashed to the east, where some huge strange metal beast was under attack by what looked like one of Darith's roving bands of mobs. The combatants fought only a pair of streets north of the road Griff, Mai, and Trevor had been taking. They had passed right below whatever ambush or trap touched off that particular skirmish, both unknowing and unscathed. Providence again, perhaps.

Best to continue on their way westward and avoid this fight. Griff didn't want to go to battle against anyone associated with the insane Herald, nor did he want to tangle against that fearsome metal beast, especially with Mai and the lad in tow. They wouldn't last a minute in such a bloody skirmish as that.

He was about to climb down and report the news to his traveling companions when he heard the faint shout of a familiar battle cry.

"FOR THE SALT!"

CHAPTER 29
BOSS BATTLE

Where Darith, the insane Herald, had been standing moments before was a thirty-foot-tall mothman kaiju with glowing bloody eyes the size of basketballs, a weird tube-shaped mouth whipping around like a sewer hose, and thick, fluttering wings covered in nasty moth dust that scattered with every twitch. In one hand, the kaiju carried a blood-splashed butcher's cleaver big enough to chop a city bus in half. In the other, he had a rusty meat hook.

"What the hell is with you people and your bug fetish?" Scott said as he hefted his mace. "First it was Roark and his creepy-ass spider girlfriend, now it's a nasty freaking moth?"

"Like it?" Darith's new voice buzzed, cut with shrieking high notes and rumbling low notes. "Just a little something I picked up for being the highest-level creature in this puny world."

GothicTerror's Jackals were still trying to tear into the monster, but they barely came up to his knees, and the damage the Undead dogs were dealing to his new massive Health bar was negligible. He shrugged them off without a problem, stomping one into paste with one weird round foot and chopping the other in half with a powerful swipe from his cleaver.

"Apparently the rules here are a little different from those of Hearthworld, but I don't mind." The kaiju Darith giggled, shaking the ground and rattling the windows in the Bell/gas station combo like a low-level earthquake. "I never bothered playing by anybody's rules anyway. And now that Lowen is gone and Marek is stuck in Terho, there's no one to put a muzzle on me anymore—just the way I like it," he tittered.

PwnrBwner, Kevin said—

No. Scott cut Helen Rose off, sick of this relay shit. He didn't have time to fight this battle on both fronts. *You get those people out of here if you have to fly into that cab and kick his ass for me. Do not take no for an answer.*

Finally, he heard the screech of brakes being released and the growl of the Witch grinding forward, out of the parking lot. A bit of tension drained from his muscles. At least this way he would know Kev and the rest had gotten out, even if he and Nessa didn't, and he wouldn't have to worry about saving a ton of innocent bystanders.

Scott rolled his shoulders and used the last dregs of his Magicka to cast Powerful Inspiration on himself and GothicTerror. Time to kick some giant moth ass.

As he sprinted toward the kaiju, Darith's giant foot—now fully the size of a sports car—rose and stomped directly at him. Would've been a helluva time to have his Magicka full. He could've cast Elemental Spikes and pinned this asshole in place, but his purple vial was sitting at zilch and he was out of Spirit Regen potions, because the universe was stacked against him. That was fine, though. The universe had always been stacked against him, yet here he was, a badass, hero, and the only thing standing between humanity and one crazy moth-er fucker. He would just have to melee the balls off this situation until his Magicka came back up to casting level.

The gargantuan foot shot toward him. Darith was a big bastard, but he wasn't fast. Scott threw himself into a shoulder roll and came up near the busted front window of the Bell.

The mothman's foot slammed into the concrete, sending out a gray-gold shock wave from the epicenter that shook the ground like a 7.8 on the Richter scale. Scott's legs buckled, dropping him onto his ass in the shattered glass bits and crumpled quesadilla wrappers.

[*You have resisted Paralyzing Stomp! Enemies in contact with the ground at the time of casting have a 30% chance of being knocked off their feet. Enemies with less than 30% Strength of caster will be Paralyzed for 2x seconds, where x is the caster's Character level.*]

The debris gritted under his boots and the palms of his gauntlets as he pushed himself to his feet. Good thing he'd leveled up so much before this fight or he would've been screwed.

By the gas pumps, GothicTerror was struggling to her feet, too. She had summoned a new set of Mummies and Jackals, but fat lot of good that was doing them. One was already a grease spot on the concrete, and the rest were frozen in place by the stomp.

The mothman chortled through his mouth hose, the humming, buzzing insect sound rattling the broken glass on the pavement.

"It's easy enough to avoid when you can see, eh?" He stomped on one of the Mummies and it exploded in a puff of bandages and skin dust. "Well, now try to dodge it blind."

Darith fluttered his grody moth wings. Clouds of gray-gold powder swirled into the air, whipping up a hot, disgusting dust storm that blew directly into Scott's eyes, nose, and mouth. It tasted putrid, and that was coming from a guy who ate Taco Bell for most of his meals and considered frozen chicken tendies fine dining. It also burned, fingers of the dust coating his teeth and tongue, trying to claw their way into the back of his throat.

"Ah, sick!" Scott coughed and spit, trying to get that shit out of his mouth.

[*You have resisted Lung Obstruction!*]

That would've been great, except his eyes were watering like crazy and he couldn't see anything. He'd been pepper sprayed once the year after he'd gotten out of high school—no fault of his own, of course. He'd been walking home after getting off at midnight and some lady had lost her shit when he passed her on the sidewalk, unloading a bright pink can of bear mace right into his face. Felt like getting hit in the eyes with a pot of boiling water; took three days before the pain was finally gone. This felt an awful lot like that.

[*You have been Blinded! Vision obscured for 30 seconds or until you rinse with a Collyrium Solution.*]

Scott rubbed frantically at his eyes, trying to get them open. He'd never even heard of a Collyrium Solution in Hearthworld, and the prompt hadn't said anything about the usual Health potion fix. Basically, it was saying he was screwed for the next thirty seconds.

A whistling sound made his pulse jackhammer in sheer unadulterated panic. Something was slicing through the air toward him, and his money said big-ass cleaver.

For a split second, fear rooted him to the spot. Scott had no idea which way to dodge. If he picked the wrong one, he could run right into the blade and finish this asshole's job for him.

Then Feral Senses kicked in. The hair on the back of his neck tingled, sensing an oncoming threat from his right. He threw out his hand, casting Shield Ward with the sliver of Magicka that had regenerated, then ducked under the swing.

The cleaver blade scraped across the magical barrier, buckling Scott's arm and taking a handful of HP with its Blunt Force trauma.

It didn't chop him in half, though, so net gain.

He dug a vial of pitch from his belt and launched it in the direction Feral Senses claimed Darith was. A second later he was rewarded with a glassy smash as the bottle shattered.

From off to his left, he heard the sizzle of GothicTerror casting some Undead spell. He still couldn't see jack shit.

"Tots, you got any Collyrium Solutions?" Scott yelled, scrubbing at his watering eyes.

"A what solution?" Her reply was hoarse. The dust must've gotten her.

"Forget it. Are you blind, too?"

Another stomp shook the ground, but this time Scott kept his feet. He didn't hear any slipping and sliding from the kaiju, so he must've avoided the pitch. Or maybe the puddle it had made was too small to affect such a huge monster. Scott grabbed a handful of the vials and launched them with reckless abandon. They smashed against the concrete, but there was no way to tell if they had landed in a good spot or not. Being blind in combat fucking sucked.

GothicTerror let out a bloodcurdling screech that morphed into a series of hacking coughs halfway through. She'd been hit, and there was no way for Scott to know how bad it was. She was still choking, but that could mean basically anything from she was bleeding out to she was still clogged up with that moth dust. He had just enough Magicka back in his gauge to hit her with a Fast-Healing Blast, but he needed line of sight or a laying on of hands to cast it.

"Tots, you all right?"

She didn't answer.

He sprinted toward the sound of choking, letting Feral

Senses lead him along, swinging his mace in front of him like a blind man's cane on steroids. The mace grazed something that growled at him.

One of Nessa's Jackals.

"Quit dicking around and attack the giant moth, jackoff," Scott snapped at it and kept moving.

He didn't have time to find out whether the Jackal would have obeyed him. A rib-shattering kick from a massive foot slammed him into the Undead canine, tearing away a full quarter of his Health and sending them both tumbling ass over teakettle across the parking lot. Scott and the Jackal landed in a tangle of armor and weapons and nasty-ass dog breath. Scott tried to shove the creature off him, but the thing must've had zero Intelligence, because its fitful struggles just made everything worse.

Moron dog.

Mothman Darith's giant cleaver whistled through the air. Feral Senses told Scott it was coming for him, but he couldn't get out from underneath the thrashing Jackal. There would be no dodging this time. He braced himself, preparing for the sharp and final bite of enchanted steel.

There was a sick *thunk*, and the Jackal yelped like a kicked dog, then went limp. Hot, sludgy, Undead blood oozed onto Scott. But he was alive, and all of his limbs still seemed to be attached to his body, which was a huge win all things considered.

Gagging at the rotting meat stench, he rolled the lifeless Summoned off him and stumbled to his feet. He couldn't hear Nessa's choking anymore; his head was spinning like crazy and there was a weird rushing sound in his ears that drowned out every other noise. Almost a whirring.

Feral Senses freaked out at an incoming blade, and Scott

threw himself out of the way, hitting the renewal on Holy Reckoning just in time.

The cleaver clipped him, slicing effortlessly through his pauldron, laying his shoulder open to the bone and making his arm go dead in the process. Scott's knees buckled from the sudden spike of pain, and the mace slipped out of his fingers and clattered across the pavement.

"Son of a—"

"You think you can defeat me?" The mothman shrieked in that earsplitting mix of high and low tones. "Darith is the new Tyrant King of this world, and you're nothing but the chattel. *King* Darith." He giggled, the sound ending on a high, almost questioning note that sent chills down Scott's spine. "Welcome to the slaughtering yard, little lambies."

An earth-shaking boom thundered off the buildings. Darith roared, and metal screamed and crunched.

Finally, the blindness flickered and light and color flooded back in. Scott winced at the sudden brightness.

Across the parking lot, the mothman was pushing himself up off the crumpled gas pump roof while white firefighting foam rained down from the ripped metal.

And... Wait... Was the douchebag bleeding?

Someone shoved a potion bottle into Scott's good hand.

"I told you Hearthworld goes overboard with the villain monologuing." Kellie's voice was tinny and canned coming from the Shieldwall-issue helmet. "But you were all like, 'No, it makes the quests more satisfying. It's totally great.' Barf."

"The fuck are you doing here?" Scott snapped. "I told your brother to get everybody out."

"No assholes left behind, asshole." Kel hefted her double-headed axe onto her shoulder. The axe looked as heavy as she was, but thanks to the strength buffs built into the armor, she handled the thing like it was a whiffle ball bat. "Stop micromanaging for one second and drink the friggin' Health potion, dingus."

"Don't tell me what to do." Scott shotgunned the potion. The Witch was parked along the far side of the Bell, stabilizing jacks down and cannon whirring into position for another shot.

That's what I was trying to tell you, Helen Rose's Message popped into his head. *Kevin said he was turning the Winch Witch around so he could get into firing position.*

Another explosion shook the world as the Witch's cannon boomed. A cannonball slammed into Mothman Darith, slapping him backward and finally ripping the foam-spraying canopy off its pillars. The Mad Butcher of LA screeched and fluttered his broken wings, but they were pinned between him and the twisted metal. When he tried to get up, his feet hit a puddle of pitch and slipped uselessly across the concrete.

Best of all, the cannon blasts had taken a massive chunk off the psycho's Health bar.

Kellie took the fall as her cue. Letting out a scream that was nowhere near as impressive as her in-game rog's berserker roar, she sprinted toward the fallen mothman and started chopping away at knees, ankles, and elbows, hitting all the major joints down one side, then running for the other.

And she wasn't the only one.

"For PwnrBwner, for Shieldwall, and FOR THE SALT!" Kaz charged out from behind the Witch with the rest of the Poser Owners following in his wake.

Scott watched in amazement as the tanks and DPS like Ninjastein, Flappie, and Buster rocked up to the party with Kaz and Kel, while the newbie casters like Tomahiro and Arjun actually stayed at range like they were supposed to and threw everything they had at the boss. Shadow Puppets climbed into the mothman's eyes and ears, fiery Meteoric Blasts rained down on him—Helen Rose even got into the fight with a double fist of Tornadic Force.

Two honks on the Witch's train horn sent everybody scrambling back. Kevin must've warned them that was the signal.

The cannon roared again, this time unleashing one of the exploding shots. It hit Darith right under the chin and detonated, ripping off most of his jaw and the firehose of a moth mouth.

"Eat a dick," Scott whooped.

He snatched up his mace and sprinted into the fray with the rest of his party.

Motion in his peripheral caught his attention. People were running across the street toward the giant boss fight. One looked like a refugee in his dumb beanie and skinny jeans, except he was also carrying an obsidian shortsword, which was weird as hell. And the other two...

Griff and Mai?

The weapons trainer had pulled out his usual sword and buckler, while the big-bodied blonde chick was wielding a frying pan like a warhammer. What in the hell was going on? Maybe he was dying and this was his brain bleeding out.

Naw. Scott was too awesome to die. After all, he was the main character, and the MC never died.

Scott forced himself to focus. Why Griff and Mai were here was something to wonder about later. After they finished this shit. And he definitely didn't need Kaz distracted. The Gourmet was kicking major ass with his Legendary Meat Tenderizer, oblivious to everything else.

Hopping over a flailing moth arm, Scott landed on Darith's chest. Feral Senses warned him in time to duck under the incoming cleaver—though this time the blow was sloppy and slow. Made out of desperation. Scott spun on his heel and swung his mace like a bat. Darith didn't have the reflexes to dodge. The blunt weapon of mass destruction slammed into the back of his hand, and Scott was rewarded with the *crack* of a giant bone breaking.

Under their combined attack, the boss-level Health bar was dropping. Down, down, down, they were eating away at it like some kind of super awesome ad for teamwork.

Which was great and heartwarming and all, but Scott was ready to end this.

Using his Ranger balance and agility, he leapt onto Darith's face.

"This is my town, motherfucker." Scott planted his feet and spammed a dual cast of Elemental Fury right between the douchebag's giant red eyes. Power surged along his arms and rammed into the downed kaiju like a freight train.

The mothman let out a bone-shaking scream as his Health bar flashed the critical below 10% warning.

Scott didn't relent, triggering Lightning Lance. Brilliant arcs of electric blue power surged through Darith's body. The giant meat cleaver fell from his oversized hand as his body seized and shook, Health dropping to 5% as Scott's Magicka ran dry. Didn't matter. He raised his mace high overhead and activated Blunt Force Barrage as he brought the weapon crashing down in the center of the monster's forehead with a sickening crack. Chips of bone and blood sprayed up in an arc, splattering Scott's armor.

[Critical Hit! 2x Damage!]

The last sliver of red disappeared from Darith's Health bar as his crazy thrashing ceased and his body finally went still. The Mad Butcher of LA was dead.

Scott smirked, covered in gore, and raised the mace overhead. "All hail Lord PwnrBwner, the Warlord of the West."

CHAPTER 30
CLOSING IN

Roark returned, transformed, to the Radiant Citadel ready to implement the rune of power the Tower had shown him. Unfortunately, fate had other ideas. The Throne Room was teeming with grim faces. Zyra, Randy, Talise, and Albrecht were locked in a heated discussion that cut off the instant Roark strode into the room. Even Mac's orange head looked a trifle abashed at his arrival.

"Is that… Roark?" Randy asked, voice shocked, eyebrows climbing high.

"The last thing I remember," Zyra said, regarding him from behind the lacy black curtain of her veil, "you were trying to find a way to put a damper on Marek's curse. Now you have six wings, a crown of fire, and armor made from bone." She tapped her bottom lip. "Which isn't to say I don't approve. I'm just curious about the how of it."

"It's a long story," Roark replied, raising his clawed hands, bringing silence to the room again. "One involving forest spirits, a tower at the center of the universe, and questionable substances."

He launched into a brief recounting of the events—his hunt

and subsequent battle against the maka-ronin, king of wolves, the meeting with Karasuno and his drug-fueled odyssey to the heart of the universe, and the shocking revelation about Marek's bloody past. Roark ended with an overview of his new Divine Soul Shaman class and transformation. The only thing he held back was the rune imparted to him by the Tower. He couldn't afford to tip his hand until he was absolutely certain the mad plan he had in mind would work.

"We knew Marek wasn't from our world," Albrecht said, shaking his head, "but a conqueror from the stars? It explains so much."

"It also tells us he won't stop until he's accomplished his goals, as if that were ever in question," Talise offered dryly. "His threat to annihilate every living soul on our world was not made idly." She unfurled a map and traced a finger along its face, finally coming to a stop at a speck of a village less than fifty miles from Korvo's fortified walls. "His army is on the march. That's what we were discussing so... *vigorously* in your absence, Roark."

"They aren't just marching," Albrecht snapped. "They're sacking every village and town from the edge of the mountains to the Hebi. The madman is completely wiping out the inhabitants, the livestock, the crops, and salting the earth behind. Frahoi's next, assuming it hasn't fallen already."

The first thought that crossed Roark's mind was that this was the reason he couldn't keep up with Marek's leveling. The death of one ordinary human couldn't afford the killer much Experience, but slaughtering hundreds, if not thousands, would grow that number disturbingly large. The bloody tyrant would also know such an act would demand an answer from Roark. In fact, he would be counting on it.

"Marek said it himself before he butchered his generals." Talise thumbed the hilt of her golden rapier. "He doesn't need humanity anymore. We were just a means to an end for him, and now that he has a better one—mobs he can spawn himself—there's no reason to keep us around."

Zyra cocked her hip and crossed both pairs of human arms. "They've been bemoaning it ever since the first half-burnt and bloodied survivor crawled into Korvo. I told them if the Tyrant King let even one of them escape, then he can't be doing a very good job wiping out the species, but they won't shut up about it."

"It's not an accident," Randy said, echoing Roark's thoughts. "He meant for the refugees to make it here. It's a type of psychological warfare that's been around since medieval times—uh, in my world, anyway. You leave one survivor from every village to tell the tale and strike fear into the stronghold you're trying to target."

"Or to act as his spy or assassin," Zyra pointed out. Her lacy black veil turned Roark's direction. "But they won't let me kill the survivors, either, which was my second suggestion."

"It's less about spying and more about morale," Randy said. "He wants to destroy whatever faith the citizens of Korvo have built up under Roark's rule."

"As far as I know, that isn't working yet," Albrecht said, his scarred face twisted into a frown. "The people of Korvo don't believe they're in any danger as long as they're within the walls. However, they are talking about rallying a band of men to ride out and defend the next villages in the Tyrant King's path." He paused, a scowl of disapproval marring his already twisted face. "The new weapons and armor you've given them seem to have created an overabundance of confidence."

Roark cursed. "That's just as bad. They won't last a full minute against Marek's forces, even with the magickal weapons and armor. Worse, they've likely got family in those villages. If I stop them from leaving to fight or refuse to send a contingent to defend the villages, I'll be seen as an insular coward only concerned with my holdings. They'll ride out anyway and force me to either make an example of them like a bloody tyrant or pretend I didn't notice and appear weak and ineffectual."

"All of which I can guarantee you Marek already knows," Talise said. "This is nothing more than a large-scale game of Rivals to him."

"So let him play," Zyra snapped. "The best way to beat a tyrant is to cut his head off and stop the game at its source." She stabbed a finger at Roark. "You taught me that. The pawns are no concern of ours unless they lead to his defeat."

Roark grimaced. Though she wasn't wrong, that wasn't how he'd meant for his tangles with the Dungeon Lords of Hearthworld to come off.

"This isn't a game, Zyra," he said softly. "The people dying are not pawns, and they won't respawn. These are my people. Half the towns and cities here hid me when I worked for the resistance, and the other half kept me fed when I was just a street rat dipping my grubby hands into their pockets. I can't leave them at the Tyrant King's mercy. I won't."

Albrecht snorted. "As if that's any different from disappearing for six months."

In a flash of feathers and hiss of steel, the tip of Talise's rapier was at the burn-scarred mage's throat.

"Don't you dare speak of my brother that way," she said, her voice icy. "He was fighting a war you cannot fathom in a world that would have crushed a pathetic seafoam noble such as yourself in an instant, and he did it all for your sake and the sake of everyone in this bloody damned world. You'll speak to him with respect, or I'll make sure you never speak again."

Though it warmed the pit in his chest to hear his sister defend his choices, Roark suspected a good amount of her fury came from her own guilt at having served Marek for so long without stopping him herself. She'd only done what was necessary to survive, but obviously she was still unable to forgive herself for those years.

Roark grabbed Talise's rapier hand and shoved the blade down.

"Marek knows what he's doing well." He sighed. "He's dividing us as much as he is the people of Korvo. If we let him sow dissention in our ranks, then there's no bloody way we can hope to defeat him." He looked to Albrecht, who was gingerly checking his throat for holes. "You said the Tyrant King's next target is Frahoi?"

"Ask your sister," he said, his voice dripping with disapproval.

Roark raised an eyebrow at Talise.

"Marek's been sending me visions of the plundering as it happens," Talise said.

"Tell your brother how the Tyrant King's able to accomplish it," Albrecht said in a self-righteous tone that made Roark want to knock his teeth down his throat. Once this was finished, the less time he spent around the burn-scarred mage the better off they would both fare.

Talise pressed her lips into an annoyed line. "Marek is still technically my Feudal Lord. Apparently, he'll remain so until I vow allegiance to another lord."

"He's messaging you from his grimoire," Roark said, catching on.

"That should be a pretty easy fix, shouldn't it?" Randy offered. He tipped his head to indicate Roark. "You just so happen to be related to a different Feudal Lord."

Talise fixed the Arboreal Herald with a flat, icy stare that reminded Roark intensely of their father. Never one for disdainful rebukes, Sir Erich had been able to silence a room with his cool gray gaze alone.

Randy shifted his weight and bumped his fists against his legs awkwardly.

"It's just... Isn't it a little much to be picky about right now? I mean, under the circumstances? If it's just sibling rivalry—"

"It isn't," she said.

"Then why in the seven hells fight it?" Albrecht threw his hands up. "There's a war going on, girl! This isn't the time for another pigheaded von Graf tantrum—"

"Von Reich," Roark snapped, "I've been civil to you for as long as I can manage. If you can't shut your bloody mouth, I'll let Talise cut you a new one below your chin." Before the mage could sputter out his affront, Roark turned to Randy. "Talise doesn't have to swear fealty to anyone."

For a moment, his sister looked as startled as everyone else in the room. Surprised gratitude washed across her face, but she quickly covered it with a bored aristocratic indifference to rival even Marek Konig Ustar's.

"In fact," Roark continued, "her ability to communicate directly with the Tyrant King solves a problem I've been trying to find a way around. Thanks to the knowledge I gained from my vision quest I have a new plan. A plan that can finish this once and for all, but for it to have any chance of success, I'll need someone who can let him know when I'm most vulnerable. Zyra was right—we need to take Marek out. Without him his army will fail and turn on each other like the disloyal dogs they are. But everything hinges on being able to separate Marek from his forces. I need to meet him on the field of battle, one on one."

"Let me get this straight." Zyra raised a hand to stop him. "You want the Undead God-Pharaoh you can barely keep level with to attack you? While you're at your weakest?" She huffed a humorless laugh. "I'm the real fool here for hoping you had come up with something sane. You'd think I would know better at this point."

Roark gave her a smirk. "Wait until you hear what I want to do to Korvo's defenses."

"Bloody Jotnars." Zyra's snowy ringlets and lacy veil swayed as she shook her head. She sighed. "Go ahead, Griefer. Shock us further."

Canting his head in a wry bow, Roark turned back to his sister. "As Feudal Lord, Marek wouldn't have to be with the armies to have a remote view of their raiding. Is there anything in the messages he's sent you that indicates he's actually moving with his forces?"

"Yes." With a wave of her hand, Talise created an opaque veil of orange light like a tapestry on a bare spot of Throne Room wall.

Blood-soaked, firelit images raced across the tapestry, showing a host of Undead chimeras sweeping through the villages of Traisbin. Roark recognized the little rustic town of Tanner's Respite alongside majestic cities like Olanspire and Wermentaer. Rabid Jackals and Sacred Bastets tore screaming humans to shreds. Homes, businesses, farmsteads, and fields burned while Soul Devourers ripped the former inhabitants into chunks of meat that they shook down their greedy gullets.

But the creatures of Hearthworld weren't the only attackers in Marek's pillaging bands. There were humans as well—not healthy, living people, but rotting muddy corpses who looked as if they'd been torn from their grave. Though the monsters frightened the citizens, these resurrected beings brought about the true horrors. People collapsed before them, weeping and shaking their heads in disbelief, unable to move or defend themselves, or worse, they ran to embrace the dead only to be torn apart by them.

"Corpsewalkers," Talise said. "He can't reanimate them

without being present, and so far he's used them at every location."

"Oh my gosh, they're family members," Randy cut in in quiet horror. "Reanimated loved ones."

Talise nodded grimly and shifted to another bloody scene. "He doesn't use the corpsewalkers often—I think even with the World Stone it takes too much power to pull them up out of the local resting places—but their presence means he was at the site of each attack."

"That's so evil," Randy whispered.

"And effective," she said. "Even the strongest warriors lose all will to fight when they see their mother or cousin or brother tearing their children apart."

Roark couldn't find a voice to weigh in. His eyes were locked on a familiar face among the corpsewalkers. Formerly golden hair hung in stringy bunches around cheeks blackened with rotting blood and pecked at by the merciless beaks of carrion birds. A thick rope abrasion encircled her neck like a torque.

Danella.

He shook his head.

"That's not possible." He heard himself speaking as if it were someone else. "I wrote her a seal. I snuck into the lime pit and put it in her pocket..."

"You know one of these corpsewalkers?" Albrecht's voice snapped Roark out of his denial.

Everyone in the Throne Room was staring at him. Roark cleared his throat and straightened up, attempting to shake off the shock.

"No. She's an illusion. She has to be. The girl I knew was sealed against resurrection and desecration." Sealing the Dead was the first writ his father had taught him, the greatest responsibility of a nobleman to his people, ensuring that nothing and no one could tear them away from the afterlife.

"I've seen the Stone do that and worse in Marek's hands, Roark," Talise said. "You need to prepare yourself for anything. Whatever you're planning, know for certain that he'll throw everything he can at you to stop it."

Roark steeled himself and gave a sharp nod. He would face down whatever nightmares Marek had to offer, consoled by the knowledge that he would make the monster pay all the more for his crimes.

"I've got some crafting to do before I can enact this plan," Roark said. "In the meantime, I have missions for each of you. To start, we'll head off the unrest in Korvo by sending out a contingent to protect Frahoi." He was tempted to restrict the company to mobs only, but knew he would only be asking for trouble if he tried. "Albrecht, tell the people of Korvo that they can join if they wish, but only if they're single men, of age, and without a parent or child dependent on them."

With a grunt, Albrecht agreed. "Though I doubt they'll be any more receptive to these restrictions than you would be if it was your family."

"I can't control them," Roark said, "but I can let them know the risks. Death is likely, and they must know that before venturing into the fray. Whatever they decide beyond that is on their own head."

"I'll lead them," Talise said.

"Absolutely not," Roark said. "Albrecht will lead them."

The scar-faced mage nodded. "A wise choice."

Talise scowled. "Are you afraid I'll desert back to Marek's side?"

"A girl who's flipped allegiances once and won't swear her loyalty to the new Feudal Lord she claims to serve is apt to do anything," Albrecht muttered.

"That's got nothing to do with it," Roark snapped, slicing a hand through the air to stop their bickering. "Albrecht is going because the villagers know and trust him. You may have been born here, but they haven't seen you in twenty years, Talise. You're nothing but a demon from another world to them, especially wearing the skin of the Malaika Heralds they saw serving Marek these last six months. More importantly, I need you here and ready to message the bloody tyrant. I want him to attack the moment everything is in place. The sooner we finish this, the less the people of Traisbin will have to suffer."

She fixed him with an icy glower, but amazingly didn't argue.

"Randy, I need you to assemble the allied Dungeon Lords of the Troll Nation. The last leg of this ploy is going to be the hardest, and we'll need their support."

"Okay, I'm on it," the Arboreal Herald said. "But what if they want to know what all that entails before they agree?"

"Tell them their part will require being ready to move—not just as a forward offensive maneuver, but their entire dungeon. They are to assemble their troops and be prepared to set up shop in an altogether new location. For good or ill, this is likely the last most of them will ever see of Terho."

Randy froze, and a tense silence fell over the room.

"If it were me, I'd leave out the 'for good or ill' bit," Zyra drawled, finally breaking the quiet.

"That... does sound pretty ominous," Randy admitted. "But also, most of the allied Dungeon Lords have gotten attached to the way things work here. I think resettling gave them a feeling of security after what happened with Hearthworld. It's going to really upset some of them that you're pulling the rug out from under them again." He reached for his missing spectacles, then dropped his hand to the back of his neck and rubbed it uncomfortably. "And honestly, I don't think any of them have ever heard that old saying about not shooting the messenger. Telling the Dungeon Lords that you're planning to displace them again kind of sounds like a suicide mission."

"They won't be seeing this world again," Roark repeated, "but that is only because they will each be getting worlds of their own. Tell them that, and I think they'll be only too happy to help."

Randy blinked. "Wow. Okay, yeah. That's a pretty good incentive." He nodded resolutely. "I won't let you down."

Roark stuck out his hand and gripped Randy's forearm. "I know I can count on you, Randy Shoemaker. You're a hero to your soul."

Lastly, he turned to Zyra. "The people of this world are at a disadvantage because they can't use magick or level up, but do you think there's any sort of potion you can create which will work on them? Perhaps give them greater strength or speed, something along those lines?"

"The Ultimate Healing Potions worked on the humans in the Devs' home world without any adverse side effects," she said. "The few people here who would let me experiment on them seemed to do well with my brews. With the right reagents and a little time, I should be able to come up with something to fortify the body. Temporarily at least. Perhaps even permanently."

"Get it done as soon as you can," Roark said. "I don't think I'll be able to hold back the defenders for more than a few hours."

Zyra snorted. "I'll have it for you long before they're ready to ride out."

With the tasks assigned, they went their separate ways, emptying the room until only Roark and Mac remained.

"Fancy a bit of crafting, boy?" Roark scratched each of the Elemental Turtle Dragon's scaly heads in turn. "The forge doesn't have a chair for you to steal, but it does have a roaring fire to curl up in."

Mac blinked, all six of his eyes managing to remain out of sync, then he chirped in happy agreement. He scampered up the wall and onto the ceiling like a beast a fraction of his weight and preceded Roark out of the Throne Room.

CHAPTER 31
WARLORD OF THE WEST

A quest notification popped into Scott's field of vision.

Congratulations! Using everything at your disposal, you have completed the quest the Mad Butcher of LA and slain Darith niet Amstad!
You have officially earned the title Warlord of the West, with all its attendant loot, perks, and responsibilities.
Activate your Dungeon Lord's Grimoire for a full list of benefits!

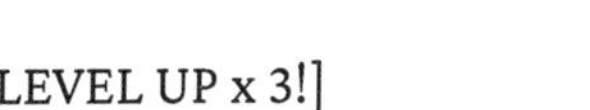

[LEVEL UP x 3!]
[You have 30 undistributed Stat Points.]

"WHATEVER," he muttered, blinking the notices away. The levels and gold weren't important right now. What was important was finding Nessa.

He shoved his way through the cheering POSes, ignoring their congrats and slaps on the back. He slipped past Griff, giving the trainer a silent nod and getting back the same. How the skill trainer had gotten here was still a mystery, but that mystery was on the list of crap to figure out later. Unlike everyone else, the old dude didn't try to stop him or even slow him down—he looked like he understood why Scott wasn't in a celebrating mood yet.

Kaz and Mai appeared in his path, the giant widow throwing herself into the equally giant Gourmet's arms.

"Mai found Kaz!" the big blue dude howled, tears racing down his fat cheeks. "She followed the clues in the videos back to her Kaz!"

Mai squeezed his huge head between her pink hands and gave him a loud kiss. "Be sure I'll always find you, my love, clues or no."

Scott didn't slow down; he couldn't deal with their PDA overdose right then. He'd rarely been happier for anyone who wasn't himself, but Kaz was a good guy and an OG brawler; if anyone deserved a happy ending it was him. Still, backslapping and ass grabbing could wait. He had to locate Nessa.

He froze for a beat, a lump lurching up into his throat and a hard knot forming in the pit of his stomach. There, by the shattered windows of the Bell... Nessa was on her side in a pool of blood, arms wrapped around her stomach. Not moving. Not breathing. Her dark skin had taken on an ugly blue-gray undertone that scared Scott more than any stupid endgame boss. She looked dead. And not the cool kind of dead goth chicks dug, the shitty kind you never come back from.

On legs that suddenly felt shaky and weak, Scott stalked to her body.

"Tots." That came out like a whisper, too scared and sick to really be his voice. He cleared his throat and gave it another shot. "Hey, Tots, you okay?"

No answer.

This wasn't the way it was supposed to go down. He was the hero. The hero got the chick and lived happily ever after, kicking ass and taking names from their Mad Max dungeon mansion in the middle of post-apocalyptic LA. The hero didn't lose the chick who'd just burrito toasted him this morning. She couldn't be dead.

Kneeling, Scott put both hands on her arm. Her skin was icy. He shook her, trying to jar her awake. She didn't resist or groan or respond in any way. With shaky hands, he rolled her onto her back and saw the problem right away. There was a fist-sized hole in her side. Her armor was dented and ripped open like a tin can, and a dark wound, vibrant red around the edges, stared at him like an unblinking eye. He bent double, pressing his ear against her chest.

Maybe...

He thought he heard the faintest *thump*. Weak and faltering. He needed a Ultimate Healing Potion and he needed it right fucking now, but he didn't have one, and Nessa was out, too. But he wasn't completely out of options. He was a Cleric, and though he'd specialized in offensive and DPS magic over spamming heals—Clerics had some badass buffs and Divine Magic was serious OP—he did have one healing cantrip that he could cast at will.

"This isn't going to work," he muttered. She was already gone and he knew it. But he wasn't going to sit there like a bitch and do nothing. "Screw it."

Scott pressed his hands flat against her chest and triggered Fast-Healing Blast.

Gold light spread across her skin like a spiderweb, making

her look momentarily better, but that faded the second the spell ended.

He swallowed around the lump in his throat. How was it possible that he could feel numb and like he'd been kicked in the balls at the same time? Worse than that. Like somebody had scraped out his guts and left him with this big hollow cavity inside. He'd won. That was supposed to count for something, but this was bullshit unfairness at its worst.

Nessa gasped and her eyes flew open wide.

Her gaze landed on Scott's face and traveled down to his hands, still planted firmly against her chest.

"Perv," she grunted.

Scott pulled his hands away with a scowl. "It's not like that."

"Yeah, I know," she replied with a weak grin. Then, with a wince, "Crap that hurt." She fumbled at her side; the skin had knit itself shut, but there was still a black and blue bruise, surrounded by a halo of ugly yellow skin. "Thanks for the heal. I always forget you're supposed to be half Cleric. You don't act like one."

Scott turned his face away and dragged a hand across his nose. "Ugh, fucking moth dust got my sinuses running like crazy."

Nessa sat up with a groan and pulled her hands away from her side. She had something white and purple clutched between her fingers. Her smashed Suicide cup.

Scott blinked. "Holy shit, did that thing save your life?"

"Are you serious?" She held it up, one eyebrow cocked at him. "This is plastic, dumbass."

"I was just asking, jeez! You had it against your wound like it was stopping the bleeding or deflecting the killing blow or something. What the hell was I supposed to think?"

"It blew over to where I landed, and I was really heartbroken about that Suicide being spilled." She shrugged. "Especially since you went in there just to make it for me."

"Yeah, I guess that does make it pretty special," he admitted. "I'm basically a pro at making them."

She snorted. "Scott, it's special because I like you."

Scott grinned, then realized he probably looked like a goober, and went for a cool smirk instead. "Obviously. What's not to like?"

That made her laugh, like almost insultingly hard.

"Whatever." Scott rolled his eyes. "Maybe I like you, too, even though you're an Uberbitch."

She leaned over and kissed him on the cheek. "You like me *because* I'm an Uberbitch."

Together, they got up and went to the Winch Witch, where Kevin and Cranko were celebrating their victory by checking the rig over—the reward for work well done was more work to do—while Kel lounged around and sharpened her axe's heads.

Scott spun the little dweeb of a driver around to face him.

"You're a dick for not listening to me and getting out of here," he said. "But your cannon shredded that loser."

Kellie rolled her eyes. "Nice way to say thanks, dick."

But Kev got it. He smiled and stuck out his hand. "No problem, dude."

Scott grabbed it and pulled him into a bro-hug, then he pulled Kellie off her perch and bro-hugged her, too.

"You two made a shitty party in-game, but IRL, you're decent. Even without magical superpowers."

"Hey, asshole, we're way better than—"

"Enough of the sticky, gooey emotional shit," Scott said, cutting Kellie off. He jerked his chin at the Witch. "How soon can she get back on the road? We've got places to be and refugees to save."

It took a while to reload the shots they'd used on Darith and make sure everybody injured had been Healed or drank a Health potion. While that was going on, Scott snuck back inside and made one last sixteen-flavor Mountain Dew Suicide. The Xiwi Xtreme ran out on him after just a little splutter, but Gothic-Terror didn't complain when she tasted it. She even snuck him another kiss, which was pretty rad.

Scott had just enough time before the convoy rolled out to distribute his stat points and go over his awesome new Warlord gains. Between the Gronions, pwning the Mad Butcher of LA and his lackeys, and the quest bonus of 50,000 Experience, Scott had jumped from Level 20 right up to Level 32. Not game breaking and still not on the level of that douche Bad_Karma, but since this was real life and not just a shitty video game anymore, that was pretty damned respectable. Probably even more respectable than Karma's hard mode levels in-game. Truth be told, Scott was likely the highest-level *real* player in the world, barring Randy—who wasn't on Earth.

Roark and Kaz were higher, but they weren't human, so they didn't count. Monsters' levels didn't translate the same way that human levels did—and based on what he'd seen that was as true in Hearthworld as it was here. Basically, what it boiled down to was that he was the best. Period. And if there were a couple asterisks next to that, then it was just because some people were so awesome that they created extenuating circumstances wherever they went.

Distributing his points was easy enough. As a Soulguard Ranger, his build was heavily skewed toward Strength and Constitution, which allowed him to tank mobs and dish out some serious blows. Even though he was a Ranger, Dexterity was his dump stat because all of his weapon damage and hit chance was based on his Strength Score—part of the reason this build was so popular. His Spell Strength was also based on his Strength Modifier, but his actual Divine Magick Reserve was still tied to Intelligence, just like a typical spell-caster type.

After getting his guts shredded by Darith, Scott decided having a little extra Constitution was probably a good thing. He dumped fifteen points in it, added five to Strength—because hitting shit hard was the best—and dropped the last ten into Intelligence, giving his Magicka Reserve and Regen a decent bump.

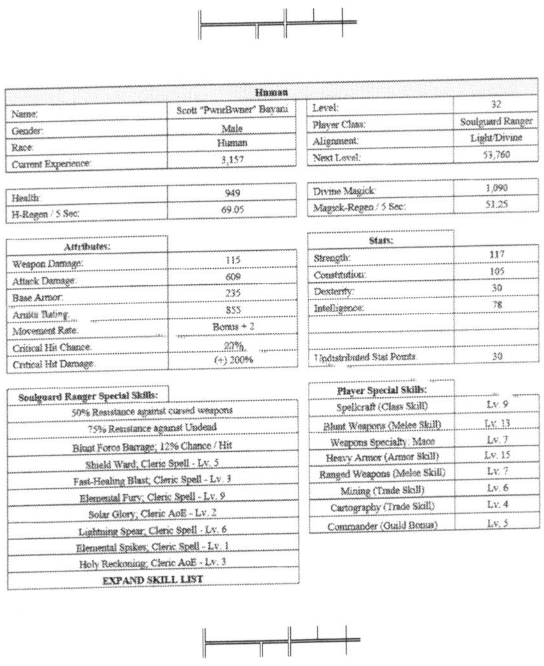

Human			
Name:	Scott "PwnrBwner" Bayani	Level:	32
Gender:	Male	Player Class:	Soulguard Ranger
Race:	Human	Alignment:	Light/Divine
Current Experience:	3,157	Next Level:	53,760

Health:	949	Divine Magick:	1,090
H-Regen / 5 Sec:	69.05	Magick-Regen / 5 Sec:	51.25

Attributes:		Stats:	
Weapon Damage:	115	Strength:	117
Attack Damage:	609	Constitution:	105
Base Armor:	235	Dexterity:	30
Armor Rating:	855	Intelligence:	78
Movement Rate:	Bonus + 2		
Critical Hit Chance:	20%		
Critical Hit Damage:	(+) 200%	Undistributed Stat Points:	30

Soulguard Ranger Special Skills:
50% Resistance against cursed weapons
75% Resistance against Undead
Blunt Force Barrage; 12% Chance / Hit
Shield Ward; Cleric Spell - Lv. 5
Fast-Healing Blast; Cleric Spell - Lv. 3
Elemental Fury; Cleric Spell - Lv. 9
Solar Glory; Cleric AoE - Lv. 2
Lightning Spear; Cleric Spell - Lv. 6
Elemental Spikes; Cleric Spell - Lv. 1
Holy Reckoning; Cleric AoE - Lv. 3
EXPAND SKILL LIST

Player Special Skills:	
Spellcraft (Class Skill)	Lv. 9
Blunt Weapons (Melee Skill)	Lv. 13
Weapons Specialty: Mace	Lv. 7
Heavy Armor (Armor Skill)	Lv. 15
Ranged Weapons (Melee Skill)	Lv. 7
Mining (Trade Skill)	Lv. 6
Cartography (Trade Skill)	Lv. 4
Commander (Guild Bonus)	Lv. 5

Not too bad, plus he'd leveled up a bunch of his skills—Spellcraft, Blunt Weapons, Ranged Weapons, and Commander.

He'd even gained two levels of Heavy Armor—probably had to do with that whole evisceration thing—and a buttload of epic benefits for earning the official title Warlord of the West.

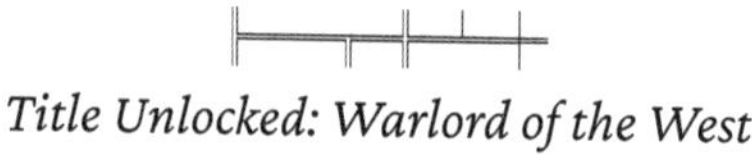

Title Unlocked: Warlord of the West

Congratulations, you have become the first Warlord of Los Angeles, establishing yourself as a fearsome force to be reckoned with. Your lessers will flock to your banner, eager to join your warband and share in the plunder and safety you can provide in this chaotic, war-torn land filled with untold dangers... and possibilities.

Stronghold Benefits

- You gain an additional 5n Layout Points to apply to your Dungeon Stronghold, Shieldwall, where n is equal to your current character level.
- Your Warband Territory now extends outward from your Dungeon Stronghold by .5n miles, where n is equal to your current character level.
- All sworn Warband members now receive the benefits from the skill *Warlord's Blessing* while inside Warband Territory.

Warlord's Blessing

- Gain an additional 5% Experience when making kills inside Warband Territory.
- Total damage increased by 5% while battling enemies inside Warband Territory.

- When looting corpses within Warband Territory, gain a 10% improved chance to receive a rare loot drop.
- Production cost for all crafted items is decreased by 8% while inside Warband Territory.

Warlord's Presence

- When battling in the immediate presence of the Warlord, sworn Warband members' Armor Rating, Attack Damage, overall Movement Rate, and Critical Hit Chance are increased by 1% + (.05n), where n is your current character level.

"This is the new reality, and I want everybody West of the Rockies to know exactly who runs it." ~ PwnrBwner

Aside from making Scott sound like a complete badass—which he was—the title gave him and his followers a dump truck worth of impressive benefits that no one else could even come close to offering. Since he was only level 32, those benefits currently only extended sixteen miles out from Shieldwall, although the Warlord's Presence buff was good wherever Scott went. He was elite status and the gear they'd looted from Darith only helped to make him even better. The kaiju moth had dropped a bunch of good shit: Blessed Heraldic Plate Armor, Gauntlets of Warforged Power, Wings of Glory, and a bunch of other miscellaneous god-tier stuff.

That shit all went to Nessa, Kev, and Kellie, which was only fair since they'd helped out the most. Scott would've spread the love around, but with most of the POSes opting to go back to "real life," he didn't want to waste his generosity. It wasn't like the government was gonna let them walk around with magical Ironman armor, anyway. Dollars to donuts, it wouldn't be more than a month before the Feds started sending in Black Ops teams to snatch and grab that kind of stuff for military use.

Scott was only too glad to see that gear go to deserving Warband members. After all, the rules were the rules, even if he was the one who'd made them up—you keep what you kill, and they had shared in the kill. He claimed Darith's meat cleaver for himself, and it shrank down to just massively oversized enough that he could wield it.

The Mad Butcher's Cleaver

One-handed Damage: 91 - 121

Durability: Indestructible

Level Requirement: 30

Strength Requirement: 100

The Mad Butcher's Cleaver ignores class restrictions and can be used as a Bladed or Blunt Weapon, gaining any appropriate bonuses.

+50 Cleaving Damage

+15% Chance of Inflicting an instance of *Bleed* on target. Bleed can stack up to three times.

Absorb +1% Life for every 5% damage dealt to an opponent with the Mad Butcher's Cleaver.

Welcome to the slaughtering yard, little lambies...

Even better, per the Quest Reward, Scott also picked up a unique scaling item, which literally had his name on it.

PwnrBwner's War Crown
Defense: 50
Durability: 99 of 99
Level Requirement: 25
Strength Requirement: 53
All Primary Stats +10
All Elemental Resistances +10%
+8% Chance to Unleash Holy Reckoning when struck

Once the Winch Witch was finally ready, Kevin and Cranko gave the go-ahead, and they loaded back up and trucked out of Los Angeles.

Apparently the majority of the mobs hadn't spread far from the city yet. They repelled a couple of attacks as they headed north on the 405, but nothing like the concentration they'd seen in LA. The biggest obstacle they faced was a major rock-slide between two hills, but Kev and Cranko managed that with a combination of cannon blasts and low-gear forward straining with the Witch's cowpusher.

The wrecker and her semi never would've made it through those tons of boulders if not for the power enhancements from Cranko's runes. Scott knew because Kevin wouldn't shut up about it that night when they stopped for a final potty break and an on-the-road Gourmet meal of Fish Soup. The soup wasn't as disgusting as Scott was expecting boiled fish to be.

Lakshya made a big deal of getting lots of reaction shots around the cookfire for her dumb show. Her buzzing around with the camera would've annoyed the hell out of Scott, but Kaz finished the show off with a last-second slam dunk that made his day.

"And so, cooking friends," the Troll Gourmet said, grinning into the camera as he squeezed his enormous girlfriend to his side, "Kaz has learned a very valuable lesson that he wishes to leave you with, as this is the last instructional video he will film."

Beside the camera guy, Lakshya's mouth opened and closed like a horrified fish out of water, but Kaz just went on talking.

"Food cannot save the world. It is wonderful and flavorful, and it opens doorways to paradises of taste sensation, but food is, after all, only the fuel. It will make the world a happier and more pleasant place while we—you and Kaz, cooking friends—save the world. For it is we who must do this, no matter which world we are in. Such is our duty to those we love." He planted a kiss on top of Mai's frilly cap. "Thank you for cooking with Kaz, friends. Now, wherever you are, whatever you are doing, turn off this video and go make your world a better place."

Slowly, the cameraman lowered the lens. "That was amazing, Kaz. I guess that's a wrap?"

"What?" Lakshya shook her head. "No way. Kaz, let's talk about this. You're on top of everything right now. People love your show. You can't stop now! Come with us. We'll make you famous. Er, even more famous."

Kaz patted her on the head with one massive paw. "Lakshya, Kaz wishes to thank you for everything you have done. Without you, Mai would never have found him. But Kaz has imparted all that he can. There is nothing left to discuss."

"Fuckin' A, Kaz," Scott said, sticking out his hand for a fist bump. "Go out like a G while you're at the top. Pound it."

"Don't listen to that loser, Kaz!" Lakshya squealed. "I'm going to make you rich. A world-wide super star. All you need to do is make one more season after this one. Please, just one. Think about it. We could travel all over the world. Taste foods from every corner of the world. You'd be international!"

Kaz ignored her.

Removing his huge Gourmet's hat, the big dude gently touched his knuckles to Scott's. "Kaz is honored to bump the fist of the mighty PwnrBwner, Warlord of the West."

"That's what's up," Scott said.

CHAPTER 32
THE TYRANT SIEVE

Roark spent the next several hours holed up in the forge, sweat pouring down his face and chest as he smelted iron and silver into useable ingots, poured them into a series of prefabricated molds, then tempered the metal, preparing each one to receive the complex series of Curses, Enchantments, runes, and portal markers needed to complete his plan. It was delicate work, and even the smallest mistake could be devastating, as he'd seen a thousand times before while crafting in Hearthworld.

He'd blown himself up more times than he could count tinkering with Curse Chains. In a world without respawn he couldn't afford a lapse in focus—not even for a second.

These plates were also far more complicated than most. Always before, the plates had been a tool meant to split and sort parties—the Hero Sieve, Roark liked to call it—but these plates were built for a single specific target, Marek Konig Ustar. A simple stun spell, fabulously effective against low-level heroes, would hardly tickle someone of Marek's level. Even with Roark's upgrade and final evolution, the Undead God-Pharaoh was still leaps and bounds more powerful than he was.

For this to work, Roark needed to "break out his big guns" as PwnrBwner often said, but doing so would create its own additional risks.

Stun spells were easy. Predictable. Spells capable of harming a creature as powerful as Marek would be unwieldly and wildly unpredictable. Roark flipped to the back of his Initiate's Spell Book and referred to the countless Curse Chains he'd already created during his time running the Cruel Citadel. The lightning bolt shaped *Yasuc* sigil, which corresponded to his Storm of Ice and Fire Curse. The maze-like square representing Sucking Miasma of Death. Arcane Soul Fire and Unholy Typhoon. Shadow Flux and Hex Shieldward. Moonlight Arrow and Celestial Hymn.

A hundred different spells that offered buffs, curses, widespread damage, or attacked a single target. In some ways, he was spoiled for choices.

He drummed his fingers over the dusty pages of the spell book.

Perhaps he had *too* many choices. Each portal plate could only support a single Curse Chain consisting of six Curses paired with up to six Active Conditions. To have any chance of success, he would need to sequence the spells in such a way to strip away Marek's untold advantages one at a time, just as he'd done against Bad_Karma—though this time on a cosmic scale. As flashy and satisfying as spells like Storm of Ice and Fire were, they would only slow Marek for a few seconds at most.

The true problem was the tyrant's Health Regeneration Rate. That was where Roark needed to focus. As a creature of the Undead, Marek would be resistant against Disease damage, but if Roark could design a stacking affliction that actively chipped away at Marek's ability to regenerate Health and Magicka, perhaps he and his allied forces would stand a chance. Past that, any damage dealt would need to be Light oriented, since it was the weak point of all Undead creatures, oftentimes preventing their recovery and further stagnating their regeneration.

After poring through his grimoire and spell book, Roark came up with a combination of spells he thought might be perfect. Curse Cloud of Dispel, Shackles of the Sepulcher, Cloud of Bloodblight, Sun Fire twice over, followed lastly by Star Nova.

Sun Fire

If an Undead creature of level 50 or higher triggers Sun Fire, a beam of divine retribution deals 10n Light Damage, where n is equal to the caster's level. When struck with Sun Fire, the target is afflicted with Star Burn, making them 10% more susceptible to Light-based magicks; duration, 10 minutes.

Curse Cloud of Dispel

Curse Cloud of Dispel unleashes a 30-foot radius of anti-magickal energy that has a 60% chance to dispel any active beneficial effect in place.

Note: Curse Cloud of Dispel does not differentiate between allies and enemies.

Shackles of the Sepulcher

If an Undead Creature triggers the hex Shackles of the Sepulcher, fetters of Light emerge from the ground, miring the unclean beast in place for 30 seconds and dealing Burning Radiance damage: 15

points of fire damage +2 burn damage/sec for the duration of the hex.

Cloud of Blightblood

Cloud of Blightblood unleashes a 30-foot-radius cloud of noxious crimson gas that deals 100 points of burst poison damage upon inhalation and triggers Blightblood Contagion, reducing Health and Stamina Regeneration by 15% for five minutes or until a Panacea Potion is consumed. Blightblood Contagion may be applied up to ten times to a given target, adding an additional 5% reduction to Health and Stamina and an extra 5 minutes per additional cast to the duration of the spell.

Star Nova

When activated, a tsunami of celestial power ripples outward, dealing 50n Light Damage to all enemies in range, where n is equal to the caster's level. Undead creatures within a 30-foot radius suffer an additional 10n Light Damage. Creatures suffering under the Star Burn affliction earn an additional 10n Light Damage for every active instance of Star Burn.

It was a devious combination of attacks. Curse Cloud of Dispel would strip away a measure of Marek's supernatural protections, while Shackles of the Sepulcher would lock the Tyrant in place, ensuring he couldn't simply bolt away. The added Bloodblight Contagion would cripple his ability to regenerate both Health and Stamina for even longer periods of time, while the double blow of Sun Fire and Star Nova would deal scads of Light Damage to the Undead God-Pharaoh. In all likelihood, Marek would survive even that, but the combination should weaken him just enough for Roark's other plans to take effect.

Now all he needed to do was construct the Curse Chain and, oh so carefully, etch them into the plates themselves. Preferably without killing himself in the process—a distinct possibility, as Roark was making one very significant alteration from his earlier portal plates. His Hearthworld Hero Sieve had been powered by the same rune responsible for creating and maintaining town portals, *Nirn,* but that wouldn't work here, not for what he had in mind. If all went according to plan, Marek wouldn't be facing a single dungeon in the fixed location of Hearthworld, but a host of them across realities. Instead of *Nirn*, Roark would be forced to use its cosmic equivalent, *Ithel,* imparted to him by the Tower of Creation.

In theory, *Ithel* would serve as the primary binding construct—fixing two points together through a metaphysical tether—creating a perfect bridge through space, time, and reality.

Hopefully, this one time, theory and practice would produce the same results.

With a tight knot of anxiety sitting in the pit of his stomach, Roark took awl to plate, beginning the sequence.

[*Any hero who meets the conditional requirements set on {Destination Plate 1, 2} is instantly transported from the Prime Transportation Plate* (designation = *Ithel*!) *to the corresponding: {Destination Plate 1, 2};*

{Destination Plate 1: If any hero or monster level 150 or greater steps on or over the Prime Transportation Plate, then they are instantly transported to the corresponding plate, equaling the value of Roth, *and trigger Curse Chain String Value: Effect 1: Curse Cloud*

of Dispel; Effect 2: Shackles of the Sepulcher; Effect 3: Cloud of Blood-blight; Effect 4: Sun Fire; Effect 5: Sun Fire; Effect 6: Star Nova.};

{Destination Plate 2: If any hero or monster level 149 or below steps on or over the Prime Transportation Plate, then they are instantly transported to the corresponding plate, equaling the value of Yiluf*!};*

If any human, mob, or hero, other than a Troll native to the Cruel Citadel, tampers with this plate, it triggers an explosion causing 150 points of fire damage (+10 burn damage/sec for 25 seconds) to any targets within a 30-foot radius.]

[*Would you like to Transmute Inscription to invent Curse Chain: The Tyrant Sieve? Yes/No?*]

Roark licked his lips. This was the moment of truth. He hit Yes.

"Boom!"

Roark flinched. But instead of a notice that his final Curse Chain had failed—*Goodbye!*—the Success page appeared before him, detailing the ins and outs of his new curse:

[*Your invention of Curse Chain: The Tyrant Sieve was successful! Accepted definition for The Tyrant Sieve has been logged in your Initiate's Spell Book under rune THE TYRANT SIEVE.*]

From near his resting place by the forge, Mac bolted to his feet and issued a deep growl, jarring Roark from his thoughts of the dead.

"Settle down, you overgrown lizard." Zyra Stalked out of the shadows. "It's only me."

The Elemental Turtle Dragon's orange head chuffed, but Mac turned around and lay back down, this time with his tail inserted into the flames. Awakened, the yellow head nipped at the blue, dribbling toxic slobber onto the floor, where it hissed and bubbled, eating pits in the flagstones. The two of them wrestled and gnawed playfully at one another for a few moments before the orange head became annoyed and barked out a gout of flame. With answering chirps and grunts, the yellow and blue heads left off their fighting and settled down to rest.

Breathing heavily, Roark dropped onto the floor and broke out into a fit of deep belly laughter. Bloody hells, he'd done it. He had a dozen more of the plates to create yet and worlds to visit that he'd never even dreamt of before the plan came to fruition, but this was the first step. The linchpin.

Zyra chuckled darkly. "You're too easy, Griefer, always so absorbed in your work."

"The day I'm not absorbed is the day I blow myself up... again. And this time there won't be a respawn."

The work had been a challenge, but one that he could appreciate. He'd been so absorbed with the meticulous toil of his hands that he didn't have time to dwell on anything else—like the long-dead, golden-haired girl he'd glimpsed in Talise's vision.

Danella. A ghost from his past, haunting his thoughts.

She was an illusion. She had to be.

But what if she isn't? some dark part of his mind urged, now that he wasn't fixated on crafting the portal plates. *Marek is powerful and ruthless enough to seek her body out to use against me. Can the World Stone have overcome the seal I put on her? Or perhaps it was me. Perhaps I failed at writing it.*

"How goes your scheming and crafting, Griefer?" Zyra asked, dragging him back from his dark thoughts.

Roark offered her a lopsided smile and hefted the first portal plate into the air, its dull metallic surface glimmering orange from the firelight.

"I didn't blow up the Citadel, so I'd say exceedingly well, all things considered. And how goes the rest of the preparations?" he asked, standing. He set the precious portal plate down on his workbench and stretched, his spine issuing a series of satisfying pops. “Is the Frahoi contingent equipped to ride out?”

“Hardly. They’re still arguing over who can go and who can’t,” Zyra said. “I give them at least another hour before they’re ready. Like you, I’ve been more fruitful with my time. I came to show you what I’ve cooked up.” She produced a series of glass vials in her multiple hands, the liquid inside ranging from vibrant purple-red to putrid green. “A few of these ought to level the gap between your frail little humans and Hearthworld’s toughest Undead creatures.”

Roark took one of the proffered vials and studied its contents more closely.

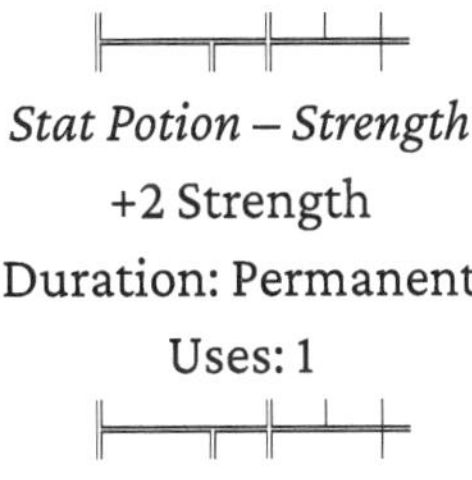

Stat Potion – Strength

+2 Strength

Duration: Permanent

Uses: 1

“Bloody hells.” He glanced at the Orbweaver Ravager. “Zyra, this is brilliant.”

“And they’re not even deadly!” she crowed delightedly. “My genius and versatility amaze even me sometimes.” She clinked a couple vials together. “So far I’ve made potions for Strength, Dexterity, Constitution, Speed, and Intelligence. The permanence makes them an especially tricky brew, but I think with a little more experimentation and some leveling of my Beneficial Draughts skill, I can raise the number of points they add.”

“How long will that take?”

Zyra tapped her chin over the veil with one vial. “Likely longer than it will take Albrecht to get the defending party sorted out. For now, I’ll focus on producing quantity and leave raising the quality until another time. From what I can tell, the bonuses stack indefinitely, so one human will get the same benefit from guzzling five of these as they would downing two five-point versions of the same potion."

"It's wonderful work," Roark said. "I'm glad."

"You might want to relay that message to your face, mighty Feudal Lord. You look awfully miserable for someone who just received good news."

"It's nothing," he said, waving a claw-tipped hand through the air. "Just found my mind wandering a bit—revisiting some unpleasant memories. That's all."

Zyra's posture changed slightly, and Roark got the feeling she was studying him through the black lace of her veil.

"It's that corpsewalker Talise showed us," she finally said. "You're still dwelling on her. She's the thief you told me about, your friend who was hung." At Roark's questioning look, Zyra shrugged. "I may be new to being an Orbweaver, but I recognize a noose mark when I see it."

"That wasn't her," Roark insisted, though it felt like a lie on his tongue. Maybe if he bloody repeated it often enough, he would finally start to believe it. "It's an illusion. Marek was counting on Talise showing that image to me. He wrote in a spell with some sort of clause to make me see someone I..." Roark hesitated. "Someone I lost. It's psychological warfare, meant to demoralize me, just as Randy Shoemaker said."

"I hope you're this certain when the time comes to kill her," Zyra said, folding her primary arms across her chest. "Because those corpsewalkers in the message certainly weren't illusions, and if what happened to those villagers is any indication, she won't spare you."

Roark flinched, surprised at the sudden sting of pain in his chest.

"Are you jealous, then?" he hurled back without thinking. "Is that it?"

"Why should I be?" Zyra laughed. "Because you loved her once? Perhaps you even still love her." She lifted the veil from her face, meeting his gaze with beautiful, mismatched eyes. "I won't begrudge you a love lost before you even knew my world existed. Lie as much as you want, I know I have your heart. There is no jealousy.

"When you came to my world, Roark von Graf, you were as jaded and suspicious as any Troll I'd ever seen—second only to me. But where I feared letting someone close enough to plant a knife in my back, you were afraid that if you let them get too close, they would be taken from you. She's the one who made you that way. You allowed yourself to get close to her." Zyra walked closer and pushed Roark's shaggy hair from his face. "You allowed yourself to love her even though you knew doing so was to court pain and heartbreak. Then she died, confirming your worst fear."

Defensive tension leaked out of Roark's shoulders.

"You're not wrong." He let out a humorless chuckle. "I was so young and stupid, and she was so beautiful. After Marek slaughtered my family, I hardened myself. Friendships, relationships, they were for the weak, weapons to be used against you. Danella, she never believed that, though. She took pity on me—which is good." He snorted. "Because I would've died without her. I was even more useless when she found me than when you did.

"I had no idea how to survive on the streets. Without Danella, I would've frozen or starved to death. She taught me how to steal and cheat to survive, showed me that there were no rules in a fight for your life. We lived like kings of the street..." He paused and glanced down at his palms, so very different from the hands that had held Danella's so long ago. "Or like only a pair of children could imagine kings living."

Zyra cocked her head, curious. "And you showed her what it was like to have a conscience. To do the right thing when you could. Just the same as you taught me. Deny it all you like, but I know you, Griefer. Your greatest weakness is that streak of idealism you're so certain you don't possess."

Roark didn't answer. He was thinking of the times he'd talked Danella out of rolling drunks or stealing from cripples and lunatics and temples, and the times he'd given in and helped her do it because he was too hungry to formulate a moral argument.

"The thief," Zyra said, her voice taking on a rare soft note. "When I saw her, do you know what struck me most? She looked lost. Alone. I'd wager a bag of gold that when you found her she thought she would never have a friend in the world, because everyone and everything was out to get her." She traced one poisoned onyx claw down Roark's jawline.

"I'm glad she had your love. I'm glad you were able to show her she wasn't alone anymore, especially in a world as cruel as this one. Marek may believe that friends are weakness, but you know better, Roark. We've only come this far because of the relationships we've made—the alliances forged through fire and hardship and shared suffering. You lost her, this thief of yours, but better such a loss than to live a life alone, sequestered from the world."

Zyra plucked her vial out of his hand and headed for the study door. Instead of opening it, however, she stopped with the handle in her grasp.

"If it were me," she said without looking back, "I wouldn't want to be forced to fight against the one who showed me what it was like to not be alone any longer. I would want to be free, whatever it took. But perhaps killing her is too much to ask of the Jotnar who loved her, and perhaps I shouldn't have suggested it."

Roark's lips turned up at the corner. "That sounds dangerously like an apology."

Zyra chuckled. "No, definitely not. Just a thought for the fight to come. Because unlike Marek, you have friends who will help you do the hard things. That is why we will win."

CHAPTER 33

DUNGEON SEEDS

The next twelve hours passed in a whirlwind of frantic chaos and focused fury. A contingent of villagers—decked out in as much magical gear as the Citadel could spare and magically strengthened by Zyra's potions—rode out from the gates of Traisbin, bound for the city of Frahoi, situated some fifty miles from Korvo's walls. Though he was no warrior, Albrecht led the group, grim determination carved into the lines of his scar-twisted face. These were his countrymen, he said, and whatever may come, he would fight with them. Despite their hardly being able to look at one another without flaring up like a pair of mountain rams defending their territory, Roark had to admit he respected the bumbling mage's dedication to the people. It was the steadfast devotion of a true noble.

Splatch the Abhorrent—a Reaver Champion and the Fourth-Floor Overseer—and Grozka the Zealot, former Third-Floor Overseer and current head of the Troll Nation's Rumble Squad, along with two companies of Trolls, rode out with the human troops. All had volunteered for the mission, knowing that the chances of success were low and the odds of forever-death extremely high. In an ideal world Roark would've sent twice or three times that number, but he couldn't afford to give any more. He would already be stretching his forces thin and relying heavily on his new Redeemer of the Fallen skill to make his scheme come together.

But neither could he abandon those who had given him aid and refuge during his time of need. He did what he could, knowing that would have to be enough. It would take the riders most of a day to cover the distance, and he needed every second of that time.

Randy Shoemaker spent the time running logistics between the various Dungeon Lords on Roark's behalf, while Zyra and Talise prepared Korvo for Marek's arrival. A tricky bit of business, that. The massive Discordant Inversion Web they'd cast to keep Marek and the World Stone Pendant out had worked wonders, but now they need Marek inside Korvo's walls.

Unfortunately, Roark couldn't collapse the defenses—doing so would reveal too much and might scare Marek away at a crucial moment. The Tyrant King needed to breach the walls, and he needed to think it was of his own doing. Marek would suspect a trap no matter what Roark did, but the despot was also egotistical and overconfident to a fault—traits that could be used against him, just as those same traits had been used against Roark time and time again.

If everything went to plan, Roark was reasonably certain Marek would proceed. He would think he'd spotted the obvious trap and could easily avoid its pitfalls, and in return, he would likely come with a trap of his own. Danella.

Roark would be ready for that as well.

While everyone else worked to execute his vision, Roark spent hours writing out teleportation scrolls, using his newly gained knowledge of the Tower, and crafting a small army of portal plates. With the first plate done, the rest went along much more smoothly. It was still a time- and labor-intensive process that required utter concentration, but the risk of blowing himself up into forge dust had decreased by at least seventy-five percent—far better odds than surviving Marek, even if everything came together perfectly.

Once the plates were done and stored in his Inventory, he roused Mac from his slumber by the forge's fire and broke the seal on the first of his portal scrolls. A shimmering violet gateway appeared as powerful magicks ripped through the temporal fabric between worlds. The portal didn't immediately suck him inward, crushing his bones to powder, which meant it was stable. Using his connection to the Tower, he'd scoured the cosmos for the right locations. He'd found them. He was certain of it.

Mostly.

"Ready for a grand new adventure, boy?" he asked, scratching Mac's orange frilled head.

The canny beast blinked and chirped contentedly.

Squaring his shoulders, Roark steeled himself for the pain that was certain to follow and stepped through the glimmering void. A brief flash of cold power washed over his skin, but there was no pain. No snapping boiling blood or inverted organs. No vast oceans of alien water waiting to crush him or deadly flows of magma ready to burn him to cinders. Even the dismantling and reassembling he'd felt on his first trip through a portal to Hearthworld was curiously absent.

His foot crunched down on a bed of lush grass that rose to his shins. Mac trundled through beside him as the portal snapped closed, his multiple heads glancing around in fascination, snuffling at the air and earth.

It was hot here, the atmosphere heavy with moisture that made his skin feel instantly slick. Thick trees with enormous fronds shaded him from the light of dual suns tracing their way across a pink sky. Eerie birdcalls echoed in the distance, and the chittering of some small creature rustling in the undergrowth nearby caught his ear. He turned and glimpsed the scaly tail of a tiny creature scampering across a row of stones and disappearing under a curtain of hanging vines.

He and Mac were in a city. Or what remained of one, rather. A vast forest had sprung up in the ruins of moss-covered arches, crumbling spires, and sprawling stone complexes that were so blanketed by creeping vines and lush foliage that it was nearly impossible to tell what had been here at all.

But Roark knew.

The Tower of Creation had been only too happy to display the worlds that had fallen beneath Marek's sword. There were hundreds of them. Asheth Kisari, where he now stood, was home to a once-great race of bipedal lizard people called the Elofinn. This city, weather-beaten and broken by the passage of long years, once stood as a defiant stronghold against tyranny. Right up until Marek's siege weapons tore down its walls. Then his armies put the residents young and old to the sword, and the Tyrant King struck down its leaders with his own brand of dark magic. All to get his hands on a sacred scroll that was but a fragment of a clue that would eventually lead him to the Tower of Creation.

This was Marek's true legacy. Worlds void of sentient life, empty and desolate. Terho would be just another on that list unless Roark stopped him.

Roark took to the skies with a single leap, his feathered wings stretched wide as he searched the ruined cityscape for a building that would serve his purpose. There was one near the center of the city. A domed palace, or a civil center of some sort, with wide pillars marching along the front. He folded his wings and dove, banking softly before touching down light as a breeze. A pair of enormous statues depicting proud-looking lizardfolk, overgrown with twisted vines, flanked an arched doorway filled with boulders and rubble. A minor cave-in, either from the battle long past or the slow damage of time.

He set to work, blasting chunks of stone out of the way, and by the time he'd cleared the entrance, Mac had caught up with him. The Elemental Turtle Dragon looked like he was having the time of his life. The blue head eagerly sniffed at the air, while the yellow munched on huge mouthfuls of colorful foliage. The orange head had a small scorched animal, larger than a rabbit but smaller than a deer, hanging from his jaws. Clearly the beast hadn't lost any of his bloodthirst with his new Evolutions.

The interior of the building was dusty and dimly lit from the cloudy crystalline dome overhead, but Roark could see enough to know that it was perfect. Thick stone walls. Huge columns, a warren of hallways and rooms whose inhabitants and furniture had been reduced to little more than dust long ago. He and Mac wound their way through the dizzying array of spaces, taking in murals and mosaic floors that offered glimpses into the lives of the lizardmen who had once called Asheth Kisari home. While they walked, Roark pulled a small talisman from his Inventory, no larger than a silver coin, and affixed it to the walls.

It took ten minutes' exploring before they found a large central chamber barred by a formidable set of iron doors studded with rivets.

The wooden beam that had once secured the doors from the inside was so rotted that it took only the slightest nudge of Roark's shoulder to open them. Inside, he found a grand stone chair, carved to resemble interlocking trees, vines, and fanciful flowers that Roark had never seen before. At the foot of the throne were the pitted bones of a creature with an elongated mouth full of teeth. Sitting atop of the creature's head was a tarnished golden crown with a polished ball of jade the size of a bird egg.

Roark knelt by the weathered bones and offered a silent prayer, then took a seat upon the great stone throne. A series of triumphant notes rang out from the air itself, startling Mac, who was sniffing at a patch of fungi growing in the corner of the room. The Elemental Turtle Dragon's blue head cast an annoyed look at Roark before returning to his sniffling.

With the crown in hand, power flooded outward from Roark in a wave, suffusing the walls, ceiling, and floors. A Dungeon Lord's Grimoire appeared a moment later, complete with maps of the various levels and rooms that composed this massive compound.

[*Congratulations! Unclaimed dungeon location Palace of Troxel the Beneficent successfully added to your Feudal Territory. Would you like to name this expanded Territory? Yes/No*]

"Troxel's Last Stand," Roark said, glancing at the bones at the foot of the throne. It seemed apt, considering the circumstances.

Roark flipped through the Dungeon Lord's Grimoire. As with the Citadel, he could tweak and change a thousand features, add additional battlements, build traps, rearrange the rooms, or create secret passages. It was a massive undertaking and one that he sorely wished he could indulge in. There was something strangely cathartic in building and designing dungeons—creating the most efficient floor plans, reviewing troop placements, adding weapons, obstacles, puzzle rooms...

Roark sighed, resigned.

Unfortunately, he didn't have time for such simple pleasures. Marek was coming, and this was but one of many worlds Roark had yet to visit. He flipped to the last page of the grimoire and saw the tab he was looking for—it strobed with angry violet lettering.

Seed Dungeon.

He selected the option with a thought, and a new page unfurled in the air.

[*Troxel's Last Stand, creature status:* Uninhabited! *This Dungeon has not been assigned a type or seeded for life. To continue, you must first select a primary race to inhabit it! In your current form, you may choose from the following race types: Troll, Necrotic Revenants, Draconic, Seraph.*

Additional selection mode detected... Redeemer of the Fallen. You may also choose to spawn Elofinn, the original inhabitants of this fallen city.

Select a type to continue.]

Eagerly, Roark chose the last option. Perhaps Roark couldn't undo all of the damage that Marek had wrought over his long and bloody lifespan, but he could damn well make sure that the tyrant came face-to-face with the consequences of his actions.

[*Congratulations! You have selected Elofinn. Would you like to seed Troxel's Last Stand with Elofinn Hatchlings at this time? Yes/No*]

Roark selected Yes, but received a flashing failure prompt for his trouble.

[*Error! Unable to complete action. Since Troxel's Last Stand is a secondary Dungeon location you must appoint an Arch-Overseer to rule on your behalf before seeding the dungeon with life. Arch-Overseers will be able to modify the Dungeon and give orders to underlings while you are absent. Please select an appropriate Arch-Overseer to proceed.*]

The prompt came as no shock to Roark. He'd undergone the same process when creating Shieldwall, back on the world of the Devs. He fished another portal scroll from his Inventory and broke the waxy seal with the claw on his thumb. This portal, twice the size of the one Roark had used to get here, unfurled in the center of the throne room. A second later Shess, the Soaring Serpent Monarch, slithered out on her fat green tail; trailing behind her was an army of scaly Nagas. Roark stood and vacated the throne, making way for the deadly Dungeon Lord.

"Welcome to your new home," he said with a small bow.

She surveyed the temple and nodded in satisfaction. "Yessss. Thisss will do nicely."

[*Shess the Soaring Serpent Monarch has been appointed Arch-Overseer of Troxel's Last Stand. In your absence, she will be able to alter the Dungeon configuration and command the forces of Troxel's Last Stand. Would you like to seed the Dungeon at this time? Yes/No*]

Roark couldn't keep the feral smile from his face as he selected Yes. Instantly, the bones at the foot of the throne shuddered to life, pulling themselves together on unstable feet as sinew and muscle sprouted, not merely reanimating the dead, but giving the Fallen a new chance at life. Marek would be met not only by Shess's Naga fighters, but by an army of fearsome Elofinn Lizard Warriors defending their home against the tyrant who had once destroyed it.

Roark pulled out a portal plate and quickly secured it to the floor, just before the throne. A second plate he handed to Shess.

"Once you're done realigning the layout to your satisfaction, place this plate wherever you want Marek to enter the dungeon."

"It will be done, my Feudal Lord," she hissed, bobbing her head. "Will you not stay to advise usss?" she asked. "You know thisss Marek better than any—your insightsss would be invaluable."

"Would that I could," he replied, pulling another portal scroll out, "but there is too much work yet to be done. Many more worlds than these. I will return if I have the time, but I trust you, Shess. You are more than cunning enough to accomplish this task. It will be up to you to finish the work before the last battle. Make him pay for every inch he takes."

Roark whistled for Mac, broke the seal, and stepped

through a shimmering purple void and onto the surface of a scorching hot world, the ground riddled by deep fissures that churned with glowing flows of magma. A towering volcano marred the horizon, rearing its jagged peaks into the sky. Carved into the base of the mountain was a stone temple, lifeless and barren. But not for long.

The Beryl King was going to love it there.

One world down, six more to go...

CHAPTER 34
MISSION ACCOMPLISHED

After midnight, Scott called one last stop. They were still five miles out of Ventura, but already he could see the glow of work lights in the distance. They probably should've stopped earlier, but he'd wanted to make sure they hadn't run into anything they needed their weapons for first. Everybody who wanted to go through the wall offloaded their weapons, armor, potions, scrolls, and any other magical items they had on them. Arjun even helpfully cast an Infinite Shadow over the cache to camouflage it from low-flying helicopters.

Ventura didn't look much like itself by the time they finally pulled into town. When the Army Corps of Engineers did something, they didn't jack around. Huge banks of work lights lit up the night, showing that half the city and its burbs had been leveled to make way for a massive fifty-foot-tall wall. The finished section extended toward the ocean on one side, while an unfinished steel framework headed east as far as Scott could see. Big earthmovers and concrete trucks swarmed the active construction site, shoving aside debris and filling in sections of wall. Workers crawled endless miles of scaffolding, riveting and welding thick steel plates into place.

"That's Couch_Warrior," GothicTerror called up to Scott as she hung up her phone. "He's the one waving us toward the checkpoint."

Scott squinted at the speck in the distance, then nodded. "All right, everybody who's wussing out and going back to civilization, act like you can't do magic. Hopefully they won't do crazy black-ops experiments on you. As long as Couch_Warrior doesn't narc on us, you should be fine. Probably."

Scott wasn't convinced of that at all. How any of the Poser Owners could possibly want to go back to the real world was a mindfuck mystery to him. Why give up being a literal magic superhero in order to work at some dumb dead-end job for a guy named Travis? All so you could save up enough money to enjoy ten years as a retiree with joint pain from on-the-job repetitive strain before finally kicking the bucket? And Scott doubted the POSes would get even that. The government was going to want answers. If even one of the refugees in the convoy spilled the beans about what had happened, there would be no normal life for any of them.

That wasn't on him, though. They'd made their choice. He, at least, was smart enough not to trade freedom for comfort.

The Winch Witch rolled up to the checkpoint and hissed to a stop as Kev put her brakes on. Couch_Warrior and one of his Reserve buddies hustled over, M4s hanging on slings. Not pointed at any of them. Yet.

To keep it that way, Scott hopped out of the turret and climbed down, putting some distance between himself and the .50 cal. A second later, GothicTerror joined him. In her sliced-up, bloody armor, and with the compound bow slung over her shoulder, she looked pretty badass. Probably almost as badass as Scott did.

"Special delivery," he said, hiking a thumb over his shoulder at the refugees filing out of the trailer.

"Dude, I can't believe you managed to pull this off," Couch_Warrior said, shaking his head at the sheer number of people offloading. "I mean, we've had a steady trickle of civilians coming to the wall, but this many is..." He blew out his cheeks. "It's unprecedented, man."

"It's sketchy, if you ask me," Couch_Warrior's buddy said, one hand now resting on the pistol grip of his rifle. "The commander's going to want a word with you."

"Tell him to make an appointment," Scott said. "I've gotta say goodbye to my peeps."

A shadow stepped out of a nearby tent.

"An appointment won't be necessary," said a wiry dude in a desert camo uniform. He had iron-gray hair and a scowl that could shrivel up an apple. "I'm here now, let's get the exit interview over with. You're the leader of this group?"

Scott turned so he'd have this commander guy in his peripheral and be able to watch the refugees filing through the checkpoint at the same time. Each and every one was being searched for contraband, which Couch_Warrior had already warned them was anything that looked like it belonged in Hearthworld. Couldn't have people running around with magical battle-axes or unregulated Wands of Fireball—that was a national security risk. But Couch_Warrior had also warned them that the checkpoint was actively snatching up anything that looked like it came out of an alchemy lab.

Health Regen Potions. Contact Poison. Elixirs of Strength Fortification. Cure Disease Draughts. Invisibility Potions.

As far as Scott had been able to tell, no one save those in his crew had innate powers, but all of the Hearthworld goodies still worked on normies. Hence loading the wonder twins up with them. He could only image what kind of bullshit the military could get up to with Health Regen Potions. Them or the big pharma companies. No thanks.

"What I want to know is if you're the leader of this group," Scott said, glancing dismissively over the patches on the dude's uniform. The commander was looking just as dubiously at Scott's scratched-up and dented armor. "Because if you're not, I've got to talk to whoever's in charge. Me and him have got a couple things to get straight about this land out here."

Like they'd agreed on ahead of time, the Poser Owners inconspicuously filtered over to Couch's inspection line. Ninjastein was the first to pass through, looking heartbroken and defeated—which wasn't all an act. The big dude had put up a hell of a fight for his katana, but finally relinquished the enchanted hunk of mall trash in favor of seeing his family again. Nerd.

"Are you referring to the containment zone?" the commander asked, pulling Scott's attention back to him.

"I'm referring to my new territory." Scott waved a hand at the area beyond the wall, toward civilization. "All that out there belongs to you and Uncle Sam. Everything back here that you guys are cordoning off? That belongs to one Scott Bayani, a.k.a. PwnrBwner, Warlord of the West," he said, tapping his breastplate so there wouldn't be any confusion about who he was referring to. "You abandoned it, I saved it. By the new rules of the West, that's all mine now, brohole. I earned it with my blood and sweat and awesomeness.

"These pansies lined up to get through processing and go back to the daily grind? They'll all tell you they wouldn't have survived five seconds out here without me. I brought them to you guys as a show of good faith, and I'll send more your way if I find 'em. And since you guys have your hands full building this puppy, I'll even keep too many mobs from finding their way out of LA before you get this wall finished. But I expect things in return."

The commander's steely eyes narrowed. "Like what?"

"Like anybody who dicks with me pays the consequences. I wasn't yanking your chain when I said this is a whole new world out here. Anybody who comes onto my territory better be prepared to fight for what they want, because they're not going to get it any other way. Rules and lawsuits... all that bullshit is a thing of the past. If people—smart people who know there's more to life than bullshit taxes and retirement accounts—want to try their luck out here, they're welcome to come. I'll be fair and let them keep what they kill, but I'm not going to babysit them. The only law that counts in my containment zone is the strong survive."

"You know I can't grant you any rights to this territory," the commander said. "Land rights aren't my department, and this Merge is bigger than either of us. It'll have to go through the appropriate channels, probably all the way up the ladder to the President."

Scott smirked. "If he or anybody else wants to fight me for it, they know where to find me. But if they step to me, they're going to have an assload more trouble than they can handle."

With a thought, he called a massive crackling ball of Elemental Fury into his left hand and Lightning Spear in his right, while surrounding himself and GothicTerror with a brilliant cloud of Holy Reckoning that radiated deadly power. GothicTerror got in on the action and raised her Rod and Staff, conjuring forth a pair of decrepit Mummies and rabid-looking Jackals that towered over every human in the area. The summoned minions posted up and silently stared at the commander, looking creepy as balls.

Over in the search lines, a bunch of refugees had their phones out and were recording, and two of the guerilla journalists were actually making themselves useful for once and streaming the impressive display of power.

"Let anybody who wants a piece know that's what's waiting

for them," Scott said loud enough for the cameras. Then with a snap of his fingers, he extinguished the spells.

"What about you, miss?" the commander asked, sizing up GothicTerror. "Are you and your magic wand-things planning to come through?"

"I don't suppose you army guys have a position open that'll keep me swimming in gold and loot?" Nessa asked. At the older man's flat stare, she nodded. "That's what I thought. I'll stay on with the Warlord, then."

It was hella cool to hear somebody call him by his new title, but Scott played it off like he didn't notice because he heard it so often.

Over at the search lines, the last of the departing Poser Owners, Flappie_Sak, had just passed inspection. The dude turned back and waved at Nessa. She gave her old friend a smile and managed to keep most of the moisture out of her eyes. To be nice, Scott didn't make fun of her for crying like a little bitch. He wasn't sad to see everybody go, either; it was just a coincidence that some idiot had kicked up dust at just the wrong time to get it in his eye.

They wouldn't get a chance to say goodbye to the POSes, which sucked majorly, but Scott could live with it. The important thing was they had all made it through without any problems, discounting a couple broken bones and minor eviscerations. Nothing a Healing Potion hadn't been able to fix up.

"Come on, Tots," he said, turning his back on the wall. "Let's go run this wasteland."

"I give you two weeks," the commander called.

Scott stopped in his tracks. "It's been less than one week and I'm already at level thirty-two. Give me two, and I'll be a fucking legend."

Commander Dickface didn't have anything to say to that.

Scott and GothicTerror mounted back up. Scott slapped the roof to let Kev know he was good to go. Kev and Kel, at least, both had the good sense to stick around, and they didn't even have magical Hearthworld powers. Good fortune really was wasted on the unworthy.

The Winch Witch growled to life and slowly turned around in the flattened ruins of the city. Scott shot the Poser Owners a cool parting wave and was rewarded with a round of whistles and cheers from both the POSes and the refugees they'd saved.

That felt pretty damn good, too.

THEY WERE five miles from the containment wall, the wrecker's tires crunching along the asphalt of the 101, when a shimmering purple portal snapped open, barring their path. The air brakes trumpeted as Kev brought the rig to a standstill. Scott, still manning the turret, swung the barrel of the .50 cal toward the portal, ready to unleash hell and hot lead on anything that wanted to start shit. They didn't have refugees to worry about anymore, but they also didn't have the full support of the POSes.

Scott had himself, which basically counted for five, GothicTerror, Cranko, Kaz, Griff, and Mai, but the only other OG POSes with powers still kicking around were 3Trenchcoat_Hobbitses and BusterMove99, who had changed their minds about bailing ship after pwning the Mad Butcher of LA. Seeing so much badassery on display had been life changing, apparently. Still, even with them, they didn't have a properly balanced party. If something big and nasty came at them, it could be trouble.

"Heads up!" Scott called down into the cab. "Kel, launch the cannon on my mark, and Kev, get the Witch ready to roll if I give the signal."

A second later something enormous stepped through the portal—a towering creature with six wings and curling horns with a halo of fire hanging above them like a satanic Christmas wreath. An enormous turtle-shelled titan with three colorful heads trundled out beside the figure, chirping and licking at giant buggy eyeballs.

"The fuck?" Scott said, squinting at the two new arrivals. He let out a tense sigh of relief and slowly eased his fingers off the dual triggers. The hulking demon had changed, but Scott had died at the hands of the Griefer a hundred times over—he'd know that cocky grin anywhere. Plus, he only knew one winged shithead with a pet Turtle Dragon, though the last time he'd seen Mac, he'd had two fewer heads.

"Should I shoot?" Kellie called up, overly eager to activate the cannon again. Classic Kel—she was a murderhobo in disguise.

Scott slapped a hand against the roof. "Naw, we know this douche." He clambered out of the turret and dropped onto the hood. "Dude, Roark, you almost got shot."

"Watch the paint!" Kevin snapped, leaning out the window.

Scott ignored the dweeb as he hopped off the bumper onto the asphalt.

Kaz blazed past him like a freight train and slammed into the approaching Dungeon Lord, wrapping his arms around Roark and lifting him into the air.

"Roark! Kaz knew Roark was alive. That he wouldn't abandon his friends."

"It's good to see you too, Kaz," Roark replied, wincing at the big dude's grip. "Would you mind putting me down?"

"Of course!" The Troll Gourmet set Roark back on his feet.

"Glad you made it back," Scott said, sidling up to the Griefer. "But you're too late to clean up the mess you made. Don't freak out, though, I took care of it. I mean, I'm assuming this's all your doing," he said, waving a hand around toward the destruction of the Merge.

"Indirectly," Roark replied. "I managed to defeat Lowen and take down the Vault of the Radiant Citadel, but not before Marek showed up. He assumed the form of an Undead God-Pharaoh—"

"From the Onyx Sands expansion?" Scott asked.

"Precisely."

"Sick."

Roark frowned. "No, it's actually quite a powerful form. He used his newfound abilities to strip me of the World Stone Pendant." He tapped his chest where the weird amber amulet usually rested. "It's back with Marek. He used the power of the Stone to do all of this."

"And Hearthworld?" Kaz asked, ears wilting.

"Gone, mate." Roark made a weird move with his hands, then awkwardly patted the Troll Gourmet on the shoulder, like he'd never tried to make somebody feel better before. "All of it and everyone who was inside. The Citadel bonded with the Vault of the Radiant Shield and was dimensionally transported back to my home world, along with anyone inside at the time of the Merge. As for the rest of Hearthworld's denizens..." He fell quiet. "I cannot say."

Scott snorted. "Yeah, well you don't have to worry about them. Turns out they're settling in just fine. Looks like all of So-Cal is the new Hearthworld. But what about that dick noodle, Marek?"

"He's grown more powerful than ever," Roark said. "He's sweeping across my homeland, putting villages to the torch and killing every human he can find to bolster his level. But..."

Oh boy. Scott knew that look.

"You think you have a way to stop him," he guessed.

Roark nodded. "But I'll need your help to pull it off." The

Griefer pulled out a talisman with an odd rune carved into the face and a handful of scrolls, all held shut with waxy seals. They looked almost exactly like Hearthworld's town portal scrolls.

"You always need my help," Scott said, accepting the items. "I'm in. We all are. Let's pwn this loser."

CHAPTER 35
BAIT THE TRAP

Marek Konig Ustar watched in annoyance as the newly arrived band of that von Graf cur's allies clashed with his Undead forces at the banks of the Hebi River. A silver-winged Arboreal Herald darted overhead, calling down powerful Earth magicks, while Wolf-Bear Hybrids, Metalwraiths, and Behemoths fought back what should have been a simple path to total destruction of another meaningless human city.

He had succeeded in forcing von Graf's hand, it seemed, but not in drawing Roark himself out of his stronghold. A truly frustrating turn of events. But no matter. If hundreds of deaths didn't catch the upstart's attention, then perhaps a hundred thousand more would. Let the pawns he'd sent to the front lines be the first to water the riverbanks with their blood.

The Tyrant King lifted his new falcate horned staff, preparing to spawn a fresh flood of Undead.

But the indicator for one unread message appeared in the corner of his vision.

Instant text communication was no innovation to Marek. He'd conquered hundreds of worlds more advanced than Terho where it had been the norm, and dozens more where that sort of messaging was considered primitive and out of date.

Of course, the number of people still living on this world who had both the mettle and ability to personally message the Tyrant King had very recently been cut down to one. He could afford to take a moment before wiping out von Graf's rescue band to see what his erstwhile "granddaughter" had to say.

Infiltration of the snake's forces has been a success. I've sabotaged the southwest tower at the edge of Korvo's defenses. Bring it down, and the rest will fail. Korvo and the Citadel will be yours.

Marek threw back his misshapen skull and laughed.

"Oh, to be young again," he said, wiping a tear from the corner of his eye with one gnarled claw. "Talise, you foolish little brat. Can you truly be so stupid as to think I would fall for this ploy?" He shook his head in mock disappointment. "It's my fault for not raising you better."

The true intent of the message was obvious. Von Graf wanted him to attack the southwest tower and likely trigger some sort of spectacular explosion or firebomb or another silly trap that only someone hopelessly optimistic about killing him would ever believe could accomplish the job. The detestable upstart was nothing if not predictable in that way.

Still, his curiosity was piqued.

He had nothing to fear from setting this trap off. Even without the World Stone, he was solar systems beyond Roark's weight class. He could take this opportunity to display the difference in their intellect and power while at the same time finally ridding himself of the upstart for good. The fool always had overestimated his abilities, and that fatal overconfidence was about to be the death of him. The fact that von Graf had brought destruction down on his own head thinking he'd done something especially clever was just an added bonus.

Marek sent a reply to his former granddaughter.

Good work, my child. Your loyalty will be justly rewarded.

Then he closed out of his messages and snapped a finger at the signalman for his forces.

"Sound the horns for a change of direction," Marek said. "Our true target has finally opened to us. Tonight, we take Korvo."

While the massive war horns blasted out the two-note alert, the Tyrant King used the World Stone to open a shimmering violet portal connecting them with the mountain range hundreds of miles to the east.

The ground shook and the air split with the answering cry from his army as their lines turned away from Frahoi and splashed back across the river in obedience. Marek chuckled as the men and mobs allied with von Graf cheered, assuming they were victorious.

A hulking she-Troll with charred black armor and impressive stag horns was the first to realize their mistake.

"They're headed for Korvo!" she boomed, raising a spike mace to the heavens. "Stop them from getting into that portal!"

A handful of the Troll's comrades rallied to her cries, hurling fireballs, casting lightning, unleashing clouds of noxious poison.

It wasn't nearly enough to stem the tide of such a large force. They shot hot lead projectiles and arrows without number, and tore across the river to stop the retreat, but all their efforts hardly made a dent in the number of Undead flooding into the portal.

Marek rolled his eyes at the arrogance of such fleas. It was as if they didn't realize or care that he could spawn another surge of loyal warriors with nothing more than a wave of his staff. His abilities were so far above theirs that they couldn't even fathom the chasm. They could slaughter his forces from dawn 'til dusk and still he would be able to replenish them with hardly the effort it took to yawn.

With a last glance back at the embattled Troll commander, Marek slipped into the portal.

He stepped out into several inches of snow, his hooved foot breaking through the brittle crust of ice on top. Before him stood the battlements of Korvo. Not fifty yards away was the tower Talise claimed to have sabotaged just for her dear granddad, standing tall and seemingly untouched.

Ranks of Rabid Jackals, Plague Mummies, Soul Devourers, and Sacred Bastets threw themselves against the outer wall of the city, but Marek squared his shoulders toward the supposedly weak point in Roark's contrived defenses.

The World Stone burned icy against his chest, and with a flick of his wrist, the Tyrant King threw a ball of force. The shot struck the tower with a thundercrack of noise. The whole structure shuddered from the impact, and for just a moment, Marek saw a fault line appear in the mortar. A curious turn of events. A second ball of force widened the crack and sent fingers racing in each direction, further weakening the stone. Eager to see what laughable trickery von Graf had in store, Marek tossed a final attack at the quickly deteriorating tower. It vaporized the mortar.

Screams went up inside the walls as the southwestern tower shuddered and crumbled in on itself stone by stone.

His army of Undead climbed over the rubble and poured in through the gap in the wall, howling in their excitement and thirst for blood.

High above the battlements and even stretching to the Radiant Citadel higher up on the mountain, a flash of light revealed a strange spell in the shape of a massive spider web. The same spell that had dealt such a painful blow to Marek the last time he'd tried to cross the threshold into Korvo. With one of its anchoring towers removed, the web flickered, then failed. No explosion followed. No trap sprung, ready to envelop him.

A smile tugged at the corners of his rotting God-Pharaoh lips. There was a hook in here, there always was where von Grafs were concerned. But this hook was proving more difficult to find. Was it possible that the girl truly had come through after all? Talise was a devious one with a knack for surviving. Perhaps she'd sensed the way the wind was blowing? Stranger things had happened. Marek braced himself and strode through the open sally port on the gate.

Before, an unseen force had slammed into the World Stone Pendant, throwing him a good half mile back from the city. Without that magickal spider's web, however, Marek walked into Korvo unaffected.

Something smashed into his right cheekbone. A trickle of blood ran down his elongated face and dripped onto his fur-lined robes.

Marek's head whipped around to find the source of the attack. A Troll Changeling hardly bigger than a human child was throwing rocks at him. The lumpy, hairless creature scooped up another handful and with a grunt of effort launched them at him.

Hardly a threat, but Marek despised the idea of the little blue piece of refuse telling anyone he'd dealt damage to the great God-Pharaoh.

Marek swept his staff in the Changeling's direction, sending the rocks whistling back toward the panicking mob. The little Troll screeched and darted away, disappearing in a flash of blue light behind a rain collection barrel.

Curious, Marek drew closer. A metal plate had been installed behind the barrel, etched with a chain of hexes that automatically transported "current humans" and "mobs with a level below ten" to the Troll Nation Marketplace. Anyone with a level of ten or higher who stepped on the plate would be transported to one of several locations across the mountain range, each of which had a name reminiscent of Hearthworld's dungeons. It took no stretch of the intellect to imagine power- and level-hungry Dungeon Lords and their underlings awaiting the transported mobs on the other side, ready to tear into the fresh meat.

Marek smirked. Very clever. No doubt of von Graf's design. Marek had heard of these devices from Lowen when the fool was still trying to get at Roark inside the Citadel. An excellent means of dividing up an invading force and tailoring your defense to their weaknesses. Marek was too smart to fall for such a scheme, though it was no surprise that the devices had given Lowen so much difficulty. The mage had always been a useful, but dull tool.

The Undead God-Pharaoh turned his nose toward the glowing golden image on the mountainside and lumbered forward, careful to avoid stepping on any of the plates. The streets were littered with them, many better hidden than the one behind the rain barrel. He knew he could easily defeat any Dungeon Lord the cur's portals pitted him against, but Marek was in no mood for trifling distractions. He wanted Roark von Graf.

As he passed through Korvo, Marek swept his staff at the surrounding buildings. Many of them hadn't been fully repaired from his first attack on the city, and he gladly demolished what was left.

Annoyingly, he heard no pained screeches or cries for help from inside the destroyed homes. The most vulnerable citizens must have evacuated before his arrival. No doubt they had fled into the sanctuary of the Citadel, praying von Graf would protect them. Indeed, the only inhabitants in the streets fighting his army of the Undead were high-level allies of the dungeon itself. Another link in von Graf's plan, it seemed. When they caught sight of the God-Pharaoh approaching, they slung pathetic spells or fired volleys of bullets or arrows at him, then quickly escaped via portal plates before he could retaliate.

Worthless vermin. Nipping away at the heals of his Health vial as if it weren't refilling faster than they could drain it. They were nothing more than mosquitoes buzzing around the head of a god, annoying but ineffectual, hardly worth swatting himself. With a wave of his staff, he spawned a fresh torrent of Undead.

Marek picked up speed, his hooves striking sparks on the paving stones, carving a direct path to the northeastern wall of the city. The battlement there had been built to withstand brute force attacks. It would have taken a lesser magick user a handful of powerful spells to break through, but Marek leveled it with a silent command to the World Stone. Half-melted stones and mortar exploded, peppering the snowdrifts.

Marek lumbered to a run, the snow hissing and sizzling as it melted and steamed beneath his every hoof-fall. Jackals, Bastets, and Soul Devourers who hadn't been transported away to some unknown dungeon raced out of the rubble of Korvo and sprinted past him, darting up the mountainside toward the golden glow of the Citadel.

For a moment, a pair of dark crow's wings fluttered across the silvery moon.

A strange feeling rolled up through Marek's hooves and into his legs. It took him a moment to recognize the rumbling.

It was an avalanche.

A mountain of snow crashed down the mountain toward him, snapping tall pines like twigs and battering the mobs who had raced ahead of him. Marek slammed his staff into the snow, anchoring himself. The World Stone turned icy against his chest, throwing out a blade of energy that cut the flood like a knife before it reached him.

As if it could sense its will being thwarted, the mountain rumbled again, sending down more and more of the deadly snowslide from every side. In seconds, Marek was buried alive in a grave of solid white.

He grunted in annoyance. The snow against his body quickly melted and refroze, locking his arms and legs in place, encasing him in a prison of ice. On top of this momentary inconvenience, the buffeting of the avalanche had stolen another paltry handful of his Health.

Was this that fool von Graf's plan? To wear him down grain by grain like a hot desert wind scouring a mountain to dust? If so, it was pointless. Unlike a mountain, Marek was being rebuilt with every second that passed. Already his Health regen had refilled the filigreed vial.

The World Stone burned with the same icy cold as the snow pinning him in place, then threw off a blast of amber force. The frozen prison exploded like a dying star, freeing Marek once more.

Overhead, the shadow of wings flashed again, and the eerie howl of a wolf rode along the wind. Another answered it, followed by a dozen more.

A moment later, a pack of lean, hungry-eyed wolves darted out of what was left of the forest, growling and barking. Seemingly without a care for their own survival, they threw themselves at Marek. His falcate staff whirled, crunching bones and slamming back the slavering canines before they could reach him.

This tactic, however, was only a distraction for their leader. A creature of fur and fang and muscle larger than a bison bounded out of the trees and leapt at Marek. Its teeth ripped into the joint of the Tyrant King's neck and shoulder, tearing away chunks of mummified flesh. Undead Scarab beetles showered the snow and pack, chewing into flesh wherever they could.

Another sliver of that bloody filigreed Health vial drained away. Marek felt a snarl rising in his own throat. The beast—a maka-ronin, according to the idiotic local legends—was too close for a staff attack. No matter. The staff was but a tool—Marek himself was the real weapon. The God-Pharaoh grabbed the creature by its shaggy head, his thumb-claw sinking into one eye as he clenched his fist and activated the World Stone.

The maka-ronin howled in pain as the amber light shredded him from the inside out. In seconds, nothing was left of the beast but a bloodied skeleton steaming in the cold night air.

Marek tossed it aside like a dirty rag and continued up the mountain. Would that he could so easily destroy the other cur harassing him.

The mountain wasn't finished with him yet, it seemed. With every step, the rocks and boulders rolled and shifted like living creatures. The wind roared and the sky clouded over. Hailstones pelted down like meteorites, exploding from the force of their flight when they hit him. Through it all, the shadowy silhouette of crow's wings fluttered overhead.

The mountains themselves seemed to be fighting on von Graf's side.

"Enough of this guiser's farce," Marek growled. He was done playing games. It was time to end this. With a command to the World Stone, he unleashed a rippling tidal wave of force that swept out in front of him, knocking down trees and buildings, scouring anything that would dare stand between him and the Citadel. Between him and Roark. He knew going into the dungeon was a fool's gambit—Roark was weak but cunning, and the interior of the Citadel could prove dangerous, even for Marek. But what was to stop him from leveling the building itself?

This was not Hearthworld, not any longer. Now that the strange web of magic had dissipated, he could rip apart the Citadel without ever stepping foot inside its wretched halls. He would bury Roark and his people beneath the very mountain that was fighting on his behalf. He raised his staff high, a snarl on his lips—

The portcullis standing guard over the Radiant Citadel lurched open, and the heavy reinforced doors behind it swung outward on silent hinges, revealing a lone figure. Von Graf was taller than he'd been before, six wings jutting from his back rather than the previous two. The impatient fool had Evolved since their last encounter, it seemed, but that made no difference to Marek. In this form or any other Roark was beneath him. A troublesome bug in desperate need of a boot.

"This ends now, Marek," the upstart said, drawing the delicate rapier at his side. "Your fight is with me, and here I am."

"You've grown bold," Marek said, composing himself. "Your most recent Evolution has made you foolhardy—more foolhardy, I should say. You must know it won't be enough."

"Perhaps not," von Graf replied, "but I can't just stand idly by and watch you kill the people I've sworn to protect."

And there was the crux of it, von Graf's true weakness. Mushy sentimentalism.

"Your sappy loyalty to those people will be your destruction, von Graf. I thought that lesson had been beaten into you long ago, but it seems you're a slow learner. Allow me to educate you one last time."

Instead of attacking, Marek thrust out a hand and conjured a shimmering violet portal. A creature shuffled through on long, coltish legs encased in muck-ridden threadbare breeches, worn thin by time and the grave. Hands, built for picking pockets and cheating at cards, were now swollen and black with stagnant blood. An embroidery of green corpse mold decorated her ragged tunic and edged the bits of rotting flesh exposed through the holes torn in the fabric by hungry scavengers.

A ligature mark cut deep into the child's slender throat, the skin tattered and ridged with the pattern of the rope's braid.

Marek watched in deep satisfaction as von Graf averted his gaze and lowered the tip of his rapier, unwilling to look at the girl he'd once loved. Marek could only imagine how many sleepless nights her loss had caused von Graf. And now, here she was, lumbering toward him like a ghost resurrected from a nightmare. The horror, the pain, the grief lingering in the air was delicious. Marek savored it like the rarest of delicacies.

"Roark..." The girl's voice was jagged and hoarse, barely a croak making it through the ruins of her throat.

Roark's voice matched it as he stammered out, "You—you're not her. This is an illusion."

"I assure you it isn't," Marek replied with a wicked grin. "Enslave the Dead is one of my most powerful spells. If I wanted, I could drag your whole bloody family out of their graves and send them crawling through the halls to tear you apart."

The rapier in von Graf's hand clattered to the ground—rendered useless by the shortcoming that was emotion. Marek's Undead minion would have no such reservations. The stringy-haired creature crept closer, pulling free a dagger dripping with golden ichor, deadly poisonous to one such as Roark.

"What I've never been able to fathom about you pathetic fools is how often you create your own downfall." Marek shook his elongated head. "Like parasites, you attach yourselves to a host, claiming love and affection, knowing all the while that your bond will only kill them in the end. It's a weakness I learned to crush before it destroyed me, but you and your lot never learn. You see it turned against you over and over, but it's as if you can't help yourselves. You're drawn to destruction like moths to the flames."

The Undead girl lurched toward the horned demon, the dagger slashing through his throat.

Except... von Graf didn't drop dead on the ground. The image of the Undying Dragonblood Seraph flickered and vanished, replaced by a spider-limbed woman. In a flash of motion, the Orbweaver threw a silken net over Marek's conjured Undead creature, immobilizing her in an instant.

Something shimmered in Marek's periphery. His eyes flashed wide as a blur of feathers and armor slammed into his side, powerful arms wrapping around his center and bearing him to the ground.

"Friends aren't a weakness," von Graf hissed in his ear. "They give us the strength to do the very things that we cannot. A lesson you never learned. But perhaps I'll be able to beat that into you yet..." The accursed upstart slapped his hand against a steel plate engraved with runes similar to the ones that Marek had seen scattered throughout the city.

A rushing *whoosh* filled the Tyrant King's ears as the world vanished around him.

CHAPTER 36

DUNGEON OF WORLDS

Roark stumbled and steadied himself as he landed inside the throne room of a Varsson great hall. Varssons were not so different from the people who inhabited Terho, save for their physical build and their unique affinity with nature—and their ability to take on the shape of fearsome creatures of the forests. They had stood against Marek for as long as they could, then like so many worlds before and after, they fell, crushed under the Tyrant King's ruthless heel.

Now, however, they had a chance to reap vengeance on the one who'd put their cities to the torch and their children to the blade.

"Is all well, Feudal Lord?" snarled a massive creature, equals parts bear, wolf, and man, who sat on a wooden throne grown from a single gnarled stump, rooted in the earth.

Gevaudan the Terrible was among the fiercest of the allied Dungeon Lords. He'd migrated his entire pack to the former world of the Varssons' and stood as Roark's Arch-Overseer of Sigelac's Hall, the new name of this dungeon.

Lingering near the throne was the hulking form of a bear, even larger than Gevaudan. Sigelac Fangbrand, King of the fallen Varssons, given a new chance at life thanks to Roark's Redeemer of the Fallen ability.

"As well as can be expected," Roark replied. "Let's see if our guest of honor has arrived."

With a thought, Roark accessed the Sigelac's Hall Grimoire, which gave him access to floor plans, trap layouts, troop placements, and a dozen other tabs and features—including the ability to remotely view any section of the dungeon.

Marek Konig Ustar crouched in a cramped room barely large enough for the Undead God-Pharaoh to stand in, weak torchlight painting him in dancing shades of orange and yellow. A thick silver cloud streaked with threads of noxious green light swirled around the tyrant and clawed at his nose and mouth. Spectral golden manacles were locked around his ankles, securing him to the floor. Marek's filigreed Health bar hung above his head like a storm cloud, fifteen percent of the red liquid in the vial already gone. It was refilling, but not at the breakneck pace it usually did. He clutched one rotting side with a clawed hand, holding closed an angry wound that leaked putrid black fluid.

Altogether, these were the work of the myriad of curses written into the portal plate Roark had activated after duping Marek back in Korvo. Curse Cloud of Dispel to undo his legion of buffs, Shackles of the Sepulcher to prevent him from fleeing, Blightblood to cripple his Regen capabilities, and a deadly combo of Sun Fire and Star Nova that would deal devastating damage while further weakening the Tyrant King against Light-based magicks. But not only that. In the room Marek was currently inhabiting, small plates crafted from solid silver and inset with Flawless Pearls were affixed to each wall as well as the ceiling and floor.

Roark activated the plates with a snap of his fingers, the many facets discharging a blinding burst of white light that slammed into Marek from every side. Although they did no inherent damage on their own, the Tyrant King staggered as the light soaked into his skin. The plates were Spell Amplifiers. Tricky and costly to make, but they'd served Roark well against Bad_Karma—and who was Marek if not an infinitely more powerful version of the Hearthworld bully?

[Spell Amplifier! *Add an additional stack of Sun Fire to selected target. Add an additional stack of Blightblood Contagion to selected target!*]

Roark felt the faintest twinge of satisfaction seeing the Tyrant in physical pain.

"What have you done to me?" Marek snarled, searching for an exit. The room was a dead end with only a single tunnel leading out through a curtain of pitch black.

"I think that would be obvious," Roark said, casting his voice through the air as he scanned the floor plan. "I've slapped you across the face and challenged you to a duel."

Gevaudan had done a fantastic job with the layout. True, it was a bit simple for Roark's tastes—too straightforward, focusing on physical dangers and less on subtlety or trickery, but that fit well with Gevaudan's personality and overall dungeon style. The wolf-bear-men were ferocious creatures that could rip and rend, tear and shred. Spike pits. Razor-sharp pendulums. Good choke points and rock-solid battlements fit their unique fighting style.

"What kind of duel is this?" Marek asked, still clutching his side.

"The kind I can win," Roark shot back. "You and I both know I can't defeat you in open battle—it would be the height of ego and foolishness to attempt to fight you head-on. So instead, you'll duel me on my terms. And the weapon of my choice is a dungeon."

"And if I refuse?" Marek growled.

"I'll call you a coward and broadcast your fear to all the universe," Roark replied flatly. "But you won't refuse. First, because your pride won't let you. And second, because you can't. Unlike you, I'm used to fighting those well above my weight class and I've rigged the game so that you'll have no choice but to play." Smug satisfaction oozed from his voice, which he knew would push Marek into a rage. "I've taken the liberty of extensively warding the compound—you won't be teleporting away, not even with the World Stone.

"This dungeon is also supernaturally reinforced—the same powers that kept you from entering Korvo are currently at work suppressing the power of the World Stone. You won't be escaping from here. You may be stronger than me, but I think we both know that I'm the superior Enchanter. If you wish to kill me—to put an end to this war—the only way to do it is to play my game. Run my dungeon. I'm waiting for you in the throne room, if you're man enough to come and find me."

The ghostly golden shackles securing Marek in place dissipated along with the choking toxic cloud filling the chamber.

"I will crush you like the pest you are," Marek said, stalking forward, into the pitch-black of the tunnelway ahead. "I fear no man. I have crushed armies singlehandedly and harvested a piece of Creation. You and your pitiful dungeon are nothing."

He emerged from the tunnel into a wide chamber lined with a series of curved wooden doors carved with intricate interlocking knots and angular floral patterns. In between each doorway were crumbling statues of strange kings and queens and renowned generals of old, all in the form of fearsome humanoid beasts. For the first time, Marek hesitated, forehead scrunching, eyes narrowing as he took in the room.

"I know this room," he said, turning in a slow circle as a hidden stone slab emerged from the floor, sealing off the passageway he'd come from moments before. "But it can't be..."

he muttered under his breath, though the Dungeon Lord's Grimoire broadcast it loud enough for Roark to hear.

"That's where you're wrong," Roark said, knowing his voice would be bleeding from the walls around Marek. "You're not the only one who's made a trip to the Tower of Creation. I've seen the monolith. Witnessed the wonder of the worlds, spinning away like a sea of fireflies on a hot summer's night. When I first saw Danella, it gutted me. It was a ruthless move—I'll give you credit for that, mate. Unleashing someone's loved ones to fight against them. A stroke of brilliance. But it also gave me an idea. You may not have loved ones to haunt you, but your closet certainly has its fair share of skeletons, and the Tower happily showed me where to find them."

The wooden doors lining the room swung inward, and inhuman wolfmen, clad in heavy armor and enchanted furs, crept into the room, lips pulled back from yellowing fangs. Fallen Varssons, reborn for this moment. A few wielded heavy axes, all etched with powerful Light enchantments, but most came armed with only their claws and fangs.

Marek dashed forward, toward the room's exit. His foot landed on a hidden pressure plate. A gout of fire erupted from small vents in the floor. The Tyrant King dove to the right—

Directly into an enormous silver pendulum, carefully inlaid with *Radiance Blast*, dealing one hundred points of concentrated Light Damage, plus added blunt and slashing damage. The blade cleaved into the Tyrant's shoulder, slicing through skin and sinew, while the force of the blow hurled him back through the air. He flipped as gracefully as an acrobat and landed on hooved feet in a crouch. His staff clattered to the floor; he was unable to hold the weapon with his ruined arm.

A wolfwoman in pearl-inlaid leather armor bounded in, snatched the staff from the floor before Marek could recover, flipped backward out of range, then darted away.

Marek scrambled toward the retreating shewolf, but the others were closing in around him like a tightening noose. She was already long gone, and so was his weapon.

"I will make you pay for this, von Graf," he thundered. "Your death will be a thousand years in the making. I'll resurrect every one of your loved ones and torture you until you plead for death."

"You can only do that if you can catch me," Roark replied. "Until then, shut your mouth, you blowhard, and atone for the crimes of your past."

Wolfmen and hulking bearlike Varssons threw themselves at the Tyrant King from every side. Claws carved furrows in his desiccated body, scattering Scarabs with every swipe, but Marek didn't panic. The Undead God-Pharaoh must have known he was more than powerful enough to kill all of them, even injured, outnumbered, and weaponless. Powerful magicks crackled from the sickly green gem between his crescent horns as he unleashed bolts of toxic green power, conjured skeletal hands from the floor, and summoned churning onyx dust devils that screamed with the voices of the damned as they ripped apart his foes. The Varssons fought with reckless abandon and fierce joy, even as they died.

Perhaps none of them would land the killing blow, but they all knew they were playing their part.

As the final Varsson fell, Roark cast a glamor, projecting himself into the narrow hallway leading off the blood-drenched chamber.

"Were these nature-loving fools the best you can do?" Marek snarled, prowling forward.

"I haven't even started to show you my best. This was just a taste. The banquet lies deeper within." The illusory Roark turned, showing Marek his back, and strode deeper into the Varsson labyrinth.

The Tyrant King roared and charged the illusion's retreating back, his hoof falls shaking the room. He careened through the conjured glamor as a stone wall slammed shut behind him. The floor dropped out, plunging the Tyrant King into a vat of boiling acid, strong enough to strip flesh from bone.

It also triggered a new cloud of Blightblood Contagion, which increased the curse's effect and duration and sapped more of his Health and Stamina Regeneration capabilities.

The acid itself barely put a dent in Marek's Health vial, but that was fine. This was a game of many steps. Roark watched as the Tyrant King pulled himself from the vat, dripping black ooze that sizzled against the stones underfoot, and headed down a series of twisting and turning passageways filled with more of the Varssons, ready to strike their blow against the monster that had killed them all so long ago. Even the most fearsome of Redeemed Warriors only gave Marek a moment of pause, but there were hundreds of them, and just as many traps.

Marek muddled through Gevaudan's dungeon. He fought through waves of Redeemed Varssons and more than a few of the Wolf-Bear Hybrids Gevaudan had brought with him from Hearthworld. All the while, Roark used his abilities as the Feudal Lord to change and tweak things on the fly, adding additional spells and augmenting existing structures and traps. Unfortunately, none of them stopped Marek for as long as Roark would've hoped.

The Tyrant King was a powerhouse—there was no denying that—and he had grown impossibly strong since Roark had gone toe to toe with him in the Vault of the Radiant Shield. It took Marek less than thirty minutes to clear the dungeon's three floors. He thundered down the final hall to the Throne Room like an enraged Stone Tiger.

"I've played your game," the Undead God-Pharaoh growled

as he shouldered open the iron-reinforced double doors standing guard over the dungeon's inner sanctuary. The metal groaned and finally ripped free. Marek smirked as he threw down the door and strolled into the Throne Room. "I've found it wanting. Now face me, cur, and perish."

"For the record, this is only the first part of my game," Roark replied casually, standing from his seat upon the tree stump throne. "Come and get me—if you can."

As Marek flew through the room, murder etched into every fiber of his being, the next portal plate triggered.

The world shattered into a thousand pieces as Marek and Roark were whisked through the stars and dropped into a new dungeon—a death maze built of fire and rock, buried in the heart of a volcano. It was governed by the Beryl King, his stony acolytes, and squat, thickset men and women with massive beards. The Dwergkin.

Fresh golden shackles erupted from the dusty ground, renewed deadly gases billowed through the air, and flashes of Sun Fire and Star Nova lit up the room around Marek as the process started all over again.

A celestial millstone, grinding him to dust.

Except this time each spell hit harder than those that had come before, not only because of the Spell Amplifiers Roark had planted in the Dwergkin's entry chamber but because his chosen curses *stacked*.

Roark could see that realization wash across Marek's face as the Sun Fire spells landed like a sledgehammer, crushing eight percent of his Health bar.

"So close," Roark taunted. "Surely you weren't fool enough to think a single dungeon would suffice? Your crimes stretch across countless realities, and so will your punishment. Come and find me, oh mighty Tyrant King. Come and see what ghosts await you in these halls and many, many more..."

CHAPTER 37
ARMY OF ONE

And so it went in a process that seemed to span days. Every portal plate inflicted a new toll, carving away another slice of his unholy power, and every dungeon was specifically designed to strip the Tyrant down further. To break him, mind, body, and soul.

After dragging himself through the Beryl King's volcanic temple, Marek replaced his ragged armor with a new set. Only to be transported to the Aerie Taiga, where he was forced to clamber through a precarious treetop dungeon—loaded with sentient vines and enormous carnivorous plants—all while being assaulted by Drokara's Metalwraiths and the strange copper-skinned Redeemed inhabitants, who rained down acidic spit that ate through the armor like fire through new snow.

When Marek replaced his lost staff with a massive Two-Edged Bronze Falcata, the Redeemed Prismatic Wyrms of a glass- and mirror-filled dungeon world snatched it away under cover of an illusory attack by Ko the Pestilent Mind-Scythe.

Marek had no more extracted himself from Ko's maddening

puzzle Throne Room than the tyrant found himself blasted by the disorienting Evermaelstrom of Rohibim's oceanic dungeon.

Roark led him on a violent chase across the newly Redeemed worlds, always just out of the Undead God-Pharaoh's reach, punishing him every step of the way. Roark never let up for a moment, never allowed Marek to regain his bearings or catch his breath—always hitting him with a new trap, a new curse, and new foes. And above all, he never let him forget that he was losing to an upstart. A no one. He rubbed each new failure in Marek's face while the angry revenants from the despot's past exacted their own form of bloody retribution.

Marek's rage drove him on despite every obstacle. His need to crush Roark—to prove his superiority—was carved into the core of his being, and it made him reckless. Just the way Roark liked his enemies.

The final portal plate carried Roark from Asheth Kisari—the jungle world where Shess, the Soaring Serpent Monarch, held court—to a barren world just half a step ahead of his furious pursuer. Heat seared Roark's skin, and livid sunlight battered his eyes. For miles in every direction, there was nothing but flat, sunbaked salt pan and dancing heat shimmers. A barren wind whistled across the ancient alluvial plain, tearing through his silver hair and rattling the Cursed skulls at his hip.

"Keep running, von Graf!" Marek sneered. Salt puffed beneath his hooves and swirled into dust devils in the wake of his now-ragged fur-lined robes. He was panting from the strain of this constant exertion, and viscous ooze and black dust poured from a multitude of wounds small and large. Marek was hurt, his filigreed Health vial hovering at just above sixty percent, and the sheer number of draining effects stacked against him was daunting. "What are another hundred thousand worlds to me?" he spat. "I know the Rune of Power, too, you fool. Wherever you go, I'll hunt you down. I'll dog your steps and paint every reality you set foot in red with blood. Flee as long as you like—eventually, you'll run out of worlds to flee to."

"No more running, no more fleeing," Roark said, spinning around to face the Undead God-Pharaoh. "The game comes to a close. There are no more dungeons to run. This is the last world, Marek. It ends here."

As he said it, the short-term Illusion spell written into the Curse Chain of the final portal plate ran out.

That hateful desert sun disappeared, draping the heavens in a blanket of everlasting night and swirling cosmoses. Where the wide-open salt plain had been, suddenly they were standing at the foot of that jagged, humming colossus of amber stone. The Tower's nimbus of purples and blues cast both Marek and Roark in cool, shimmering shades.

The silver links holding the World Stone around Marek's neck snapped with a thin *twang* that was nearly lost in the low hum of power coming from the monolith. The Tyrant King's eyes flared wide in shock and what might've been genuine fear. Roark had caught glimpses of uncertainty as Marek waded through the various dungeons, but never fear. Not until this moment. The Tyrant King clutched at the pendant, caught its chain. But his arms shook from the strain of holding it back. The World Stone wanted to return home, and it was far more powerful than Marek.

After a fruitless few seconds of struggle, the chunk of amber broke free from his grasp and tumbled end over end toward the Tower. Rather than crashing against the structure's side, the World Stone slipped perfectly into the fist-sized wound from where it had been extracted so many eons before.

Time and the clockwork of universes surrounding them stood still as brilliant light poured from the edges of the damaged section. The constant, resonating hum of the Tower intensified until it shook Roark's rib cage and stole the breath from his lungs. Marek was driven to his knees with his hands clamped to his decaying, tattered ears.

Slowly, the reverberating note tapered off and the light waned.

The Tower stood before them, whole and unbroken once more.

"No." Marek stumbled back on his hooves. "Can you even begin to understand," he whispered in a voice radiating cold fury and rising with every word, "how hard it was to carve off a piece of this damnable Tower?" He finished in a roar that echoed through space. "I had to wage a war across centuries and galaxies just to assemble a weapon powerful enough to harness even that tiny chunk!" He reached out with one empty, bloody hand as if to strangle Roark. "You will live to regret this. I am supreme, you pathetic worm. I am a god! Even without the World Stone, I am still worlds more powerful than you!"

God Mode

The Tower of Creation is under assault from Tyrant King and Undead God-Pharaoh Marek Konig Ustar. As Tower Guardian, you are expected to protect it by defeating this would-be deity.

Objective: Kill Marek Konig Ustar while protecting the Tower of Creation.

Reward: 100,000 Experience, Immortal Blessing of the Tower

Failure: Die at the hand of Marek Konig Ustar or allow the Tower to be damaged.

Penalty: No respawn.

Accept quest? Yes/No

To defeat a monster, one must become a monster. What then must one become to defeat a god?

Roark braced himself and accepted the quest. As the parchment dissipated, he activated his new Draconic Celestial Form. The iridescent feathers of his wings spread, covering his body, their inky blackness now shining with pinpricks of starlight. His spine stretched and grew into a tail studded with glowing purple spikes as jagged as broken glass. A third set of limbs joined his others, giving him six enormous legs tipped with deadly talons that shined with celestial power.

Marek laughed. "Do you think I don't know the same trick? I can play that game better than you could ever hope to. I've waged this campaign for centuries! Deal any card you like, I've beaten a thousand hands just like it—crushed a thousand enemies just like you. Even your best is nothing to me."

Onyx sand whirled from the sickly green gem between Marek's crescent horns, enveloping him. At the eye of the sandstorm, the Undead God-Pharaoh's already huge form began to grow and twist.

Jagged yellow fangs erupted from his jaws. Enormous decaying wings ripped from the rotten flesh of his back, scattering a shower of Scarab Beetles upon the ground. His crescent horns lengthened and the gem tripled in size. His gangly limbs stretched and thickened, his bony torso extending and hunching forward until it forced him down onto four legs that ended in massive paws tipped with wickedly curved, sand-dusted claws longer and sharper than a newly forged sword. A tail as thick as a ship's anchor chain whipped behind him; at its end was the fanged, hissing head of an adder, mindlessly searching for a target to strike.

The decaying sphynx prowled forward, advancing on Roark with a wild light in his glowing cat's eyes. Even damaged and cursed, he was a force of nature to be reckoned with. Roark just hoped everything he'd done had been enough.

Marek circled right, then pounced, a cat going in for a kill.

But Roark was no defenseless little mouse. His draconic muscles coiled as he leapt up to meet the Undead God-Pharaoh. As their bodies collided, booming peals like thunder rolled through Creation, shaking the universes in their endless spin. They tore into each other, ripping with tooth and claw, hammering with ferocious wingbeats, blasting one another with gouts of Venom Spray and jets of Supernova Flare—Roark's newest ability as a Draconic Celestial.

They careened into the side of the Tower and dropped, Marek gaining the momentary advantage and landing on top.

"You have no hope, von Graf," he growled, claws digging into Roark's throat. "Not of victory. Not of survival. All of your pathetic preparations, every soul you've thrown against me is for naught. You will die here, a minor footnote in my history, and there's nothing you can do to change that. Against me you were always destined to lose."

A wry smirk bared Roark's draconic fangs. "It's true, in a fair fight, you'll beat me every time," he choked out.

With a thundercrack whip of his tree-trunk tail, his jagged spikes tore open Marek's jaw and ripped the cat's claws loose from his neck. Roark thrust hard with all six of his Draconic legs, kicking the sphynx off.

"But I've never fought fair before, and I don't intend to start now," he finished. He pulled a runestone pendant from his Inventory. It was a small silver talisman with an odd rune carved into its face, *Yuduor*. A simple spell that twined this pendant to every other pendant forged from the same batch and marked with the same sigil. It began blinking with a purple light—and two dozen other pendants scattered across the universes began blinking in turn.

Violet portals shimmered to life, one at Roark's left, a second by the tower, a third at Marek's side. Four, then five, then nine, more and more, until a small army of holes in reality stood gaping around them.

Marek let out a short bark of laughter. "I thought you said no more running?"

"These aren't exits for me," Roark said. "They're entrances for—"

"FOR THE SALT!" Kaz bellowed, charging out of the portal closest to Marek. Instead of his trusty Legendary Meat Tenderizer, the Feral Hellstrike Knight wielded a massive Obsidian Glass Warhammer enchanted to deal an equally massive dose of Light Damage with every blow, a weapon Roark had smithed just for fighting the Undead.

Marek spun, letting out the earsplitting yowl of an attacking lion. The gem between his horns rained black sand like a shattered hourglass.

The Troll Gourmet's charge slowed to a crawl as the earth around him shifted and flowed into thigh-high waves of sand crashing into him, forcing him back. Kaz's battle cry turned into a roar of effort and his face twisted into a frustrated mask as he fought to barrel forward while the sea of sand battled him back, refusing to give him a clear run at the tyrant.

A blaring double-honk split the air, a sound that Roark had recently learned came from an air horn. On the heels of the strange sound came the earth-shaking boom of a cannon.

The ball slammed into Marek's bony rotting flank and exploded, taking a deep bite out of his already hemorrhaging Health bar and blasting a jagged hole through one of his leathery wings.

The Winch Witch—covered in enough steel and spikes to armor a company of Trolls—rumbled out of the portal, the drum on her cannon rolling noisily over to load the next shot.

A smug-looking Ranger Cleric was riding atop the Witch, manning the beefy .50 caliber machine gun. He opened fire on the God-Pharaoh turned giant sphynx, strafing him with hot lead.

"What's up, loser," PwnrBwner said in between bursts, jerking his chin at Roark. "Calvary's here."

"It's 'cavalry,' doofus." In the turret beside him, his lieutenant GothicTerror fitted a Light-Enchanted arrow—another fresh resupply from the Citadel's armory—to her bowstring and fired it at Marek. Like all of the weapons Roark had passed out to his allies over the last twenty-four hours, the arrows and Kaz's hammer had been crafted to take down Aczol the Eternal NecroDragon, but their magicks would work just as well against the Undead God-Pharaoh.

And the floodgates opened.

From the portal at Roark's side, an Elemental Turtle Dragon waddled out leading a series of somewhat smaller, newly evolved Adolescent Turtle Dragons. Mac threw back his orange head and chirped out a gout of flame. As one, the shell-covered dragons stampeded toward the sphynx, harrying the Undead God-Pharaoh.

Through another portal marched the Witchdoctor Ick and the Paragon of Light Yevin, leading a contingent of their best students.

"Fall into formation, you lousy toads!" Yevin barked.

The front line of Light students backed the Paragon, hurling spells and curses at Marek, while in the back line Ick and a chorus of Night students raised their voices in a buzzing, insectile song, flowing through a series of accompanying postures to add to the buff's power.

Silvery moonlight shined from Roark's skin and surrounded each of his friends as Strength poured into his limbs.

[*You and all allies of the School of Night Magick within a 50-foot radius have been Strengthened by 21% with Nimbus of the Night; duration: 2 minutes.*]

From the gem between his horns, Marek conjured green-black streaks of lightning, hurling them at the Turtle Dragons. With a graceful, powerful thrust of both palms, Ick effortlessly countered the spell, casting a web of Discordant Inversion to intercept the deadly bolt. Instantly, its opposite shot backward and slammed into Marek's battered, decaying hide.

A silver streak swooped through the air—Randy Shoemaker, clad in shining armor. The Arboreal Herald stretched out his palms, suddenly surrounded by a halo of emerald Earth magick. He clenched his hands into tight fists, and brilliant green vines erupted from the ground, twining around each of Marek's legs. The sphynx roared and tore free, but the momentary distraction had left an opening for Talise to drop in from above.

A Light-enchanted rapier danced in her golden hand, further whittling down the Tyrant King's diminishing Health. Marek spun to fire off a deadly blast of black-green lightning at the raven-winged Malaika Herald, but as he did, Kaz laid into Marek from behind. The Troll Gourmet had finally broken free of the quicksand and made it into striking range of the Tyrant King.

The despot was being hounded on all sides, his Health eaten away in the same death-by-a-thousand-cuts manner that Roark had faced when he attacked the maka-ronin and his pack, leaving him no time to regenerate. Between the relentless onslaught, the Bloodblight Contagion, and the endless number of Sun Fire afflictions, Marek didn't stand a chance. His decaying flesh hung in tatters from his bones, and his limbs trembled as if all strength had left them. Even the Scarabs crawling beneath his desiccated skin were abandoning him, scattering like rats deserting a sinking ship. He looked as if he were at death's door.

A sound rumbled up from the Tyrant King's throat, but it wasn't a death rattle or cry for mercy.

He was laughing. Deep, rumbling, menacing laughter.

Bubbles boiled along the surface of his rotting flesh, swelling and twitching, looking for all the worlds as if he were about to pop.

"So this boss-level bullshit is universal now?" PwnrBwner spat and opened up on the seething mass of sphynx, but Marek's undead body swallowed the bullets like dry earth lapping up raindrops.

Heat waves flowed off the Tyrant King, and a red glow shined from him as if he were burning from the inside out.

"Get back!" Roark roared. "Now! Everyone away from him!"

But it was too late. With an ear-shattering report like a monolith cracking in half, a huge bubbling tumor tore itself free from the massive sphynx. Roark expected the disgusting meaty growth to explode, but the reality was far worse. It grew teeth and graying hair and human limbs, slowly taking on the bored aristocratic face and form of the Marek Konig Ustar who had subjugated all of Traisbin.

"Did you think I wouldn't have prepared for just such a contingency, von Graf?" this human Marek growled. "That I didn't know how much you love to drag others into your pain and destruction?"

Another hunk of boiling flesh leapt from the sphynx. Gray, bristling hair covered the lanky, muscular form of a werewolf, who was also Marek. Or perhaps had been at one time. Close on this beast's heels was a chunk of Marek that became a brawny bipedal shark with gnashing bloody teeth. Following that was a monster like a cross between a great metal hornet and a praying mantis, with a pair of scythe arms, buzzing transparent wings, and a massive stinger dripping with venom.

"With every iteration, I became stronger—a more distilled,

better, deadlier version of myself, but I never cast off the previous versions," the humanoid Marek said, his sphynx body still vomiting up more of the strange and diverse creatures he had once been. "The Tower of Creation exists at all times, in all places, and here so do all of me. You forced me to confront the skeletons of my past, but now you will face those same skeletons. The Tyrant Kings of a multitude of worlds."

While he spoke, a skeletal wraith on a bone stallion broke free, then a massive squid with razor-sharp pincers at the ends of its tentacles and a snapping, hungry beak. A scaly blue-green monster with webbed hands coated in endless suction cups sprang up, followed by a radiant cloud of swirling gases and a glassy crystalline creature that crunched and clanked with every movement.

All Marek. Every one.

"You hero types always think you're so wise, relying on your friends and allies to save you, dragging the ones you care most about down to the depths with you," the humanoid Marek said, chuckling as if he'd heard a clever turn of phrase at a courtly party. "But you see, I'm beyond that. I don't need friends. I have myselves."

CHAPTER 38

DEATHBLOW

For a moment, stillness reigned at the center of that kaleidoscope of swirling realities. The Tower looked on as the many iterations of Marek Konig Ustar stood gloating over his latest play while Roark and his friends looked on in horror and tried to formulate a new plan.

Then a gunshot echoed across the universes.

Half of the human Marek's handsome, aristocratic face was ripped off in one violent jerk. Bone and blood sprayed onto the shoulder of his finely cut robes.

Zyra's Tattooed Colt 1911s belched muzzle flash and gun smoke as she fired again and again, emptying her magazines into the Tyrant King. With Marek's level, the Cursed shots should have been no more troubling than a beesting to a rampaging bear, but instead of only pilfering tiny slivers from his Health bar, each bullet stole away great heaps of red.

"And yet you take damage like a first-level mob," she drawled, ejecting a clip and tipping the pistol back to her shoulder so one of her extraneous spiderlimbs could reload it from above. "Doesn't seem like that brilliant of a plan, splitting your Health between each of your selves."

"What?" Marek's brows furrowed in confusion and fury as he prodded weakly at his gushing gunshot wounds. "No! That's not possible!" He dropped to one knee. "I am all-powerful!"

Kaz lunged forward, swinging his massive hammer down with a crunch on the kneeling humanoid Marek. His head squished inward, neck snapping.

"Zyra is right!" Kaz stepped back and watched as Marek's Health bar flashed a critical warning, then ran out as the body went abruptly limp. One version out of the fifty of him dead. "He is many, but he is not as strong as when he was one!"

"Aw, hell yeah!" PwnrBwner swung the Winch Witch's turret gun around and opened up on the squid Marek. "Let's shoot some asshole fish in a barrel!"

Sensing it didn't have much time left, the squid snapped its beak and raced for the Ranger-Cleric, quickly eating up the distance with its writhing tentacles. Not perturbed at all, Pwnr-Bwner sawed the gun back and forth, nearly cutting the squid in half with his spray of bullets. GothicTerror finished him off with a Light-blessed arrow, which lodged itself in one giant, oversized eyeball.

Battle broke out once more, all of the Mareks suddenly springing to life, frantically flinging spells, attacking with varied talons and fangs, or shooting strange weapons.

But Roark spotted the problem right away.

Marek had never truly depended on another, and it showed in his fighting. Instead of working as a well-rounded party, the lot of them fought as individuals, each Marek fancying himself the hero—and the other versions of himself mere cannon fodder. He was a man who sent others to die at his behest, who preserved himself at all costs while throwing away the lives of countless meaningless lackeys. Ensuring his own survival was more important to him than anything. Including, it seemed, protecting the other versions of himself.

Had the Mareks joined forces, they might've been an unstoppable force, but Marek wasn't one to take orders. Separate, they were vulnerable.

Kaz crushed the glassy crystalline Marek with a massive blow from his hammer while the scaly blue-green Marek, close enough to have intervened and maybe even killed the Troll Gourmet, turned tail and ran as fast as his webbed feet could carry him.

Zyra snared the radiant ball of gases in a poison-drenched web, giving Talise time to swoop in and blast that version of Marek with a burst of lawless orange magick, all the while going unmolested by the shark Marek, who could have snuck up behind either one and attacked, but who had gone after one of the weaker Turtle Dragons in a bid to escape.

With a ground-shaking thud, all twelve hundred pounds of Mac landed on the fleeing shark. The toothy Marek put up a fight, but as a group the small herd of Adolescent Turtle Dragons and their vicious three-headed leader savaged the muscular shark, tearing him to pieces and swallowing great fishy chunks of meat as their reward.

"This changes nothing," the sphynx Marek growled, sidling slowly around the fray on decaying paws.

Roark fell into the circle, his fencer's footwork less agile in his new Draconic form but still instinctual.

"And that's why you're going to lose," he told the Undead God-Pharaoh, his spike-studded tail flicking. "In all this time, you've never really changed. You wore different faces, but inside you've always been the same. Selfish, vain, caring for nothing and no one except yourself. Should've learned to adapt, mate."

Roark dove at the sphynx, his powerful wings pushing him to blazing speeds, and opened his fanged maw wide, blasting Marek with a concentrated Supernova Flare. Marek bellowed in retaliation and batted the wave of celestial flame aside with one paw, the stink of scorched meat filling the air. As Roark slammed into the sphynx's chest, the adder of a tail whipped over Marek's shoulder and struck, once, twice, three times, faster than Roark could blink.

[*Clearblood Ring has resisted Venom of the Adder.*]

The flurry of strikes ate through a sliver of Roark's Health, but at least the venom didn't take. Finally, the bloody ring had come in handy for something besides thwarting his lover's poison-happy moods. The fact that Roark was protected against all poison, disease, and blood-based magickal attacks, however, seemed to infuriate the serpent tail. It struck for Roark's eyes, and though it missed with its fangs, it managed to spit a healthy dose of venom into them.

Roark cursed, blinking and shaking his head, still locked in combat with the colossal Undead sphynx. Resisting the poison damage wasn't worth much when his eyes were burning and clouded with adder spit.

[*Your vision has been obscured by a foreign substance! Vision reduced by 65% for 30 seconds or until you rinse with a Collyrium Solution.*]

A massive paw crashed into Roark's feathered jaw, ripping open the scaly flesh and busting fangs from their moorings. Roark exhaled another gout of Supernova Flare while simultaneously slashing at Marek with his talons and battering the sphynx with his powerful wings. Without his vision, though, it was next to impossible to avoid Marek's attacks. The sphynx slipped beneath one of his wild swipes and launched a ferocious counterattack, laying open Roark's stomach with feline claws, spilling out ropes of innards.

His filigreed Health vial flashed as it plunged below fifty percent.

"Don't worry, Griefer, I got you," PwnrBwner yelled through a break in the gunfire. "Warlord PwnrBwner to the rescue."

With a bellowing shout, the Ranger-Cleric cast Fast-Healing Blast over the battlefield.

[*You have been healed for 160 Health Points.*]

The spell wasn't much, but it stemmed the blood loss and allowed Roark's natural regeneration to kick in, boosting him back to the sixty percent mark. Another blast of Divine healing magick helped put Roark's insides back into his belly where they belonged, just as his vision finally cleared. He'd taken a nasty beating during the blind brawl, but then so had Marek. The Undead sphynx was down to forty percent red and still plunging.

Roark frowned in confusion as he cast Meteoric Blast, another of his temporary Celestial abilities. The spell conjured a shower of flaming comets which each landed for +25 Fire Damage and 2n Light Damage, where n was equal to Roark's character level. Each blazing rock had the potential for 223 total damage, and there were more than two dozen of the projectiles. A powerful spell to be sure, but even that didn't account for such a huge dip in Marek's Health.

Perhaps it was the cumulative effect from all the Sun Fire afflictions burning through the Tyrant's filigreed vial? No, even that wasn't enough. Marek must have close to 5,000 total Health and a normal regeneration rate of a hundred HP per second.

Then he saw Ick and Yevin teaming up to cast Shattering Illumination and Deadly Nightshade on a Marek of shadow and smoke. The creature exploded from the inside out, dying in a blast of sunlight and moonbeams.

As the shadow-smoke Marek's red bar emptied, a fraction of the sphynx Marek's Health dropped, too. All across the battlefield, a myriad of Mareks flinched as a slice of their Health was stolen away. Killing one version of Marek was detrimental to them all.

Finally, understanding clicked into place. They were all connected, every version of the tyrant.

The sphynx's adder-tail lashed at Roark's throat, opening a new gash. Wind whistling through the bleeding hole beneath his chin, Roark cursed and let go of the sphynx. When the adder lunged again, he caught it by the jaws, prying them open, wider, wider, until the bottom jaw tore free. The adder head spasmed, spewing out a fountain of harmless venom—harmless to Roark, at least—then fell limp, dead.

Below, the scaly webbed-hand creature's corpse detonated from a combination death blow of Elemental Fury and Exploding Corpse dealt by PwnrBwner and GothicTerror.

A bloody, flayed-looking thing wrapped in webbing succumbed to Zyra's poisoned knives.

Kaz took the head off a tottering Marek with a deft swing of his hammer.

Randy and Talise, fighting back-to-back with Earth magick and rapier, took out a Marek apiece.

Griff shield-bashed another Marek in the teeth, creating what looked like an opening in his guard. A fool's opening, a *chiamata* that invited attack. When that Marek lunged into Griff's measure, the old skill trainer deftly danced to the right and thrust his shortsword into that Marek's heart, killing it on the spot.

Just like that, the tide shifted. Suddenly the only Marek left was the Undead sphynx battling with Roark.

Roark saw a spark of panic ignite in the Tyrant King's feral cat eyes. He was losing, and he knew it. He was surrounded by his enemies. The World Stone Pendant was gone. He was well and truly alone.

The sphynx hesitated, momentarily distracted as the Winch Witch skidded into range.

Roark attacked, darting in low and spinning fast, bringing

his spiked tail around in a vicious arc. Purple spits of hardened bone slammed into Marek's side and sent the monster reeling on drunken feet. His Health bar inched lower, flashing out a critical warning as it dipped below ten percent at last.

"No!" Marek bellowed, steadying himself. "This is not the way it ends. I won't go down alone! If I am finished, then I'll take you, the Tower, and all of Creation with me!"

A whirlwind of black sand swirled to life around him. Green, necrotic lightning arced from the sickly gem between his crescent horns, blasting Roark backward in a wave of thunderous concussion.

Roark smashed into the ground, tumbling over and over again. His Health dropped precipitously as Marek's cancerous magick gnawed at him like a living beast.

The air lit up with toxic green energy—a deadly aura shining from Marek's skin.

"He's got the Nuclear Corpse ability!" GothicTerror shouted, a frantic edge in her voice.

"Oh shit!" PwnrBwner wheeled his arm toward the Winch Witch. "Everybody haul ass behind the Witch! He's gonna blow!"

"That won't help," GothicTerror argued. "The truck isn't enough! Every living thing in the blast zone—"

The sandstorm whipped to a fever pitch, drowning out her prediction of unstoppable doom. The gale snatched up the sphynx and carried him toward the Tower at eye-blurring speeds. Roark wasn't sure what the Nuclear Corpse ability did, but he knew Marek well enough to be certain that he couldn't let the attack succeed. Ignoring the warning, Roark picked himself up and leapt into the air. He had to stop Marek from taking out the Tower of Creation, whether it killed him or not. Hoping his friends had listened and were getting clear, Roark triggered Planar Flight.

Instantly, his Stamina was cut in half, but he shot like a bullet at Marek, slamming into the Tyrant King's left flank. The two of them tumbled end over end and crashed into the Tower with a deafening thud.

Agony bolted up Roark's spine as his left wing was crushed and a good number of ribs splintered. His Health vial dipped dangerously, dropping into the critical zone.

[*You have suffered a Broken Wing! Flight is hindered for two minutes, or until an Ultimate Healing Potion is consumed. Dexterity reduced by 9% for two minutes or until an Ultimate Healing Potion is consumed.*]

[*You have suffered a series of Fractured Ribs! Movement Speed is reduced by 10% for two minutes or until an Ultimate Healing Potion is consumed.*]

The timer for Roark's Draconic Form ran out a heartbeat before Marek's sphynx form melted back into the battered Undead God-Pharaoh.

Marek cackled, rotting black blood trickling from the corner of his mouth. "It's too late, you wretched cur. Kill me if you like —my body will detonate the moment I die, like one of your Cursed heads but multiplied immeasurably. Nothing and no one will survive the blast. The Tower will be leveled, and when it falls, all of Creation will fall with it. You may have won this paltry battle, but I've won the war."

"Wrong again, mate," Roark wheezed, pulling a spell scroll from his Inventory and breaking the seal with his thumb. A shimmering purple hole tore through reality.

Roark didn't hesitate. While Marek stared stupidly at the rift, Roark locked his arms around the Tyrant King, planted his feet in the dirt at the base of the Tower, and shoved with every ounce of strength he could muster.

Together, they tumbled through the portal into a vast dead world. This was one of the many worlds that Roark had visited during his initial search, one that was truly dead. No sun lit the extinguished planet. No life grew upon its surface. No breeze stirred the air. There was nothing but a bleak emptiness in every direction. It wasn't suitable even for a dungeon.

It was, however, a perfectly appropriate location for the death of Marek Konig Ustar, the ruthless tyrant who had destroyed it.

Roark pulled a Light-enchanted Kaiken Dagger from his Inventory. Its wickedly contoured blade and unassuming hilt was so unlike the elaborately smithed weapons he'd grown accustomed to. It was far closer in appearance to the mundane Lyuko dagger he'd tried to assassinate Marek with back in the abandoned von Graf manor house so many months ago. From nowhere, a familiar thought flitted through his mind, the same one that had occurred to him that fateful night—that this was a fitting final gift from the half-breed son of a murdered *tsarina* and nobleman.

"Do it!" Marek roared, sadistic glee burning in his eyes.

Throwing his weight behind the dagger, Roark drove the blade home. It cracked through Marek's breastbone, flashing with Light Damage as it plunged into the tyrant's black, shriveled heart.

"Ready to die for the last time, von Graf?" Marek choked out, black sludge oozing from his desiccated lips.

"Not quite," Roark said, casting Undying Soul on himself. Power flooded out from his center as his limbs turned a ghostly opaque and an intensely painful arctic chill settled into his bones. It was misery, neither life nor death, but a liminal state waltzing between the two. For a full minute he would spin through that in-between realm, unable to kill, unable to be killed.

The Tyrant King's eyes widened as he realized what Roark had done.

"No, you can't—"

The last remaining dregs of red liquid drained away from Marek's filigreed Health vial, robbing him even of his final dying words. A blinding nuclear blast of green light erupted from the Tyrant King's corpse, gouging an immense crater into the surface of the dead world and propelling Roark from his feet. The planet rumbled in angry protest, then shattered like a dropped porcelain bowl. A whirling, sucking black hole opened, summoning a maelstrom of crushing gravity and blistering fallout.

Unconsciousness swarmed in from the edges, threatening to pull Roark under. Apparently just because he wasn't able to be killed while Undying Soul was active didn't mean he wasn't able to feel the equivalent amount of pain. But Roark was accustomed to pain and darkness in equal measures—he'd spent his entire life fighting tooth and nail against them, and he wouldn't be thwarted now. Not when he was so close to the finish.

Roark gritted his teeth against the agony—against the darkness and the crushing weight of that ravenous black hole—just long enough to pull out an emergency scroll. It took every ounce of strength left in his body to break the seal with his thumb, summoning one more portal—this to whisk him away from the dead planet's final, violent obliteration.

A cool breeze whipped through his hair as he fell through time and space.

With a thud, the portal dropped Roark von Graf back at the foot of the Tower, alive but only just.

CHAPTER 39
AFTERMATH

The moment he could see again, a sudden influx of notices flooded Roark's vision.

[*You have suffered Radiation Burns! -33 HP/sec for two minutes or until an Ultimate Health Potion is consumed.*]

[*You have suffered Retinal Burns! Vision is Obscured for two minutes or until an Ultimate Healing Potion is consumed.*]

[*You have suffered Internal Trauma! -4 HP/sec for two minutes or until an Ultimate Healing Potion is consumed.*]

Over the smell of his own burnt flesh and feathers, Roark caught the sweet scent of deadly coquelicot flowers.

"I should withhold these potions for that self-sacrificial gambit. Of all the reckless, overly ambitious Jotnar schemes, that has to have been the most foolish I've ever witnessed." Zyra's boots scuffed the ground near his head and her voice grew closer as she knelt beside him. "You have no idea how lucky you are to have me to feed you Ultimate Healing potions. Drink this."

"I sure as bloody hell do know." Roark rolled over to face the Orbweaver Ravager, unable to stifle a grunt of pain. "And not just because you're the only one who can make a potion strong enough to save me from all my reckless Jotnar schemes. Even if you couldn't do anything to help me destroy my enemies, I'd still bloody love you."

There was a moment's silence, then her lacy veil brushed his face and soft, warm lips gently pressed to his, giving just a hint of her fangs. Although it aggravated his Radiation Burns, Roark slipped his fingers into the soft white hair at the nape of her neck and pulled her in for something much hungrier. They had just saved the universes and survived a potentially reality-ending war, after all. A little celebrating seemed to be in order.

When Zyra pulled back, Roark huffed a laugh.

"Just so you're aware," he muttered, "if you poisoned me, it probably *will* kill me this time. I'm hovering over critical health at the moment."

A stopper squeaked from a bottle.

Zyra chuckled. "I did level my Envenomate ability enough that your precious Clearblood Ring can't save you any longer." She wiped a trickle of blood from a fang mark on his lip with her thumb. "But I skipped the poison just this once. You're a pain of a Jotnar to love, but I do."

Glass was the next thing to kiss Roark's lips, and syrupy Ultimate Healing Potion flowed down his throat. As the injuries healed and his Health vial refilled with crimson liquid, he sat up and stretched the kinks out of his back and neck. They protested with a series of crackling pops.

He suddenly felt very tired. He'd spent a lifetime searching for a way to defeat the Tyrant King, and while he fully intended to celebrate the end of that dark, terrible era, a nagging part of him couldn't believe it was over. He was free. His family's spirits could rest easy. All that was left to do was properly inter Danella, as she deserved. Then? He could finally move on with his life.

But what would he do with that life? He'd spent so much of

this one fighting that he didn't even know where to begin. Honestly, he'd never expected to live long enough to see the end of Marek's bloody reign. He'd seeded dungeons across several worlds, but maybe there was more work to be done. It was impossible to undo all the damage that Marek had wrought, but with his Redeemer of the Fallen ability, he could take a stab at it. Visit more of the worlds Marek had ravaged, seed dungeons, give the inhabitants of those fallen worlds a chance to live again. To rebuild a portion of what they'd lost.

As he mulled over the thought, a new scrap of parchment appeared before Roark.

[*Eternal Resonance offered. Compatibility: 100%. The Tower of Creation, having accepted you as a Guardian, is offering to bind Temporal Location Radiant Citadel with Eternal Location: Tower of Creation.*

Do you agree to this binding? Yes/No?

Warning: Binding a Temporal Location to an Eternal Location will raise its Temporal status to Eternal, potentially inviting a new and more powerful range of foes to the Location. The foes who would launch an attack on an Eternal Location are vastly stronger than those who would attack a Temporal Location.

Warning: Binding Temporal Locations to Eternal Locations is irreversible.]

Roark's breath caught in his chest as he read and reread the prompt. The last time he'd tried this, Hearthworld had imploded and the Cruel Citadel had ended up transformed and stranded in the mountains high above Korvo. That time, the Compatibility had been well below one hundred percent, but accepting was no guarantee that the Citadel as he knew it would survive.

The gravity of the decision settled around Roark's shoulders like a weight. If he accepted, he would be the defender of the endless galaxies that made up Creation. Realities he had never dreamt of would depend on him—and not just on his faithful protection, but on the strength of the entire Citadel. He would have to remain vigilant for as long as he lived—perhaps even find a successor when his ability to watch over the Tower drew to a close.

Whether or not he was up to the task wasn't in question. No one was up to such a task, and any who believed they *were*, most assuredly *weren't*. But this wasn't a hypothetical situation—the option had been presented to him, and Roark had to believe he'd been selected for a reason. What better way to spend a lifetime than preventing another Marek from rising to power and preventing untold worlds from suffering in the process? It was his duty, and he would see it done.

Steeling himself, Roark agreed to the Binding.

[*Binding accepted. Universal Forge activated. Creating new Eternal Location... Designation: The Celestial Citadel...*]

The Tower rumbled and groaned while blinding amber light radiated outward in pulsing rings of power. A deep, echoing hum filled the universe like a royal decree. Unlike before when it was reabsorbing the World Stone, the low, resonating tone the Tower sent out this time was refreshing and warm, the sound of all Creation working in concert. Reality itself rang with the note, until Roark could feel the vibrations deep in his bones calling to him, telling him he had a purpose.

"What's happening?" Zyra asked, drawing her Colts. "Is it another attack?"

Roark shook his head. "More like the forging of a new alliance."

The boundless spinning cosmoses surrounding them flickered, replaced with the gigantic bioluminescent mushrooms, softly chiming grass, and rolling hills of the Citadel's fifth floor. In one corner, Roark caught just a glimpse of the Troll Nation Marketplace, in the other, the looming shape of the Keep, considered the Citadel's sixth and final floor, though it was technically within the bounds of the fifth. Then everything flickered again, and the pale, glistening light of the mushrooms was replaced once more with the vastness of space.

[*Adding new level... Designation: Seventh Floor. New level accessible only by way of the Celestial Citadel. Deleting all other external entrances...*]

Slowly, at the far edges of the interminable clockwork of realities, a ceiling became just barely visible, dark as the abyss and sprinkled with shimmering sapphire, violet, and jade space dust.

At his side, Zyra let out a soft sigh.

"It's beautiful," she whispered, her weapons and fear forgotten.

Silently, Roark nodded, then rolled the last vestiges of tension from his shoulders. Perhaps he was already becoming accustomed to the added weight of infinite worlds.

A new notification appeared before him.

LEVEL UP!

[*Congratulations! You have completed the quest God Mode! Receive 100,000 Experience Points and Immortal Blessing of the Tower!*

Immortal Blessing of the Tower: For as long as you defend the Tower of Creation, you will be granted Immortality. Health and Magick Bonus, +1,000 per 100 Character Levels! Health and Magick Regen Bonus, +100 per 100 Character Levels! 100% Resistance against non-magickal weapons.

Additional Properties:

Soul-Forge – Imbue the undead with life and will.

Current Creation Tower Authority: Greater Vassal 11/150; Lesser Vassal 68/1,000

Property: Glamour Cloak – Use arcane power to disguise your appearance even to the keenest of eyes. Cast 1 per day; duration, 3 hours.

Property: Transmute Energy – Meld and merge the primal energies and magicks in the world around you to your will.

Property: Transmute Flesh – Twist and shape the very fabric of living flesh, crafting unspeakable creations fit to serve your bidding and will.

Property: Temporal Binding – Form, shape, and stitch together the fabric of reality itself, bending time and space as you wish.

Warning: Immortality is not *Invulnerability. You will no longer age, but you are still capable of being killed by enough physical, mundane, or magickal damage. Use the gift of Immortality wisely.*]

Wonderingly, Roark opened his grimoire and turned to his updated Character page.

Undying Dragonblood Seraph Overview

Name:	Roark
Gender:	Male
Type:	Undying Dragonblood Seraph
Current Experience:	1,232

Level:	100
Player Class:	Divine Soul Shaman
Alignment:	Infernali
Next Level:	440,000

Health:	3,954.25
H-Regen / 5 Sec:	548.325

Infernali Magick:	5,090
Magick-Regen / 5 Sec:	401.25

Attributes:	
Weapon Damage:	163
Attack Damage:	1789
Base Armor:	125
Armor Rating:	1592.3
Movement Rate:	2.5 x Speed of Opponent
Critical Hit Chance:	32%
Critical Hit Damage:	(+) 300%

Stats:	
Strength:	173
Constitution:	243.65
Dexterity:	200
Intelligence:	310
World Stone Authority, Greater Vassal	11/60
World Stone Authority, Lesser Vassal	85/225
Undistributed Stat Points:	10

Draconic Special Skills:
Rapid-Regen
100% Resistance against non-magical weapons
Stunning Blow; 22% Chance / Hit
Infernal Necro Shield; Draconic-Hybrid Spell
Necrotizing Infernal Torment; Draconic-Hybrid Spell
Necrotic Invigoration; Draconic-Hybrid Spell
Infernal Undead Temptation; Draconic-Hybrid Spell
Raise Thralls; Draconic-Hybrid Spell
Infernal Necrotic Breath; Draconic-Hybrid Spell
EXPAND SKILL LIST

Player Special Skills:	
Spellcraft (Class Skill)	Lv. 15
Bladed Weapons (Melee Skill)	Lv. 12
Weapons Specialty: Rapier	Lv. 9
Calligraphy (Trade Skill)	Lv. 5
Blacksmithing (Trade Skill)	Lv.13
Tailoring (Trade Skill)	Lv. 8
Enchanting (Trade Skill)	Lv. 17
Enchanting Specialty: Cursed!	Lv. 15

His Health and Health regeneration had both increased by leaps and bounds. He was still killable, as the warning had declared, but it would take far more work to finish him off than it had before, and his total invulnerability against non-magickal weapons would make him a force to be reckoned with against even formidable technological weapons, such as guns and tanks.

Huge arms grabbed Roark from behind in a crushing grip and swung him around as if he weighed nothing more than a rag doll. Roark felt his bones creaking beneath Kaz's grip. It was a bloody good thing he'd started out this hug with a full Health vial.

"Roark was so brave!" the hulking Troll Gourmet cried, weeping tears of joy. "Kaz feared he would lose his best friend, but against all odds, Roark survived!"

"A little easier, Kaz." Roark winced. "I might have leveled up, but my bones aren't made of steel."

With a last shuddering sniffle, the Hellstrike Knight set Roark on his feet and beamed proudly at him out of teary eyes.

"Roark has triumphed over evil!"

"Not just me, Kaz," Roark said. "All of us. I couldn't have done it—I couldn't even have made it this far—without your help." He looked at his friends who were gathering around. "Without even one of you, this wouldn't have been possible. Thank you all."

"So modest! So kind!" Kaz scrubbed at his streaming eyes. "Roark is truly a great friend and leader!"

PwnrBwner shrugged. "He's all right, I guess. And he's definitely not wrong about us helping him. We pulled that one out at the buzzer. All in all, we make a pretty killer team."

The Ranger-Cleric stuck out his fist, and Roark, who had

recently learned that the gesture was one of solidarity and congratulation, bumped it with his own, gauntlet clanking against gauntlet.

"You're way less of a douchehole than I originally thought." PwnrBwner glanced up at the infinite swirling worlds in all their glory. "And the grandness of the universe is pretty cool, too, I guess."

Roark nodded. "You're also less of a childish ass than I first assumed. You make a powerful ally, PwnrBwner, and I couldn't have left Shieldwall in the hands of a more capable Dungeon Lord."

"I prefer Warlord," PwnrBwner said. "It's got a better ring to it, and I earned it myself through sheer awesomeness; I didn't get it handed to me by anybody. No offense. I'm glad you picked me to run Shieldwall, and I'm doing a kick-ass job and all, but I want everybody on my planet to know who the boss is."

"Warlord PwnrBwner it is," Roark agreed with a lopsided grin.

A wiry hand clapped him on the shoulder.

"You did well, Griefer," Griff said, fixing him with his piercing blue eye. "Mayhap you took the long way around to get past your troubles and regrets so's you could, but you came out the other side a stronger man who oughta be right proud of himself."

"I had quite a bit of help along the way," Roark said, clasping the older man's scar-crossed forearm. "And excellent advice from a wise weapons trainer."

Griff gave him a wry grin. "Well, a weapons trainer, anyway." He hooked his thumbs into his sword belt as he solemnly considered all of reality stretching out in front of them. "What will you do now?"

Roark glanced up at the gleaming amber Tower, now stowed away in the deepest reaches of the Citadel. It was whole and hearty now, but where one power-hungry tyrant could rise up and threaten all of Creation, others would eventually follow. Perhaps not for years or even centuries, but in time they would come.

"Keep building up the Citadel and her defenses," Roark replied, happy to have a purpose once more. "Watch over the Tower. Stop any would-be Tyrant Kings who come looking to carve off another piece of it."

Kaz cleared his throat. "Before Roark does that, may Kaz suggest a celebratory feast?"

CHAPTER 40
ENDINGS AND BEGINNINGS

The feast Kaz and Mai prepared now that they were reunited with one another and their beloved Flavortown spanned a full week and was the most joyous—and lavish—Roark had ever attended. This was in part due to the added festivity of Kaz and Mai's wedding, which took place halfway through the revelry. Delectable foods from across the Devs' home world, Traisbin, and Hearthworld were passed around alongside multiple recent culinary innovations by the Troll Gourmet and his plump new wife.

All of Korvo and much of the quickly recovering Traisbin attended the festivities, along with the Troll Nation and the remaining Poser Owners. Relations were strained at first. No one seemed quite sure how to proceed. There were a few awkward throat-clearings and much glancing up at the starry galaxies that now populated the sky up beyond the fifth floor's bioluminescent mushrooms. The unease, however, was put to rest in short order when Mac and the locals' dogs began frolicking and playing together in the chiming grass. Soon the pet owners followed suit, albeit with a little more aplomb, swapping stories and engaging in some good-natured competitions.

Randy Shoemaker reluctantly officiated one such drinking contest between Grozka the Zealot, Zyra, and a motley assortment of former nobles and commoners from across Traisbin. Luckily, Roark was on hand to protect Randy when his pronouncement of a winner caused an uproar. The Arboreal Herald was very gracious in accepting Zyra's apology later.

The attendance of so many delegates from across the land had the added benefit of allowing Roark and the Elders from many of the major cities to discuss reinstating the Council of Traisbin as the ruling authority. They gathered in the Throne Room around the repaired golden table during one of the quieter nights of the festivities.

Roark sat at the head of the table of voidglass, with the infinite clockwork of Creation wheeling silently at his back where brilliant golden walls and garish stained glass once stood. Fluted columns of the same voidglass now supported the dark vaulted ceiling, but the room wasn't cast in shadow. The subtle glow of the Tower on its distant world lent the Citadel a ghostly amber light that seemed to both permeate everything and emphasize the immeasurable vastness of the space that now hung behind him.

Awed though the Elders were at the beauty, they eventually dispensed with the gawking and got down to the work of deciding who would sit on the restored Council. It was tedious work, with as many opinions as there were faces at the table, but they managed to sort it before the night was out.

"You're certain you won't be a part of the new Council?" Morgana asked, twisting the opal ring on her gnarled knuckle. "There's still one seat left to fill, and it's well known that your father advised the previous Council from time to time. Perhaps you could make his place a more official one."

Roark favored the old woman with a tight smile.

"I don't have the stomach for these sorts of politics," he

said, though he was thinking that what he truly didn't have the stomach for was withholding information from the world, even when that information might be dangerous. But it amounted to the same either way. "In any case, I'll be busy dealing with external threats. I do, however, have a suggestion for the final member of the Council. I think Talise would do well in the seat."

A murmur swept through the mostly elderly people around the table—Albrecht and himself being the younger exceptions—but it didn't sound as violently opposed as Roark had been preparing to counter.

"Granted, she's young for the position," he conceded, "but she's seen the inner workings of despotism and should be able to recognize more of the same before it gains a foothold in our world again." He glanced at Morgana and chuckled self-consciously. "You'll also no doubt find she's got a considerably cooler temperament than her older brother."

"Appointing a younger sibling seems like the perfect way to keep the country dancing on your puppet strings," Albrecht scoffed, folding his arms across his chest as he glowered at Roark.

Roark remarked to himself with bitter amusement that he could add the pompous scar-faced mage to the list of reasons he would be better off staying away from the Council.

"Think what you will, von Reich," Roark said, keeping his reply civil with some effort. "But don't forget that Talise never vowed her allegiance to me, even when the rest of you happily bent the knee. With Marek dead, she owes fealty to no one, whereas yours is still pledged to me."

That silenced the buffoon's protests.

A vote of the current Council members approved Talise for the final seat almost unanimously.

When he relayed the news to her later, Talise took it with a somber frown.

"What if there's a true threat and they refuse to listen to me?" she asked.

He smiled and put an arm around her shoulder. "I think you are more than capable of badgering them into seeing things your way. You always did have a way with words. And you haven't got an older brother for nothing, Talise. I told them the truth—you don't owe me anything, but I'll always be there if you need me."

She nodded slowly, accepting the answer. And for the fourth time since he'd begun talking to her that evening, her attention strayed across Flavortown's common room to where Soileau and his beat-up hurdy-gurdy were leading a jouncing head-to-head duel against a troupe of laughing local musicians. Something of a line of local musicians waiting to challenge the bard next had formed. So far, he was unbeaten, a status Roark doubted anyone would best.

"And you can start by taking my advice," Roark said. "Stay away from the bard. He's left a trail of broken hearts from here to the Devs' home world. He might be handsome, but he's trouble of the first order."

The ghost of a smirk turned up her lips. "My heart's not as fragile as most. In any case, it wasn't the bard I was watching."

Roark looked again, beyond the dueling musicians. He was just in time to see Randy Shoemaker hurriedly avert his gaze from Talise and take a guilty drink of ale.

He looked askance at his sister. "The Herald?"

"Randy's intelligent and kind, and he cuts an impressive figure in his newest evolution."

Roark sized the Arboreal Herald up. He supposed Randy had put on a bit more muscle, but there was still an underlying awkwardness to the man that put Roark in mind of a gangly half-grown pup that hadn't yet learned how all its appendages worked together. Despite that, he seemed to be drawing a fair number of admiring glances from female mobs and humans at surrounding tables. Having the countenance of an angelic being probably helped a great deal on that front.

"Besides," Talise said, "someone planning to wed a bloodthirsty spider shouldn't throw stones." She smiled at his expression of shock. "I heard you in the forge while you smithed the ring. Talking to yourself is a bad habit, mate."

Roark scowled, his face heating. "I was talking to Mac."

"Even so." She shrugged. Then she leaned forward conspiratorially. "Do you have it with you right now?"

He shook his head. "It's not finished yet. I'm still working out the slapdeath mechanism."

"Sounds as if she's going to love it. As Father would say, you're a well-matched pair."

Roark snorted. "I'd forgotten he used to say that."

"I think he would approve," Talise said, turning serious. "Mother... If she could get past her utter revulsion of spiders, maybe she would have as well."

"Randy's not a bad choice, either," Roark admitted. "Brave and good-hearted as anyone you'll come by, in this world or any other."

A hulking shadow fell across their table.

"Did Roark and Talise say they desired more spiced pears?" Kaz waved a platter of delicious-smelling fruit dishes beneath their noses. "Flavortown has more than enough for seconds and thirds. It is Kaz's mission to see that none go hungry while he is in this world."

"I don't think you've got to worry about that, Kaz," Roark said, patting his stomach. "I've eaten far too much every day since you returned. It's been excellent fare, but I can't take another bite."

"Perhaps another tankard of Kaz's special Honey Orange Ale?"

"I'm already swimming, mate."

"I'll take one for the road," PwnrBwner said as he and GothicTerror squeezed through the masses to join them.

Kaz's ears dipped sadly. "PwnrBwner and GothicTerror are leaving so soon?"

"Well, it's been a week, dude, and the containment zone ain't gonna run itself." PwnrBwner shrugged. "Warlords gotta warlord, amiright?"

"Yeah, pretty sure you've had enough already," GothicTerror said.

"It'll be fine," PwnrBwner said. "You're driving."

She rolled her eyes.

Kaz hustled off to the kitchen, the sea of bodies parting for him.

Griff ambled up to the table as well, but shook his head when Roark pulled out a chair and offered it to him.

"No, Griefer, I reckon I'm gonna head out with these two," he said, hooking a thumb toward PwnrBwner and GothicTerror. "Oughta save some time and Magicka if we take the same portal. I said my goodbyes to Mai, and now I figure it's time I take my leave."

"You're leaving?" Roark asked, both surprised and a little saddened. Griff had been a true friend and a wise counselor when Roark had needed both. He'd hoped the old man would stay on.

Griff scrubbed a hand down his whiskery jaw. "This new world and its... containment zone, as PwnrBwner was calling it..." The older man paused to collect his thoughts. "See, the folks there are nothing like the heroes I knew in Hearthworld. Half of 'em don't know their backside from a hole in the ground, and the other half don't know whether they're coming or going.

I spent most of my life after the arena working out what I'm supposed to do with these old bones, and turns out, I'm a guide. It's just who I am. These Earth folks... well, they need a guide. Somebody to point 'em in the right direction and help 'em get their head on straight."

"They couldn't find a better guide," Roark admitted, standing up to see the three of them out. "I hate to see you go, Griff, but I hope it's everything you're looking for. Know you're always welcome back."

Together, their small group squeezed through the revelry and out of Flavortown.

Randy Shoemaker saw them leaving and caught up to them at the door.

"Headed back, huh?" he said.

PwnrBwner glanced sidelong at the Arboreal Herald. "You could come with us if you wanted, man. It's a whole new world out there. The Wild West on steroids. You could be a Mad Max Kin, bro."

Randy shook his head. "I don't think that's for me. I kind of like this pseudo-medieval lifestyle." He smiled and awkwardly stuck out his hand to PwnrBwner. "It's been an honor. Take care of yourself. And uh, take care of Earth for me?"

"No way, Rando." The Ranger-Cleric knocked Randy's hand aside and dragged the Arboreal Herald into a back-slapping hug. "We hug in this guild."

"Jeez, you're a sloppy drunk," GothicTerror said.

"I'm not drunk," PwnrBwner said, clumsily turning the hug around so that he could face her over Randy's shoulder. "But I'm working on it." He gave Randy one last squeeze, then let go and pointed to Roark. "Dude."

Roark put up his hands to forestall a hug. "I think we've said the appropriate goodbyes."

"Listen, if you ever get yourself into trouble like this again, hit me up. I've got your back."

"I'll keep that in mind."

As Roark cast the portal to return the trio to Earth, Kaz came bounding toward them, the grass chiming wildly beneath his massive feet.

"PwnrBwner's ale for the road," Kaz said, offering him the drink with the fondness of a father presenting a new babe.

"You're the man, Kaz," the Ranger-Cleric said, bumping knuckles with the Troll one last time.

"And a special surprise for GothicTerror, Kaz's newest creation inspired by our conversations at Shieldwall—a charming Bakeless Blueberry Cheesecake on a Buttery Crumble Crust. GothicTerror is right, it is much better than the baked version. But please do not tell Jordan Bamsey that Kaz said so. He is quite adamant about the virtues of baked cheesecakes."

GothicTerror laughed as she accepted the dessert. "We don't all know each other just because we live on Earth, Kaz."

"Of course not." The Troll Gourmet nodded emphatically. "But when you see him."

"The odds of that are—"

"Don't kill his dreams, Tots," PwnrBwner said, patting her on the arm. He took a sip of his ale, then nodded at Roark. "Later, bro. Let's get this show on the road, Screamo. The wasteland ain't gonna run itself."

The Ranger-Cleric hopped through the portal. GothicTerror gave Kaz a quick hug, then followed PwnrBwner into the shimmering violet light.

With a final clasp of Roark's forearm, Griff hefted his trusty buckler and shortsword onto his shoulder.

"Watch over Mai for me, lad," he called to Kaz over one shoulder. "She's something else. But then, I suppose so are you."

"Kaz will do his best to give her everything she could ever want," the Troll Gourmet vowed as solemnly as he had the day he married her.

Griff cleared his throat and nodded a final farewell to them all. The portal closed behind him.

Randy shifted his weight awkwardly, then glanced back over his shoulder toward Flavortown as if he'd heard someone call his name. For a moment, a faint green glow suffused his silvery skin, then disappeared.

"I, uh, think I left something in the tavern," he said, reaching for his nonexistent spectacles. "I'll see you guys."

He started to go, but Roark stopped him.

"Randy, are you messaging my sister with Heart of the Forest?"

The Arboreal Herald's eyes grew wide. "No! Well, yeah, but... not anything obscene or... Talise just said she wanted to get some of my views on governing strategies and systems... We're not, um..."

Roark smiled and let him go. "I probably should've given you the warning about heartbreak."

"Heartbreak?" Randy blinked. "I would never—that is, Talise is a fine young woman and I wouldn't treat her with anything but the utmost respect and—"

"See that you do," Roark said, clapping the Herald on the shoulder.

Finally released, Randy Shoemaker hurried toward Flavortown as if he'd been shot out of a tank.

"She's going to eat him alive," Roark said, shaking his head.

"One never knows what strange ingredients combined will produce a gourmet meal," Kaz said, watching the Herald go, "just as one never knows what strange beings thrown together will create a great and enduring love."

A raucous cheer went up in the direction of the revelry.

"I think I've had enough feasting for now, Kaz. I'm going to take another look out—make certain there aren't any new threats inbound."

"Kaz will join you."

Together, they headed for the Keep.

Zyra and Mac were on the ceiling of the Throne Room waiting for them, playing a game that seemed to consist of the Orbweaver throwing bits of Rooting Boar bacon to the Elemental Turtle Dragon. It seemed to be proving more challenging than usual as Mac's attention was divided between the smoky meat, the occasional explosive bursts of distant dying stars, and the playful bickering among his three heads.

When the silly beast realized Roark and Kaz had arrived, Mac dropped down, landing in a scaly heap on the floor, and nudged Roark with all three of his heads, demanding attention.

Roark laughed and scrubbed at the overgrown Salamander's beards.

"You missed the farewells," Roark said to Zyra.

The veiled Orbweaver spun out a thread and gracefully lowered herself to the ground.

"I'm not much for sappy goodbyes," she said. "Unless they're over a corpse."

"Zyra would not have liked this, then," Kaz said helpfully. "Everyone was alive."

Roark took his seat on the dark voidglass of the Celestial Throne and looked out into the vast swirling machinations of endless realities, searching for threats.

Zyra joined him, leaning lazily against one spire of the seat and playing with something shiny on her finger.

"What is that?" Frowning, Roark leaned over to see it better.

"A slapdeath ring." Though her face was hidden behind the veil, Roark could hear the laughter in her voice. She held it out to better admire the venomous purple and green jewel in the setting. The icy light of a passing comet glinted off the stone. “Your sister’s not the only one who can overhear things she’s not supposed to. And I’m much better at hiding.”

“It’s not finished yet,” Roark insisted, trying to take it back.

Zyra used Diurnal Prowl to avoid his reach. “I’m just trying it on.”

“Strange loves indeed.” Kaz sighed, his big chest inflating and deflating as he gazed up at the starry expanse. “Oh, the wonders Kaz has seen. The foods he has tasted. The friends he has made.” He grinned. “Kaz and Roark and Zyra have come a long way from the pair of scared Changelings and the scary Reaver in the Cruel Citadel.”

“Farther than you realize,” Roark said, finally giving up on his fruitless attempts to get the ring back. “And we’re not done yet.”

He opened his grimoire. It was time to get down to the business of preparing the Celestial Citadel for greater, more powerful enemies. When a new threat arose, they would be waiting.

THE END

Celestial Citadel

The Rogue Dungeon Book 6

James A. Hunter
Aaron Michael Ritchey

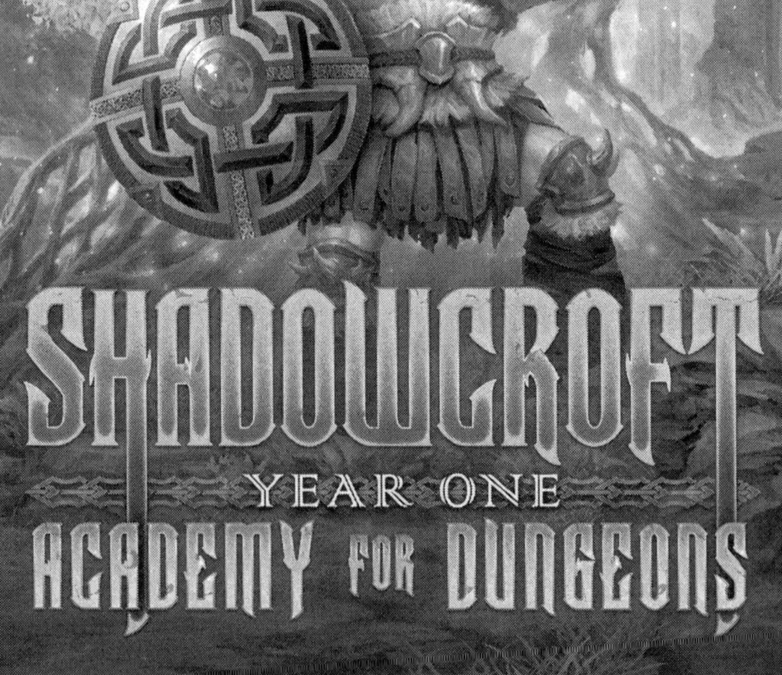

MORE DUNGEON ADVENTURES...

Looking for more exciting dungeon adventures, and need them right this minute? Check out *Shadowcroft Academy For Dungeons: Year One*.

Build a Dungeon. Slay Heroes. Survive Finals.

Wounded Army vet Logan Murray thought mimics were the stuff of board games and dungeon manuals... right up until one ate him.

In a flash of snapping teeth, Logan suddenly finds himself on the doorstep to another world. He's been unwittingly recruited into the Shadowcroft Academy for Dungeons—the most prestigious interdimensional school dedicated to training the monstrous guardians who protect the Tree of Souls from so-called heroes. Heroes who would destroy the universe if it meant a shot at advancement.

Unfortunately, as a bottom-tier cultivator with a laughably weak core, Logan's dungeon options aren't exactly stellar, and he finds himself reincarnated as a lowly fungaloid, a three-foot-tall mass of spongy mushroom with fewer skills than a typical sewer rat. If he's going to survive the grueling challenges the academy has in store, he'll need to ace the odd assortment of classes—Fiendish Fabrication, Dungeon Feng Shui, the Ethics of Murder 101—and learn how to turn his unusual guardian form into an asset instead of a liability.

And that’s only if the gargoyle professor doesn’t demote him to a doomed wandering monster first...

From James A. Hunter—bestselling author of *Rogue Dungeon*, *Bibliomancer (Completionist Chronicles Expanded Universe)*, and the LitRPG epic *Viridian Gate Online*—and Dragon Award Finalist Aaron Michael Ritchey, comes a brand new Dungeon Core novel, like nothing you've ever seen before. Funny, funky, and full of Gamelit goodness, this is one novel you won't want to put down.

BOOKS AND REVIEWS

If you loved *Celestial Citadel* and would like stay in the loop about the latest book releases, deals, and giveaways, be sure to subscribe to the Shadow Alley Press Mailing List.

www.ShadowAlleyPress.com

Sign up now and get a free copy of our bestselling anthology, Viridian Gate Online: Side Quests! Your email address will never be shared and you can unsubscribe at any time.

Word-of-mouth and book reviews are beyond helpful for the success of any writer, so please consider leaving a rating or a short, honest review on Amazon—just a couple of lines about your overall reading experience. Thank you in advance!

You can also connect with us on our Facebook Page where we do even more giveaways: facebook.com/shadowalleypress

BOOKS BY SHADOW ALLEY PRESS

ENTER THE SHADOW ALLEY LIBRARY to take a peek at all of our amazing Gamelit, Fantasy, and Science Fiction books! Viridian Gate Online, Rogue Dungeon, Snake's Life, Dungeon Heart, Path of the Thunderbird, School of Swords and Serpents, the FiveFold Universe, and so many more... Your next favorite book is waiting for you inside!

ABOUT THE AUTHORS

James A. Hunter

James A. Hunter is a man of many talents. He's a former Marine Corps Sergeant, combat veteran, and pirate hunter (seriously). He's also a member of The Royal Order of the Shellback—because that is totally a real thing. In addition to all of that, James has also been a missionary and international aid worker in Bangkok, Thailand. His latest mission? Taking care of his two kids and writing full time. He is the author of the Yancy Lazarus Urban Fantasy series, Legend of the Treesinger, Rogue Dungeon, and the bestselling LitRPG Epic Viridian Gate Online!

eden Hudson

I am invincible. I am a mutant. I have 3 hearts and was born with no eyes. I had eyes implanted later. I didn't have hands, either, just stumps. When my eyes were implanted they asked if I would like hands as well and I said, "Yes, I'll take those," and pointed with my stump. But sometimes I'm a hellbender peeking out from under a rock. When it rains, I live in a music box.

But I'm also a tattoo addict, coffee junkie, drummer, and aspiring skateboarder. Jesus actually is my homeboy.

Made in the USA
Columbia, SC
02 July 2025

60222522R00250